SIX MORNING KISSES

A novel

DIANA ELLIOT GRAHAM

Cover design: Diana Elliot Graham

Publisher: Arrobehu (aka Diana Elliot Graham)

To anyone looking for the love of your life,
it is found in the love of your life.

To anyone looking for their happily ever after,
don't wait for the end of the story.

Chapter One

HAPPILY EVER AFTER

Bancroft

I'm staring down the path at the brightly painted front door like it will magically open on its own.

If I stand here long enough maybe it will. He'll notice, opening the door with that all-knowing smile. Leaving me with no choice but to cross the threshold through the currently closed front gate and walk the rest of the way up the path where he will greet me with the same obligatory kiss one comes to expect.

Unless, of course, he's in the basement buried away. Hiding from the reality of it all. He probably is. He has been.

God—I'm such a hypocrite. Hiding is exactly why I haven't taken a step. Why I've been ignoring his calls. Because I knew that as soon as I answered he would hear it in my first breath, and I wasn't ready to admit it yet. Too scared of what it all means when I tell him the truth about my plans.

My fingers wrap around the wrought iron gate as I look across the front lawn. The front garden looks impossibly green, like someone's been spending way too much time nurturing it lately. Probably as a coping mechanism, thinking maybe it would be different if he could just keep the basil alive.

They say the grass is always greener, and from where I'm standing, it certainly looks like it.

The late summer heat is making my sundress stick to my back, and somewhere nearby I can hear birds judging my life choices, making a mockery of me not walking into my own house, and realize my grip has tightened around the gate the way it often does when I grip the steering wheel trying to motivate myself to go inside after a long day at work.

Come on, Bancroft, just fucking do it. One foot in front of the other. Basic human skill. You've got this.

I take a breath, pushing the gate open and I hear it creak with memories I wasn't prepared to think about now. *Thanks for that, gate. Really helpful.* So I take a step to escape them. Then another and another, finally climbing the handful of stairs and landing right in front of that goddamned painted front door. Like I needed the reminder of this all-consuming love.

This house used to be perfect, I remember when it was. There was a time it used to feel like an old Nancy Meyers movie, just the right amount of chaos, lived in sofas with indentations of me curled up with a book.

I've walked through this doorway more times than I can count, but not more than I can remember. And like all the times before, the smell of home overwhelms me. Down the hallways lined with pictures, my life is framed on these walls. I think about what I thought it would be. I was wrong, and now I have to suck it the fuck up and just fucking tell him once and for all.

I'm leaving.

"Hello?" Not exactly a scream, but it will carry down the narrow hallways and find him wherever he is hiding, though he used to never hide from me, we'd hide together. The hurried footsteps racing up the stairs means he's as shocked that I'm here as I am fucking petrified to be here.

He rounds the corner to where I'm sitting at the kitchen counter and I force a smile. He said I could always come home, but turning up without notice feels wrong now. I bite my lip to assuage the anxiety and he spots it.

"Sterling," I say, trying for stern but landing somewhere around about-to-emotionally-combust.

"Bancroft," he replies with matching faux-severity, but there's more concern in it as he asks *'What are you doing here?'*

He knows.

Well, he knows something.

"I need to talk to you." I might be buzzing with nerves, but his tell is just as visible in response. I can see it on his hand. His thumb spins the gold band on his ring finger and my hand reaches for the diamonds on mine. These two rings forged for the same reasons, now missing each other in separation.

"Then let's talk." He pulls out the stool next to me after making a fresh cup of tea for both of us. The small comfort he always offers. Lemon for him, sugar for me.

And it all poured out of me. All the things I'd been too afraid to tell him. He didn't interrupt, didn't say anything. He just let me speak. And I did. I think I blacked out as I explained it. This wasn't the way I imagined things, as he always told me to imagine things. But here I am. Telling him that I'm moving across the country. That I'm leaving, *him*.

He pulls me in for a hug, and I cry on his shoulder as I have over so many things before. I feel his chest inhale a deep breath. It's unfair for him to be the one to comfort me now that I'm scared to go. But when he says things, I believe him, I've always believed him, maybe it's why I'm so terrified now, knowing whatever he would say might not be honest, but it would feel like it is.

Chapter Two

HAPPILY EVER BEFORE

Arden

There's a distinction between making love and fucking someone. I've done both, and all manner in between, even some form of copulation that landed on either end of the spectrum. But I've been the woman held and caressed and I've been the one relentlessly fucked in primal desperation. Which is how I know even through the glass of the window and across the street that's what's happening in the bedroom that mirrors mine. I can somehow see the ripples of passion as the beads of sweat roll down the muscles of his back. I know it's in my mind. Not the movement of his body, that couldn't be clearer, but the detail that is crafted by the orchestral conductor of my brain to create something symphonic in place of the song that has been on loop.

I'm not a voyeur. I never have been. That's far from my kink. Though I'm not sure I would have referred to myself as particularly kinky in general. Sex I've had plenty of. Both as a single girl looking for whatever validation or gratification I could claim from a night in bed with someone, and the more regimented and routine relationship sex that I've found exclusive consistency in.

And in all the years since I started having sex never once have I derived pleasure from anything that could be considered voyeuristic. *Until, perhaps maybe now.*

It's not that I've ever intended to watch him. It's not that I know anything about him. Besides which apartment is his and that he can last anywhere from seven to thirty-nine minutes depending on a few factors, including partner. *Not that I'm timing him.* His apartment is also on the fourth floor. And much like me, most of his activities take place at night. Though while *my* sexual partner lays next to me in that post-come-contentment, cumtentment if you will, I usually default to picking up whichever book is keeping me company in the moonlight. Allowing myself to trust-fall into the romance of a happily ever after where the characters ride off into the sunset and the pancake-breakfast style epilogue is just as sticky sweet. But some nights lately, as someone snores in that monotone metronome kind of way, I can glance through my bedroom window and it becomes less about this primal man and more about me.

I don't even know how long he's been there. Maybe he appears whenever I get bored, manifesting around the same time everything fizzled out here. That first night I thought he could have been a figment of my passion starved imagination and I think that's why I still wonder if it's just a delusion my mind is projecting while maybe I'm actually asleep. Except, of course, I don't sleep. And thankfully, neither does he. I don't recall seeing him before a few months ago, and I definitely would have noticed him. But then again, I haven't really seen him, he's always shrouded by darkness, I wouldn't be able to identify him in a line up. The image my brain has invented of this man is just an amalgamation of the men I've known, intimately and otherwise, cherry picking their best qualities to construct recognizable sexual prowess of this complete stranger. *Does he have music playing? Is that his favorite position? What is he saying? Does he love her?* Who knows. But it's a nice distraction.

The moonlight streaks across the hardwood floors of my bedroom, catching only my feet, leaving the rest of me in shadow and I'm lured back into the reality of my own apartment and out of the fantasy of this stranger by the vibrating breaths coming from the man next to me. I chance one more look across the way and I think about how his body moves against hers. If I look away now, it's not voyeurism. That's what I've told myself recently each time I'm in this exact situation.

I reach for my phone to check the time, though I can tell by the way the sky is lit there aren't many people who would call this *morning*. Barely 5 AM, I throw myself back into my pillow, and as usual, my bedfellow is unbothered by the movement.

I'll lay here long enough for our hero to grovel following the third act break up, and then I'll start my day in the hopes of finally feeling that early-twenties-movie-montage I'd been promised my entire life post graduation.

I crick my neck up just the smallest bit over the pages of the novel in my hands, peering over it subtly as if I'm not hidden in all meaningful ways. No movement, no lights, whoever he is, they are, they're gone now. Or maybe, my brain just turned them off and they were never really there.

———

It's amazing what creatures of habit human beings are, even against their own self-interest. I hit the street and the not-yet-morning spring air is wet with a chill, but so familiar. It didn't use to be. It's not hard to remember a time that weather like this would chill me to my bones, but since then, I've seen enough leaves hit the ground and perfected the art of light layers, that crispness of the Cambridge air is more refreshing than anything else. My feet have walked these streets for years and the pattern of the city remains intimately familiar, even in this predawn darkness.

The Coffee Haus doesn't open until six, but I know better, and manage to shamelessly press my face against the glass and knock when I see a man pop his head up from behind the counter. His face morphing from aggravation to understanding in a matter of seconds. The door opens with a chime from the bells above as I sneak into the almost entirely dark space.

"Couldn't sleep?" Rush asks. His name is my second favorite thing about him, because it has always felt incredibly ironic, that he is in fact, *never* in a rush. No long line can motivate him to work at any pace faster than what can only be described as leisurely at best. My first and most favorite thing about him? He lets me in before they officially open. Maybe because he got tired of me hanging around outside the door checking my watch every five minutes willing it to change, maybe because he liked the company when he got everything sorted to open up in the morning. *Even if that means tolerating the philosophical debate that a flat white is just a more arrogant latte.* Either way, I'm not about to look a gift horse in the mouth. Especially one that hands me a fresh cup of coffee without prompting.

"Unfortunately not," I say as I slouch into the booth they've built against the wall near perfectly positioned in the window. *Seriously, creatures of habit.* Sitting here is different than it once was, but I'm not often haunted by the ghosts of my past, unless of course one walks through the door. Which given the radius I am from where so much of my formative life has been lived, isn't an impossibility. But this is still my favorite coffee shop that's walking distance, and sometimes, *usually,* my feet recall the path even in the dark. I saw the preview of the email when it came through last night while I was a bit more *indisposed* but I figure there's no time and place like the present to read it. Popping open my laptop and I click on the familiar, though far less frequent, name. There are changes after all these years, new paint on the walls, new students on campus, and old ones off, *and I now occupy the seat that he used to prefer.*

It's as if I can hear his voice as I read the latest email. We exchange them and some supporting texts a handful of times a year, a pattern that has ebbed and flowed as we settled further away from each other and into our lives. But I was the one to initiate most recently based on the latest at work, because despite all the key players in my life, he's been a good sounding board for decisions, always pragmatic.

The correspondence saved in a folder is probably the only part of him I allow myself now. There is something that inspires a specific brand of self-loathing about hearing from him while I sit here, even though he's not *really* here, just whatever memories are clinging to this place we sat when we were more than we are now.

It's the correspondence that lives in my drafts, going all the way back to the initial break up, that I sometimes click through in an attempt to gain a better understanding of who we were and how I was left so shattered that is the saddest representation of our friendship.

He moved to San Francisco a couple years ago when the company he works for established headquarters there. From his limited social media use it seems like he's doing well. Surprisingly some of the juiciest updates I got for a time came from my old roommate Stella through his best friend Austin. Austin who still is roaming the streets of Boston's financial district charming his way through life after Stella rebuffed him time and time again. He always had a clear thing for her, unbothered by any romantic attachments she had, and chased after her like a love-sick puppy. *Maybe more of a dirty hound dog.* But for me, it meant that after Reid broke up with me, even though we said we'd be friends, there was a back channel of information.

That summer following my freshman year was the hardest I can remember. I spent nights in hotel rooms with my mom crying, her hopes that spending days prancing across the art museums of Europe would inspire me in some ways. And then, I would email him, telling him about the latest thing I saw or ate, acting like it was fine. He had asked me to keep in touch. So I did.

Even as my European adventure went from hotels and suitcases with mom to hostels and backpacks with Ethan and Stella. I tried, because I thought that it might mean when I got back to campus that fall we would feel like we hadn't missed much. But he didn't miss anything. When I got back to Cambridge, he was gone. He left this city, and me with her.

I called my mom, and she said *'it was for the best'*. I didn't believe her at the time, but eventually...

In all the emails *sent,* he never expressed regret for the breakup. And one night after too much Ouzo and adrenaline from us dancing on tables trying to teach a group of Greeks the *'Cotton Eyed Joe,'* I wrote the email that has lived on ice in my drafts for years. I used to check on it. Like it was something I needed to feed. I'd open the draft, read what has been seared in my brain since it happened, and eventually close it. Knowing it wasn't worth it. Knowing that I had already thrown myself at him once, any preservation or hope for the future now would mean I couldn't default to being the needy, childish, girlfriend he broke up with. And while he's always remained the model of respectful distance, and kept his word in being friends post breakup, for so long I wished he hadn't. But his friendship is what I asked him for, and after all, he always only gave me what I asked for.

He's remained in my corner like that email has remained in my drafts.

But now, before I open his latest, I might as well check social media to see if there's any indication of what his update might include. *Nothing notable.* I scroll through and see some of his recent posts. Photos of him in his new place in San Francisco, *no piano in sight*, photos with friends, *the kind that look like they are grabbing an after-work-drink,* and several photos of his new kitten, *I should really get a dog.* Between the sporadic emails and infrequent social media posts, we follow along at a distance, staying well out of the bounds we set at the end of my freshman year.

I know the contents of his email are a follow-up to my question about work, as he once interned where I now collect a paycheck, he knows where some of the bodies are buried. Namely, the upcoming 'Thompson Challenge.'

The Thompson Challenge is named after an account that was under management more than a decade ago, pre-dating either of our employment at the firm, but became sort of management consulting lore. The story goes, the Thompson Solutions only really ever solved one thing, copy and fax machines. Which, for a time, *was* incredibly lucrative, *until email of course.* They stayed focused on their path, focused on the original products, never willing to jump on board the digital disruption that could actually help them grow. Until that fateful day that some predecessor's predecessor's predecessor of my current boss positioned the floundering company as the way for the Patrick Bateman-esque wannabees of the office to fight it out for a promotion. Rumor has it (*as do the files that I've looked up, because who doesn't love a corporate fairy tale*) that Max Harrison won by proposing a merger where Thompson Solutions would partner with an up-and-coming document management system. And much like fairy tales, it was a match made in heaven and everyone lived happily ever after. Especially Max Harrison who was not only promoted but coined the term Thompson Challenge for us all to live through now.

That's why I emailed Reid. I know it's coming, I could use a bit of that pragmatic wisdom. Because despite my best efforts, navigating this landscape of bro-fessionals often leaves me as the odd one out, struggling to even be heard in a meeting, let alone taken as seriously as I take myself.

I can almost predict his response, likely that's why I emailed him in the first place. But it doesn't stop the momentary pause where I imagine it as something entirely different, the apology I spent months wishing for after he broke up with me. It was almost masochistic choosing his friendship at a time I was so desperate for his love. But after spending the summer away from the red brick buildings of Cambridge, Massachusetts, in just a matter of months, the heartbreak I first felt became secondary to so much else I was trying not to feel. How much easier it would have been if choosing numbness was possible, but it wasn't. And when I came back to campus that fall and he was gone, it became easier knowing I wouldn't be holding my breath in fear of the casual bump-in. I got custody of this place, and *thank god*. I watch as Rush casually fills the machines with coffee beans and the buzz of the shop mixes with the air to trigger the memories I've made here since. Not the ones from before. It's become the place of a hundred first dates, cram sessions, cry sessions, new friendships, old friendships, and like this morning, escapes. So despite the pause, I take a deep breath of the morning grinds, a sip of my coffee, and open the latest exchange.

Dear Arden–

Things in San Francisco are, as you would say, "West-Coasty" but I am well. I began a new role about a month ago and that means I'll be traveling even more. Already scheduled to head to meet with a media corporation next week. I will let you know when I'm in your area if you want to grab a coffee.
I know how much you must want to see the Thompson Challenge as the ticket to promotion, but promotions don't happen overnight in companies this size. My advice: Number one — There are people there who have been working towards this longer, they may be positioned to take it. Number two — Don't be afraid to find a partner to support, you can still show everyone what you've got. Number three, most importantly — Slow down and pace yourself, your career is a marathon not a sprint, you'll get there.

Yours,
Reid

Not in romance, but as plainly as this email. He looks older every time I've seen him. Just ever so slightly in ways you don't expect to notice. The small changes you don't see when you sleep next to someone nightly, but are screaming at you when they aren't. I guess that makes sense. I am older too. Though I've never felt it. Somehow the idea that I'm aging feels more defined by everyone's increased expectations and my added responsibilities than it does in any way of my actual psyche.

The first time we saw each other, almost a year after he dumped me, I plastered a smile on my face and acted like I was fine, in some ways I think I might have been, but then I cried the whole way back. But if he was sitting here now he would be dressed like he was coming from work, a suit, maybe even a tie, because he's always working. If he's in the area it's only ever for work, and he does me the favor to squeeze in a hello. He'd order his coffee, and sit across from me. He'd say *tell me about work* and I would kick off into a run-on stream of consciousness explaining the corporate ladder I'm desperate to climb, and how there's a promotion that I think I absolutely deserve but will be competing against all the other bro-sephs for it. Instead, I just put the abridged version in the email, because that's what we are, the abridged version.

Hey Reid!

I managed to sneak out before the crack of dawn and am currently sipping the *perfect* latte in a familiar place. I don't know the last time you were here but even though the Coffee Haus is entirely different the coffee is still the best around, *andddd* I've managed to, um, let's say convince one of their baristas to open up early for me.

Your email makes a lot of sense, I just get incredibly frustrated watching the same copy and paste versions of Brads, Chads, and Thads, all on what seems to be a clear growth path, meanwhile I am struggling to even get an idea heard in a meeting. I know what you must be thinking, when have I ever had trouble making sure I'm heard, but let me tell you (though you already know), this corporate life isn't for the faint of heart.

I'm glad you're happy in San Francisco! Have you done any of the touristy things? The Golden Gate, Alcatraz, if not, you should definitely play hooky for a museum day, there are some great ones. Thanks for everything! Definitely let me know when you're in town!

Best,
AB

I stare at my sent email for longer than I care to admit, analyzing every exclamation point like they're evidence in a crime scene. Because that's what corresponding with an ex feels like sometimes, trying to strike the perfect balance between *I'm thriving*' and *I'm not trying too hard to show you I'm thriving.*' It's emotional gymnastics, and I never did gymnastics.

The truth is, Reid's emails always leave me feeling like I'm still that freshman girl, desperate to prove I belong in his spaces that weren't built for me. The one left on the back porch of a house party while her boyfriend decided she was too immature. And now, his pragmatic advice which so often has felt like wisdom, while *technically* sound, has the same energy as a fortune cookie telling you to 'be patient' when you're already running late to a meeting. Thanks, but I've been patient. I've been so patient I could teach a masterclass in watching mediocre men fail upward while I perfect the art of nodding supportively in meetings.

Rush slides another latte onto my table without asking, because he's either psychic or he's noticed my descent into an email-induced existential crisis. Probably both.

"You're thinking too loud," he says, and I wonder if maybe he should have been the psychology major instead of Stella.

"Just trying to navigate the delicate art of proving to my ex that I'm living my best life while simultaneously asking for career advice," I say, closing my laptop with perhaps more force than necessary. "You know, normal Tuesday stuff."

Chapter Three

HAPPILY EVER BEFORE

Will

There's humor in sneaking out of your own apartment at 5:47 a.m., especially when your middle brother is passed out on your couch, reeking of expensive whiskey and poor decisions. Alfie showed up at my door some time around three in the morning, tie askew and wedding ring suspiciously absent, here to lecture me about life choices while making several questionable ones of his own.

I grab my running shoes, *bright orange ones that my mother once called 'aggressively pedestrian' with the same tone Hugh Sterling uses to discuss my career,* and slip out like a teenager missing curfew. Like I'm eighteen again, choosing art history over finance at orientation, watching my father's dreams of continuing the Sterling financial dynasty crumble with each additional art history class I took. I'm really only sneaking out to save myself from another remix of last night's speech about family duty and corporate responsibility.

The air has that specific Boston bite in spring as my feet carry me toward the Charles River. The river path unfolds before me, a familiar loop that's carried the weight of countless crises and family disappointments. Check. The black sheep running from his golden cage yet again, while my older brother Cal runs the M&A division and Alfie handles risk management, both of their roles really just head of something or other in the family name. Titles that have them perfectly slotted into the lives we were groomed for.

I pass the footbridge just as the rowing team begins their morning practice and can hear their oars slice through the water in perfect synchronization. It creates a rhythm that mingles with my breathing, becoming my playlist this morning. The city itself, a chorus of early commuter trains, the whisper of wind across the river, the soft thud of other runners' feet hitting the pavement. *I wonder what they're running from.*

I do this loop almost daily, one of the few routines I have. It gives me space and time to think about the rest of my day. In a few hours, I'll walk through the doors of one of the most prominent museums in the city, through the modern structure donated to present the past, and into the space where thousands of stories are preserved in paint. And people come from all over to just revel in it.

Being a Sterling in the art world comes with its own peculiar weight. The name is on plaques in half the museums in Boston, even some buildings. Generous donors, patrons of the arts, and let's not forget, tax write-off enthusiasts. But when their youngest son saw this as more than a way to offset taxable income? Suddenly it was all *'But Will, that's not what Sterlings do.'* Because apparently, Sterlings can buy art, can donate art, can use art as a conversation piece at charity galas, but God forbid I actually find value beyond societal and financial gain. *Then again, that is how they measure the value of most things.*

Which of course, brings me back to Alfie's drunken rant about the board seat they need me to fill. Eight weeks until the Memorial Day Weekend party at the Newport house, where the Sterling Financial Group will parade their united front before announcing their latest acquisition. Eight weeks to decide if I'm willing to be the final piece in my father's corporate chess game.

I breathe out as my feet pick up the pace heading toward the bridge, partly because I know what's coming. In about three miles, my right shin will start its familiar protest, and reality will come crashing back. The reality that this Memorial Day is viewed as especially critical, my father needs to show 'strength on the Sterling front' before the board votes on the acquisition. A vote they can't win without filling that family-designated seat with another compliant Sterling.

I curve past the bronze ducklings standing in their perpetual parade. There's something accusatory about those ducks, lined up in perfect formation, following their mother exactly where they're supposed to go. They gleam as the sun comes up, polished to a shine by decades of tiny hands and countless photo ops. I wonder if they ever wanted to break formation, if one of them ever thought about waddling off to become a swan boat instead.

My father would hate this metaphor. He'd say I'm being dramatic, that comparing myself to wayward waterfowl is philosophical nonsense.

As my laps start to slow, I follow the path towards the coffee shop where the morning crowd is starting to trickle in. I'll pick up an herbal tea and just ease my way back to my apartment before having to confront the conversation waiting for me at home. I just know Alfie will be in my kitchen by now, double-fisting caffeine like it's going to wash away his sins from last night, ready to deliver whatever speech our father programmed into him this week.

I can't tell much about the woman at the counter from the back of her head, except that she is arguing with the barista about the difference between a flat white and a latte with the kind of passion not usually expelled on coffee, but the two of them seem to know each other by the way he threatens to *'withhold her fix'* and she backs down with a *'see you tomorrow'*.

As she turns to leave, our eyes land on one another in a passing moment, and there's a spark of recognition.

She brushes past me on her way before I can say anything. Not sure what I would even say, maybe offer up some support in her latte argument, though it doesn't look like she needs any help from me. Then again, as I glance down at myself, sweaty, fabric clinging to my body, and my *'aggressively pedestrian'* sneakers, is this the look of someone you want to make casual conversation with before the sun has even fully risen? Doubtful. *But fuck it.*

"Excu—" I begin to turn and speak to her, but as I do my name splits the air.

"Will... I have an herbal tea for Will."

I see the narrowing of her eyes as she turns back towards the door and exits. Perhaps that I don't have the coffee-legs to stand on to support her case, and she walks out the door.

"Thanks," I say, grabbing the cup from where it's waiting to be collected and sip my tea the rest of the way home, in absolutely no rush to pick up where Alfie and I left off. *Hopefully just more sober this time.*

The thing about being the black sheep is that they see my job at the museum as some sort of extended rebellion, a phase I'll grow out of once I realize the importance of *'real work.'* Without any recognition of the very real work I do.

By the time I make it back to my apartment, the sun is fully up, and my tea is long gone. I dragged it out as long as possible, taking a few extra laps around the block to be sure. I rest my forehead against my door, breathing hard, knowing exactly what waits on the other side. Alfie, ready to remind me that some people would *'kill for the opportunities I have.'* One of his favorites. And he's right, of course, which only makes it worse. The problem isn't that I was born with a sterling spoon in my mouth. The problem is that they see my choices as if I am choosing to dig in the dirt with it, rather than stir my father's corporate tea.

When I push open the door, I'm proven right. My brother,

the poster child for 'work hard, play harder,' looks like he got into a fight with a bottle of whiskey and lost. Spectacularly.

"We need to talk," he says, as if he didn't barge in here last night doing exactly that.

"I don't have time for this." I'm already stripping off my shirt, heading for the shower. Behind me, I can practically hear him straightening his shoulders, preparing to deliver the family gospel. He wants to know what I'm up to. What my plans are. How much longer I'm planning on drawing this out.

This being my life.

My answers are the same as usual, a version of *'none of your business.'* And his answer is the junior version of our father's, *'it being my business is exactly why we are in this position.'* The *position* they refer to is this archaic ideal of old-school standards of living. All paved paths.

My father is one of those men that people consider successful because he's managed to turn money into more money. He likes to fashion himself as a *'pull yourself up from the bootstraps'* kind of man, but that's just an excuse for a form of selfishness I don't subscribe to. It's genetic. My brothers Alfie and Cal have the same distorted sense of reality.

The world is your oyster? That idiom is about me. For all intents and purposes, I've experienced nothing preventative in my life. I know it. That's the difference, *I know it.* My brother stands in my kitchen bothered by a laundry list of things, when the man has never done a load of laundry in his life. And while I can look back at him and acknowledge the advantages to being on the gold-plated hamster wheel, those wheels exist in cages, gold or not. And my father has done well to make sure his children remember that.

"Did you have a *guest* last night?" I can hear him rustling around in my space, flipping through the books on my desk where I've been researching for upcoming exhibits.

"No." I respond flatly. *I did.*

"Huh, I coulda sworn I heard–" *She snuck out before I did.*

"You didn't." *I reaffirm.* "You don't care about my sex-life Alfie, what do you want?" *Let's get this over with.*

"No one has heard back from you," he calls after me, his voice carrying that specific note of disappointment that is practically carried in our DNA.

"What did you expect to hear?" I step into the shower, letting the hot water blast away the morning's miles. Unfortunately, it does nothing to drown out Alfie's voice.

"It's a single board seat, Will," Alfie says, as if he's explaining something truly that simple to a child. My brother has always tried to emulate our father's way of making everything sound like both an offer and a threat.

"And when that vote turns into another? And another after that?"

"That's generally how responsibility works," he snaps back.

My father Hugh Sterling, built an empire out of our great-grandfather's already existing empire. Despite my lack of interest or involvement, it's my name just as much as theirs. I may not have an active interest in what they do, but by birthright alone, I have shares.

I don't pay as much attention to the details as they'd like me to, and even if I wanted to, the fact of the matter is, my brain never wrapped around numbers the way it does a brushstroke. Most of the time they let me hide away within the walls of the museum, only turning up for the occasional gala, where everyone is reminded that the name on my badge is not just a coincidence.

But this time, as I've been told *too many times to count,* this merger is a game of numbers, board seats, and *that* is why this round of disappointment holds a great deal of resentment as well.

The problem is that Sterling Financial needs a supermajority vote on the board to approve the wolf of an acquisition in the sheep's clothing of a merger. And right now they're one seat short. According to the company charter, that seat must be filled by a Sterling family member, a provision my great-grandfather put in place to ensure family control. *Hasn't been a problem until now.*

"Here we go..." I say to my shampoo bottle, which is probably the only thing in this apartment that doesn't have an opinion about my education, my job, what I have for breakfast...

"It's a big deal, you know that. Or you would if you ever came home."

"I *am* home." The words come out harder than I mean them to, but they're true. Home isn't the lobby at the Sterling Financial Group, it's not the Westchester house or the one in Newport, all with their rooms of carefully hung expectations. Home is here, in *my* space with quiet mornings, late nights, not lectures from the president of the board of directors of my life.

Alfie yanks back the shower curtain. His eyes catch on my newest tattoo, a small rendering of Kandinsky's *'Several Circles'* that would give our mother heart palpitations.

I started collecting tattoos in college, they began small, and I kept them hidden beneath fabric so as to not cause more dismay in the proverbial family newsletter.

"I'm really not asking." His voice has that edge to it, the one that means he's channeling our father. "You like to pretend you are better than the rest of us, but this is family we are talking about. At the end of the day, you have obligations and you'll do right to remember that when the time comes."

"Oh yeah, Alfie? And would you call whatever you were up to last night family obligations?" I yank the curtain closed, but not before catching his flinch. "What *would* Olivia say about that?" We both know that his nightcap with his old college buddies in the area, turned into something that would undoubtedly make his wife question her decision. Or, at least ask for more caratage.

"You've got eight weeks. I'm serious."

I hear Alfie take a swig of mouthwash, probably trying to wash away the taste of hypocrisy, or the whiskey. The sound of my front door closing tells me he's gone, off to transform back into the Sterling heir apparent.

Chapter Four

HAPPILY EVER BEFORE

Arden

If someone had told me that my entire sense of self-worth would be reduced to a spreadsheet and a passive-aggressive email chain, I would have laughed.

I always think of that scene in Mean Girls where Cady is talking about life in Africa and the animals around the watering hole. She's talking about it in relation to students at the mall, but working in an office is the same. I don't exactly know what I was expecting. My points of reference for corporate-life didn't come from my mom and dad, whose careers took a different path than mine. My friends weren't much help because our interests couldn't have been more different. Stella stayed in Europe after a semester abroad, on more of an *'Eat Pray Love'* journey than a career one. Ethan turned his love of anything outdoors into a career writing about it. The man of few words turned out to have no shortage of them. I made friends in some of my business classes before graduating, but most of them are the tadpole versions of the now finance-frogs that cluster across the room at the water cooler.

The office is less Silicon Valley startup, more Gordon Gekko's wet dream with a bull-pen that feels like a gladiator arena. Though twenty-something women are about as common here as unicorns in a Wall Street trading pit. I'm one of three, which means I've perfected the art of being simultaneously invisible and hyper visible.

This is meant to be my chance to prove I'm not just another millennial with an overpriced degree and an embarrassing number of dead houseplants. I mutter it in part to myself, because apparently talking to myself is my primary form of motivation these days. Talking to the plants that I continue to buy despite having no success in keeping them alive doesn't seem to be working. For either of us really.

My desk is a beautiful disaster, that's not an insult. Worse things have been said about me. Multiple half-empty water bottles, sticky notes with cryptic things to remember, and a new succulent I named Pricktor, after my boss Victor. Because, well, he's also a prick. He's the lead singer in my collection of ill-fated plants, though his backup band isn't looking much better these days.

This just isn't what I thought it would be. Or at least, not what I hoped. It's a far cry from the idea of being thirty-and-flirty-and-thriving, except I'm not thirty, and is anyone really thriving? I will be, right? This is just the beginning of the story. The main character always has some kind of work-hurdle before they get everything they've ever wanted. I just would like to feel like I am something more than a collection of student loans, attachment issues, and 3 a.m. dread.

I suppose Reid is right, it takes time. No matter how much I want to skip ahead.

Victor, the man not the succulent, who possesses all the charisma and subtly of one of those STD posters you see in the T station urging you to get checked, calls an all-hands meeting. And just like that the office transforms. His voice has everyone scurrying from the bull-pen of cubicles towards the large glass conference room with a view out into Boston herself.

The room has about as many seats as the Titanic had lifeboats, and who gets them works similarly. Not 'women and children' because again, unicorns, but it's based on seniority and importance. No one with a title below Director takes a seat while the rest of us stand gathered around the backs of the twenty seats as if we've picked allegiances.

"The Thompson Challenge," he declares. It's the word across the screen behind him and the only thing he says to silence the chattering amongst the group.

"As you know, every year this firm holds what we refer to as 'the Thompson Challenge.'"

Every poor schmuck here knows exactly what that means. The Hunger Games, where even golden boys like Reid emerged victorious and promptly fled. You can still see the difference in wall texture where first-year analyst Nathanial Wells got stabbed in the back (metaphorically, I think) and then punched the wall.

"The Vulcan Manufacturing account has been under management for three years. Take a brief, review it," he continues. "They are hemorrhaging money worse than one of you at a craps table. The CEO is stubborn, only a client of ours after pressure from the board."

I take a brief from the pile being circulated, immediately scanning through. Vulcan, with their clever reference to metalworking for a manufacturing company, has been losing market share faster than I lose bobby pins. Which considering I'm down to three from a pack of one-hundred-and-fifty I bought last month, is pretty alarming. They're stuck in the manufacturing equivalent of using a horse and buggy. Appropriate with their mythological inspired name. They might be functional, but it's embarrassingly behind the times.

And there it is. The real challenge isn't just figuring out how to improve market share, but getting them into the 21st century with a CEO that is interested in security of what's known.

I can practically hear the murmurs across the room already, planning for acquisitions, looking for the quick escape hatch.

"I don't care how you get this done. I care that it's done. Draft a proposal for acquisition and submit it by the end of the month." Victor continues. "This quarter we have two open seats for new associates..." He scans those of us standing in the back, the group that would undoubtedly be up for this type of step up. "Two of you," he repeats curtly. "This is how we will decide. The best strategy will be promoted. It will also become their first account under management."

I already work like an associate. I'm the one turning off the lights in the office, and this will be how I prove it. I'm scribbling notes on the yellow pad in my hands while Michael and Brent-number-two are standing next to me smirking with the same smug *I got this in the bag* face they give themselves when talking to a woman at a bar.

Victor carries on for another ten minutes before the command of 'back to work,' has everyone running back to their cubicles. I return to mine and find Brent-number-two leaning against my desk. This is exactly the kind of behavior that got him the number-two spot to begin with. I find the other Brent far less offensive, if only because he at least pretends his eyes don't drift south during meetings.

"Bancroft." He sings through his far-too-white-teeth.

"Oh wow, you remember my name, super impressive." I say, and by the way his lip pulls up and his shoulders shrug, I don't think he realizes I'm being sarcastic.

"I've been thinking..."

"Careful, I've heard that can be dangerous." I yank my chair out from where he's got it trapped and take a seat. He laughs again, but I think our interpretation of the joke is different.

Brent-number-two, because apparently, we've reached a point where men are so interchangeable they require numerical categorization, deciding this is the perfect moment to grace me with his professional proposition.

My silence here is strategic and has him filling the space with the same blubbering babble he has in meetings when he has nothing to say but wants to be heard. Usually when I play the game of mental buzzword bingo to see how many of the same corporate empty words are bandied about between them.

"You know we have great synergy," he starts off, in a way that suggests this is peak seduction. Though from personal experience from a happy hour last month, I know full well what his peak seduction looks like and to be fair, it is about as appealing as his use of the word synergy.

I resist the urge to explain that 'synergy' is corporate speak for 'I have no actual plan.'

"Is that what we're calling it?" I cock my head ever so slightly to the side in a way that makes him shift between his feet. I've learned that hesitation is a language all its own and I'm becoming fluent.

My friends think I'm playing some elaborate game. Maybe I am. But this isn't just about a promotion. This is about proving that the girl who loved her business classes isn't going to become another statistic, another twenty-something who settles. There are enough ways in life women are expected to settle. With pants-pockets, in bed, my career won't be one of them.

Those 'Thirty Under Thirty' lists are psychological warfare, by the way. They're basically telling an entire generation that if you haven't changed the world by your thirtieth birthday, you might as well start collecting cats and giving up. Jokes on them, I'm much more of a dog person anyway.

A partnership would be an inflated way to describe what I think we could pull off, but watching Brent-number-two lean against my desk with a jawline and fortune-500-future-CEO smile, I know exactly what I'm doing.

Guys like Brent have connections that run deeper than merit while being the kind of handsome that makes people forgive his mediocrity. The type that peaked in his fraternity days but still maintains the confidence that comes from never having under-stood the word 'no' in his life.

His smile widens as I agree *we should totally work together on this.'* The words taste like compromise, but I swallow down the barbs of it. He's a shortcut wrapped in a Brooks Brothers suit and I'm just being pragmatic enough to use that. After all, Reid did say to find a partner.

I watch Brent swagger away, already mentally rehearsing how he'll tell this story to the other bros at their next happy hour.

Machiavelli would be proud. Or at least mildly impressed. He was more focused on being feared than loved. Fear seems to be a non-starter here on the basis of sex alone. And love? Well, that's not even on the docket. So sorry, Machiavelli, in this case, it might be best to be underestimated.

Chapter Five

HAPPILY EVER BEFORE

Will

Everything feels more real before the crowds come, before the space fills with shuffling feet, whispered conversations, and the occasional teenage boy laughing at an exposed breast.

Mack has been guarding these halls long before I ever strolled through the door. He gives me his usual nod as I walk in. "Morning, Mr. Sterling."

"Will," I correct him for probably the thousandth time. "We both know the *real* Mr. Sterling has set foot in this wing exactly *twice* since donating enough money to get his name on it."

"Whatever you say, Mr. Sterling," Mack says. He's been here long enough to remember when I was just another rich kid here for the galas not the galleries, before I fell in love with these walls and everything they hold.

There's a wooden bench in the center of the main gallery that sits like a well-loved centerpiece. Its oak surface burnished to a soft glow by countless visitors. More than just a place to rest, it's positioned perfectly to take in the art from every angle, as if it were placed there by someone who understood the need to pause and absorb beauty.

I lie down and stretch out across it, my feet hanging off one end, my head propped against the other. *Mack won't tell.* He's seen me in here too many mornings, trying to find answers in brushstrokes and gilt frames.

People come to sit here for all sorts of reasons, I just have the benefit of doing it after hours.

Every Wednesday there's the retired art teacher who brings her sketchbook to draw shadows that are reminiscent of Sargent. Her hands might shake more now than they did in her youth, but she still catches the nuance in every shade.

Then there's the businessman who started showing up a few times a week during his lunch breaks after his divorce. For a while, he just sat in silence, staring at the walls like they might hold answers. I pretend not to notice when he wipes his eyes.

My favorite is the young couple who come every Saturday morning and make up the stories behind the paintings. Never actually caring about the historical accuracy, just telling tales between themselves more outlandish than the last.

Sometimes college students cluster on the bench with their laptops, writing papers. Sometimes they find themselves in the company of professors who help them do it.

Last week, a young girl in light-up sneakers sat here with her grandfather and asked the question we've all wanted to know since the dawn of portraiture, *'Why do they look so serious?'* she asked. *'Because sitting still that long makes anyone grumpy.'*

"Rough night?" Mack asks, making his usual rounds preparing to open.

"My brother paid me a visit." I fold my hands behind my head, staring up at the ceiling. "Showed up to remind me that I'm throwing my life away, you know, *the usual.*"

"Ah." Mack's been here for enough of my family drama to fill a soap opera.

"Apparently, it's fine to throw money at art, but god forbid you actually decide to make that a career." I gesture vaguely at the massive Sterling plaque by the entrance.

I'm lying here in a wing my family paid for, surrounded by art they raised money for, while being the family disappointment for loving it too much.

From my horizontal position, the painting takes on a different perspective. The four sisters seem to float in their dim interior, their white dresses glowing against the shadows. I've given probably hundreds of tours of this painting, explaining its composition, its historical context, its influence on portraiture. But right now, all I can think about is how the youngest daughter is half-hidden in shadow, like she's trying to escape the frame entirely. *I get it.*

"You know what kills me?" I say to the ceiling, to Mack, to the girls in the painting who've been listening to my problems for years. "When I applied for this job, I didn't tell *them*, I wanted this, on my own, and when I got the offer I was overjoyed with a sense of accomplishment. I was sure it was the gallerist pun I made that solidified it. It wasn't until I was leaving that I was told to *'thank my parents'* for their latest contribution."

Mack and these paintings have heard more of my confessions than any priest.

"You know what's worse? I actually studied art history. I interned at three different galleries. I wrote my thesis on *'The Role of Museums in Shaping Contemporary Art History.'* But none of that matters now, does it? It's all just window dressing on what everyone assumes is another trust fund hobby pretending to be a real job."

There it is. The quiet part I don't often say out loud. It's privileged and uninteresting, but it's the lens through which I know I'm viewed by more people than I'd want to admit.

The museum will open in an hour. Soon, these quiet halls will fill with visitors. There will be tourists clutching guidebooks, students with their sketch pads, and locals who've seen these paintings a hundred times but keep coming back. The magic of the early morning will fade into the busy rhythm of a regular day.

I stand up, straightening my shirt, cuffing my sleeves just

enough to let some of the *'Hands of God and Adam'* make an appearance.

'Leave the art on the walls,' my mother said when she first spotted it. As if I haven't made my entire body a gallery of the things I love.

The room develops from dawn to actual morning, like a sharpening polaroid. Soon, Marian from the gift shop will arrive, singing show tunes under her breath as she arranges postcards and art books. Dr. Wilder will sweep through on her way to her office in the conservation department, already talking about light exposure and humidity levels.

The museum will wake up, like a living thing stretching out its limbs.

I check my schedule for the day, three general tours, one specialized tour of the Impressionist collection for a group of art students, and a private tour for some donor's family that the development office begged me to take.

"Time to earn my keep," I say, standing up. "Better get ready," I say to Mack, resuming professional posture. "Your adoring public awaits." As I nod to the door where they are just being opened. Mack being one of those institutions in a place like this that will outlast us all.

I check that my badge is visible, run a hand through my probably hopeless hair that dried on the walk over here, and head towards my office to grab my notes for the day.

Chapter Six

HAPPILY EVER BEFORE

Arden

I'm sitting across from Gabriel, at what he assures me is 'the best new fusion place in Boston.' We found ourselves in a relationship of convenience. The only thing making it a relationship is really the exclusivity and consistency of schedules. I don't know precisely how long it's been a thing— I've made it a habit not to keep track since discovering relationships are easier when they don't survive past the two-month mark. But a thing it is, though his lack of leaving behind even a phone charger is a constant reminder that he also is just here for the adequacy of it rather than some great love story.

For that, I have books.

There was the momentary meet-cute in the elevator at work when we both reached for the same floor, and his smile and warm hands implied there might be this divine intervention of serendipitous timing. But alas, by the feeling of it now it is just more likely that I work in a densely populated office that is a merry-go-round of men.

He's fine, *really*. Tonight is just one of those days I'm far more critical of those around me, likely in an effort to distract myself.

He's spent the last twenty minutes explaining inflation to me in the tone of voice usually reserved for explaining shapes to toddlers. Every so often I throw out a harmless *'can't we just print more money?'* to really get him going as I order another glass of wine and he swirls his finger in the air to the waiter to indicate he'd also like another.

When did it happen that all dating feels like everyone is either trying too hard or not trying at all.

Ordering for both of us. *Trying too hard.*

So now I'm staring at what appears to be deconstructed sushi that's been reconstructed into abstract art. I'm a fan of art. I'm a fan of sushi. I'm also a fan of sustenance after a long work day which is why the most appealing thing to me is the plate of crispy, salty salvation in potato form.

Truffle fries that he ordered but never offered to share. *Not trying at all.*

In the last few months, we went through the standard this-is-a-date motions. Lucky me, now he knows my middle name. Not like he'll ever need to use it. We got to know each other just well enough to get to the point of sexual compatibility. Which is one area he is better than most, probably the reason this has lasted as long as it has.

But the rest of it?

My mind wanders most when unstimulated by company. And given the happening recently with the Hunger Games at work, it's easy to be distracted as Gabriel prattles on.

I think about Reid's emails, about pacing myself, about marathons not sprints. *Funny, we never made it to the finish line.* But watching Gabriel meticulously dissect another french fry, I can't imagine this is what I am supposed to slow down for?

"And that's when I told the investors—" he pauses mid-sentence, probably for dramatic effect, and I realize that I've been staring at his fries for so long I've completely lost track of his monologue about disrupting the whatever industry.

"Sorry," I say, not sorry at all, "I was just thinking about how this reminds me of something I read recently about the intersection of technology and human connection." *It's a complete lie*, the fact that I was thinking about it, not that I read the article, which actually was really interesting. But his eyes light up like I've just given him enough runway to keep going.

"Exactly!" he exclaims, launching into what I'm sure will be another riveting monologue. I let my mind drift back to my email exchange with Reid, thinking about how he would probably approve of him on paper, they'd maybe even be friends. He's ambitious, career focused, clearly knows how to network...

But Reid would have asked if I wanted one of his french fries.

It's a dangerous thing when you start measuring people by who they aren't. And sometimes, like tonight, you measure them by the simple fucking ability to offer you a french fry. It's probably not a metric a psychologist would endorse, but then again, I don't imagine many of them have watched a man eat french fries with a knife and fork while explaining the Econ-101 principles to a woman in the same field.

I check my watch, wondering if it's too early to fake an emergency. The night stretches ahead like his pitch deck, *endless and full of questionable projections*, which of course he has taken me through page by painful page. Not asking for my opinion, *of which I have many*, just enjoying that supportive nod I've mastered at work.

Which I do, until I can run out the clock and then just run out.

Despite hoping there would be chemistry during our meeting, the only buttons we'll ever push together would be each other's.

Chapter Seven

HAPPILY EVER BEFORE

Arden

"What is it about every single movie that makes it seem like these are supposed to be the best years in our life? This can't be it..."

I'm laying on the floor in my living room, limbs spread out like a starfish clothed in the remnants of my office-job. I try to go for more of a Devil Wears Prada are-those-the-chanel-boots look, but honestly, none of the men I work with have seen that movie and I certainly cannot afford Chanel anything at this point. Like everything else in my life lately, it's all carefully curated appearance with nothing substantial underneath, much like whatever this thing with Gabriel was supposed to be.

"I'm just saying... I thought it would be different than this... didn't they make it seem like it would be different than this? Do you know how many times I was asked to get coffee today? Do you... and it's not about getting coffee, it's about the fact that no one with a penis ever gets asked. As if the thing between their legs prevents them from balancing a tray, if it was actually as big as any of them liked to pretend maybe they could use it to balance the tray but no..."

To send your voicemail, press one. To re-record press two.

"Shit shit shit." I sit up quickly and the phone falls from where it's been propped on my boobs as I ramble for what the voicemail gods have obviously deemed 'long enough.' I hit one on the keypad and send the voicemail off to Stella where it will sit in an unanswered inbox like so many of them. I don't blame her. After our sophomore summer, she signed up for an exchange program and after graduation she decided that her calling was in Italy. And that's where she ran as soon as she could. Her degree now sits in her back pocket as she is more focused on perfecting her pasta making technique than being a psychologist.

Which basically means we've been playing a game of telephone tag for as long as I can remember. Much like my houseplants, our friendship exists in a perpetual state of barely hanging on, both requiring a kind of attention I can't seem to maintain from a distance. It's easier to watch things wither than to admit I'm not good at keeping things alive once they're out of arm's reach.

"Ugh." I sigh loudly and dramatically let myself fall back to the floor. No one is here. I live alone now. And while this apartment is nothing to write home about, it is mine. Alright, not mine mine, but mine, because every month I send off most of my hard earned coffee-getting money to some dude I've never met. But it's the perfect space. Close enough to all the places I've loved without being trapped in them.

I don't think enough people talk about the weirdness in living alone. It isn't something anyone prepares you for. Or rather, the weirdness that becomes you. It's not always loneliness. Though, that creeps in also. The quiet is kind of nice. But the all out weirdness of knowing you're not beholden to any other living thing so long as you are alone in these walls. Probably why I've defaulted to staring up at the ceiling fan and watching it spin with my boots kicked off and bra thrown across the room but I'm still dressed just enough because the complete paralysis of having to take off anything non-essential has me rooted to this spot.

It's nestled on a short street lined with buildings just like it.

When I graduated I could have left the city like everyone else. This city is transient and moves in waves. You see it every fall as the bright-eyed freshman land amongst their new peers. You see it every spring when the grads pack up and leave her behind. While all the buildings here have survived hundreds of years of students, she's used and then set aside for the glitz and glamor of the big siren cities that come calling once degrees are in hand. Reid heard that call too, joining the exodus that happens every spring. Maybe that's why I stayed. *Our* relationship wasn't over yet, not with the city, at least.

Having just crammed the contents of my day into another inbox, overstuffing it into the void like I do so many things, I'll just lay here a little longer waiting for return phone calls I know won't come.

I watch the fan circle. Imagining how fast it would need to be moving before it spun right off its rotator and came crashing down on top of me. The only sound I hear besides the non-stop self-narration is the whooshing with each rotation, or maybe every several rotations, I'm not sure. It's the kind of mindless thought that allows me the hyperfixation needed rather than focusing on all the things I need to be doing and thinking about.

When did this become my life? Too tired to move. Alone in silence. Sometimes the only meaningful conversation I have in a day is with myself. This didn't used to be my life, back in college when the halls were filled with friends and laughter. Now the only sounds are those from the apartment itself and my growling stomach.

Today was exhausting. Not because work is hard as much as it can be frustrating. Frustrating to watch all these men around me, throw their dicks on the table to see whose is biggest. Spoiler alert, none of them. I know this because if they had anything meaningful between their legs or between their ears, they wouldn't compete in this ongoing cock fight. It's almost comical. Or it would be if I wasn't always the one left watching them bro-eachother-off. The way they all pat each other on the back for a job mediocrely done is just a frat-boy circle jerk. Even my succulent, Pricktor, seems to be withering under the toxic masculinity, and those things are supposed to be impossible to kill.

Speaking of cocks... there's something I need to do.

I take a deep breath as I swat my hand blindly in hopes of finding my phone within reach so I don't have to move again. Leaning into the physical and emotional atrophy that's occurred now. There should be something grounding about having my spine on the floor and my limbs stretched out like this. I think it's supposed to help a chakra, or balance, or anxiety, which I have been newly diagnosed with.

Not officially diagnosed, but more of a general, *'do you ever feel anxious'* question during my last physical, *'don't most people?'* was my reply. Apparently, most people *do not*. Or rather, they just don't admit it. *Lesson learned.* I took down the recommendation for a therapist, called my mom, and filed that away. I'll tell you what won't help my anxiety? Another hour taken from me each week to talk about all the things that already happened. The only ancient history I'm interested in is occasionally actual ancient history, never my own.

I prop my phone back on its boob-perch so perfectly positioned that it sounds like I'm putting effort into this call while in actuality it just means I don't have to pick my head from the floor. I uncomfortably glare down my nose to scroll through the contacts to find his name so I can rip off this bandaid. *R.I.P.*

Rip is a fucking stretch. It's like one of those loose bandaids that hang from your heel and you're not sure if you're better off exposing the blister or forcing it back down as you shove your foot into the high heel you know will cause your toes to be numb and filled with blood by whatever time you stroll in. Only to slip on the more practical work shoe a handful of hours later. In this case I've decided. Blister it is. I hit the call button, switch the call to speakerphone and lay it against my sternum so I can feel the vibration of the ring.

Dropping my arm back to the wood floor and resuming my

position as full starfish. Gabriel and I have had this pseudo-casual semi-consistent relationship on the back-burner for long enough.

Three rings.

"Hello?" he answers with more of a question. Probably because we spend so little time on the phone.

"Hi," I say with more confidence in greeting than he did. The beat of silence goes on longer than I should let it. I've gotten in the habit of giving people the breath to catch up, to fill the silence. Unsurprisingly, he doesn't. And that's my cue...

"I don't think you should come over tonight."

"Working late?" *Fair question considering I am typically either working late or lying about working late as the go-to excuse.*

"No, I'm already home, I just, I think I need a break, this isn't really working out."

"This?" he says with such incredulity, like the idea that there even was a *this* is shocking, or maybe he's offended that it isn't working out. *He couldn't actually see this as going well, could he?*

"I just think we are looking for different things," I continue, trying to let him down more gently. But this whole thing has been gentle. This whole thing has been based around convenience, reasonable compatibility. And it's been fine for both of us, working within schedules, but laying here for the last hour the flurry in my stomach at the idea of seeing him later was more at the inconvenience of shaving my legs than it was any sense of excitement. There was a time that was part of the appeal. Perhaps knowing that even the best version of him could only ever result in the worst version of us, and I would never find myself in a position trapped by the addictive comfort of love. *It wasn't love.*

"Arden, seriously? Are you even listening to me?" *Wow, I guess not.*

"What do you want from me? You're busy, I'm busy..." *It's not a lie.*

"What do I want?" he laughs, chortles almost, "I want a girlfriend..." he says. *A girlfriend. Not 'you'. Which is how I know this is the right decision.*

We were both placeholders, and worked well enough, but the thing about using people as placeholders, is that there's clearly something you are keeping them in place of. And eventually, you realize it just isn't enough. The shape of whomever you're holding as the cardboard cutout in your heart, isn't shaped in a way this person can walk through. Not without going full KoolAid man and crashing through. And let's be honest, there's nothing about Gabriel that makes him an I'll-crash-through-a-wall kind of guy. That has been part of the appeal. That, and again, the convenient scheduling.

He sighs in defeat, and it's honestly more of a fight than I thought he would have even put up.

"You want a break, take your break, but I won't be waiting around for you to decide this is something you want."

This.

Maybe if we had ever seen each other as more, we would be talking about each other as people, not just the semi-frequent sexual encounters and meals we labeled a relationship.

"I'm sorry" I offer in consolation.

"You're not and I don't need you to be."

And with that the line goes dead. I curl my head up from where it's remained on the floor during this whole call, and yep, *Call Ended.* Relationship, too. I should probably be more disappointed than I am. But I don't feel much of anything. It never took hold. It never got far enough into my bloodstream to infect the rest of my cells, it never pumped its way to my heart. Which is for the best, this all is.

I let out a dramatic groan that sinks into the floor with me as the ceiling fan continues its metaphor for my life. *How profound.*

My phone buzzes against my chest, and for a split second, I think it might be Gabriel having an emotionally mature revelation. But no, it's just my birth control alarm. Predictable. Right on schedule.

The wood floor beneath me has gone from grounding to just plain uncomfortable and I can feel the secondhand embarrassment from the houseplants in various stages of decay. I should probably move. Order takeout. Feed myself something other than the stale crackers and spite that have been sustaining me all day.

With heroic effort, I peel myself off the floor, my skirt making that distinctive sound of synthetic fabric separating from wood, like velcro but sadder. The apartment feels different now that I've officially ended things with Gabriel. Not emptier, exactly, but more honest. Like it's no longer pretending to be a space that might someday house a real relationship.

I shuffle to the kitchen, my stockinged feet sliding on the hardwood like I'm doing a very lazy impression of Tom Cruise in Risky Business. The contents of my fridge are a perfect represen-tation of my life choices at the moment, half a bottle of cham-pagne I nabbed from a work celebration, three different types of mustard from three different take out orders, and a yogurt that expired yesterday.

The city sparkles below me, all potential and promise and overpriced real estate. The sky is turning that specific shade of purple and orange that makes everything look like it's being filtered through an Instagram preset called Millennial Disappoint-ment. Below, students are starting their Thursday night migra-tions between bars, their laughter floating up to my window like a reminder of when I used to be that carefree. Or at least drunk enough to fake it.

I open the champagne with a pop that sounds like the excla-mation point to my day. The end of a chapter, maybe. I don't bother with a glass, that feels too civilized for a woman who just ended a relationship while essentially planking.

Somewhere out there, Gabriel is probably already updating his profiles, adding himself back into the pool of eligible men who list 'adventures' as an interest but really mean 'golf.' And some-how, watching the lights flicker on in apartments across the street, I feel more connected to this city full of strangers than I ever did to him.

Chapter Eight

HAPPILY EVER BEFORE

Arden

The swift double knock on the door could only be one person. The only person left now. What once was a vibrant social life has boiled down to me, and my former, whatever-you-call-the-person-you-had-casual-sex-with-at-eighteen. Somewhere between then and now, we became the only two left, and he's only here part of the time, though he always says Boston feels different from everywhere else he's been, that he could see himself coming back here someday. All of our other college friends are gone in one way or another. And while he doesn't live his life with the same permanence and doesn't believe in planting roots, he's turned that into a career that he seems to find incredibly fulfilling. *I guess someone is thriving.*

I read along with his name in the byline of his travel journal series, as Stella and I text back and forth fawning over the latest photo of him cliff diving or eating some kind of insect on a stick.

His knock comes right on cue. Always unannounced, always perfectly timed.

Clinging to the remnants of people in the form of texts, voice-mails, and emails, is a digital shell of something that used to be more. And sometimes when I'm only getting the highlights on delay, I think about how these relationships used to just be easy, it didn't require effort. Now, every single one of them is constantly on life support. There is some passive effort, but every contact just is a little farther apart from the previous. The time zones and heartache keep the distance in place, but what exists between the walls of time and space are the memories that keep me trapped in this pocket of nostalgia.

My friends have all found themselves in what they do. This all just isn't what I thought it would be, it isn't quite right. And for the hundredth time this week, I wonder if *anything ever will be.*

Another knock on the door and I'm sure it's part of the reason why he's here. His eyebrows knit together fiercely. He's assessing my well being. His hair falls in his face with a tilt of his head and a short double nod to match his knock, he breaks into a smile and wraps his arms around me. It's been months. He only returns now because his moms live just outside of the city. A bear hug like no other, with a bag of what looks like Thai food swinging from his hand at my back.

Ethan Hayes stands in my doorway not that different than he was at eighteen. Hair perpetually wild, skin tanned from all the ways he exposes himself to the world, brown eyes still carrying the same unshakable restlessness, as if he's forever on the edge of something.

"All good, kid?" he asks and it sounds like he already has a sense of the answer. I don't remember exactly when he started calling me kid... probably around the same time we stopped sleeping together. 'Sleeping together' being a complete euphemism considering we never slept. It's not that he has any real seniority here in terms of age, none, in fact. I've got him beat by a couple months. But as our physical relationship dissolved and became the most natural friendship, everything before that had been wiped away. That shifted dynamic resulted in him tossing out the occasional *'kid'* as if a reminder. I had never given him the credit he deserved in being my friend. But he always was. And sometimes now, especially when my relationship with Stella is just a game of phone tag, he feels like the only one left.

"I'm *fine*, E," I say as I grab the bag and make my way into the kitchen, careful not to trip over the collection of shoes that are reproducing in the middle of the room while he cues up a playlist so the silence isn't so silent.

"You finally broke up with him." It's not exactly a question, definitely not an accusation, but a confirmation that it happened. Ethan was never a huge fan of Gabriel, but tolerated the idea of him enough whenever I'd give him the abbreviated update on my dating life. His feelings on the man are not too dissimilar to my own.

"Can you really even call it a breakup?" I ask as I roll my neck from shoulder to shoulder.

"I don't know, you never did with us, that doesn't mean it wasn't." He reaches into a container and grabs a couple of spring rolls offering me one with a smile. And while it might have the bite of a sarcastic remark, remembering a few years ago, there never were any hard feelings. Any reference to it now is just honesty.

"Break up implies broken. Nothing was broken between us. Why do we all treat it like there are only ever two options, a classic happily ever after or someone totally shattered and broken." I nab the spring roll and tap it against his, in a rehearsed *cheers* motion before taking a bite.

"What do you want me to call it?" he asks as he pops the rest of the roll in his mouth.

"I don't know. It just feels sad when you call it a breakup, and as I recall, neither of us were sad." My response makes the corner of his mouth quirk up with amusement, and a bit of memory.

"There was *nothing* about us that was sad," he says and it's true, there never was. He pops the lid to another food container, and hands it to me, my stomach more eager to participate in this conversation than either of us.

"Well, whatever you call it, it's over now. It was time. Not just because of him, but because of me. I've been dating forever, in some form of the word. And I'm exhausted. It's all predictable, just following the same patterns. *He's interested, I'm interested, we learn each other's favorite colors over coffee, maybe he asks me my middle name on our second date, I force myself to sit through a movie, we go to dinner, I talk about my job, he feigns interest. He talks about his career, or band, or recent golf game, all while we are just dancing around the big question of sexual compatibility.* It's all so superficial. I know that and I get that it takes time, but the idea that this is what's out there, it just feels like I've been misled by every romance I've ever read. I don't see myself with anyone now, because even when I was with him, I wasn't *with* him. You shouldn't be alone when you've got someone in bed with you. I've tried, I've done the love thing, and maybe we will again, but I just am not going to force this same stale but comfortable version of companionship when everything I got out of that relationship I can just as easily fulfill being on my own."

I take the breath needed to fill my lungs as I complete the rant I just word-vomited at his feet. That's fine, he's seen me *real* vomit.

"How did he take it?"

"About as well as he did everything...pretty agreeable. There was a moment there I thought he might prove me wrong, but nope. Once again, I was right."

"Then it sounds like you got what you want, and you're on your own, kid."

He says the words aloud, words I served up on a silver platter, but even that, like everything else, doesn't feel quite right. We let the silence hang between us, until I force myself to break it as usual.

"I don't want to talk about this anymore, I want to talk about you," I say, "Where to next? *Who* to next?"

His laugh barrels out of him as if I don't know a big portion of his travel is because he falls fast and follows whomever he can across any borders, to the tops of mountain peaks, or the depths of underwater caves. And his journalism degree does the rest. But he always jumped in, heart first, and for being so fueled by passion and people, he always just enjoyed the ride, regardless of the destination.

"You didn't think Thai was a coincidence, did you?" He nods to the container of pad thai. "I'm still here a few more days if you want to go for a run tomorrow morning," he offers, already knowing my answer.

"I'm running up enough hills at the office trying to keep up with the boys club. I'll pass."

A familiar song comes over the speakers, and despite that saying about *old habits dying hard* he just hits skip and instead asks me about work.

Chapter Nine

HAPPILY EVER BEFORE

Arden

Some days, I look around the office at the men in their perfectly pressed white shirts and wonder if they feel it too. That low-grade panic bubbling just beneath the surface of the glass ceiling they don't even realize is in place. One day, they'll just be able to ascend through without any concerns of cracks, leaving it fully intact for those below them. I imagine them staring at their screens, fingers hovering over keyboards that produce profitability rather than poetry, wondering if they are secretly doodling marginalia to remind them of the imaginary friends they abandoned along the way. At some point the only keys they remember are QWERTY not pianos, and the only notes they have are the ones for their powerpoint presentations.

Men don't seem to do tortured soul-searching the way women are expected to, they are too busy constructing their own narratives while we're just trying to survive the ones they've written about us.

This isn't *bad*, I remind myself. It's exactly what I wanted. Or at least, it's what I thought I wanted before wanting became this complicated algorithm of compromise and desperate ambition.

"Arden," The use of my name has me swiveling around in my chair. Pricktor, *I mean,* Victor appears like my subconscious conjured him.

Despite the Thompson Challenge running in the backgrounds of all our minds, it's all still business as usual. It's really quite brilliant, a win-win way the company gets to overwork everyone with the possibility of just a slightly more golden carrot at the end of the race.

"Did you finish the analysis of which areas are under performing?" *Right now, I think I'm the under performing area.*

"Yes." I flick back to the screen, trying to ignore how he's moved to hover behind my shoulder, his cologne is too sharp this close and we both know it. "There are two departments that are responsible for about 37% loss."

"Excellent." His reflection feels like it's looking right at me. "I'll have you present your findings and the resulting termination plan for the employees in those domains."

I spin my chair to face him, "Did you say termination? We're firing them?"

He arches an eyebrow, the same look he gives when someone presents a report with a typo. "What did you think the purpose was?"

"I thought we were going to improve productivity? Improve performance?" My voice sounds smaller than I'd like, and I hate that. I force myself to maintain eye contact as I continue, "I didn't know we were terminating..." I look at my screen once more to confirm the numbers, the figures now feeling less like data and more like faces, "terminating one hundred and three jobs!"

Victor adjusts his cuffs that need no adjusting, just like when he points out an unneeded correction on a document just to remind you he can. In this case, it's a tell that he's gearing up to deliver something *he* considers mentor worthy.

"Sometimes things can't be salvaged, it's important to know when to cut your losses. You'll benefit from learning that early," he says flatly.

I have a pit in my stomach, and the way he's still standing there, expecting grateful acknowledgment of his wisdom, only makes it worse.

————

The city is a living metaphor, historic buildings nestled behind contemporary facades. A physical representation of the internal landscape I'm constantly negotiating. Duality has always been my love language, and this place speaks it fluently. So today, I'm choosing to get lost somewhere that isn't the labyrinth of my own overthinking.

The contemporary pavilion stands like a protective guardian over the historic building behind it, a glass-and-steel preserving something delicate and profound. I'm not going to spend too much time unpacking the painfully obvious parallel to my own emotional architecture. Some metaphors are best left unexamined, like the one you know you shouldn't keep texting but definitely do, especially after your third glass of wine, or an all around shitty work day. *Who am I kidding, I already have an email drafted ready to send him, no wine necessary.*

I slide my expired college ID across the ticket counter, wearing my most charming I'm-definitely-still-a-student smile. The intern, who looks like he's running on nothing but cold brew and unresolved career anxiety, doesn't bat an eye. Only grunting one word, *'tour?'* He points to the sign up sheet. *'I'm good on my own.'*

We're in an unspoken pact, he'll give me the discount, I'll pretend I'm not essentially committing museum fraud, and we'll both get on with our day.

The croissant hanging from my mouth is probably not helping my sophisticated-art-patron-vibe, but some days, survival is about choosing your battles. Today, that battle is definitely not with this chocolate-filled pastry that I need for physical and emotional sustenance.

As I move through the glass-enclosed walkway, the modern

world starts to dissolve. It's like stepping through a portal with each step taking me further from financial briefs, closer to something that feels more like breathing.

The space opens up like a revelation. A soaring glass ceiling floods the interior with light so pure it could resurrect Renaissance dreams. Ancient Roman sculptures stand like silent witnesses, flowering plants softening the edges of marble and memory. These are Babylonian gardens hidden in the heart of a city that moves too quickly to notice. Fountains murmur their eternal conversations, blending with the hushed voices of fellow time travelers, though they might just consider themselves tourists.

The great rooms with their golden frames are humbling in a way that feels almost cellular. Each room has an intimacy within it to remind you how intentionally curated this space is.

The combination of carbs and canvases has become my go-to coping mechanism for early-twenties ennui, a habit that started that fateful rising sophomore summer. There's magic in places like this, there's also heartbreak, and tragedy. Maybe that's why it can strip you of your own. It gives you someplace to feel things rather than your own tortured heart. This is the closest reality I can find to the ones I create while dreaming at my desk, remembering books with protagonists whose lives never escape the pages.

In college I took more than one art history class. The first was for a required credit, the second and third were just because I loved them. Which is why on a good day, I know my way around a museum. On a bad day, I get lost in them. Two guesses which kind of day today is? I take another bite of my contraband croissant. *Definitely not meant to be eating here.*

I weave through a motley crew of museum-goers. The retirees with their comfortable shoes, the wide eyed tourists, and a handful of college students who look like they're one coffee away from a breakdown. *Been there — spoiler alert, it doesn't end when you graduate.* We're a jury of mismatched peers, bound together by nothing more than our shared proximity in this one momentary intersection.

The painting before me seems to glow from within. No doubt why they put her where they did, positioned precisely where the sun can illuminate all the indecent brush strokes. It's an unwritten rule, the bright thing always centered for everyone to see. She's massive, though it really isn't the size that overwhelms you first. It's the light. The way it seems to pulse from within, like somehow her pale body glows in spite of everything going on, even as the fabric of her dress commits the ultimate betrayal and exposes her, leaving me to feel like I'm witnessing something I shouldn't be.

It's not just me watching. The tour guide stands at the front radiating a kind of practiced authority that screams *'I've memorized every possible fact about this painting.'* His all-black outfit is meant to be museum-docent but is giving much more of an art world rebel vibe. I always thought these jobs were reserved for retired professors, but in the glimpses of him, he doesn't look much older than me, if at all.

"Before us, we see a luminous woman with billowing red silk as she twists away from a white bull charging into a stormy sea while cupids weeping in the golden sky above." He explains the top level of paint, his voice a perfect blend of warm academic passion and performative drama.

"This masterpiece," he continues, "depicts Jupiter, *king* of the gods, who spots a gorgeous Phoenician princess, Europa, and decides that his best move is to transform himself into the most beautiful bull anyone's ever seen... We're talking flower garlands, soft fur, the kind of bull that makes you temporarily forget everything you've been taught about *not* approaching strange animals."

There's a sense of comedy to his explanation, a punch on certain words to emphasize the hilarity of the mythology and keep everyone engaged. Though I suspect his face keeps people engaged enough as is. Through the glimpses and cracks between guests in front of me, I can see him. He carries himself with a rare mix of easy confidence and genuine enthusiasm, like one feeds the other, making even the most obscure facts sound like secrets he's only sharing with you. It's how everyone is enraptured by him as he speaks. How he commands a space, where even the security guards nod as he passes with his group. His voice carrying just enough to keep everyone engaged without disturbing the sacred quiet of the gallery spaces.

But as he does, his voice shifts to something more reverent.

"That's exactly what is captured here. This is the pinnacle of Titian's Posies. How he captures both the violence and the ecstasy of divine intervention, while being a representation of one of the most enduring myths of the ancient world. It's a stunning allegory of divine desire, power, and the inevitable clash between mortal innocence and overwhelming forces."

I look up at this painting in front of us as I hang near the back of this tour group.

"Now, for infinite bragging rights, and a free Museum-Geek t-shirt from the gift shop... who can tell me what inspired this piece?"

It's clear who in the group are the students, though with every answer they lob at him, I watch as he shoots them down in that *nice try* kind of way.

I miss school sometimes, and just as often as I consider getting bangs, or chopping my hair into a bob, I also wonder if I should just enroll in graduate school. Put myself back in an environment I know I can thrive in, as I always did. School being the one place where overachievers seeking validation can control exactly their own destiny. Rather than the workforce where charm plays a heavy role, and in most cases, not even charm as much as male-comradery. But in school I always knew the answers, and a right answer satisfied something in me that even people can't.

A scoff escapes me. It's part eye roll and part involuntary commentary at the idea that out of this group, no one knows the origins of Titian's Europa. Her luminescence is only as valuable to them as her exposed breast, no one considering more depth in her source than feminine beauty.

His eyes sweep the crowd, laser-focused and intense. And when they land on me, rather than admit I've been caught, I shoot my hand up as if it was intentional all along.

But with my hand raised and my gut starving for the small validation of, well, being right and in this case getting some free swag, I'm able to get a clearer view of him. And for all the things I expected him to be, familiar isn't one of them.

"It's based on the novel 'Leucippe and Clitophon' by Achilles Tatius," I've barely let the smug smile broaden across my face as his lips press together and he shakes his head with an apology.

"If there are no other guesses, it is inspired by a scene from Book II in Ovid's Metamorphoses. Now, before we move on, any other questions?"

He's wrong. *Wrong wrong wrong.*

My hand shoots back up again horrified at how boldly he dismissed what is clearly the right answer. I've stayed on the outskirts of this group, intentionally not trying to immerse myself. But I'm pulled towards the center now. Charged with the challenge of his dismissal and needing to be closer to the pulse of the conversation.

"Yes?" he directs back to me, also taking a step closer.

It's as he approaches I am able to understand the shape of him, broad in a way his shirt pulls tightly across his chest, and taller with each step. I don't let the distraction of his soft stubble prevent me from educating him on his inaccuracy. All while scanning his face and trying to place what feels like it exists in an unvisited corner of my brain.

"Ovid was hundreds of years earlier, Leucippe and Clitophon would have been much more influential." I cock my head to the side ever so slightly as he narrows his eyes in response.

"Ah, but you're talking about influence, I asked what inspired it." Now he is the one that is smug.

"So you're rejecting my answer based on... a technicality?" I have no doubt the disbelief is all over my face, but his is full of something much more.

"No, I'm saying that influence and inspiration are two different things...I asked about inspiration. This isn't the Price is Right, I'm not about to give out the most coveted prize of a Museum Geek t-shirt based on the closest guess." He's weaving through the others, and coming nearer to me where I have also taken a stance.

It's as though those around us have taken a step back as we each step further into each other and the arrogance of this argument.

"That emotional quickening you feel right now, *that* is inspiration. You couldn't keep yourself from answering, even if you were wrong, you were *inspired*. It wasn't something you could keep restrained. Whereas *influence* is my ability to tell this story, and provoke your changed opinion." He's provoking alright, in more ways than I care to admit, but the look on his face tells me he knows them.

"It seems you think you've changed my opinion." My eyes drop to the waist of his pants where his name tag is clipped and hangs like a badge of honor. He spots my eyeline at his waistband and strategically slips his hand into his pocket, using his forearm to hide his name from view.

"And it seems you think you know something I don't," he says, taking a half step closer. The movement shifts the air between us.

"I *clearly* know a few things you don't," I shoot back, tilting my chin up to maintain eye contact, unintimidated by his proximity but absolutely engulfed by the way he's looking at me.

"That's probably true in most cases, but this isn't one of them," His voice carries a hint of amusement that makes my fingers itch to wipe the almost smile off his face.

Up close, he's devastatingly attractive. All cheekbones and barely contained intellectual energy. The closer he approaches the better the glimpse of his eyes, which radiate blues similar to the sea on the canvas behind him. And based on how we've both seem to have goaded the other into this public display, I can tell it's not just physical similarity he carries to the sea behind him but depth able to swallow you whole with each response.

While I'm fueled by this interaction, I'm also desperately racking my mind for any indication how I might know him. I'm not sure that I do, unable to pull out a name, but there's this overwhelming sense that this isn't the first time I've seen him.

"And while we're at it, The *RAPE* of Europa," I emphasize, "It's clearly about female resistance, more than some 'enduring interpretation of power and divine intervention.'" In the moments we've stood here the hunger for validation turned into frustration and provocation around his original presentation. Just another man constructing the narrative while the woman in the painting, like all of us, tries to survive the story being written about her.

I can see him inhale and I can feel my lungs do the same like our organs are in a competition all of their own.

"Yes, and while that is a recorded view, there *are* historical letters between Titian and Philip II that actually document the painting's intended meaning."

"Ah, yes, because a period-specific record mansplaining a woman's experience makes it inherently accurate. *Got it.*" My reply is heavy in sarcasm and his laugh is unexpected. It's a sharp, quick sound that makes me want to do the same. I *am* inspired. "Or," I step closer, our proximity crackling with something that definitely isn't just art historical tension, "he was showing how Europa maintains her autonomy even in the moment of terror, but didn't think his '*Renaissance-bros*' would have gotten it." *The air-quotes included selling how I really feel at this point.*

"Well," he says, leaning closer so that I can smell a hint of something warm and clean, "since you're such an expert, perhaps you'd like to take over the rest of this tour?" His hand sweeps across the space, encompassing our impromptu audience who've been watching this verbal sparring match with poorly concealed interest.

"Oh," I breathe, "I'm finding your... misinterpretation... far too fascinating to interrupt."

I had forgotten the steps to this dance, more often than not, just finding myself alone in the center of the dancefloor. The tour members fade into background noise, forgotten extras in our own private performance.

We're standing close enough that I can see the glare in his eyes that suggests he's enjoying this far more than he should. And that he can likely note the same in mine, in this light, mirror images of each other.

"I'd think sneaking onto this tour would have been enough," he says through a smile, "but it seems you won't be satisfied until you've dismantled my career *and* called me a misogynist."

Busted. Completely, utterly busted.

"Next time," he continues, "try not to call attention to yourself by fighting with the guide. We usually frown upon that sort of thing."

"And *I* usually frown upon inaccuracies," I counter, "so I guess we're even."

He brings his hand to his mouth and drags it slowly up his jawline as he laughs through it. His hand, like the rest of him, looks more and more like it belongs amongst a sculpture, the only adornment, a signet ring on his right pinky. He pulls his hand away from the fullness of laughter on his lips with an offer.

"You can stay, on one condition..."

"I promise not to fight with the guide?" My own voice dripping with insincerity and eyelashes fluttering in mockery.

"Meet me on the bench in the gallery when the tour's done," he says, gesturing his head towards the building as an indication. When I say nothing in immediate reply, mostly out of shock, he lifts his eyebrows ever so slightly.

I nod, in a momentary check, not defeat, because the alternative, walking away from this, is absolutely not an option.

He leans closer, his voice is low, a gravelly whisper meant only for me.

"And Arden.. I *want* you to fight with the guide."

When he pulls back and winks, I catch a glimpse of ink creeping from his cuffed sleeve. As he positions himself back at the front, he speaks through a different smile now, and something tells me, I'm sporting one to match.

I have no reason to stay to engage with this know-it-all-too-attractive-to-be-a-tour-guide tour guide. And yet, here I am, already googling gathering information like armor. Because despite my best attempts to blend in, okay, maybe not even my worst attempt, he saw me.

It's only then I realize, he said my name.

He turns his attention back to his group as if nothing out of the ordinary has occurred. *'Now, if you'll follow me to Botticelli's Lucretia, we can discuss how Renaissance artists handled sequential narrative—'*

The tour moves on, but I stay behind for a moment, looking up at Europa's face.

In those few seconds when he leaned close, he offered more than just an *albeit incorrect* art history lesson. The way he looked into my eyes, it felt like he was reading something deeper, something I've been working to keep carefully hidden.

And Europa help me, I let him.

Chapter Ten

HAPPILY EVER BEFORE

Will

Unfuckingbelievable. I laugh my way back up to my office to grab a couple of things. My laptop, a couple reference books, a Museum Geek t-shirt, and a breath mint for good measure. The tour ended and I answered a few of the additional questions from other guests as she stood off to the side. It looked like she was deciding what to do, but I saw her stomp off towards the gallery where I said to meet on a mission.

I've been contradicted on tours before, usually the arrogant professor who doesn't like a modern interpretation or some young kid trying to be funny. This wasn't the first and certainly won't be the last time. It comes with the territory when you're part art historian and part performance artist. I'm pretty sure that's what it said on the job description. But this was different. This was the first time I've ever wanted to be wrong, or, more accurately, the first time I've wanted someone else to be right so badly I could taste it with every word she shot my way.

By the end of the tour, she'd transformed from potential troublemaker to the most engaged participant I've ever encountered. Her questions weren't just smart, they were sharpened to cut deeper, to challenge the narrative I've gotten comfortable present-ing. The audience is usually interested in the more superficial anecdotes, not her.

She wasn't subtle in the back of the crowd, but it was bold to jump in and think I wouldn't notice her. Then again, I don't think she noticed me with the same memory. To be fair, the last time I wasn't usually the one on the receiving end, but the memory is still seared into my brain in a way that made her imme-diately recognizable.

Spring semester, 2008, Art History 201: Histories of the Renais-sance and Baroque.

She always took the same seat, perfectly positioned near the front of the class while I was always the complete diagonal in the back. I spent most of that term with a better view of the back of her head than I did the searing look she gave me today.

I'm not sure that it was intentional or if she just accidentally found herself in the middle of a tour ready to go toe-to-toe before just totally fucking stealing the tour.

I don't think she has any realization that we know each other. Know is a stretch, but that semester I spent weeks watching this woman whirlwind her way around every other person in the class, myself included, and occasionally the professor. Then as the fates would have it, to just never have another class with her again.

Fates are funny things.

The glass gallery awaits. Complete contrast to the rest of the space. This is the most modern addition of the museum, different from the deep tones and ornate frames. This space is far more industrial, cleaner, meant to showcase the items hung here as well as the people who spent the money to be immortalized by it. *Trust me, I know.*

There she is. Sitting on the bench staring up at one of my favorites. Most people don't know the history of this place, and the woman behind it who bought art in a way Boston society frowned upon, but left this incredible legacy. It is the story behind what hangs in every gold frame, and even the frames that hold nothing, that is the most moving.

Her shoulders drop ever so slightly and the fierceness on her face fades to fragility as she tilts her chin up to allow herself the space to absorb the painting in front of her.

She isn't dressed like this was her intended day plan, much more like she escaped an office like the one I'm constantly pushed towards. But you know what they say about intentions. The road to hell is paved with good ones. Looking at her in this light, I don't have any problem with that being the destination.

I take a seat next to her on the wooden bench. The same one I lay across some mornings when I get here before the world wakes up. I just exist in this space and think about all the people who have sat here before us. Now I can add us to that list.

"Here, I marked the page for you." I hand her one of the reference books I brought down and she starts flipping to the tabbed page. The book looks heavy on her lap, but her long fingers flutter through the pages like someone playing an impossible instrument racing against some internal clock. She reads as if she's starving, as if knowledge is a competition she's determined to win. Meanwhile, I open the laptop to pull up some digitized images.

"I am right!" She taps her finger on the page, exactly why I brought it down. "I knew it! I have this book!" Her face pinches slightly, and juts her head back before closing the book cover to read the title and confirm what I knew when I saw her. "Wait, I *have* this book."

Of course she does. It's a college course book from years ago. Figured it might jog her memory, also the reason she felt so adamant about her answer.

The book only distracted her momentarily as she put the pieces together. I can tell she is trying not-so-discreetly to place me.

"Check this out," I say, quickly pulling her attention to the laptop. "You see here? I would bet this is why you were misinformed. That book quotes an interpretation that has been widely referenced for years by professors in colleges in this very city, can you believe it?" The hint of taunt in my voice draws her closer, like a fencer advancing for the perfect strike. I see the moment that all the pieces are falling into place.

"Can I see that?" She reaches across with no regard for the way our bodies are closer than makes sense. She just focused, zooming in and scanning the rest of the images, to confirm upon closer I said. Her arm is pressed against mine and be it the smell of her laundry detergent, her shampoo, or just her, it fills the smallest crevices left between us.

"Fine," she says as she shuts the laptop and book simultaneously. "We're both right."

Straightening back up and facing me dead on. I could give it to her, the compromise but why would I settle when clearly she is getting off on the thrill as much as I am.

"No, this time, I'm right." I shake my head slowly, and her lips pop open with a sense of disbelief.

Despite the vast space, we're so close that I can feel the vibrations of her skin against mine as she moves to parry my argument with one of her own.

"But don't you think because–," she begins.

"I think that maybe, at least this once, you'll have to take the loss and admit I am right." My tone is playful knowing she has no interest in backing down.

"I'll admit you give a decent tour, but that's about it."

"I've been called a lot of things in my life, decent isn't one of them."

I can see it, when she quirks a smile pulled from the corner of her mouth, and changes tactics.

"Do you practice those little speeches of yours in the mirror? Complete with hand gestures?" Her hands wave like she's trying to mimic me earlier, but in fact it looks more like her long fingers are attempting to cast a spell. *And with every flick it's working.*

"Only on Tuesdays. The rest of the week, I practice looking disapprovingly at irreverent museum-goers."

"Ouch, is that what I am? *Irreverent*?" Her hand reaches for pearls to clutch that aren't there, but the dramatics make me smile all the same.

"There is nothing irreverent about you, Arden."

Her eyes are locked on mine. I won't tell her how easy it was for me to recall her name once she was there tearing down the tour I deliver multiple times a day with a full audience. But neither of us is willing to admit directly that this isn't the first time we've been in each other's orbit.

"Sterling!" The voice refracts off the wall of windows. Slicing right through our conversation.

"Good, good! You're still here. There's a donor who's just arrived, and despite advising that there are no more tours for the evening, you know how they can be..." I sigh, both because I don't want to leave the conversation, but also because I do know exactly how they can be. I also know the likelihood that my last name has some benefit to being the one that walks them through the museum. Surely about to result in numerous versions of 'I saw your father for golf last week' or 'give our love to your mother.'

"I can take them, but I have plans, so I won't have long." He nods emphatically and scampers off. Thankful that he won't be the one required to make forty-five minutes of small talk with someone who could have him fired out of boredom. He's a small, anxious man, and having all the education to justify his title but none of the nepotism, means this task is always left up to me. Because I have both.

I stand gathering my things, acutely aware that Arden has done the same. Taking it as her cue to make her own exit. Brushing her hands down her dress as she stands and tucking her hair behind her ears I can see her face even more clearly now.

"Well, Will Sterling," she says with emphasis through a victorious smirk. "I appreciate the over-intellectualized Art History 201 lesson, but I better get going."

"Have coffee with me. I'll even tell you all about the great art heist," I say, watching the most imperceptible smile try to contain itself.

"Are you asking me out after trying to prove me wrong?" Her eyes drop ever so slightly before meeting mine again, and there's a visible pull toward saying yes written all over her face, but something else too.

"Is it working?"

"Not really, plus I've already heard a decent version of that story." She emphasizes 'decent' in a way that makes me want to prove her wrong about everything.

The museum is nearly empty now leaving our voices to echo slightly in the hall. My fingers brush hers as I hand over a Museum Geek shirt, a peace offering of sorts, and that simple touch sends electricity up my arm.

"Consider it encouragement to come back for another tour. Maybe next time you'll actually sign up and I can save you a spot at the front."

"Careful, next time I might actually ruin your credibility." She takes the shirt, her fingertips lingering against the fabric and I imagine how they would feel against my back.

"Worth it," I say.

For a moment, I forget about every masterpiece I've spent years studying. I just let myself appreciate this unexpected one standing in front of me, more enthralled with the brushstrokes of her mind and the theory of her eyes.

"You know, in Europa's time, it would have been a cup of wine, not coffee," she counters.

Wine, coffee, fuck it, we can fight our way through the post-impressionists and drink absinthe, all sounds good to me.

"True, but I find coffee leads to fewer tragic endings," I say instead, wondering if she can hear the hope in my voice.

"That's what you think." There's something in her tone there, vulnerability leaking through like pentimento showing through the layers.

"Then just come back and fight with me some time."

"Surprisingly tempting," she replies, "but I'm not available."

Chapter Eleven

HAPPILY EVER AFTER

Bancroft

We've spent hours talking about it now. Fuck, I've spent hours before now, having the same conversation.

Averaging about two hours a week, for the last year, excluding some scheduling conflicts, holidays, and the days I decided to talk about everyone's favorite related therapy topic outside of one's love life, daddy-issues, that brings the total hours I've paid to discuss this to a whopping hundred hours of someone nudging me forward towards making a decision.

The decision, the logistics, even covering the guilt.

And when Dr. Harvey asked what was holding me back most, it was the fear of this conversation. How do you tell someone who loves you so much that it's time you leave him behind? That all the walls of this house feel like a museum of what we lost. That you stayed long after you should have gone, watching him try to preserve everything exactly as it was, while you were suffocating under the weight of all that preservation. That if you don't leave now, you'll *both* be trapped here. You've tried so hard to be enough. But this isn't supposed to feel like obligation. Even when it's kept you tethered to this city far longer than you should have stayed.

Of all people, I should have come to him, knowing who he is, that this way of hiding my problems from him has only ever backfired. It's embarrassing really, because if he loves me as unconditionally as he's always said, will this really change that? Transcendent of circumstance. He has proved that in the past.

Being here now, it feels like home. The way my thumbprint is pressed into the mug from all the times it's been in my grip before.

He turns away from me, facing the sink, and I can't see if he's looking out the window, I imagine he is. So much time was spent in the garden, and so much of it is overgrown, the basil overtaking the back corner, and I think of the few clippings that were tucked into my bouquet.

He stands there washing his own mug, and I can see it, I can hear it, the faintness of Elton John playing in the back of my mind, the shape two people so many years ago formed at the kitchen sink. Two people so in love dancing with soapy hands.

The rarest love and even that has proven impermanent.

He turns around grabbing a dish towel to dry his hands. No one is dancing today. He's been alone in this house since I left, maybe he figured I would come back. No clue what he could be thinking now as I tell him I'm taking a job three thousand miles away.

"Isn't it hard for you to be here by yourself?"

"Sometimes more than others," he says somberly.

"It's hard for me." I say, and I wish it wasn't true. I wish I was braver but sitting at this island like nothing is different feels like a lie. Like the happy couple that lived here doesn't haunt the home and overwhelm my senses. Maybe I should be grateful, but it's hard not to have resentment when that love is such a memory, and no longer graspable the way it once was. The way he seems to stand just a little less tall indicates he feels it too, like gravity has gotten stronger, weighing more than it used to.

"Let's go somewhere else then," he says as if it's that simple to run away.

———

"Hey Mack, do you mind if we–" He smiles and gestures beyond the security guard who recognizes the request immediately.

"For you? Of course, Mr. Sterling," he says as he unclips the velvet rope meant for keeping out museum patrons and lets us pass through. "I haven't seen you in a while, Ms. Bancroft," he adds as we take steps into the galleries.

"I know, I've been away," my partial reply offering very little detail, but how much do I really owe anyone.

"Well, Ms. Bancroft, he looks happy to have you back." I look over and I'm not sure I'd say the same. He looks... *something*, but happy isn't the word I would use. Especially because, I'm not *'back'* beyond organizing the remaining logistics of my life.

"Thanks, Mack, you on duty all night? I'm not sure how long we'll be," he asks.

"Take your time, I'll be here." With that, Mack walks off, likely to continue rounds. It's not lost on me how uncommon a privilege this is, being here without the hoards of people. Perks of the old job I suppose.

The magnitude of this space has always matched the magnitude of him.

Maybe that is why this was his favorite place to come. Despite it being his job for so long, the passion he found in the arts was beyond worldly, beyond logic.

The grandiose works on the walls, massive pieces by masters, commissioned memories, biblical references, historical retellings. But our favorite spot in this entire building is in the center of the room, the wood bench that feels at the center of our universe, with a small gold plate engraved with a memory.

TAKE SEATS TOGETHER AS STRANGERS AND STAY

LONG ENOUGH TO FALL IN LOVE LIKE WE DID.

I look at him, as he stretches his legs out in front of him, and I do the same. Maybe I was right, he's shrinking in that house. His body stretches to a full long length, leaning back on his palms, like his spinal cord isn't compressing him in this room, he can be his full self here.

"Hey stranger," he says, "now, let's talk about you leaving."

Chapter Twelve

HAPPILY EVER BEFORE

Arden

Social media keeps people familiar in a way you are never really sure if you remember them. It took me longer to place him than I would care to admit. Each scroll through old photos felt like flipping through a yearbook where faces blur together, was he just background in tagged photos, or did he have a presence in chapters I didn't often re-read?

When he brought down those books at the museum. That's when I finally began to put it together. Somewhere in my adult-prologue he was there, unexpected to ever be anything more than a passing character.

'I'm not available.'

The words had tumbled out before I could stop them, my standard defense against anything that might matter. What the actual fuck does that even mean. Besides the fact that it's not true. Unless of course we're talking about emotionally. I am very much available.

'Then come back and fight with me some time.'

And as he said it, his eyes sparked with the same intensity

they'd flared with during our *disagreement* that had me eager for more.

He handed me the heather grey t-shirt from the gift shop with only two large words on it, MUSEUM GEEK, and the only thing I could imagine, was him taking it off.

It was the beginning of the smile I saw forming on his lips as he turned away from me that had me crane my neck as if it would let me see the rest of it.

The thing about watching a stranger walk away is that they can be whoever you want them to be in that moment. They can be the perfect happily ever after, because watching a stranger walk away is a lot easier than someone you weren't prepared to love. It's when you see the back of someone you know that it all comes shattering to the ground.

And that's how I'm able to think about him the whole way home.

Will. The never-called-decent-docent.

———

Everything about my life should be pulling me down to the wood floor so I can watch the approximate three-hundred-rotations-per-minute of my ceiling fan. I did the math once during a particularly desperate bout of insomnia, armed with nothing but a stopwatch app and the usual am-I-doing-enough dread. And yet, rather than returning to the invisible starfish outline I often inhabit in the center of my living room, my signature contemplating-life-choices pose, it's not long before I'm standing at the bar, margarita in hand. I lick the salt from the rim, capturing it on my tongue and momentarily all feels right in the world.

The bartender knows me, which is what happens when it's your bar. Not in the 'I have equity' sense, but in the 'I've cried in that corner booth' sense. This is where my friends and I have celebrated new jobs, commiserated over failed relationships, and conducted what we used to call strategic romantic reconnaissance missions aka tipsy people-watching aka-aka looking for a hookup.

The group in the back corner have their blazers draped across their booth seats like shed snake skins, as they all clank glasses and drop shots of Jäger into their beers. Men and bombs, seriously, you'd think Oppenheimer did enough on the bomb front to satisfy the male population for eternity. But nothing is ever enough for them.

Tonight, I'm not sure what I'm doing here. I called Stella, but as usual, my voicemail landed in the same place all our secrets seem to now. I meant it when I told Ethan I think I'm better off on my own. I can be on my own, and I prefer that to the alternative of being lonely and with someone, which pretty much sums up the last few months.

But the most safe I am is either predictable or alone. I've done predictable for long enough, which means now it's time for *alone.*

"Barkeep! I'll take two of whatever she's having!"

The man's voice is loud enough to make me wonder what he thinks he's auditioning for. It's not even that loud in here yet, the rowdy college crowd won't roll in until eleven at the earliest, bringing their distinctive bouquet of body spray and poor judgment. I remember those days, *most of them.*

And seriously, who says 'barkeep?'

What. An. Asshole.

He's clearly with that group in back, probably the one who drew the short straw, intellectually and otherwise, and was tasked with the next round.

When did I get so cynical? Have I always been like this? Maybe it's not age that's made me more skeptical and less patient with men. I think it's happened around the same time I started fucking them. I mentally sigh, wait, maybe I audibly sigh, and try to soften my approach before turning to him with a smile. I do it softly, though there's nothing about me right now that feels soft.

"I'm alright, thank you though." My voice aims for polite but firm, landing somewhere between 'customer service representative' and 'kindergarten teacher explaining why we don't eat glue.'

"It would be my honor." *Your honor? Really? Is this a bar or a medieval court? Should I be curtseying?*

"I appreciate it, but—"

"But if the price to pay for your company is a couple of margs, then I would say I am the luckiest S-O-B in this joint." *Maybe just the most obnoxious.*

"I'm sorry, but it looks like tonight won't be your lucky night after all."

"Why is that, gorgeous?" The bartender hands him two margaritas, and he slides one to me like dealing cards in a game I have not agreed to play.

"First of all, I cost far more than just a 'couple of margs.'" I say that and immediately realize I've just made myself sound like a very specific type of female-sex-positive-entrepreneur.

"And second of all, I'm waiting for someone." *Great, that doesn't help.*

"Come on, that's as much a blow off as any I've ever received."

Now he's the skeptic, and rightfully so. Technically, it is bullshit. A margarita used to be more than enough for me to consider a conversation with someone, sometimes even more, and I am absolutely, unequivocally, without a doubt, here by myself, unless you count my never ending stream-of-consciousness commentary as company.

It's not easy to extract yourself from situations like this. It should be. It shouldn't require a song and dance. But the lie isn't for his ego as much as it is my own safety. Because regardless of the year, and what other pseudo-feminist talking points he might have memorized for his dating profile, men in bars respect an unseen man a lot more than the woman in front of them saying no.

He takes a step closer as he leans against the bar. My hand on the wood of the bar top as my fingernails scrape against the grain with a pit suddenly in my stomach as I back into the stool behind me.

And then, as if the goddess of serendipity herself decided to throw me a bone, or maybe she just got tired of watching this tragic scene unfold, she cast a spotlight over the swinging door.

I see him.

And for lack of all sense that I've held, I doubled down on possibly the most dangerous idea I've had to date.

"There he is..."

Our eyes meet when he is about ten paces from me, and this time there's no mistaking the spark of recognition, the same intensity from our earlier art debate now mixed with something darker, more possessive. His stride doesn't break as he approaches, like he's been waiting for this moment since I walked away at the museum.

"Sweetheart," I stress the endearment as my hand reaches around his bicep. "I was just telling my new... friend? No, friend feels like the wrong word, like calling a paper cut a flesh wound, but I was just telling," I motion my hand waiting for him to supply his own name.

"Gerry," he says with a sense of confusion beyond his own existence.

"I was just telling Gerry that I was waiting for you after he was nice enough to buy me a drink.... Gerry, this is my boyfriend."

The lie rolls off my tongue easier than it should, probably because it feels like the kind of romantic comedy moment I've been training for at 3 a.m. book in hand.

His stare crawls up and down my face as I speak, from my eyes to my lips and back, a mirror of how he'd studied me earlier when I'd challenged his point. Before landing firmly on my gaze, offering me a smile that acknowledges the ruse he's willing to play along with, and possibly suggesting he's better at improv than I gave him credit for.

"Oh Arden, darling." His voice croons in a way that wraps around me like a cardigan, as he leans down and places a kiss on my cheek. The gesture is deliberate, lingering just long enough to make it clear this isn't just about saving me from an unwanted advance.

There's a fullness to his lips that leaves an imprint on my skin and feels like it might be permanent while the words sink into the depth of my stomach like a stone in a wishing well.

Gerry glances back across the bar to his group of actual friends, indicating less subtly than he intended, motioning to the bartender who is lining up another twelve shot glasses like they're attempting to recreate the Last Supper but with Jägermeister.

His eyes narrow on Will, as if that will help his ability to see through the drunken haze. But Will's arm reaches across me to grab the fresh drink on the bar, the margarita just delivered to me at Gerry's request, and tips it to his lips. He drinks it down completely before returning the empty glass back to its cocktail napkin and pushing it back towards him.

"Thanks for the drink." He runs a knuckle over my cheek as if he's checking for the remnants of the kiss, the gesture carrying the same confident authority. "I think it's time you head back to your friends."

"You're her boyfriend?" Gerry asks with a sense of skepticism.

"More than you'll ever be." Will's voice is sharp enough to cut glass. His response is to Gerry, but his eyes are on me, dark and intense with something that looks like possession mixed with pride.

"Maybe next time, Gerry." I offer in consolation, immediately feeling Will's glare like a physical touch, hot against my skin.

"Oh no, darling," his voice dropping to a register that ripples across my skin, "...there won't be a next time." His jaw ticks ever so slightly as he takes my purse from where it lay on the bar counter, and shifts his body around mine. Putting himself between me and Gerry and gently guiding me away from the bar towards the booths against the opposite wall to the commotion.

We fall into an easy step, like that of two people who have walked through life together before. His hand snakes across my lower back to rest on my hip. I slide into the booth, and he takes the seat next to me without hesitation, turning his back to the noise of the bar, facing me dead on like I'm the most interesting thing in a room full of distractions.

"That was a nice show, *darling*. I didn't know you were an actress." His voice carries an amused lilt that makes me wonder if he's enjoying this as much as I am.

"I'm not, *sweetheart*, but I do believe in self-preservation. And you seemed like my best bet." I'm aiming for casual, but my voice betrays more truth than I intended. As it has seemed to more than once since meeting him.

"You want to bet on me?" There's something in his tone that makes it sound less like a question and more like a dare.

"Is that a problem?" I counter, wondering in what split second this stopped feeling like an act and took the shape of something more sincere.

"Depends who you ask." His hand comes down over mine on the table, and his thumb strokes the skin, gently turning it over in a way that his fingertips follow my life lines searching for spoilers to our story.

"Will!" There is a voice that laughs around the word, and his head snaps around toward the suited-heat-seeking-missile of a man b-lining it right for us.

"I'd preemptively apologize... but remember, you were the one that started this."

"What do you mean? Who is that?" Though based on the matching jawlines, I already know the answer.

"Exactly who you wouldn't ask... my brother."

Chapter Thirteen

HAPPILY EVER BEFORE

Will

No doubt Gerry put two and two together the second he got back to his seat, probably congratulating himself on his elementary school math skills. I'd spotted my brother the minute I walked in. Kind of hard to miss Alfie when he's holding court like a corporate King Arthur with his nights spent around tables, but it didn't matter.

She quite literally called to me.

Beckoned me over with those desperate eyes, and when I saw how visibly uncomfortable she was being cornered by one of the lackeys, I would have been willing to do a whole lot more than just a quick intervention.

She did say she was unavailable earlier. Was that because we were jumping right into a full-blown relationship? Sounds good to me. We probably would have gotten there anyway after a handful of walks in the park, a couple of dinners, and well, whatever else you might want to call those moments when you realize someone could absolutely ruin your life.

If I'm right, *and I try to make a habit of it,* Gerry, is also known as Fitzgerald Addams. *Yes, like those founding-fathers*

Addams, though his family tree has about as much revolutionary spirit as a corporate tax return. He's about seven years my senior but has been in prep school with Alfie since they were teenagers. Just enough intersection in our lives to make me identifiable in a way he could scamper back and tell him I was here. And worse, that I'm not alone.

Alfie isn't someone I'd expose just anyone to. He's a model of my father in all ways but one, actual backbone. That has been replaced by the sterling rod shoved so far up his ass, he only knows which way to turn based on dad's adjustment of it. It's like watching a ventriloquist act where the dummy got an MBA.

Arden looks confused, maybe she thinks *he's* confused.

"I'd preemptively apologize... but remember, you were the one who started this," I say, trying to sound lighter than I feel. Of all the people who would bet on me, my older brothers aren't names I'd add to that list. Unfortunately, they have reason not to.

As far as they're both concerned, I broke the cardinal family rule and haven't handed in my corporate conscription card yet. Each delay causes more shifting in boardrooms that I don't have any interest in, like I'm somehow responsible for keeping their Earth's axis tilted correctly by showing up to quarterly meetings which I have no plan to attend.

The latest ultimatum came packaged with a Memorial Day deadline. The perfect timeline for them to announce their merger with my name freshly added to the board seat they've been dangling like a golden noose. Nearly a year of pushing back against this particular power play, but the expectation was always that I would return to take *my* seat at the table regardless of what my diploma said when I graduated. My Art History degree was something they considered a compromise, when I considered it my choice.

After our last conversation, I texted Alfie looking for some version of reconciliation. Or at least hoping I could get him to drop this whole thing once and for all. The last thing I need is any sort of countdown clock for the prodigal son's return. I've made the same mistake more than once thinking I could appeal to some sense of brotherhood, but his allegiance is never rooted in the same nostalgia mine is. Where every conversation turns more into a hostile negotiation over my soul than a chat between brothers.I had never intended, fuck never even considered, Arden would be here for it.

Alfie reaches the booth and slides in across from us, the smile on his face more concerning than if he'd showed up in anger.

"I didn't know you were bringing your girlfriend, Will... I'm sure you would have mentioned that." Some combination of curiosity and condescension laces his tone

"I didn't know you were bringing all of your apostles, Alfie... you definitely didn't mention that." The group of his followers crane their necks more likely curious about Arden than any brotherly love they might miss out on.

"Oh no, I don't mean to be rude..." he pivots toward Arden and my body tenses, but her fingers lace with mine and she pivots right back.

"Well, what do you mean to be then... because you're doing a pretty bang-up job at rude," she says without an ounce of hesitation.

People don't usually defend me, not about this. They see the Sterling name and assume I'm throwing away a golden ticket, turning my nose up at privilege. *And yet, here she is.* Perhaps the freedom of being someone's momentary fake girlfriend absolves you of the stress of meeting the family. Even one such as mine.

She's putting back on the mask of an actress and potentially repaying the favor despite the unease and unawareness she has in what's playing out right in front of her.

"I'm at a disadvantage, I didn't know you existed, let alone that you were coming tonight," Alfie says as he motions at the bar for a drink, his signet ring catching the light like a warning signal. The one I wear on my pinky to serve as a reminder of who I am, and more importantly who I'm not.

"What's your name?" he asks her.

"Arden," I jump in, feeling protective. "This is my older brother Alfred."

I bring our interlocked fingers beneath the table, into the darkness of her lap and release them so she's not trapped in this conversation or my grip. But she doesn't let go. Instead, she brings her other hand below to wrap around them as she shifts her body in the seat closer into me, like we're co-conspirators in a great art heist of our own making.

"Arden what?" He asks the question in a way that's so loaded and the smile she lets creep across her face tells me she's clocked the intention.

She tosses out the dismissive 'Only child, and you wouldn't know my parents' with the kind of confidence that makes me want to applaud.

I can see him mulling it over, tossing the idea around in his brain, searching for her in his mental contacts like she's a LinkedIn profile he can't quite place, but he notably comes up empty. In his world, not being able to place someone in the social hierarchy is like finding a glitch in the Matrix.

"Is she staying or going?" he asks, giving her the exit from being a bystander to this.

"Staying." she says without hesitation, like she's claiming her spot in this story. She kneels on the booth and leans across me, holding up two fingers to the bar to get us a couple of drinks as well. When she does, her body presses against mine in a way that indicates she also feels this sense that we're meant to be touching in any way possible.

It's silly. I felt it, when our arms pressed against each other and she didn't pull back, but the lack of hesitation feels like we're just meant to know each other. Like maybe we always have, in some parallel universe where I'm not the family disappointment and she's not my impromptu girlfriend.

She plops down in the seat and smiles as she's handed the two bottles of beer.

"You can put those on his tab," is all she says, and I wonder if she knows how much I'm already in debt to her presence.

"Will, how many times are we going to have this conversation?" Alfie crosses his arms maybe in a show of strength, but that's how he and my father will always be different. My father just exudes the power that Alfie tries to emulate, like comparing a lion to someone in a lion costume.

"Looks like at least once more." I take a slow sip from the beer and feign indifference, though I wonder if there's any of a childhood bond left that lets him see through it. The fact is, I'm fucking exhausted by it. I've had the same conversation with Alfie, and Cal, and of course our father.

The 'time is up' conversation.

The 'playtime is over' conversation.

But what none of them seem to understand is that this isn't playtime, this is my life. And sure, maybe I live it more freely than they do, but that's my choice to make. Whatever business deals they have lined up because they think they need another Sterling to sit in a boardroom isn't one I'm particularly inclined to make.

"You wanted to take time off after college, we let you." The way he says 'let you' makes my jaw clench. Like my life is something they graciously permit rather than something I own. Like I took a joyride in a stolen car, not that I show up everyday as a contributing member of society. But to them, it's not a caliber of career that can be considered anything more than *time off.*

"It's time to put on a suit and show up for the life you're meant to have. Regardless of what you've got going on here."

With that he glances over to my right, where Arden is lazily strumming her fingers against the bottle like she's playing a tune more entertaining than this conversation.

What a funny concept, the life I'm meant to have. As if the life I'm meant to have is anything different than the one I'm choosing to live.

"Will, shouldn't we get going? We *do* have that dinner reservation and it sounds like we really need to talk about your future."

Arden interjects, it's coated in sarcasm and mockery at the idea of a grown man being lectured about his plans by his brother. But my name falls from her lips like a match into gasoline as Alfie's eyes narrow looking for cracks.

Her hand finds my knee under the table, and the warmth bleeds through my jeans like sunlight through stained glass.

Alfie's eyes narrow, the cogs of suspicion turning behind them. He stands, straightening his jacket, a gesture that transforms him from brother to businessman in one practiced motion.

"This conversation isn't over."

"It never is," I reply, but he's already walking away, back to his disciples of dividends and their communion of corporate climbing.

The moment he's gone, Arden's shoulders drop an inch, but her hand stays on my knee.

Chapter Fourteen

Arden

Some encounters slip in quietly, like a pickpocket stealing away your carefully constructed narrative before you even realize what's happening.

When Will first appeared, or rather, when I first noticed him, I was certain I knew exactly who he was. Confident, arrogant, with a polished veneer that suggests he'd never truly been challenged. But Will Sterling is decidedly not that man. He's blooming into something more complicated, suddenly a Russian nesting doll of contradictions wrapped in tailored clothing and unexpected vulnerability.

His brother just left, dropping verbal breadcrumbs that hinted at some of it. And here we are, tucked into a booth that feels like our own private universe, playing a game of conversational chess where each move reveals something deeper. The booth creaks each time shift as I peel my skin off the material of the seat and the worn wood table between us bears the scars of countless nights like this one. Rings of glasses, initials carved into its surface like evidence of all the people who sat here before us. Eventually fading into the mere suggestions of past nights, past

82

conversations, and past possibilities, just like this one will. Beyond our alcove, the bar thrums with movement. *Clinking of glasses, bursts of laughter, the steady pulse of bodies moving through spaces too small to contain them.*

"Well, I definitely didn't anticipate a family reunion tonight," I say, swirling my drink. "Is this how you normally spend your evenings? Ambushing unsuspecting women with impromptu family drama?"

He leans back, that infuriating smirk playing at the corner of his mouth. "I think it would do you well to remember, you started this whole thing."

"Impressive time management skills," I deadpan. "Balancing museum tours, family confrontations, and whatever elaborate game of flirting we're currently engaged in."

"Bold of you to assume," he says, "that this is either a game or flirting, you said you weren't available."

"Isn't it?" I match his raised eyebrow. "Because I've been on the receiving end of enough of it to recognize the signs. You are *definitely* flirting."

He leans in, close enough that I can see the gold flecks in his eyes that might otherwise be lost to the deepest blues of them. The same eyes that have tracked my every movement since I walked onto his tour.

"I thought asking you out would have made that clear."

His brother's earlier comments haven't evaporated from the space, and certainly not my interest in wanting to understand the root of them. The fragments of the conversation suggest Will is running from something, hiding behind museum walls and witty deflections. But right now, in this moment, he is more present than anyone I've been with in months, years even. Including any tortuous conversation I have with myself. Even though I also know from past experience, that present doesn't mean permanent.

I sat here and played along to the bit that I first introduced, having no clue it would land us both in this situation. But when it did, it felt like the least I could do. Although, I'm not actually sure if I made it worse.

"Well, I definitely didn't think we were going to jump right into meeting the family." I say where maybe I owe him an apology.

"Wasn't the plan, but now I'm thinking we can just plan a January wedding," he quips. I shake my head, this man is quick. Catching the tail of whatever I say. I saw it earlier also, the unbridled interest in me mid-argument. He laughs and inches closer to me in the booth. His back is towards the rest of the bar, shielding me from all the Gerrys and Alfies of the world, or at least in this space. Maybe because he knows them better than I do.

Yet, he's so deeply invested in this moment, in me. I've seen men look at me before. They have for years. But this time feels different, because for the first time in a long time, I feel invested back.

Maybe it's nothing more than the alignment of the stars or the recent loss of the dead weight I've been carrying around in the form of Gabriel-the-convenience-boyfriend. But investment in this moment will not make any of it enough.

"Speaking of college..." I begin to position the question.

"We weren't speaking of college..." Will says without his eyes breaking the connection with mine.

"Oh, that's right, *well*, now that we are..." I trail off deliberately, and he laughs a rich, warm sound that sinks into my stomach as I lay the foundation of the question I wanted to ask earlier. "That's it, isn't it? How we know each other?" I wonder if I sound more vulnerable than I intend to, but I'm looking for confirmation over what I'm fairly certain of. But I'm afraid speaking the connection into existence might make it disappear.

The way he's looking at me now, half-smiling like he's been waiting for me to piece it together, and pleased with me that I have.

"Yeah, though I'm pretty sure back then you were too busy calling the professor an 'pedantic drone,'" he says through a smile, maybe with more memory of a previous interaction than I have.

"Had I known that today I would have ended up on the receiving end of that same style of public flogging, I would have stayed home."

His fingers move against mine, mindlessly, like our hands are locked in a conversation of their own.

"No, you wouldn't," I say with certainty.

"No," he pauses and the air between us is thick and warm, "I wouldn't." His smile engulfs us both. Reaching for his beer to sip slowly, an act of restraint for the electricity flowing between us.

I think back to the class we would have shared, and I have guilt for not noticing him then.

This city has more than half a million people in it. More than 150,000 of them are students. It's not surprising that I would have crossed paths with a few of them. Though, this feels more than a coincidence of census. I put that thought to the side. Knowing that even if I had known him then as I do now, with the indisputable sense of lust and interest that I have in this moment, in this man, what would ultimately have changed? It always ended the same, with me bolting before it could really take root. *Well, except that one time.* And rather than spending time conducting another full post-mortem on college romances, I tuck myself in closer to him now.

Our bodies shift in small ways to touch each other. Not in the way that I do to gain a man's attention, a small touch on the arm, or a graze of the leg, but like a thrumming of electricity that would have made Franklin reach for a key.

"How about you, besides hiding out in museums, what do you usually do with your time?"

"I wasn't hiding, I don't actually even have a lot of time." I say with some incredulity at the albeit accurate accusation.

"Ah, that's right, you're not available. I had you pegged as much more of a runner than a hider anyway." I cross my legs beneath the table as he stretches his out to tangle further with mine.

"And what makes you such an expert?"

"Because I do the same thing."

There's silence between us, he doesn't force it with chatter, and while we have cocooned in this back booth, I am anything but trapped. I watched him as he walked up to the bar to order a couple drinks, watched as he leaned against the same spot he rescued me from not long ago. I know there are people around, but it's like everyone else moves to the outskirts of my mind, my peripheral sight, as he stands there, surprisingly commanding. The combination of tailored and free. His arms crossed, as he nodded along to the conversation being made next to him, possibly to him. Grabbing the drinks from the bar, and parting the red sea of people crossing to return to this booth where I remain shrouded in darkness of the wood partitions.

But then there's this pull. This maddening, tethering, pull. Is it curiosity, is it the vulnerability that showed through with his brother, or is this just my old M.O. slipping through the cracks I've kept sealed since college.

Time in space shared with him becomes ignorant of the surrounding world. We just sit here and nurse a couple of drinks. They serve as the added props to this conversation right next to the stale pretzels he also snagged from the bar.

"What was all that about?" I ask with the gentle nod back towards the location of his brother and all that went along with it.

"All that," he breathes with an exhaustion that tells me more than I have any right knowing, "is just the same fight I've had since I graduated."

In my lack of reply, he continues.

"My family is less than enthusiastic about the choices I make, and because of that, I don't see them often. They think they know what's best, and maybe they do, but I've yet to be convinced."

I remember being in a place once, where I struggled with the idea of expectation, only to realize they were my expectations and no one else's. Though, based on the encounter, and what he's saying now, it doesn't feel like he has the same blank check of emotional support that I have from my parents.

I look at him and the way I can see his mind running. Even though the core of his body is so still next to mine. The hint of gold in his eyes counter to the silver of his name, but the flecks like that of the gilded frames surrounding the great works he dedicates his days to.

His eyes narrow perhaps, like I am, deciding how dangerous this is.

"Why did you turn me down earlier?"

"I told you, I'm busy, I just..."

"Are you? Or are you sabotaging yourself for the chance to be anything other than busy. Because being busy is a hell of a lot easier than being happy."

"There's nothing wrong with 'busy.' I'm not unhappy, as much as I don't think of happiness the same way I did when I was a kid. It's just the disillusionment of adulthood. I'm fine."

This conversation escalated, and I know I'm the reason. Opening the door to more than light banter. But it's dripping with an intense sincerity that's indescribable.

"You don't strike me as the type of person to settle for anything, let alone fine."

"I'm using it exactly as the word was meant to be used. As in, *'Will, you gave a fine tour today.'*"

"I thought we'd been over this, I'm better than fine... and from what I see, so are you. That's what I don't get. You came in today in a daze, with a bag of food, *you're really not supposed to eat in there by the way,* and you just strolled around, picking up steam, eventually clearing the fog of whatever it was keeping you cloudy the moment you thought you had a viable challenger." He smirks slightly. He clears the gruffness in his voice, "And I'll take that challenge, any day, anywhere."

He's coated with passion in more ways than one and it's collecting like dew across skin.

"So no, I don't think fine is something you'd settle for in your life. Fine dining, maybe. Fine jewelry, sure. Fine people, fine career? Fine, *happiness*? I don't believe you. And I saw you there waiting for me, gearing up to double down on the fight for no reason other than the principle of it, or maybe the thrill of winning. Why would you do that if you weren't looking for more? Why are you still here, right now... looking at me like that, if you're not available."

"I really wanted a free t-shirt."

"And yet here you are."

"Here I am," I agree. "Though I recall you also said you were meeting someone, what would you have done if I said yes earlier?"

"Cancelled." And he looks at me like it was an obvious answer, as if there wouldn't have been a plan he wouldn't have me wreck.

"You caught me on a weird day. Work just, it feels like I'm constantly trying to learn the rules of a game while everyone else is changing them. And I finally have a chance to actually show everyone there that I'm just as good, actually that I'm better, but that means that no matter how easily I used to fall into the arms of a devastatingly handsome distraction, I can't afford any right now." While part of what I said came across as a taunt, there's truth in my avoidance, and I can see the moment he recognizes it for what it is. And I watch as his Adam's apple moves slowly to swallow it down

"You think I'm handsome?" *His hand is spread across my thigh.*

"I think you're devastating." *My legs intertwine with his.*

"I think you're avoiding the question." *His fingers knead into my skin.*

"And I think you're missing the point." *My eyes narrow on him as I say it.*

The way everything between us escalates quickly, it makes sense why I would consider it a distraction.

"What are you afraid of being distracted from, or is it what you're afraid of being distracted by?" He asks, perhaps the most terrifying question yet.

"I thought I would know what I wanted to do, and I don't. At eighteen I knew everything, and now, despite the degrees, I feel like just a child with a bank account. And every decision causes an emotional overdraft fee. It just feels like I'm watching everyone else get to where they want to go while I'm sitting at the bus stop waiting patiently, terrified I'm going to board the wrong bus. I thought I would love my job, I want to solve problems, I want to grow something someday. But I can't even keep Pricktor alive."

"*Pricktor?*" he asks.

"My succulent boss."

He nods in understanding as an indication for me to continue now that I've clarified my aptly named boss inspired desk-plant mid-fucking-ramble.

"I know, things take time. I know, 'Rome wasn't built in a day.' Trust me, I know how the story goes when you try to sprint before you've learned to walk. I've heard it all... but I'm so bored waiting."

There's something freeing about confessing all this to a stranger, someone who exists outside the carefully constructed narrative of my life. And he just takes it in, our earlier banter transforming into something weightier, more real.

"What if you're wrong?"

"I'm never wrong."

"What if you're meant to run, and all these careful steps are just ways of talking yourself out of your own strength? I'm just looking at you, and I can't understand why you would deny yourself anything."

"Says the man running away."

"Guess that makes me the expert then."

The tension between us pulses like a living thing, expanding and contracting with each breath. His proximity is a gravitational pull, not the performative lean-in of desperate courtship, but something more geological.

Tectonic.

Our bodies are land masses slowly, inexorably converging, carrying millennia of unspoken history.

Chapter Fifteen

HAPPILY EVER BEFORE

Arden

We're standing in the dimly lit hallway, leaning against opposite walls, waiting for the bathroom.

The crowd has turned over, and he didn't exchange any version of a goodbye to his brother when he left. We've just spent the last hours engrossed in conversation spanning topics from all quadrants of the New York magazine approval matrix.

The noise of the bar reaches us but is drowned out by the pulsing I can feel as my heart beats out every other thought every time I get a glimpse of him. The idea of his lips on my skin is overwhelming in a way I can't justify, and don't want to ignore.

I've spent years choosing the safety of predictable men who couldn't surprise me, but standing here with Will, those walls feel paper-thin, ready to dissolve at his touch. The clean scent of his laundered shirt mingles with the gritty bar, much like how the roughness of him seems to soften only when he looks at me.

There's something voracious about him, or maybe just me being near him. Has this been here the whole time? Not because of him, but me? Have I hidden this piece away too afraid to stoke it myself? I thought this was part of growing up. The idea that you leave behind the pieces of yourself that were too much, too wild. So that's what I did. But to whose benefit? Because looking at my life recently, I'm unconvinced it's been my own. There was a time I wouldn't doubt my interest in a man, and I wouldn't deny myself the pursuit of it. Not if it was something I really wanted. So what really changed, besides me of course.

The space between us is thick with possibility, an electric current passing from one side to the other. Absorbed and returned from our bodies.

The bathroom door opens and our gaze is broken momentarily as a person passes between us. We might be separated, but not for long. And each lightly pushed ourselves off the walls we leaned against to take a slight step to the middle.

He looks at me and curls his fingers around my ear, wrapping the loose hairs behind it, and dragging them along the curve of my jawline. Each lifting slowly from the path, until his long index finger draws up under my chin ever so slightly encouraging a glance up towards him.

"What if..." *I take a breath.* "Tonight, I'm not unavailable after all." The words slip out in a whisper amongst chaos meant only for him. Too afraid to admit even to myself what this sense of immediate gut churning interest could mean.

It couldn't have been more than a blink when I stepped into his arms. And he consumed me. He leaned down into me, pulling me against him as my hands held his face and his tangled in my hair. My feet are off the ground as I'm in his grip.

Wrapped in a kiss so deep and full I've forgotten completely where we are.

His lips are generous and I'm greedy for each movement his mouth makes against mine.

"Bathroom." I say, as he lowers me, but I'm far from grounded.

He leans down again, kissing me with intensity I've craved, crackling voltage beneath my skin, as his hands hold mine. He walks backwards a few steps refusing to take his eyes off me, and when he's in reach of the doorknob, pulls us both in. And the sounds of the bar are turned down another notch as our commingled breaths are the only things I hear.

Our kiss is fueled by something unrecognizable. Or perhaps more terrifying, something I'm afraid to recognize.

Powered by an energy I can't source.

And as he locks the door behind us, his hands move to the backs of my thighs, and wordlessly, I'm hoisted into his arms. My back pressed against the door and legs locked around his back.

He exposes a grin so devilish it drips down my throat through my stomach right into the pulsing, tightening, core of me.

His lips find mine, though they were never lost to him. As he pulls our weight off the door and spins us until I feel cold ceramic hit my slightly exposed ass his hands climb my back.

He's standing over me as he leans in for another kiss, pulling my lip into his mouth and twirling the tip of his tongue against the same spot I just had my teeth.

His kiss lowers, his tongue leaving the trail along my jaw, down my neck, and across my collar bone.

My hands hold his face and pull him into my view and trace my thumb across his bottom lip, smearing what remains of my lipstick that is blooming across his face. Imprints of passion that *I was here* even if they say something else tomorrow, but right now, in this moment, I couldn't care less about tomorrow. I can feel his smile more than see it. We're existing in some liminal space between propriety and complete wanton abandon.

My free hand is sliding up his chest, counting his heart beats against my own. They are two drumsticks on the same snare.

He captures my wrist, his thumb pressing against my pulse point in a way that makes me wonder if he can read my thoughts through the rhythm of my blood.

The way he looks at me now, it's the same intensity from the museum, that focus turned carnal. His hands slide into my hair, cradling my head with a gentleness that contradicts the hunger in his gaze and what I'm sure is matching in my own.

"Tell me to stop," he breathes against my mouth, not quite kissing me, just sharing the same air. "Tell me this isn't what you want."

"This is exactly what I want." I close the last whisper of space between us, and this kiss is different. Deeper and darker, like we're both trying to taste the truth on each other's tongues. His hands tighten in my hair, and I arch into him, propriety be damned.

The only words muttered are logistical ones. And now, and he wordlessly maneuvers his mouth over my skin, I see his body lowering as I remain perched on the sink.

His arms moving around me, hands tighten across my ribs, following the dip into my waist before finally hitting the hem of my skirt. Which he lifts, now eye level, and between my legs.

He looks up at me, a smile, as he says "I don't have a condom."

I bite my lip and nod. Kneeling in front of me, as I'm precariously balanced, his fingers grip the band of my underwear. Slipping my leg through, and he hooks it over his shoulder before mirroring the motion to the other side.

He presses his full lips against my thick upper thigh, making his way higher up my leg. Deeper towards me.

His arm wraps around my thigh as it drapes over his shoulder. His finger presses into my skin, and I'm sure they will leave a mark for me to revel over tomorrow.

The current that has flowed between us all night, picking up frequency, picking up speed. And reverberates through me as I feel his lips press varying degrees against my skin.

"Don't tease me."

"I have every intention of teasing you," he says as he drags a finger slowly up the middle of me. Gathering the moisture that has collected there. Not only in the moments leading up to this one, but truthfully from the moment he arrived at my side tonight.

The irony that in giving into a desire as strong as this one, it was now going to be teased out of me, is thrilling beyond belief.

My mind is void of any of the earlier stresses. Just watching this man, kneeling, for me, as he dips in. Tauntingly. Teasingly. Until his breath hovers against me. He slides another finger in and leans his lips against the aching parts of me.

He has me braced against the sink. His head pressed between my legs. As his arms locked around my thighs, I feel his fingertips sinking into my skin now, as his lips suck against me. Releasing my right hand from the ceramic I'm perched on, sinking it into his hair. Which is thick and full in a way that matches him.

Full of life. Full of passion. Full hair. Full lips. Full eyes.

They are hooded in lust, darkness and desire, but offering it all to me on the altar of this bar bathroom.

My fingers twined with his locks tighten as does his grip on me.

There's a knock on the door. A pounding in actuality. Though the real pounding is taking place in here.

The knock comes louder.

I can feel it when he smiles against me. Smiles inside of me.

"Coming!" I scream back at the door. And his smile becomes a throaty laugh. That motivates him beyond teasing. He releases my right leg from where he held it, letting it fall to the floor, though I have no stability beyond what he's providing. And presses his fingers deep back into me. Curling them, moving them, pulsing them.

And I do. I come with his lips on me making passionate promises against my skin, and the desperation I have to feel him. All of him.

He was right, there isn't anything I should deny myself. Especially if what I have been denying myself is him.

We break apart, both breathing hard, and I can't help but laugh at the complete disaster I've made of his mouth, his jaw, his collar. He looks thoroughly debauched and utterly unrepentant about it. My face must look the same, smudged of color from the red lipstick I'd forgotten I was wearing and flush with desire.

I don't come down from my orgasm, even as my breathing steadies. His hands offer me support as he allows my body to slide down and land in his lap as he sits back on his feet. Arms wrapped around my back pressing his lips to my ear.

"I'm wondering," I say, my voice rougher than I expect as his teeth tugged on my earlobe "if this is just another form of running."

"Maybe," he admits, "but its better than standing still."

The immediacy of the attachment I have to him is over-whelming. Terrifying.

I used to be casual about sex. And then I grew up. Instead prioritizing the comfort of simple companionship until I ran out the clock. But Will isn't simple.

There's no relationship we could have that wouldn't have just started with him going down on me in a bar bathroom.

Despite his exterior, he's soft. Not in that way. In fact, in that way it's painfully obvious even through the thick black denim covering his lap, that he wants me. I move against it, grinding myself onto him, as his teeth drag down the column of my neck. Teasingly, as he said he would.

"We can't stay in the bathroom forever" I stand from where I was seated in his lap. His hands remain on me, looking up at me from his knees. Lifting the hem of my skirt so he could place a final kiss on my thigh.

"We can do whatever we want."

"You and I live our lives very differently then."

"Maybe, but we don't have to." He stands, reaching his full height, and grips my waist, hoisting me back up onto the sink. Stepping between my legs as his hands brace either side of the column of my neck. He dampens a paper towel and carefully cleans the smearing of makeup across my smile as his thumb drags across the line of my jaw.

"If you want to stay here, I'll barricade the door and call this home."

Chapter Sixteen

HAPPILY EVER BEFORE

Will

Was it my plan to go down on her in the bathroom? *No.* Not at all. Condom or not, standing in that hallway my mind might have been consumed by her, but it was full of thought beyond some quickie in a dive-bar bathroom. She stood there across this invisible barrier of air that we shared and then she crossed it. Threw down the gauntlet, and I'll be fucking damned if I was not going to rise to the challenge.

Coming down from going down isn't the easiest considering it only heightened a desire that's been building between us for hours. Fuck, if I'm honest, since I met her, or re-met her. She's facing the mirror, so all I can see is the back of her, but I feel with some sense of certainty that it's written across her face as much as it is mine. The slight tremor in her gives away her breathlessness, and I fight the urge to wrap my arms around her waist.

Come on... turn around... show me I'm right.

I don't know if it's some temporal twine that's tied us together, but I know her subconscious hears mine when she turns around to face me. Sure enough, the flush on her cheeks isn't the giveaway as much as the glint in her eye as she looks me up and down. Challenge, invitation, warning, all at once.

Go right ahead.

She steps forward and into my arms. I wouldn't call this cuddling per se, but given the surrounding it feels as close to spooning after sex as one could replicate in this space. No, she's giving me a hug. *An actual hug.* And her head fits perfectly beneath my chin as if it was sculpted that way just for this fraction of a moment.

It's barely a movement to kiss the crown of her. Her head tilts up, and she looks up through her lashes. Another kiss on her forehead. Her smile broadens slightly. Each time I pull my lips away, they beg to be returned with a sense of desperation. She rolls her head against my chest as her hand presses against my heart. I kiss her temple and she breathes out against me, her eyes closing with the pressure of my lips in their vicinity. Her skin has the path illuminated for me. I kiss the pad of her full smiling cheek. The kiss I plant on the tip of her nose nudges her head back. Her lips part with the smallest pop, and when I press my mouth to hers they know each other intimately.

She turns her body so I'm pressed against the door, and I will gladly keep us both here forever. I wasn't kidding. If she wants to hide out in here, I'll damn the outside world for as long as she wants. I'm not exactly eager to go running back towards impending responsibility.

She lands back on her feet and I release my hand from where it's clinging to the column of her neck.

"What if there are people waiting?" she whispers. Perhaps at the realization that this exit might be more public than the original frantic need for each other accounted for when we shut the door behind us.

"What?" I ask, but she's smiling in a way that I'm starting to realize might be my undoing.

"I'm just thinking about how many people are going to know exactly what we've been doing when you walk out of here."

I lean in close again, my lips brushing her ear.

"Let them."

"You don't care if there are people just gathered on the other side of the door when we both skulk out of this *single* bathroom?"

"Do I care what a bunch of strangers think? Not particularly. And we aren't going to skulk. I'll scope it out if you want, but I have no reason to sneak out."

"You don't think this is embarrassing?"

"It's only embarrassing if you're embarrassed." I lean down and whisper, "and there's nothing embarrassing about knowing you were trembling against my tongue."

The coast is clear as I open the doors and step out, reaching my hand behind my back in request of hers. I'm not interested in letting go yet. She slips her fingers between mine, interlocking them together, confirming she also isn't ready to snap the line. We step into the bar and it's bustling with people. Over at the bar some poor sod who thought he had a chance with her. He'd have killed to see her in the form I just did, I'd bet most of the men and even some of the women in here would as well. Hearing the whimper escape from her as she came, feeling the tightening of her around my fingers as her leg tensed on my shoulder. I'm already desperate for more.

"I have to go," It's loud in here, but she says it over the surrounding crowd.

"What?" My voice snaps with disbelief.

"I said, I have to go..." She repeats louder as if the volume of her voice was the issue.

"I heard you..."

"Then why did you ask?" She's straightening her stance. This dynamic here isn't one sided, she stepped into me, even now she is keeping us connected.

"Call it disbelief that you're running already when your fingers are still grasping at my waist" She glances down where her subconscious is keeping us connected in a way that she was clearly unaware of until I mentioned it. She drops her hand and I pick it up, our fingers weaving together of their own accord. "Arden, if you want to run, tell me now."

She raises up on her toes to reach my mouth, and I would never keep it out of reach of her. She grants me a kiss that builds into something more without question, regardless of the obnoxious level of PDA it's resulting in.

"I want to see you again." It's a whisper that can reach me despite the commotion, the hoots and hollers of rowdy bar-patrons. "But you should know, I just ended a relationship. I'm not looking for another one."

"What *are* you looking for?" I ask, though it's a pointless question. She clocks it. The look on my face tells her there's no circumstance that could prevent me wanting her.

She is all fierce uncertainty and raw honesty.

"I no longer have any fucking clue."

"I'm in."

Chapter Seventeen

HAPPILY EVER BEFORE

Arden

"Hey Stella, me again... I thought I would catch you but I guess this is just our life now..."

Not that long ago, she wouldn't have been a phone call, she would have been here in bed with me as we snacked our way through a debrief. I guess this also gets filed in the category of 'relationships you leave in college dorm rooms.'

The voicemail hangs on a telephone line that seems to have been severed somewhere around the same time we packed ourselves into the last boxes of our college youth.

I don't know that she would admit it so bluntly, I don't think she would say there's anything wrong. But I also don't think she would know. Which in and of itself, proves the point. Our messages just go into the same black hole where we pick them up, but each time, they are just a little bit less than before.

Now I lay here alone and reach for my latest read. Its predictability is a comfort as the softness of my salt lamp casts soft shadows across the wall. Reading as the main characters struggle through their middle to get to their happily ever after. Maybe that's what's happening here, too. Struggling through the middle. I just didn't think it could be so lonely.

Loneliness is the most dangerous type of hunger. It means that anytime anyone shows up with a hot meal you let them in thinking they will feed whatever is missing from your soul. And sometimes it does, for a time. But it also means you're eating a lot of things that *maybe* you don't really want in the hopes it will sustain you.

I wasn't running from him when I left the bar, but standing there tangled with him, the pit in my stomach felt like fear. It wasn't going to be the *happily ever after* kind of love, love stories don't start with a public argument and definitely not a public bathroom.

I know myself, despite how much self-awareness I'd tried to pack away in recent years, I know how easily I could fall into a relationship. Just about as easily as I jump out of them. There was a time I wouldn't even call it that, pretending that in some way casually dating excluded me from heartbreak. *But it didn't.*

I stare at my phone in the dark, his message glowing accusingly on the screen. The timestamp mocks me, three hours and counting. He texted me immediately, asking when he can see me again. The blue light illuminates the carefully arranged photos on my nightstand, memories of simpler times when I wasn't afraid of my own desires.

But here's the thing, *I'm fucking terrified.*

It's like standing in a room full of gunpowder and feeling the static electricity crackling at my fingertips. One wrong move, one spark, and we will both go up in flames. The scary part isn't that I might get burned, I've been burned. And while those scars don't exist topically in a way for anyone to see, I remember the pain of them.

The thing that scares me most is that part of me wants to strike the match just to watch it happen.

I've prided myself on control. It is part of the reason I started dating as I did. Looking for consistency. Preferring to keep myself in labeled boxes and tucked away from the risk that goes along with all that.

But the way our bodies gravitated toward each other in that booth, it wasn't just attraction. It was physics, chemistry. The kind of reaction that changes the molecular structure of everything it touches. His hand on my thigh wasn't a touch, but a catalyst.

It's not the possibility of getting hurt, but the certainty that this thing between us could consume everything in its path. My carefully laid plans, my professional ambitions, and after listening to his brother lay into him about *his* life, it would burn up what sounds like his own hard-won independence. All going up in flames burning away in the inferno of whatever this is.

I feel so far from who I was when I first moved to this city. In many ways I am. In others though, I'm just a few blocks from some of my best and worst memories. The intersection of them is the most ironic of all.

Graduating college was supposed to be liberating. But it just reset the goal post. *How bullshit is that.* My entire life has been a series of marathon finish lines and the second I break the ribbon, I can see a new one off in the distance. And again. And again. Until when? I thought I had slowed down and focused, but I didn't. I just ended up suppressing myself in a way that made navigating my life feel like I was trying to run through mud when there was perfectly good pavement if I just looked up.

I look up and out the window scanning the glass for invitations into other people's homes. Okay okay, never really invited, *but lured.* Every one of them is in darkness. The only story I'm crafting now is a memory, not a dream.

The moment his lips first landed on mine, how his fingertips felt against my skin, how they felt inside of me. I sink into the collection of pillows on my bed, and slip my fingers under the band of my underwear.

My teeth dig into my bottom lip wishing it was him.

And that's why I know, for my own self interest, it can't be.

Chapter Eighteen

HAPPILY EVER BEFORE

Arden

The very same message Stella and I used to mock receiving is now
the one I send. The intention is clear as day because it's the middle
of the night.

me: are you up?

It's some time after one in the morning, and while I've run
through the motions of the rest of my day, I didn't find myself
merging with the floor when I came home. Instead I manic
cleaned my entire apartment looking for a distraction, ate some
grapes, tortilla chips, and a cheese stick for dinner standing at the
sink, and since then, for the last three and a half hours, I have been
lying here pretending I'm not obsessing over the idea of him.

My thumb hovers over the send button. This is exactly why I
left him at the bar. Why I tried not to think about what
happened. Because I've seen what being drawn to someone can do
to you. But at some point between then and now, my resistance
has crumbled into dust.

At least until approximately two minutes ago when my will power snapped. His response is instantaneous.

Will: yes, tell me where

Instantaneous and clear.

I pause a moment, wondering if I should have more hesitation about sending him my address. I should, probably. But here we are. So I fire off two messages. One to him. And one to Ethan explaining that if I'm murdered he should donate my books to the local library.

Will: you've got to be fucking kidding

The text comes through minutes after the original, the same time there's a soft knock on the door. No time to slip into some-thing sexier as one would say, no time to make it seem like I'm casually lounging around, not expecting any company in matching red lace. But there's no real expectation to set here, is there? We both know what this is. It's a 'you up' text and a sure-thing fuck.

I open the door and he's standing there, his smile dripping with desire.

"Are you the fucking Flash or something?" I look at my phone, check the timestamp of the message. "Three minutes. Literally. You got here in three minutes."

"I would have been here sooner if you let me." His voice is thicker than it was, likely because he can taste this thing between us just like I can. A thirst we both have that goes beyond hydra-tion, and satisfies a different reciprocal need.

His eyes drop from where they were narrowed on me, and they run down my body. I bite down on my lip to contain the smile because I know why his face is lit up now. He takes a step forward into the narrow hallway of my apartment and I'm in arms reach of him. Something he makes me fully aware of when his large hands land on the bare skin of my hips as he slips them under the t-shirt and pulls me into him.

"I like your shirt." He says between kisses.

"I won it off some tour guide."

"Some tour guide, eh?"

"Yeah— he was fine." I smirk, tauntingly as his hand crawls up the column of my neck and tilts my head back ever so slightly. Stepping us further into my apartment.

"I'm not here for fine."

"Good, because I don't settle it."

And with that his mouth is on mine. A kiss fueled by desperation of only a day, and yet, I was unable to wait, and clearly neither was he. We are an unrehearsed movement of limbs and lips as I lead him backwards towards my bedroom. There's coordination in the air around us as we crash into each other. Frenzied and starved.

My hands grab for his belt as his are in my hair. The advantage that I'm already home, barely dressed, isn't lost on either of us. But he doesn't move to help me strip him any faster. Instead keeping his hands on me. He steps out of his shoes, and I move to the buttons on his shirt. He breaks our kiss and spins me from where I face him. He wraps himself around me from behind, as I feel his left hand crawl under my shirt and cup the curve of my breast. His free hand threads his fingers between mine, his palm swallowing the back of my hand as he lifts them together and presses our joined hands against the window I'm standing in front of.

His kisses direct my head, rolling it to the side as his lips move across my skin, landing right back where he seems to have a direct line into my thoughts.

"Did you know, Arden?" The depth of his tone drips down my throat landing within me. Pooling somewhere deep I know he will find.

"Did I know what?" My breathing is shallow and eager in response.

His mouth reaches for mine again as he says "I don't know how you could have, but god what an incredible thought."

I'm so lost to him. Whatever he's saying, perhaps some argument he's having with himself, but with each breath from him, my knees feel just a little bit weaker, and his grip of me tightens in a way I'm sure he's holding up more of my weight than either of us are actually aware.

"Look," he says, pressing my hand flat to the window, his long finger taps the glass. "You see that apartment? Fourth floor, just like this one. The apartment that you can see into perfectly. You wonder how I got here so quickly? Because *that's* where I was. That's where I've been. Apparently just waiting for you..."

My head lulls back against his chest and I can hear him breathing in a pattern that's expressing increasing torment at the constraint of his clothes. His hand flexes against the glass.

"So tell me darling, did you know?"

"I didn't know it was you." I let out. "But I've watched."

"*What* have you watched, Arden?" He gently pulls down my underwear and they fall to my ankles. I hear the groan from behind me, feel his hardness pressed through his pants against me.

"You." I say, without shame.

"And right now, do you think anyone can see us?"

"I..I don't know." His fingers find me as easily as they did earlier.

"Do you want them to?" he asks as his foot knocks mine, spreading my legs apart for him.

"Yes." I say, again, not an ounce of shame as I'm standing in his arms.

He doesn't release me entirely as he steps out of his pants, and I hear the tearing open of a condom. The 'you-up' text, really doesn't leave much to the imagination. Though, there was no way, *this* is what I had imagined.

He bends me forward where both my hands are pressed against the glass, and my eyes are wide open. But the only place I can look is into the depths and darkness of his apartment. The one I've stared at for months in question, in lust, in loneliness.

I feel him slide into me slowly, but like everything experienced between us, the escalation intensified beyond understanding. His hands knot in my hair as he fucks me deeply lacking any modicum of modesty or restraint. It's as his hand reaches between my legs, teases me as he thrusts, I come apart completely in his arms, and he, right behind me.

Chapter Nineteen

Will

When the text came through my hand was already drafting one of my own. Then I saw it. The address that placed her 300 feet from where I was. I was out the door and standing at hers faster than she could comprehend. And when she opened her door, in nothing but the consolation prize t-shirt, I lost all manner of self control. I've been told before I don't have any. That's not true. I just don't allow *them* to control me. That's the difference.

I've never seen in this window, as she admitted to being able to see in mine. Maybe I just wasn't looking. But I'll be looking now. I should also consider investing in curtains. I turn my head towards the faint glow from the moon and with very little adjustment I have a straight view into my bedroom.

We're laying in her bed, more on top than in. Just where we landed after being tangled in each other for the better part of this morning. All of our clothes remain scattered across her bedroom floor as her body is strewn across me. Her face pressed into my chest as her lips hang open, the corner of which is collecting the smallest amount of drool.

I take stock of the room. Two books on the bedside table. *I make note of them.* A small tv on the dresser that isn't angled in a way that she watches it much. A framed print hanging on the wall. She's let me into her home. *She doesn't seem unavailable.*

What would the didactic plate say of this image? I close my eyes and freeze the mental image of us, now. Imagining the bird's eye view of us in this bed. I can see it in black and white, a highly contrasted photograph, the kind that highlights the brilliance of human experience in the commonality of it.

'Man and Woman Entangled'
Artist: Unknown Photographer

When we landed last night, we didn't pass out immediately as one would think. We laid there in some cloud of sweat and complete fantasy. She'd drag her finger across the ink on my skin, and ask for the details. When I got my first tattoo it was reckless. It was just something I wanted. And from there, it grew. Some end up connected, some independent and done on a whim. She played my skin like it was a map she was trying to memorize. I've loved art for most of my life. I was surrounded by it in a way most people in my position take for granted. But simply having the thing is not enough. It should be appreciated, often. And for me, that turned into committing it to skin. The wings on my shoulder blade from 'Winged Victory,' the outlined bridge below my collar bone from 'The Scream', 'The Hands of Adam and God' across my forearm. Pieces I've seen that have left me marked by their impact. She dragged her tongue across 'The Storm on the Sea of Galilee' and never have I been happier about the placement on my upper thigh as it resulted in her dragging her tongue across more than just the ship's mast.

Moments from last night are painted across the ceiling, and if I were to close my eyes I'm sure I'd see the brushstrokes come to life.

The sun begins to rise and she stirs ever so slightly with it. I need to do the same. The second I move from underneath her eyes struggle open, blinking rapidly to adjust, but landing on me without reproach.

"This time I have to be the one to go," I say.

"Are you running from me?"

"I'll run right back the second you say."

Run from her? Ridiculous thought. Normally I would start my day with a literal run, but I preferred the time spent pinned beneath her.

I pause, weighing the words before I let them out. "There's this thing Saturday night, come with me."

She studies my face for a moment, and I can see her wrestling with what this invitation means.

"I can't, I'm —"

"Unavailable, I know." I let it sound casual, let her keep the security she needs in the distance.

I pull on my underwear and jeans, and grab a blanket she has draped across her reading chair. She doesn't move from bed as I stand over it. Snapping the blanket in the air so it can flutter gently down on top of her like the dusting of a snow flurry. It would be so easy to just crawl back in bed, as I lean down to kiss her the temporary goodbye, with each press of my lips it's harder to go as she nuzzles deeper and smiles into them. But I eventually do.

Chapter Twenty

HAPPILY EVER BEFORE

Arden

I'm tagging along to a surprise birthday party of someone I don't know thanks to Ethan who abandoned me as soon as we walked through the door. *Fine*, abandoned is harsh. I decided to hang back closer to an escape than the center of the room.

Our host's name is Rosalie, Ethan gave me the rundown before we got here. College sweethearts who moved here when he got a job. She followed him. And when he decided to quit, to start his own company, she followed him into that, too. From the look of things, it was a gamble that seemed to pay off. At least so Ethan says. They just celebrated their IPO. Though despite all that, he swears they are more down to earth than Forbes will paint them to be.

This city is known for making people like them. The Mark Zuckerbergs of it all. The *disrupters* with their hoodies and laptops clamoring in this wild wild west of business. *A new age.* Meanwhile my day was spent with versions of monopoly men who worship at the altar of JP Morgan in a way that should genuinely terrify everyone.

Rosalie gives Ethan a greeting that is full of comfort as he motions to me for the intro. She's sleek in so many ways but also visibly uncomfortable. Watching her move through the space like a bird caught in an unfamiliar cage despite this being her home. I can't explain it fully. Like there are too many people in this space for her to be able to have oxygen. So I don't force a hug, instead just smile and stick out my hand to shake hers.

Nails bitten down, but also a hair not out of place. A contradiction of personalities that I'm fascinated by.

"This is my friend, Arden Bancroft," Ethan says as exchange hellos. "We go way back," he offers her and she gives him a sideways glance and smirk that tells me she knows too much but would never dare say a word.

"Thanks for coming, the more the merrier they say." Her voice sounds like she's trying to convince herself she isn't drowning in the number of people that are here.

"Just because they say it, doesn't mean it's true." I say, offering the acknowledgement of the invasion. The small huff she lets out is an indication of her agreement, and confirmation of my assessment.

She's gorgeous really, with her hair tucked behind one ear and falling just below her chin. Her brown eyes are friendly but the way they bounce around the room looking for some kind of stability. I know that must be her looking for him, being the thing that grounds her, even though she knows he isn't here yet. I think about what that must be like. The human lightning rod that will take all mother earth has to charge. Your energy source without giving up any of themselves.

I've existed in spaces and crowds for long enough to know how draining they are. There was a time I convinced myself I was energized by them. I used to tell myself that I would get that volt of electricity and light up a room from it. I would be the disco ball. The one people can't keep their eyes off of. Wherever I perched myself would be where the small cluster would form. They never realized why, as much as just felt it, the electricity, the spark, the sparkle, that since has faded and dimmed to a place it doesn't reflect light in the same way.

Now, I spend my time amongst a room full of strangers searching the room for who has taken my place. There's always one in the crowd, I can spot her in the way of looking for myself. I can hear the boredom between the giggles and read the look on her face as her cheeks blush on self-command. She's playing the role society instructed her to, the one that she believes will get her far, and keep her safe. It's everything we're ever taught as women. The perceived agreeability in femininity that gives us the illusion of control over social settings dominated by men. But it's just that, an illusion, no different than the mirroring of their own selves or rather who they want to be, in her shiniest of reflections.

I look at the girl who I feel more kinship to than most. I want to be her friend. The kind she might not realize she needs yet. Because right now, she knows everything. Who she will go home with, who she is going to become, what to say to get the audience of suitors and jesters to respond. She thinks she knows who she is, but the painful reality will eventually catch up with her in the way that everything she thinks she knows gets washed away one morning when you wake up in the bed you made but can't recognize anymore.

I used to have that charm. But it cost me so much more than I thought it did at the time. Swiping my card at every interaction, but it was feeding their accounts while draining mine. I used to think I was energized by people naturally. It's not until I stepped out of that light that it became clear that natural doesn't mean easy, and doesn't always mean good.

I stand here as a bystander to Rosalie and Ethan as she eases into conversation with him. He has this superpower that is so disarming, comforting in a way that you wouldn't expect. But the presence of him just offers relief in whatever form is needed as he has to me in so many ways over so many years.

She checks her phone and frantically tries to quell the crowd.

"OKAY EVERYONE! He's almost here," she shouts in a whisper. "Hiding places!"

And with that she runs to flip the lights off and everyone scatters. Ethan and I dart in opposite directions and I drop behind the sofa.

There's something joyously juvenile in physically hiding. I've become far too comfortable in the alternative.

My knees are exposed on the rug and I peek up ever so slightly knowing I have the perfect view of the door.

"You look like someone who might be able to help..." The voice is distorted through whispers but as I glance over my shoulder, no one forgets a face like that. One so good looking it's actually laughable and time has only been kind to him though it's been years since we've been this close. Never having reason to share spaces after Reid dumped me.

"You see, there's this toast I'd love to give about honor, I heard it once before, but I can't remember how it ends..."

And just like that, the crackle and flicker of the old disco ball sparks on in memory for Austin Becks.

"And you look like someone I might know, but it's hard to say... I'm going to need you to strip down to a gold speedo and cover yourself in body glitter to be sure."

"Those days are behind me, I'm respectable now... Unless you ask nicely, *of course.*"

He laughs, and it sounds like the shared memories of Rocky Horror Picture Show in the cold Cambridge nights of my freshman year.

"Were you always this much of a flirt, Austin?"

"Always," he says with a smile that is seen even in the darkness of the room. "It's been a while since I've seen you in the flesh."

"I can say the same to you." Tipping my chin towards his fully-clothed-self.

We haven't seen each other in some time, even longer since it was purposeful. Our lives stopped intersecting. It's always funny how that can happen. I'm struck by how much time pleats people and places together at the strangest times, crouched behind a sofa waiting to yell surprise for someone else's milestone.

And while Austin never tried to be deeper than a puddle of water he is giving me a look that tells me he remembers more than he's let on. Instead just playing along with the game of memories that I'm willing to trade.

Someone across the room makes violent shushing gestures, there's a frantic last minute shuffling while people duck behind curtains and behind walls, as footsteps and laughter come from the hallway.

"How've you been, Arden?" The whispers of banter from friendships past subsided, a genuine question now on his lips.

"I'm good... how's..."

"SURPRISE!!!"

The door opens and the lights flick on. Our instincts have us on our feet with the rest of the crowd regardless of narrowly avoiding a trip down memory lane. Not like we'd be skipping down the street arm in arm, but at least we're both past the point where we'd cross it to avoid each other. Something I'm ashamed to say happened once before I was ready to deal with the implications of everything beyond the updated relationship status.

The noise around the room picks up, and the man who walks in with a backpack on his shoulder, hair a hint of red, ignores every bit of sound and every figure taking up space until he spots her. *Like lightning.* He absorbs it all and passes through the crowd to where she stands. I can see her mouth *'happy birthday'* as he smiles into their kiss. Whispering into her ear something only for them. Before turning to the room full of people.

"I don't know who you all are, and I don't know who to thank more," he says, "You for being here... or my Rosie for putting up with you!" He slips his arm around her waist and I think she stands a little taller by him, smile broader, shoulders no longer at her ears like earrings. *Her lightning rod.* The crowd laughs a bit, the music comes back on.

"What were you saying?" Austin asks. But I'm completely lost to anything besides Will standing in the doorway. A narrowing of his eyes is penetrating in a way that is indescribable and becoming more and more frequent.

"What?" I turn my head slightly to acknowledge Austin's question, but my eyes are elsewhere. The delayed impact of understanding that I had abandoned mid-thought no longer of any interest. "Oh, uh, nothing worthwhile."

Austin, who was once a back channel of information I found valuable, but not anymore, and certainly not now.

Now, the only things I want to know are 'what is he doing here' and 'can he read my lips?' Can he see that this conversation is nothing or is he intrigued at the idea it might be *something*? Is it jealousy that has my stomach rolling despite our distance or is it the very recent memory of his hands on my skin that has the tightness deepening in my chest?

He stands there somewhere between the same shock and fascination that I have.

I would be lying to myself to say I hadn't replayed the other night more than once. But the idea of all of that had me unnerved to the point I've ignored his texts since. Attraction that strong always combusts. In some form or another, everything goes up in smoke. Either I strike a match and it sets everything on fire or the slow silent gas leak fills the air until the smallest spark blows up the happily ever after house.

It takes all of my attention to untangle my stare from his. Blinking as if that will clear my vision.

You know that feeling when a camera flashes and you blink really fast to try and clear from your sight. But it doesn't dissolve. The shadow of still obscuring whatever you look at. That's what happens when I see Will. No amount of blinking can clear his shape from my sight.

"It was nice to see you, Austin," I give him a hug and I think we both know its meaning.

"You too, Arden," he responds in kind. The same agreeable, friendly, we-have-a-weird-reason-for-knowing-each-other, *good-*

bye. The kind that indicates, despite crossing paths, we may never see each other again, as I walk towards the only thing calling my name.

Will took steps as I did, meeting me in the middle of the room. Standing there toes to toes, no more steps to take. Except the one that has my lips tingling. I tilt my chin up with a smile and he reads it for what it is. His hand lands on the side of my face as he presses his lips to mine in a crowded room full of people with no remorse.

My eyes open and the sunspots that blurred my vision are gone. It's just him now.

When we finally pull apart, his eyes hold an intensity that makes my knees weak, full of tenderness and a barely contained wanting. The corner of his mouth quirked in a half-smile. And while his text remains unresponded to, I've drafted more than one in reply. *Just never hitting send.*

"Hi," I whisper into his mouth. He freckles a pattern of kisses up to my ear.

"Hello."

It's when he pulls away I drop my hand from where it planted on his chest, but he catches it in his palm. Like it was waiting there.

"Fancy meeting you here," he murmurs, his thumb tracing circles on my wrist in a way that makes my pulse jump. "Though I should have known, you seem to have a knack for showing up exactly when I was thinking about you."

"Is that so?" I managed, trying to sound "And how often is that?"

"More than I should admit in public." His voice has a rough edge to it that makes me want to drag him away from all these people, find some quiet corner where we could just exist in our own little world like we did before. "But apparently not enough for you to respond to my texts."

"Oh? Was I supposed to?"

Ethan bumps into Will from behind, momentarily breaking

our bubble. *They know each other. I'd even go so far as to say they are friends.* The look on my face must say it all, as the shock of the proximity of Will Sterling in my life just grows.

The party surges around us, with laughter, music, and the clink of glasses.

"Excuse us," he says to Ethan as he wraps his fingers with mine and pulls me down the hallway beyond and into a small office. The door shuts behind us and we've both clearly possessed by the ghosts of bar-bathrooms-past. The wordless exchange of kisses and breaths going beyond reason.

But when my back hits the wood door, I feel it. The wood grain against my spine. My breath gets short and his eyes open.

I see his face marked with confusion as he takes a step back.

"I'm sorry, I..." he begins to offer immediately as he scans me to understand what's shifted.

"Don't be... I- I just, I get a little claustrophobic."

It looks like he doesn't know if he should believe me. I don't know if he should. Claustrophobic. Skittish. And about a dozen other things I am that have absolutely nothing to do with him despite how much I want him right now. These things that come up like food poisoning. You don't know it's there until you're emotionally vomiting it over someone else's shoes.

I look down at our feet, but they are all clean.

I should step back. I should make an excuse. I should do anything except stand here, letting the gravity of him pull me closer while my mind screams about all the ways this will go wrong.

But then he shifts his weight, and even that small movement eases me into him.

"You know," Will says, as he steps back to lean against the desk, "for someone who keeps running away from me, you have an interesting habit reappearing."

"Well, maybe the universe just has a twisted sense of humor," I counter, following him like my feet have their own agenda. I hop onto the desk beside him, letting my legs dangle.

"That's what we're calling party-crashing these days?" *He shifts his pinky finger toward mine.*

"I'll have you know I was invited!" I say with mock indignation.

"That's right, you're Ethan's friend." *His pinky loops under mine.*

"No, not just Ethan. Rosalie and I are the *best* of friends." The lie rolls off my tongue with surprising ease, even as my pinky curls around his in what feels like a secret.

"Oh, really?" His voice drops a register. *"Do tell."*

"We go *way* back." I continue, doubling down on my obvious fabrication. But he knows Ethan, *through run-club or something,* and I can't let him be the only one with the advantage of a shared acquaintance. Not to mention the fact that lying feels better than the alternative of appearing like a complete psycho who just keeps popping wherever he is.

"Fascinating," he says, reaching across the desk with his free hand. "Then you'll definitely remember this." He produces a framed photo of himself, Rosalie, and Simon, at what appears to be a marathon finish line, all three grinning and holding up medals.

He laughs, the sound rumbling through his chest. "You are absolutely terrible at this, you know. It would be so much easier to just admit you're obsessed with me."

"Fine, you've caught me." I say.

"Not yet I haven't."

"For all I know, you've been the one orchestrating this whole thing, and *you're* the one obsessed with *me*." I raise an eyebrow.

"I am." His free hand finds my hip, pulling me closer with a confidence that makes my breath catch. Two simple words exhaled into the space between us as his lips land against mine for the briefest of moments. "But if I had that kind of power, you would have said yes to coffee."

"Ah, but where's the fun in that?" I manage, despite the way his proximity is scrambling my thoughts. "This way, you get to keep pursuing me dramatically across the city."

"You do realize," he says, his voice softer now, more serious, "that this is the third time you've ended up in my arms after technically turning me down. I'm starting to think you like the chase more than the catch."

"Maybe I'm just worried about what happens when the chase ends." The words slip out before I can stop them, more honest than I mean them to be.

His eyes meet mine, and there's understanding there.

"Or maybe you're more worried about what happens when it doesn't end at all." The audacity in the statement doesn't make it any less true, but I'm swallowing down the disbelief that he would say it.

"That's...That's a lot of certainty from someone who barely knows me."

"Is it?" His thumb traces circles on my hip where my shirt has ridden up ever so slightly to expose a patch of skin to him. "Because it seems like we've been missing each other by minutes or miles. And suddenly, every time I turn around, you're there. It's starting to feel less like coincidence and more like inevitability."

"Inevitability is just another word for lack of choice," I whisper, but even I don't believe it anymore.

"No, you always have the choice." he says, tucking that errant strand of hair behind my ear. The weight of that truth sits between us, heavy with possibility.

"How about this, third time's a charm," he says finally, breaking the tension. "Have dinner with me."

"It's almost midnight, I've already eaten."

"Breakfast then."

Chapter Twenty-One

HAPPILY EVER BEFORE

Arden

The diner glows like a beacon, all harsh fluorescent lights and worn vinyl booths that had heard a thousand stories. Will slides into one side, I take the other, our knees somehow finding each other beneath the laminate table that has seen better decades.

"Breakfast at 1 a.m.," I point out, picking up the sticky menu. "Clearly the most responsible decision we've made yet."

His lips pull to the side, desire and desperation still pinking his cheeks.

The waitress approaches, her name tag 'Greta' likely from decades before, and sporting a look of mild exhaustion that suggests she's seen everything this late-night crowd could offer.

"Scrambled eggs with rye toast and a cup of coffee, please." I hand her back the menu and she just tucks it casually under her arm while scribbling the order onto her notepad.

"Can I have the Denver omelet, double bacon, a biscuit, and" he takes a pause and looks at me before proceeding with what he already knows is a good decision. "A side of fries for the table."

And then we just sit here in silence.

Our earlier intensity has mellowed into something more

contemplative. But the look on his face tells me his mind is flashing back to moments between us like mine continues to.

When our food arrives, Greta tops off my coffee, and I wonder what story she's made up about us in her mind. We look like we could be on a date, though not dressed for this one. There's a pulse here that I can feel just being in his proximity, and I wonder if strangers can also.

He pushes the plate of fries to the middle of the table.

I'm acutely aware that this is exactly how it starts. The casual intimacy. The shared food. The way he tilts his head when he's about to tell a story about a museum guest that he knows will make me laugh, the way we are tracing all of our paths knowing how closely they've been crossed for longer than makes any sense.

It's dangerous.

That's the problem.

The absolute crisis of this moment. He's sincere, he's charming. And not in the social media kind of way, but in the way that suggests he actually listens. That he finds the weird, quirky parts of a conversation fascinating rather than something to be politely ignored. All wrapped up in a smile that looks crafted just for me. The conversation flows like the diner coffee. Warm and slightly bitter, but unexpectedly smooth.

"You know," he said, taking a fry, "I didn't expect tonight to end like this."

"In a diner. Eating carbohydrates. At an hour when most sensible people are asleep?" I thread it with sarcasm and hopefully he picks up on that rather than the bit of fear in my voice that I, too, am completely and utterly surprised. Cards on the table, *fries* on the table, I didn't see him coming.

"Precisely," he repeats, mimicking my earlier tone. "But I'm not usually called sensible."

There's something almost hypnotic about the casual way his fingers move, how they remind me of those same fingers trailing across my skin.

"So," I say, dunking a fry in ketchup with perhaps more

concentration than strictly necessary, "do you make a habit of seducing women and then taking them out for breakfast in the dead of night, or am I special?"

Will's laugh is low and rich in reply.

"One more and I get a free grand slam breakfast... and you said no to coffee, and dinner..."

I try not to smile but fail miserably. The remnants of our breakfast-at-night are scattered between us, and I'm struck by how comfortable this feels. Dangerous territory, that comfort.

"Well, I certainly didn't expect it to play out like this..." I swirl my hand in the air hopefully to capture the undefined *this* in my statement. "So I'm not exactly sure where things went wrong."

"Oh, I'd say things have gone surprisingly right." His voice reaches across the laminate table top as his feet entangle mine beneath it.

Greta swings by with more coffee, forcing us to untangle our feet as she leans between us to pour. The steam rises in lazy spirals between our faces and I notice how she smiles knowingly at us, probably adding our story to her mental catalogue of late-night diner romances. *If only she knew the half of it.*

"You know what I think?" Will says after she leaves.

"I'm sure you're about to tell me."

"I think you're trying *very* hard not to like me." The honesty in his statement has me almost choke on my coffee.

"*Excuse* me?"

"You keep throwing up little walls, these clever remarks designed to keep me at arm's length. But then you laugh, really laugh, and I can see you forgetting to maintain the distance." He's saying all this while finger painting the condensation of his water glass like it's the most casual moment, not the accusation it is.

"That's..." I start, then stop, because damn him for being perceptive. "That's a lot of psychological analysis for some whose day job is giving a decent tour." *And damn him if he isn't proven right by my instinct to deflect him with a taunt.*

His lips pull to the side in smirk as he shakes his head near imperceptibly. Clicking his tongue in disapproval. He leans back, stretching his arms along the back of the booth, and I definitely *don't* notice how it makes his shirt pull across his chest. *Except for the fact that I do.*

He might have a lot to say about me putting up walls, but he has just as many witty deflections as I do, with the added bonus of a self-admitted habit of running away.

"You're right, I do like you." And with those words the smile blooms across his face. "But I think we should just enjoy this for what it is. No pressure, no expectations. Just two people who hooked up in a questionably clean bathroom, had great sex, and now find themselves enjoying each other's company with absolutely no expectations for the future because we both have enough of those." Our laughs betray us both in different ways.

"When you put it that way, it sounds almost reasonable." He reaches across the table, his fingers brushing mine.

"Well, I think we've already established that neither of us is particularly sensible," I murmur, elbows propped on the table.

"True. Sensible people are definitely asleep right now."

"Exactly. So why don't we leave sensibility to the sleeping masses and just..." I pause, gesturing vaguely with my free hand as the other reaches for a fry, "see where this goes?"

"And *tonight*," he breathes, his voice dropping lower, "where do you see this going?"

"Well," I hesitate, watching his eyes darken, "I was thinking we could start with pie." *Start with pie. Because we both can tell where this will go.* There's something infectious about his joy, about the way he seems to take everything in stride without taking anything too seriously.

He flags Greta down with a wave. "A slice of apple pie, please. À la mode."

"Look at you, making executive decisions," I tease, settling back.

"Don't tell my father," he confides, eyes full of a teasing

mischief, "but I can be very decisive when it comes to important matters."

"You're doing that on purpose," I accuse, heat rising in my cheeks.

"Doing what?" he challenges, innocence belied by his foot against my ankle.

He accepts the pie from Greta with a thank you that makes her beam, though his gaze remains fixed on me.

"Lucky for you," I say, watching him, as I deliberately taste the ice cream, "it seems to be working."

He is just as transfixed as I am. There's that look again, a gaze heavy with promise.

"Don't push it," I warn.

But he does push it, metaphorically and literally, sliding the pie plate slightly toward me in offering. The diner is quieter than before, just the soft clink of dishes from the kitchen and the vibrations of the lights overhead. It feels like we're separate from the real world with all its complications and consequences.

The front door opens with a jingle of a bell, and the new patrons have me glance outside for the first time since we walked in. And while the sun isn't up yet, she's beginning to yawn in that lazy way you do before you're ready to wake up. When I see the clock on the wall it's clear, we found a mist to get lost in for more hours than I could have imagined.

"We should probably go," I say, though I make no move to leave, waiting for him to confirm.

"That would be sensible" he agrees, then flags down Greta for the check.

As we slide out of the booth, I feel a sudden reluctance to let this night end. Which is ridiculous, because this isn't anything. It can't be anything. It's just a random connection, a spark in the dark, temporary collected moments of madness.

Outside, the street is quiet except for the distant sound of traffic and our own footsteps on the sidewalk.

"So," I say, because what else is there?

And before I can build another wall or make another joke, he's kissing me. It's different from our earlier kisses, which have all been heat and urgency. This is slower, sweeter, tasting more than coffee. His hands frame my face like I'm something precious, something worth savoring, and I let myself melt into it just for a moment under the spill of the gossiping street lights.

Chapter Twenty-Two

HAPPILY EVER BEFORE

Arden

Offices echo. Don't they realize that? The way their voices carry around corners and through doorways, bouncing off glass walls and landing right where I'm pouring *myself* a cup of coffee.

That's how I hear them, Brent and Michael, their voices drifting over the partition of their cubicles like they've forgotten sound travels.

Or maybe, they just don't care.

"Her Thompson plan is never going to work," Michael says, in a strain of corporate condescension that I'm tired of translating. "But you know how she gets when she thinks she's right."

I freeze. My coffee cup halfway to my lips. Afraid if I actually take a sip I'll end up with a spit take of coffee. The coffee was mediocre at best before. Now? It's practically sweetened with printer toner. *Whatever that actually is.*

"Yeah, but Victor likes her." Brent replies.

"Victor likes to look at her, there's a difference."

"Can't fault him for that." And they laugh like there's a joke in it.

It's me. I'm the joke. The punchline they've been waiting to deliver since I first walked through these doors. I've played their game. Giggled at their jokes. Nodded along to stories about their weekend boats and weekend women. I made the right small talk at happy hours while carefully counting my drinks. All while they looked at me like my education was just an MRS. degree and expensive hobby to fill the time and get a diamond ring.

I thought if I played it right, the perfect balance of competence and compliance with just enough 'one of the boys' they might actually see me as an equal. But here they are, voices carrying across corporate carpet, revealing what they thought all along. I'm just another girl who dared to think she could sit at their table instead of serving drinks at it.

"We just have to go along with it, let her prepare to present the pitch for Vulcan, and when it's D.O.A, we'll have our plan."

I've spent weeks on this proposal, sacrificed weekends, skipped plans. And here they are, dismissing it like it's a child's art project they'll hang on the corporate fridge out of pity. All while patting my head, *or my ass,* telling me *'good job'* not meaning a word of it.

My phone vibrates on my desk, another text from Will.

After dinner, *or actually breakfast,* I stopped avoiding him. Our agreement, that we will just *'see where this goes.'* And that seems to end up with some pretty aggressive public displays of affection around friends and strangers alike. For now this casual yet consuming way we want each other, is insatiable. While I have a pretty solid idea of where this will go eventually, he will fall in line as men always do for opportunity, move on to chasing someone or something else, and I'll be left here clamoring on my own.

Our conversations have become run-on. Much like we are. Anytime we are within feet of each other, picking up the end of the previous moment like there was no gap in time or space.

I should be focusing on the Vulcan account, on finally securing that associate position that's been dangling just out of reach. Instead, I'm thinking about the way his hands crawl up my body like they are memorizing the paths of each curve like it was sculpted.

And *that* is exactly the reason it can't be anything more than whatever it is.

It's not about the distraction now, but the one that will result in me being absorbed into my bed aching at the idea of him and crying about a future I was foolish to hope for.

I'll just run out to grab lunch and come back and eat at my desk with *Pricktor*, who sadly is *not* doing super well despite his ice cube breakfast.

The cafe is busy with the lunch rush when I arrive, all the pre-made sandwiches from the display case are cleaned out. *Of course.* But there's one perfect, golden-brown chocolate croissant left. As I reach for it, another hand appears in my peripheral vision.

"Oh, sorry!" she says, *though she's not sorry at all*, snagging the last croissant. And then laughs in that awkward way strangers do when they're trying not to be rude.

The other woman has the kind of hair that suggests she's got better things to do than worry about it, a laptop covered in stickers, and she's wearing a sweatshirt that reads *'Practice Shelf Care.'*

"Listen, I don't mean to be rude, but I have..." *I check my watch* "exactly seventeen minutes to scarf down anything I can to power me through the rest of my day, *which sucks by the way*, so I'm really going to need that..." I say, pointing to the croissant in her hand.

She purses her lips and moves them side to side in thought.

"This would make a great meet-cute," she says, then immediately blushing. "Sorry, I'm a writer, or going to be, or am in the process of becoming one," she rambles at me while grabbing two small plates from the counter. "You see, I'm working on my first romance novel. So, everything's potential material."

She finally takes a breath.

"I'm Amanda," she says, grinning. "I'm absolutely putting this in a book." She doesn't give me a chance to protest, taking the croissant and splitting it down the middle for us to share. We claim a tiny table, the croissant divided into precise halves between us as Amanda pulls out her laptop and starts typing. *Perhaps documenting a version of this encounter for her main characters.*

My phone lights up the space between us with a vibration that is less discrete than the actual ringer.

Will: Someone seriously just argued that Sargent was over-rated. You'd appreciate the audacity.

She looks at me like she can read the pining that's written on my face as the message comes in. *Perhaps she can.*

"Boyfriend?" she asks as if it's that simple. I let out a chuckle and huffs of air rather than words.

"No. Definitely not."

"That face coulda had me fooled, but what do I know, I just write happy endings," she says with a shrug.

"We're just, *seeing each other.* I have other priorities, and he has..." *I don't even know how to explain what he has. Pressures from family? A likely exit strategy when the time comes?* So I continue as if she's asked for the whole story. "I have this promotion to focus on. And my bro-workers are already waiting for me to fail. Chanting for it even. So this thing with Will..." I pause, picking at a croissant crumb, "I can't afford for it to become a real some-thing, because real *somethings* fall apart. I've done the falling apart before, and it's not great for productivity."

Amanda slides a business card across the table that says her name and 'Author of Works in Progress' beneath it.

"What's this?" I ask, twirling it between my fingers.

"I write romance novels because I believe in love. Not the perfect, fairy-tale kind, but the messy, wild, cant-get-enough, kind. The kind that shows up when you're busy making plans and it refuses to be ignored... and it sounds like you could use a friend,"

And with that, my phone buzzes again against the tabletop

exactly in that can't-get-enough-refuses-to-be-ignored kind of way.

I haven't stopped thinking about him. I called Stella and left her a series of voicemails explaining what happened. The one I finally got in response was just a scream of excitement as she hopped on a moped clinging to the back of someone, promising to 'catch up soon.' Though we both know it's the easier lie.

Will and I are tangled in a game of lust, and we are both playing it between rounds of real life. I think we've seen each other daily in the pockets of time we take as breaths as we run.

Despite every self positioned obstacle we haven't stopped messaging. A long thread of commentary about our days, about each other. He isn't testing the waters in a coffee shop and asking me my favorite color. He tells me how he's desperate to see me. I don't ask him his middle name. I tell him I want to feel him between my legs again. He agrees to be free of labels which is ironic considering how this all started. But it's for the best, we both are clearly focused in other areas, and based on the little context I have, it sounds like his focus will be shifting soon anyways.

I remember when I was sure I knew it all, when I had everyone around me figured out. How is that possible when now, with each day, I'm sure I know less than the day before. Including who I thought I would be. Maybe it was because I didn't realize how much there was to know.

Sitting at my desk moving formulas around an excel file has become background noise to the thrill of seeing his name flash across the screen of my phone. It's a sense of all-consuming obsession you think is reserved for first-loves. But there's not a single vibration that I don't hope is him. This type of passion is just that.

Vibrations.

An oscillating phenomenon deep within me. And when I gave myself the freedom to experience it, I remember what it's like to have someone look at you like that. It's beyond interest, beyond desire. It's engulfing. I've seen it. Remember it. But the safety I thought I was experiencing by keeping the fire small, was stifling. When I was younger, I knew everything even if I didn't, and because of that, I let myself experience so much more than I do now just because 'I know better' now. It's all bullshit.

This feels like one of those pivotal moments where you stare at yourself in the mirror, or in this case computer screen, repeat some affirmations, 'I'm thirty and flirty and thriving,' or something. Except, I'm not thirty. And is anyone really thriving? Am I one of those people who loves their job? Not yet. But I will be. *Right?*

Will does, Ethan does, Amanda, *whom I've barely known longer than a sneeze,* does, and Stella? Even Stella just loves. Whereas I feel a combination of inadequacy and resentment I was never expecting.

I look around the office and see the gaggle of mid-twenties post grads gathering around the water cooler. What a cliché representation of men in the wild. Here I am. At my desk. Actually working while they talk about their golf swing. *Come-on it's so clearly a metaphor for your dicks.*

I am like most people who find themselves post college, pretending that the grind and the hustle are really all they are cracked up to be. The normal text I would send would have three-thousand miles to travel to the west coast. Reid has had some passive consistency in helping me through situations like this. But I can almost predict what he'll say. He'll tell me that this is pretty standard. That I'm smart and doing a good job. He'll tell me not to rush decisions.

But today sucks. It's actually that simple, so I send a simple text.

me: I hate my job
Will: meet me after work. we'll celebrate

Chapter Twenty-Three

HAPPILY EVER BEFORE

Arden

He said we were celebrating, that was the word he used. Maybe he has something to celebrate. I don't. His message told me to come straight from work, and that's what I did. Standing on the side door of the museum waiting for him to let me in.

The door cracks open and his hand reaches out for mine. My grip slides into his without question and I slip into a non-public entrance. It's a fluorescently lit hallway but the light that surrounds us is golden. His hand tightens on mine, as he steps back and lifts our joined hands, he whips his wrist and me into an unexpected twirl right into him where he catches me with both arms. *He's unexpected.* He was as soon as I met him, and amidst the big moments of my days he fills the in between in all ways. It causes me to break into a smile and throw my arms around his neck with a kiss that is slow and mindful, one that feels like he's telling me his secrets.

He guides me down the hall and up a few flights of stairs, using his id card to bypass locked doors, never once letting go of my hand.

"Is anyone here?" I ask, feeling in some way we're doing something wrong. I know the museum is officially *closed* for the evening. "Am I even allowed to be here?"

"You're with me, it's fine."

"Oh... it's *fineee* is it? I thought we shouldn't settle for fine." I say tauntingly. He stops from where we are hurrying through the maze of secret passages.

"You know what, you're right."

"Usually." He steps towards me and his thumb tilts my chin up toward him.

"I've noticed." His lip curls in a delicious smile, and he shares it with a kiss. "Now are you ready to celebrate?" he asks as he pulls away.

"What are we even celebrating?" I ask.

He swipes his card and pushes open the door, the room is empty. Not a soul. Except maybe the ones preserved in paint. Just a bottle of champagne left on the bench where we first fought.

"We're going to sit there and figure something out."

We don't sit as we did the day we met. The bench is wider than one you would see at a park or somewhere with a singular focus. This is meant to allow many people facing all different directions to share the space. But the only space we share is each other. He sits cross-legged and I do the same. Not looking towards any of the walls, but he's looking only at me.

"Alright Arden, you hate your job, your day sucked..." he starts, his hand wraps around the neck of the glass champagne bottle, while the other one begins to delicately untwist the wire top containing the cork.

"You want me to drink champagne because I hate my job? I know shitty jobs can lead people to drink, but that's not really what I'm going for."

"No, I want you to sit here with me, drink champagne from this bottle, and realize that there's something that happened today for you to celebrate. Even if everything else is terrible. Right now, it's just us and this bottle of champagne, and we can't waste it. We need to come up with something, no matter how small, to drink to. For starters..." and with that the bottle *pops* as he pulls the cork out, immediately raising it to his lips catching the overflow in his mouth. "For starters, I'm going to celebrate that this cork didn't go flying and hit one of these paintings."

I reach for the bottle. Our knees are touching, and I don't think I knew we were so close. But somehow we always seem to be connected.

He clicks his tongue and shakes his ever so slightly. "You have to come up with your *own* reason before I hand you this bottle."

"It can be anything?" I ask.

"Anything," he says.

"I..." I think about my day, the big boulders of it not worth even the worst champagne.

"Come on *darling*," he prompts in jest, "I can see something working behind your eyes. I want to hear one thing that made you smile today."

I'm not sure if this was part of his ploy, but the only thing I want to celebrate is him. But I don't say that. *I can't say that.*

"I found my missing chapstick!" I nearly scream with excitement. He leans forward and we meet in the middle across our laps for a kiss. The taste of champagne lingering on his tongue. The taste of my chapstick on his lips.

"Cheers to that." Is all he says as he pulls away and hands me the champagne. I take a swig from the heavy glass bottle. The bubbles hit my tongue, and he might be onto something. I look around the room, the gravity of it as we sit here in solitude.

"I found a heads-up penny on my walk to the train." *sip.*

"I...this is hard..." I say, a bit defeated already.

"Come on, you've got something else," he prods as his hand comes down across my thigh, as he slowly moves to coax it from me.

I think about some of the moments of today that might be worth celebrating, and the overwhelming sense is that I might be sitting here wasting this bottle. When I just want to crawl into his lap and have him kiss me in the way he robs me of all stress of the outside world.

"Today I got clarity." *sip.*

I hate that this is my response, but I did. The kind of clarity you can only get from hearing your colleagues prepare for your failure like it's already pencilled on their calendar. At least now I know that the list of people I can trust at work, starts and ends with me.

"I spoke to a couple today that has been married for sixty-five years and every week they come and sit right here..." He takes a sip and as he tilts the bottle back, his eyes darken so slightly not breaking my stare. "They said if you sit here long enough as strangers, you can fall in love."

He says this as I tip back the bottle and get a rush of foam, choking down a swallow as the bubbles hit my throat. I burst into a fit of coughing and he puts the bottle down to free me from the added burden of holding something while I'm gasping for breath wondering if champagne is coming out my nose. His quick assessment returns that I'm not actually dying, as he brushes the hair from my face, catching some remaining drips from the corner of my lip. I pull it under my teeth, almost embarrassed. But his smile is slow, not cautious, as it spreads across his face and guides mine to do the same.

His hands reach for my face and the pull toward him isn't in his grasp, but my body. The way it comes to life with him. His tongue moves against mine, unbothered by the audience of portraits and lovers who were once inspired to do the same. So much so they were immortalized in paint for us to revel. I'm wrapped around his body as his hands move against mine, laying me back down against the wide wooden bench. His kisses find their way to my neck as my hands slip up his shirt.

"We can't do this here," he gruffly whispers, the warmth of his words brush against my skin. His kisses transform from the deep passion filled ones, to softer presses of his lips, slowing down as he straightens us both back upright. Our feet are on the ground now, facing the portrait in front of us as he slips his hand into mind.

"Did you know, she was his mistress, in fact for a time he paid for her... *affections*?" Will looking ahead at the portrait of a woman, nude, but glowing. "Would you have been able to tell the nature of their relationship without research?"

I rest my head on his shoulder in a way that feels natural and inhale him.

"This looks like it was painted with love."

"It was, his marriage wasn't one he wanted, they say she was the love of his life, and she made the choice to be in his life in any capacity." His thumb strokes and swirls the skin on the back of my hand.

"Are you asking me to be your mistress, Will?" He looks away from the immense painting in front of us and curls his head to meet mine with a kiss on my forehead.

"I'm telling you, I'll be anything to you. Your mistress," he laughs "your champagne," he takes a sip, "your friend," I catch my breath, "I'll be whatever you want to call it, but I want this."

"I do too... I just don't know what that means." I'm concerned he will be hurt, scared this is going to be pushed into an ultimatum. I can't force him to stay in the inbetween.

He smiles and takes a slow sip as we near the end of the bottle before passing it back to me.

"What are you celebrating?"

"Us, *darling*."

We pass the bottle back and forth until it's empty, but we are both full. And by the bottom of the bottle my terrible day was drowned out by sips of champagne and my lungs are full of him.

Chapter Twenty-Four

HAPPILY EVER BEFORE

Will

Arden is standing in my living room, and watching her explore my space feels like watching someone read my diary. As her fingers trail along the spines of books I've collected over years, many from college, even more since.

In the last weeks we've always landed in her space rather than mine. She'd text me and I'd come running. It wasn't far, but I would have gone regardless.

We sat on the floor of her apartment eating takeout.

Sipping champagne as she showed me her plant collection.

Trading details of our day like secrets.

Finally ending our nights tangled in a way that our bed sheets could only tell the story of in the morning. And yet, she'd never been here. It was like some last threshold she's been unwilling to cross.

Until now.

"So," she says. Pulling out a dog-eared book with the kind of gentle reverence that indicates her own relationship with reading is much deeper than just the late night companion by her bedside would imply. "You *read*?"

"No, actually," I say, unable to resist teasing her. "I just collect them for aesthetics."

She rolls her eyes in that way that somehow manages to be both exasperated and endearing, carefully sliding the book back into its exact spot, as if she wants to leave everything exactly as she found it. Terrified that any record of her would be left behind.

"You know what I mean," she says, turning to face me. "I just... didn't realize you *enjoyed* reading."

"You never asked." I'm leaning against my kitchen counter, watching her methodically, carefully, comb through this space. "Though I'm curious what gave you the impression I was illiterate."

I have books that are stacked in towers on the coffee table, some with paper markers protruding like multicolored flags marking territory in an academic war zone, preparing for the next tour, assisting in some research at the museum.

"Well, you do spend an awful lot of time staring at pictures," she teases, pulling out a hefty one on Renaissance art. "This looks more like you are moonlighting as a professor... Docent by day, distinguished academic by night?"

"Not distinguished at all." I move behind her, my chest pressed against her back, as I drag my fingers across her neck sweeping her hair away from the nape, pressing a kiss in its place.

She spins in my arms to face me, the book she was holding the momentary barrier between us wraps around my back as she reaches up on her toes to knot her arms at my neck.

Speaking secrets onto my tongue, and smiles into my kiss.

"Let's run away" she says.

"Where do you want to go?"

She drops down to her feet, face full of joy and presents me with the book she just retrieved from the shelf.

"Narnia."

So we do... for hours with her head against my chest, and my breath against her forehead, we trade the pages back and forth.

———

I know that knock, that irregular, too-heavy rhythm that means Alfie decided that a bottle of whiskey wasn't going to finish itself after a long day. He does this about once a month, sometimes more, sometimes less, depending on what deals are going through or what fight is going on at home.

While there's not much about our lives we share, he turns up here knowing that regardless, I'll open the door under some misguided familial obligation. Even though it often results in the same fight the next morning when the whiskey wears off and he's faced with his own reality.

I carefully extract myself from Arden, who is sleeping peacefully in my bed, her hair spread across my pillow like melted gold.

Before I can reach the door, Alfie's voice booms through it, followed by a kick and an expletive that slips through the crack in frustration as he jiggles the door handle.

"WILL! Open up."

"Shit," I mutter, rushing to open it before he wakes the entire floor. "Alfie, what the hell?!"

He stumbles past me, reeking of the same bad decisions I've come to expect. Those bad decisions wear a much fruitier scent than his wife does.

"Had a great night," he announces, too loud for the hour. "Closed a massive deal. The kind dad would've—"

"Keep your voice down," I hiss, trying to guide him toward the couch. "It's the middle of the night."

"Oh, you've got company?" He chuckles dangerously as he's rummaging in my fridge for another beer. He slams it against the counter to open and the bottle crashes to the hardwood spilling its contents to be a sticky memory in the morning.

But Alfie's already noticed the second wine glass on the coffee table, the unfamiliar coat draped over my chair. His bloodshot eyes narrow with something that looks alarmingly like contempt as he takes thunderous steps towards my bedroom door.

Despite the length of my stride and my desperation to keep her safely behind that door, it's all too late.

It cracks open with sleep and Arden is standing there rubbing the confusion from her eyes. She's standing there in nothing more than a t-shirt of mine and my chest aches at the innocence on her face. Her lips are pink and full with sleep still pressed in the patterns of her cheek.

"Oh this is too good, you're still playing house with that girl from the bar." Alfie drawls, leaning against the doorframe despite the fact that I've immediately stepped between them.

"It's all okay, just go back to bed." I cup her face and try to speak just to her.

"I just want to hear how she convinced you..." It's not just a drunken statement, he says it with every intention of grabbing her curiosity.

"That's enough." I grab his arm, but he shakes me off and from the voice behind me, it's clear he's got her hooked.

"Convinced you of what?" she asks, a voice that's scared of the answer, but directing the question to me all the same.

"That this" Alfie waves his arms around at dismissal of the space, "is worth giving up his life." I've yanked him back by his shirt, as he spouts actual nonsense. But it's just emboldening him. Making him meaner. If I didn't know better, I'd even say he's jealous.

I push him onto the couch and he throws his hands up in the air in submission.

"I, I.. I should go." Her voice barely above a whisper.

"Arden, please." The words feel desperate on my tongue. But Alfie's face broadens with a cruel smile that looks genetic.

"No, stay," he croons. "You know he's not really this person, right?" He directs at Arden. "This whole artistic soul thing? It's just his latest way of running from responsibility. And you're just the latest girl in his bed helping him pretend."

"You don't know what you're talking about." I snarl, putting more space between them.

"I know you're throwing your life away!" he shouts back, face reddening. "Talking about other people's accomplishments instead of making something of yourself! And for what? For *her*?"

When I look back, Arden's already hurried herself into a pair of jeans and is gathering her things.

"Arden, wait!"

"Don't," she says, and the tremor in her voice kills me. "Just... don't. I know better, I, I *knew* better."

She pushes past us both, and I can hear her bare feet on the hardwood as she runs. *Literally this time.* Shoes in hand. The sound of my front door slamming reverberates through the apartment like a gunshot. *Feels like one too.*

"Are you happy now?" I run my hands through my hair with barely contained rage.

"Someone had to say it," he mutters, but the fight's gone out of him, replaced by a dull glaze that to anyone else that could look like drunken momentary regret. It's not.

"Don't fucking move." I say, already grabbing my keys, and his, because the last thing he should do is put any of this drunken judgement behind the wheel of a car.

I don't wait for his response, just race after her. She's fast, but I catch up to her at the elevator where she's frantically jabbing the button to escape.

"Let me explain," I beg, my voice getting to her before my feet do.

"Is he right?" she bursts out, whirling to face me. *Is he right?*

"Alfie doesn't know what he's talking about." I insist, reaching for her desperately. "He's drunk and angry and—"

"But he knows you," she cuts in, backing away slightly from my touch. "Maybe he's right. Maybe I'm just... maybe this isn't..."

The elevator arrives with a cheerful ding that feels like mockery. She steps inside and I follow her. The two of us enclosed the space, a short ride in silence as we reach the ground level. Staring at our distorted reflections in the metal doors.

"Look at me, of the three of us, I can promise you *he* isn't right. I know how that sounds, I know what you must think, but he doesn't know me, you do, and I know you, too."

As the doors open, so do her eyes. More awake that she was in the last minutes of this whirlwind.

"There's a reason you walked into the museum that day." I continue softly. "There's a reason I walked into that bar that night. There's a reason you showed up at Simon's party. All while being right across the street."

"And what reason is that?" she breathes. My hand reaches for her, intertwining like it's the most natural thing in the world, even in a moment where she's uncertain.

"Because sometimes two people are tied together without ever realizing it," I say drawing her closer, "and the universe continues to take the strands of their lives and weave them together. That's why. I can't stay away from you, and I don't want to. That has nothing to do with what Alfie thinks, my dad thinks, that has to do with me and you."

We're standing on the street between our buildings, she's got a decision to make, if she is going to take steps farther from me. Cross the street and leave me on the other side of the crack that would put between us. She's quiet for a long moment, I don't let the silence fill with any of the voices in her own head telling her different.

"And there is no part of me I'm going to convince to stay away from you when the whole fucking universe put a giant gold frame around this tapestry of our future."

"I want to run." she whispers, her voice even in the most hushed tones wraps around me in the night air.

"Okay, but I'm coming with you."

She steps into my arms as I press her head to my chest. Maybe she can feel my heart beat pounding its way to her.

"I'm sorry for him," I whisper into the crown of her head. And I feel her nodding against my chest until her face tilts up and pulls me into a soft kiss.

"Me too," she says, and it sounds like pity. "But that's the last time I'm staying at your place."

Chapter Twenty-Five

HAPPILY EVER BEFORE

Arden

The memory of Will's words on the street still rings in my ears, *'the universe put a giant gold frame around the tapestry of our future.'*

My phone feels heavy in my pocket, I've been wanting to call Stella all morning, needing to process everything that happened.

Straight to voicemail, of course.

"Hey Stells, it's me, again. I know you're probably..." I pause and release a breath that sounds suspiciously like a laugh. "I actually don't know anything." And hang up. We've been playing this game of friendship ping pong for too long now, and it's becoming less and less tenable.

Thinking about last night, after everything settled. How Will and I ended up back at my place, how he held me like I might disappear if he let go. His brother's words should have scared me more than they did. *'You're just the latest girl in his bed helping him pretend.'*

But there's nothing about him that's pretending. We both agreed to what this is. We set the expectations from the beginning. Which means we absolve ourselves from any pretending.

His brother's intrusion could have been the excuse I needed to bail, to protect myself from getting in too deep. Instead, it showed me just how deep I already am.

Will: He's gone. I won't let that happen again.
Will: Let's celebrate tonight.
Me: I'll grab the champagne?

Last night, after we got back to my place, we lay in bed talking until the sky started to lighten. About his brother, about his family, about the life he's choosing, instead of the one that was planned for him.

'They just want you to be successful,' I said.

'I am. Just not the kind they recognize.'

The afternoon stretches ahead, filled with meetings. The Thompson challenge isn't just a proposal anymore, it's become my personal crusade. My calendar glares at me from my computer screen. Three more meetings, two client calls, and a mountain of emails to scale before I can even think about escaping. But for the first time in forever, I'm not looking for excuses to work late. The presentation can wait until morning. The world won't end if I don't respond to every email in my inbox tonight. It's a strange feeling, this shift in priorities, like watching the tide change direction.

"Working late?" Brent asks as he passes my desk, his tone suggesting he expects nothing less.

"Actually, no, I have plans." The look of surprise on his face is almost as satisfying as the confirmation on mine when I see him sit down at my desk as I walk away.

I pause around the corner, counting his predictability like heartbeats. One, two, three... and there it is. The soft click of my mouse, the subtle shift of his weight in my chair. Through the reflection in the glass partition, I watch him navigate through my desktop with the kind of entitlement that makes men think they can take whatever they want.

He finds it exactly where I knew he would, the file labeled 'VULCAN-Presentation.Final-final-really-final.pptx' sitting right there like a gift-wrapped trap. I bite back a smile as he clicks it open, practically salivating at the thought of getting his hands on weeks of my supposed work. Work that I stopped sharing with him around the time I realized there never was any 'synergy' here. I give him another minute to dig himself deeper, to feel that surge of victory as he thinks he's gotten the upper hand as he occasionally scans the room for bystanders.

And I turn and walk away, leaving him to his petty corporate espionage.

Because I really do have plans.

———

We show up to the bar hours late, just in time to meet Ethan and the latest love of his life. It's magical to watch really, the way Ethan just dives head first like he knows there's a body of water waiting to catch him. I don't know how long their soul-mate ship will last, but he seems happy for now. And in some ways, happy for now, is really all any of us ever have.

This comingling of friendship is an inner circle of intimacy. *Though in some ways, that happened before we ever did.* Ethan and Will have become closer in a way I wasn't able to predict. Will's friend Simon stopped by with his girlfriend Rosalie, old friends from prep school. Simon is so much like Will in that he seems to reject a lot of the people associated with that life.

I scratch my nail into the bartop, the wood is old and soft, and takes the imprint of the half moon easier than I'd expect. Will watches me, he *sees* me, I don't think just at this moment, but as he has from the beginning. A hyper vigilance to any move I make.

The music that fills the bar overtakes the conversation, and we all turn our heads at once to see the bustling near the front where two microphones and a screen are being set up. The problem with your local bar being your local bar, is that the locals don't always change. Many of them cycled out in the last few years, otherwise I wouldn't be here, but I've never run from places the way I've run from people. Places hold memories and they are easily replaced by new ones, people? You can't replace the feelings caused by people as easily.

An emcee makes his way to the front, calling the attention of the bar-goers in a fashion that feels like it should be reserved for a camp counselor, but it makes me laugh as he rallies the crowd for what sounds like it's going to be a lively round of karaoke.

It's the round of tequila shots that motivates us all to put our name on the list. I've never hidden from a microphone, usually more to say something clever or punny with a red-solo cup, singing is not my talent, but can anyone really call karaoke singing? The first man stumbled up to the stage with his beer in hand, and as soon as the first note came on, I knew his rendition of *'I Will Always Love You'* was going to be a complete shit show. Seems like he learned the same lesson so many women are encouraged to learn early on. A shit show is still a show, and a show means people are paying attention, which, for women, is one of the things you're meant to crave.

"How are you with late-80's one hit wonders?" Will whispers into the crook of my neck.

"I guess we're about to find out."

It's when he raises the microphone to his mouth, the smile that broadens across his face is another promise.

'*... When I wake up, well I know I'm gonna be... I'm gonna be the man who wakes up next to you. When I go out, yeah, I know I'm gonna be... I'm gonna be the man who goes along with you. If I get drunk, well, I know I'm gonna be... I'm gonna be the man who gets drunk next to you....And If I haver, hey, I know I'm gonna be... I'm gonna be the man who's havering to you.*'

For a song that's cheesy and a performance that's cheesier, he's singing it to me. It's packed with humor and has me laughing from the dark corners I normally hide in. It's so much more than humor though, and it's not even a full verse before I'm singing and dancing with him on the stage unaware of everyone else. As we always seem to be devoid of any awareness of anything but the moment we exist in together.

You would think we rehearsed it. But you can't rehearse this kind of joy.

Simon spent a good half hour talking to me about some of the technology of his company and the joys of start-up life, all the while turning back to the quiet woman tucked into his side, with remarks like *'It' was all Rosie's idea'* or *'she's the real brains.'* I see why Will likes him, they are similar in that way, the disregard-the-status-quo way. Choosing happiness as their measure of success. I wonder if it's harder for men like this to choose happiness? Knowing that it sometimes contends with success as we know it. But as they laugh, something tells me it's the reason they are friends. Because regardless of outcome, they wouldn't change the joys in their life.

That's why he stood there, stood down his brother, stood up to me. Because the things he finds valuable are in moments like this. The ones where we are tangled in each other, where he's making a cup of tea in the kitchen, or texting me mid-day to tell me about the latest thing he learned about a piece of art. It's the way he looked at me when I woke up with my cheek pressed against his skin, like I was his best friend. And every morning when he leaves for his run, it's the kisses he presses across my skin.

I'm watching Will at the bar as he orders us all another round. He's cool in a way that is commanding the attention of more than a few women here. And they haven't even heard him open his mouth. He's attractive in his own right while there's a casualness to it that feels like you know him, while at the same time, he's unlike anything anyone has ever seen.

Ethan says something and I have to tear away my focus from where it has become glued to the back of his head. As the two of us sit together like we don't have our own ancient history mere paces from us now. I told Ethan the whole thing as quickly as I could when we had a moment alone earlier, and clearly he's been waiting to get to the meat of it. But he was there the last time. He saw me get so wrapped up in someone that I was left hanging upside down as the world went on without me. He's seen me love someone, and he's seen someone love me, and neither time did he have as much to say as he does now as Will and I just cling to the parts of each other that don't require the severity of love.

"We've been friends for a while. You're one of my favorite people in this world, and I've seen a lot of it. I love you, kid." I'm a bit taken aback by this expression of more emotion than we normally exchange. It's not new information. Our friendship may have had the kind of origins that only a show on the CW would indicate is possible to sustain, but somehow we have. Which is why I believe him, I trust him in what he's gearing up to say.

"Yeah, E. I love you, too." He places his hand on top of mine and squeezes and I think back to that night in Greece years ago where we sat in a dark corner not too dissimilar to this.

Despite the city, country, or year, you can always find somewhere to run and hide. I had been chatting with some young Greek college student who looked like a god and had a name like Stravos, or Nikos, or something that would have been especially good for the *Good Boob Years* memoir. But when he backed me against the bar and tried to kiss me, I panicked. I blinked as quickly as I could to be sure my vision was clear. I pushed him back in a way that Ethan was able to spot in the small bar, and he intervened immediately when Mr.-Athens-2008 threw his hands in the air and backed off without another word. Except for what I imagine equated to *'crazy bitch'* in Greek muttered under his breath as he walked away.

We sat in the back corner of that tiny Greek bar, and I don't know how, but he knew. Maybe it was because despite the numerous offers, I hadn't so much as kissed anyone since that night. I think in the beginning he assumed it was Reid. That my heart remained so broken. But the more time we spent together, culminating in that moment, where he looked at me like he knew it was more than missing someone. *'Do you trust me?'* he asked that night. '*Of course I do.*' I replied. '*Why didn't you tell me?*' '*There was nothing to tell…*' I replied. '*Then why does that nothing give you nightmares?*' he asked. There wasn't a way to explicitly say what was wrong. I'd thought so much about it in a way I could never even explain. Apparently so much so that my subconscious in the smallest windows of sleep screamed for help. We never talked about it again. But I wonder if he's always had this sad awareness since then.

But right now, he's gearing up to say something. Deliver a point that he often would have reserved.

"I know you're afraid. But for the first time since I can't remember when, you seem like you're living your life. I get you're afraid of what it means, but you love him. You've been treading water for a long time now. It's like you forgot that you actually know how to fucking swim."

"You can't know that." I yank my hand from under his, as if it will disconnect whatever source of information he is drawing from.

"Sure I can." His eyes soften with a shrug like it's obvious.

"Why, because you've seen it before?" I press firmly. Rolling my eyes in a way to hopefully dismiss the accusation I'm not in a position to accept.

"No, because I've *never* seen you like this before."

Chapter Twenty-Six

HAPPILY EVER BEFORE

Arden

I'm fixated on my bedroom door. *I fucking hate that door.* You'd think it would be higher quality given what I pay in rent, but no. It's not the fixation that makes sense, but it's my reality. But that door, that fucking door. It makes me think about love in a way that's irrational. The only real similarity between the words is that they are both four letters. But it's as if the grains on the wood form memories I try to forget, and some I already have. Maybe it's not irrational. What's more symbolic of love than the door you're able to walk out or worse the one that you can't.

Will takes a seat next to me on the bed and his eyes fixate on the same spot mine are glued. I wonder if he can see what I see. *How could he?* For people like him, doors look like opportunities. He doesn't read the knots the same way I do.

"What are we looking at?" he asks.

"Different things."

"Show me yours then," he says.

"You've seen mine," I elbow him, but he catches my arm, catches my face, catches a kiss. The way his eyes scan my face are looking for what I'm not saying.

"What is it?" I don't even know if I have the words to really explain.

"I just really hate that boring fucking wood door." His eyes narrow in a way that he knows I'm not being completely honest. But I can feel him in a way that doesn't feel forced. He slips his hand into his squeezes twice.

"Call the restaurant and tell them we're going to be late."

"Where are we going?"

"We're taking care of that door" he says matter of factly, as he pulls out his phone searching for something.

"What time do you close?" I hear him asking the person on the other line as he checks his watch. "Okay, we're about ten minutes away... I'd really appreciate it, promise we'll be in and out."

Will grabs my hand, checks for some cash in his wallet, and smiles as he pulls me out the door and down the street. We're hurrying somewhere I have no idea. Not until he turns down one of the side streets and stops in front of a hardware store. The sign of the door says closed, but he doesn't seem to care, knocking loudly enough to get the attendant from the back.

He cracks the door open and points to the clock. Four minutes past nine. As if to say *just missed it.*

"Hang on, before you *rightly* shut this door in our faces, so you can go home after what was undoubtedly a long hard day," he says, "what will it take for you to grab us a gallon of paint and two brushes? That's all, I can pay cash. We don't even have to come in."

The man looks annoyed. Our outfits definitely don't scream *we're about to embark on some home-improvement projects.* And maybe takes pity on us for whatever reason would cause us to turn up here, at nine-o-four on a Saturday night.

His pause gives Will the opening he's looking for, grabbing his wallet.

"Listen, I've got..." His hands fiddle with the cash trying to count it out frantically. "I've got two-hundred and... ninety... two hundred and ninety eight dollars, for a gallon of paint and two brushes."

"And that plant!" I add in quickly. Through the crack in the door, I can see there's a small rack of small potted herbs that feels like it needs a home with *'the Photosynthesizers'*, the name of the miscellaneous plant band I keep scattered across my apartment.

"One gallon of paint, two brushes, and this..." Will reaches past the man and grabs it, "basil."

"Wait here," the man says, returning just moments later with a large bag and canister of paint, the bright marigold marked on the lid indicates what's in the can.

"Someone didn't pick this up." He does a sweep to see if anyone is around, before extending his hand, like we are completing some illegal transaction.

"What do you say, are you a fan of yellow?" Will asks looking to me for confirmation.

"More than I ever imagined."

Will empties his wallet of the cash, even hands over a Coffee Haus gift card as an extra thank you for the coveralls and primer he included. He carries our supplies past brick buildings that have seen two centuries of similar night wanderers, though probably fewer carrying the same marigold paint. The streetlights catch on the wear-smoothed cobblestones peeking through modern pave-ment, little reminders that this city has layers upon layers of stories beneath our feet, no different than us. As the air has that specific Cambridge weight to it, where academia hangs in there like invisible ivy, even when you're no longer tangled in it.

"I can't believe you just spent almost three hundred dollars on paint and this plant," I say, cradling the small plastic potted basil.

"Worth it," he says matter of factly as he runs the thick pad of his thumb across the leaf. "I can't believe you're worried about the paint when you've got a history of premeditated plant murder to answer for." He bumps my shoulder playfully and wraps his around me to pull us closer. "Should we talk about the recent *incident*?"

"I'm not a plant murderer" I say. "That was succulent-suicide. Prictor knew what he was doing when he jumped off my desk."

"Sounds more like first degree horticide."

"*Ifff anythinggg*, it's more like second degree plantslaughter."

"Right, and I suppose the peace lily just happened to develop an anxiety disorder?" *Who hasn't?*

"Listen." I shift the basil to hold it a little more securely. "Some plants just can't handle the pressure of living up to their names. That peace lily had war in its heart."

"You know what this means, right? We're going to have to name this one something with low expectations." Will laughs, the sound echoing off the brownstones on our walk.

"Barry the Basil, who's probably questioning his life choices right now?"

"Speaking of questionable choices, are you ready to commit a crime against your security deposit?" he asks as we reach my door. But walking into this space of mine feels ever so slightly different when walking through the door with *him*.

"Alright, first thing's first. Barry needs a home that isn't your hands, preferably somewhere high enough that he can't make an escape attempt." He reaches for the small basil in my grip and places him on the kitchen counter, well away from any edges, as he begins to unpack the rest of the supplies.

"Now he can watch us destroy my rental in comfort."

"He can watch us do a lot more than that," he says through a kiss, "the little voyeur."

The color hits the wood like liquid sunshine, transforming the door I've spent too many nights staring at into something new. Something that doesn't hold the weight of memories that never existed here.

We finish the first coat, and while we wait for it to dry, Will sits on the floor with his back against the wall, pulling me down to sit between his legs. The paint fumes probably aren't helping our already questionable decision making skills, but there's something perfect about this moment. The way his arms wrap around me, the way the yellow door seems to glow in the apartment lights.

"You know," he says, his chin resting on my shoulder, "I think this is the first time I've committed property damage in the name of love."

Love. He used the word so casually. As he brushes the hair back from my eyes, and buries a kiss to grow as my head lulls back across his chest. There's music playing in the background, a version of *'Lay Lady Lay'* I haven't heard, as he hums it into my hair. His breaths are smoother than the coats of paint, and my body follows his with each rise and fall like they've come to for the last weeks.

We sat there as the paint dried, something notably, mockably, known for being painfully dull. And yet, I have no interest in moving.

The second coat goes on smoother than the first, and with each stroke, the yellow warms my bedroom. And with each stroke, I tell him why. Reasons I've barely admitted to anyone, especially not myself. But the same reason I unexpectedly feel a pit in my stomach when my back hits a door, or why I sometimes find my fingernails scratching into wood grain just to feel the density of it.

By the time we finish, it's late, our dinner reservation replaced by a delivered pizza. We're covered in various shades of yellow and white, and my boring old door has transformed into something that looks like it belongs in a story about new beginnings rather than old endings.

"So," he says, cleaning off his brush, "do you still hate it?"

"No," I say, reaching for his paint stained hand. "I think I might actually love it."

Chapter Twenty-Seven

HAPPILY EVER BEFORE

Will

I stopped listening about ten minutes ago. I wonder if he's noticed, not likely. He always preferred those around him in silent agreement. I'm not sure what Alfie relayed, but whatever it was, that, combined with my lack of reply to anyone's messages, has caused my father to show up here. A building he only sets foot in once a year to satisfy my mother and the annual patrons gala he doesn't even realize they sponsor.

He's still talking, something about quarterly projections and family legacy, but my mind is elsewhere. Specifically, it's in my bed this morning where I left Arden with her laptop and a cup of coffee cursing under her breath about her upcoming meeting. The memory of her there, hair wild, is infinitely more interesting than whatever lecture I'm currently enduring.

Boston isn't that far of a drive while they are staying at the Newport house for the season. Of course, as usual, kicking it off Memorial Day Weekend. It's still one of my favorite places, the beach as well as the house itself. Memories of us as kids there hiding from the parties rather than being forced to attend them. I've thought about taking Arden out, *obviously not when my parents are there,* but just the two of us holed up in the pool house for a few days.

It's been two months of this. Pretending the insatiability between us is just physical, but it's not. She falls asleep in my arms almost nightly.

So much of us seems to exist in beds. *Beds, bathrooms, cars, the occasional stairwell.*

But it goes beyond any sense of reason, that's why I know despite what she said early on, this isn't just about sex. Her unavailability is an election she's made, and while she's let me see pieces of why, she does not yet seem willing to admit anything to the contrary. We came to terms in the gallery downstairs. I told her what I am willing to be, I meant it and still do. *Anything.*

"Will." My father's sharp tone cuts through my reverie. "Do you hear me?"

I meet his eyes, the same ones I see in the mirror every morning, though mine, I've been told, have a habit of looking amused even when they shouldn't. *Like right now.*

"Of course, I do. You need me to sign away my life for this merger, Memorial Day weekend is paramount, and my current life choices are...*impressive?*" He huffs in a way to remind he doesn't share the same sense of humor. "That's right, *disappointing.*" I correct. "Did I miss anything?"

"I'm not here for my health. I didn't come all this way to take another lap around this place."

"You should, we have a new exhibit in this place and your name is slapped all over it."

The number of didactic plates mentioning the 'Sterling Collection' is almost laughable considering he has no idea what his donations to the arts actually mean. Actually, I think he just doesn't care.

"That's your mother's doing, not mine." His retort is spit out as an insult, it's not to me, it's one of the few things she and I share. I think her love of the arts comes from the social standing it can achieve, whereas mine is something entirely different.

"The position is waiting for you," my father says, like he's offering me salvation rather than a sentence. "You're expected to take your place by the end of summer."

"The board expects, or you expect?"

He ignores my question, the way he ignores anything that doesn't fit his narrative. "This is your legacy, William. The Sterling name means something."

"It means something here too." I gesture to the gallery beyond my office walls, ironically also possessing their name.

"Yes, well." His fingers drum against my desk, a habit I inherited but hate recognizing in him. "If you continue to resist what's best, certain... reallocations of resources will need to be considered about any peripheral ventures."

The threat lands exactly as intended. He knows exactly which strings to pull, which dominoes to threaten. After all, he spent years setting them up.

The knock at the door has us both turn. It might be a sixth sense at this point, the way I can feel her orbit. The unexplainable force that roots me in place when she's anywhere.

He yanks the door open as if he has any authority here, probably because there aren't many places he doesn't.

Fuck. I would have preferred to avoid this. The Alfie-show was enough, and almost scared her off, Hugh Sterling actually has the bite that Alfie pretends to.

"What," he says with a harshness that wouldn't be befitting of a greeting to anyone, let alone her. I'm on my feet, not sure that there's anything to do as she squares her shoulders against him. Readying herself for a fight she has no context for.

"This is my—"

"Arden Bancroft." She steps forward with the kind of confidence that makes my heart skip, extending her hand as if my father wasn't currently trying to incinerate her with his glare.

"Fine," he says, ignoring her hand. "I'll see you both next week. For godsakes Will, wear a fucking tie for once." He moves toward the door and Arden steps right by him, landing at my side as her body instinctively angles toward mine, a movement so slight only someone looking for it would see.

His eyes narrow on me and I'm only looking at her. The devil can keep my soul, my stock, and whatever else I need to sign away. There's no deal worth giving that up.

"What's that about?" She takes a seat in my desk chair, immediately spinning it once before facing me. "I thought he was going to burst a blood vessel."

I lean against the desk, unable to help my smile as she continues to spin. "You're making me dizzy."

"You love it," she says, reaching out to grab my leg to stop herself. She handles my father's disdain the same way she handles everything, with that mix of defiance and wit I've heard her use in her own battles. "Besides, your office chairs are way better than mine. I might have to steal this one."

My father's words about 'reallocation of resources' creep in as I watch her spin. She has no idea that her own workplace politics might be easier to navigate than the ones waiting for us at the Newport house. At least in her world, the threats are clear and the battles are fought in boardrooms, not at family dinner tables.

"You already steal my clothes, and my sanity. Now you want my furniture too?"

"Don't forget your heart," she says with exaggerated batting of her eyelashes. She's teasing, but in the joke there's honesty.

"Yep, you have that too." I stop the chair's circles, and catch her between my arms. We're practically nose to nose. With her cheeks flushed from laughter, I lean forward and pull the chair closer to me.

"That... would be my father."

"Though the resemblance is uncanny," she teases, reaching up to trace my jawline. "You're much prettier though."

"And we've been summoned." There's never been an inopportune moment to see her, which is probably why she just showed up here, but this was less than ideal.

"I can get you out of it," I say hurriedly.

"You don't want me to meet your parents?" Her face falls the slightest amount. Almost imperceptible, before she snaps it back to mask what looks like it could have been momentary disappointment. *Fuck.*

"That's not it." I lean forward to take her face in my hands. "Of course I do, but it's not an easy situation, and I don't want you to be subjected to it if you aren't ready."

"Please," she scoffs, but leans into my touch. "I think I can handle your parents."

Her fingers crawl into my hair, interlocking to pull my face to hers. "Besides," she whispers against my lips, "I already have an in with their son."

"Ah, that's where you've miscalculated… they don't trust my judgement, *remember*?"

The most beautiful thing to exist is the transformation of strangers into this. Whatever this is. It's the unnamed underpainting of something extraordinary. And one day, the layers will all be there. It will be framed in gold and strangers will sit in front of it just like we do, trying to understand the depths of what they cannot see but know is there.

"Just promise me one thing," I murmur against her lips.

"Hmm?" she breathes against mine.

"Whatever happens, you and me, we're on the *same team*."

Her laugh breezes through my office like wind chimes in a gallery. She might not realize just how serious I am being, but she agrees.

"Same team," she says.

Chapter Twenty-Eight

HAPPILY EVER BEFORE

Arden

Six forty-one a.m. and I'm already on my third coffee. The conference room glass reflects the image I'm trying to. Blazer pressed, hair polished and twisted into submission, lips painted in a power red, but today feels more like a 'fake it till you make it crimson.' I check my laptop one more time, though I've already verified the files twice this morning. The real presentation sits innocuously in my email drafts, while the decoy has lived on my desktop like the poisoned apple it is, perfectly tempting.

I noticed Brent for weeks circling my desk like a vulture, waiting for his moment. Men like him are nothing if not predictable, why did I ever consider that to be a safety? They see what they want to take, and they take it. The fact that what they're taking might be exactly what you're letting them have never crosses their minds.

My phone buzzes as if hyping me up in preparation.

Will: Break a leg, or break their spirits. Your choice.

I smile despite the knots in my stomach. He knows exactly

what I'm about to do, even said he wished he could be here to watch.

The conference room fills the way it always does on Thompson Challenge days, like a courtroom where the jury's already made up their minds. The usual suspects take their assigned seats in their unofficial territories, everyone knowing that this isn't just a presentation, it's a spectator sport. Faces I see every day have a slightly different shape today. The same people who've watched presentations crash and burn, who've witnessed careers made and broken over PowerPoint transitions, are now the audience waiting for blood in the water.

Victor arrives last, and his presence shifts the energy in the room from anticipatory to frozen over. After all, he's the one who actually will make the decision. Everyone else is just here for the show.

And I know how to put on a show.

Brent is already here, huddled over his laptop, but straightens up when he sees me. The smirk he gives me makes my three, *okay four*, coffees curdle in my stomach, but I force myself to smile back. Let him think he's won. Let him think the file he stole, the one so clearly labeled 'FINAL_REALLY_FINAL_CHALLENGE_WINNER_v3.ppt' is my best work.

I always wondered how villains in movies spill the whole plot, like they are so emboldened by their confidence that they just assume there's no way for it to backfire. Then I heard Brent and Michael, detailing their little scheme like it was foolproof.

'Her presentation will be D.O.A.,' Brent had laughed, 'But just to be safe, we should probably get our hands on her deck. Make some... adjustments. That way when she crashes and burns, we can swoop in with the right strategy.'

I hate that some of what they said took root, that I'm looking at our boss, Victor, wondering if the reason he's watching me gear up to present is more about the cut of my jacket against my waist than eagerness to see what I have to say.

"Let's begin," Victor says, gesturing to Brent. "I understand you and Arden have been working on this together."

I watch him connect his laptop, noting how his fingers tremble slightly with anticipation. I can tell, he thinks he's about to humiliate me, that he's gearing up to have a good ol' boys laugh at me.

The first few slides are exactly as I left them, surface-level analysis, obvious solutions, nothing that would raise eyebrows. I see Victor's attention already wandering.

"As you can see," Brent continues, growing more confident with each slide, "our recommendation focuses on conservative cost-cutting measures and minor efficiency improvements..."

"If I may," I interrupt, standing smoothly. My heart pounds but my voice stays steady. "I believe there's been some confusion about which version we're presenting."

The silence in the room shifts from bored to alert as I connect my laptop to the secondary projector. "This is actually our final recommendation."

The real proposal appears on screen. Not the safe, timid approach Brent stole with the intention of torpedoing, but a complete reimagining of Vulcan's business model. Vertical integration. Strategic acquisition of their main supplier. A transformation that would drag them kicking and screaming into the modern era.

"As you can see, this updated approach..." I continue, unable to resist glancing at Brent, "it's a bit more than just something pretty to look at."

I launch into the real analysis, watching expressions shift to interest.

"But the key," I say, pulling up the financial projections I'd triple-checked last night, "isn't just the immediate cost savings. It's the positioning for future growth. We're not looking for an easy win based on playing it safe." I turn to glance at Brent.

"That's not..." Brent starts, then stops, realizing he has no way to finish that sentence without admitting what he did.

"Not what?" Victor asks. "Not the version you found on Ms. Bancroft's computer when you accessed it without her knowledge?"

The room temperature seems to drop ten degrees. Brent's mouth opens and closes, but no sound comes out.

"I have to say," I continue, as if I hadn't noticed the exchange, "I was surprised anyone would think Vulcan's salvation lay in minor efficiency improvements. Especially since our preliminary research indicated that approach would be, what was the phrase you used?" I pretend to check my notes. "Ah yes, *dead on arrival.*"

I lean in close, as if sharing a confidence. Watching his expression and all the color drain from his face. "Funny thing about that though," my tone is hushed but not a whisper, "when I fuck something, I usually prefer it not be *dead*. I didn't peg you for having such specific tastes."

The next thirty minutes are excruciating for Brent and exhilarating for me. Every question from the table I answer with precision. By the time I finish walking them through the implementation timeline, I know I've got it in the bag.

"Bold," Victor says finally. He glances at Brent, then back to me. "Though I have to wonder why you didn't present this strategy together, given you were meant to be working as a team."

"Oh, we did work as a team," I say, keeping my voice light. "Brent was kind enough to demonstrate exactly why we can't afford to play it safe anymore."

In Victor's office, he sits back in his chair with that inscrutable expression he's perfected over years of breaking bad news to clients, while breaking the souls of employees. I force myself to stay still, to not fidget with my blazer or check my phone where I know Will is waiting to hear how it went.

"That was quite a show today," he says.

Being praised by someone like Victor has its own cost associated with it. It never feels *clean*. Which is in part why I'm sitting across from him fidgeting more than I'd like to be. The conference dispersed and every contestant and observer alike scattered back to the safety of their own desks.

Stop fidgeting. Stop fidgeting. Stop fidgeting.

"I prefer to think of it as a strategic reveal." *Am I crossing and uncrossing my legs too much?*

"Indeed." He shuffles some papers on his desk.

"Congratulations. You and Brent will both be promoted."

"Both of us?" The words escape before I can stop them.

"Yes." Victor leans back, studying me. "He may have fumbled today, but he's valuable to the firm. He played the game as you did, and whether you like it or not, he pushed you further to deliver something better. There were more dramatics than need be, but you both delivered."

Both.

I'm not sure what infuriates me more, that we *both* get awarded an equal promotion, or the fact *my* success is still attributed to him. Not just that he clung to my coattails, but that his contribution was motivating to me in anything other than rage.

I walk back to my desk in a daze, equal parts triumphant and troubled. I got what I wanted. The promotion, the raise, the satisfaction of watching Brent realize he'd been outplayed. And then each one of those things was invalidated.

"Well, we got the promotion," I tell Pricktor. Though he has yet to respond. If I'm being honest, he might be barely clinging to life. At this point he really is only a small amount of dry dirt in a pot held together by scotch tape. *Aren't we all?*

"We sure did, Bancroft." Brent strolls into my cubicle which now feels immeasurably smaller. "Thanks for that, by the way." Voice carrying the same smug certainty of someone who's been able to fail-up his entire life.

"Not the type of synergy you hoped for," I reply, keeping my eyes on Pricktor's wilting form rather than giving Brent the satisfaction of my full attention.

"All worked out in the end" he shrugs, straightening his tie with nonchalance, the real kind, not the kind I practice. And for people like him it always does. The world bends itself into pretzels to ensure men like Brent land on their feet, no matter how far they fall.

Even in victory, I'm still being defined by a man's actions. My strategy wasn't brilliant on its own merits, it was brilliant because it outmaneuvered him. My promotion isn't because I'm exceptional, it's because I proved I could play their game. Everything I achieved today will be viewed through the lens of how I responded, not as something I accomplished on my own.

They're probably already spinning it. 'She handled it well' instead of 'She developed an innovative strategy.' Even my cunningness in setting the trap will be seen as reactive, a woman protecting herself rather than orchestrating a win.

The mirror of my computer screen is the worst of all. But I can't look away, wondering if this is what success will always feel like. Achievements that come with asterisks.

Another text from Will.

Will: How'd it go? Did you crush them or just their egos?

I stare at the screen, trying to figure out how to explain that I proved I could be just as calculating, just as ruthless as any of them. And while it worked, there's a bitter taste of defeat regardless of the victory.

Chapter Twenty-Nine

HAPPILY EVER BEFORE

Arden

"I need to pack, I need your help... which dress says *'I'm casually dating your son and I just want to make a good impression because this seems to matter to him even though he looks physically uncomfortable every time he mentions you so maybe my charms and this dress will distract you from the fact that he doesn't want to be here and I don't want you to hate me?'"* I hold up two versions of cocktail dresses where Will sits leaning against the headboard making notes for the latest exhibition, waiting for me to throw the last items in the bag.

"You're expecting a lot from a dress that you are more than capable of saying out loud." Will observes, setting aside his exhibition notes. But I've found there are times that fashion can really do most of the talking. This may be one of them.

I'm so far three for three on negative encounters with his family. I'm not blaming myself for that, in fact, all three times I wasn't even supposed to be there. *This time* I've been invited.

I just take them both, plus a few extras, along with the bathing suit, a handful of summer dresses, a pair of keds, and whatever else felt like a necessary last minute addition to my frenzied packing.

He grabs our bags, his car keys, as he shuts the door behind him.

'Oh shoot– I forgot to text Amanda to water Barry for me when we're gone.'

'We're only going to be gone for the weekend, how often are you watering these plants?!'

––––––

The drive to Newport isn't bad, though that might have more to do with the company than the actual journey. Will insisted on driving, claiming it would give us time to ourselves before the impending chaos of his family, but I suspect he also wanted control over our arrival time and access to an easy escape. Two hours of watching him drum his fingers against the steering wheel of his SUV while belting out increasingly terrible renditions of Journey songs has somehow both flown by and felt endless in the best possible way.

The landscape has been slowly transforming around us, from Boston's busy streets to the kind of wealth that announces itself in perfectly manicured hedges and wrought iron gates. Newport in late May is like watching old money bloom.

"Look at me," Will says, taking his eyes off the road to meet mine. His voice is heavy with a weight I've rarely heard, making my stomach drop. We're driving through what can only generously be called a 'neighborhood,' though that seems far too common a word for what surrounds us. These aren't houses but mansions that have witnessed a century of summer parties and scandals, standing proud behind gates that seem designed less to keep others out and more to keep their secrets in.

He turns his head toward me, the road ahead is clear, *because of course it is,* who else would be driving through this museum of American aristocracy? His free hand has been drawing lazy circles on my thigh where my dress has ridden up, and I wonder if he's even aware he's doing it anymore. Touch between us has become as natural as breathing, which is probably something we should talk about someday. *Not now though.*

He's wearing a vintage Rolling Stones t-shirt, paired with dark jeans that look deliberately lived-in. His tattoos peek out from under his sleeves, a beautiful mess of art that drives them crazy, which is why despite the current rebellion, I know he will throw on a different shirt right as we arrive to save himself the confrontation.

The houses we pass are like something out of an Edith Wharton novel, all Newport stone and ivy-covered walls that have watched over a hundred summers of society parties.

Will squeezes my thigh gently, pulling me back to the present.

"Before we get there, I need you to understand what you're walking into."

The worry in his voice makes my chest tight. His father only said a handful of words to me that day in Will's office, but they weighed enough to leave him unsettled since. He's never been particularly forthcoming about his family, I know enough. *Old money, older expectations, and a son who'd rather spend his days surrounded by art portfolios rather than stock.*

We pass through streets, their mix of tourist shops and high-end boutiques, all preparing for the summer invasion. The air smells like salt and money, and as we wind our way up to the even more exclusive areas, the roads become narrower, more private, as if they're trying to discourage unexpected visitors.

The houses are architecturally stunning reminders of America's Gilded Age. Some have names rather than numbers, which seems both ridiculous and perfectly fitting.

Will's grip on the steering wheel tightens as we turn onto what must be his family's street. The trees here form a canopy overhead, their new leaves casting patterns of light and shadow across the hood of the car. The Sterling house is waiting somewhere ahead of us, and with it, all the expectations and complications he's been trying to prepare me for.

The SUV slows as we approach a bend in the road, and suddenly there it is, the Atlantic Ocean, spreading out before us like nature's very own display of wealth in contrast to what's been built upon it. The mansions here face the water like they're in conversation with it, their windows reflecting the late morning sun. Memorial Day weekend in Newport is like watching American royalty wake up from their winter sleep, and we're about to walk straight into their court.

"I know what I'm walking into," I say, even though I probably don't. "But I'm walking in with you." His smile breaks through the storm clouds he feels gathering.

"Yeah." Is the only response he can muster for the moment. I think for the first time I'm understanding the gravitas of it all. It sounds naive to say, maybe I am, I knew the name, I googled them all. And yet, seeing *this*, being privy to it, paints a very different picture than the one I've been convincing myself of.

"My mother is sweet, but agreeable to the audience. She'll only be your ally if it suits the masses, *or my father*. My brothers will *both* be there with their significant others. Alfie you know, and is the one they deploy most often to do my dad's bidding, both in the boardroom and in life. And Cal, well, Cal is a lot more observant than he lets on, he plays games with people."

The way he talks about his family is like he's going into battle. It's not something I can relate to. Looking at him, I can read his body intimately, his breathing is forced as he prepares himself. His grip is keeping him grounded with his fingertips on my thigh.

Then it hits me, maybe *I'm* the reason he's like this. He had no intention of coming this weekend, or if he did, he had no plans for me to come with him. It all came to a head when I showed up un-fucking-announced. *Damnit, Arden. You know better.*

"Will, who do they think I am to you..." His head snaps at the question as he turns down another street.

"Who do you want to be, Arden?" *What a loaded question.*

"We're just... keeping it casual, right?" We've not called this a relationship. We've kept it casual. Casual in the sense of exclusive and non-stop, all-consuming, cant-get-enough, casual. But despite what we might have told his brother that first night, he's never called me his girlfriend.

"They know I'm bringing someone. You can call it whatever you want, but no matter what you call it, it's me and you. No matter what happens, we're on the same team."

He shifts in the seat ever so slightly, trying to remain calm, not to give me reason for concern. Though for the first time, I am concerned.

He turns into a driveway and punches in a code and the large gate opens in slow motion. I can see it on his face, the contemplation to turn around and run.

"You want to run?" I ask.

"More than you know."

"Okay, well, where could we go..." I tap my index finger on my pursed lips, and I make a humming noise to indicate thinking. "How about New York?" He laughs and his fingertips flex on my leg.

"Too close, that's only a drive."

"Okay okay, what about... Paris... we could go to the Louvre, and eat baguettes, wear berets..." *It actually sounds like a dream, the two of us in Paris walking along the Seine.*

He reaches for my hand, and interlocks his fingers with mine.

"Then we're in Paris," he says. Raising our hands to his lips, kissing the back of mine.

The long driveway leads up to a house, his childhood home, correction, one of his childhood homes. This one, the beach house. But I can't imagine him growing up here, not for any amount of time. So much of who he is, and who I've seen him as, grew out of his own mind. As we pull in, and despite all the exposure I had in my life to people and parties, this is different. This is a category of wealth that supersedes just old money. They didn't just have money, they made it. Not in the sense that they worked hard and made their fortunes, but more that their families go so far back in American institutions I would be unsurprised to find out that they were descendants of a founding father. Designing the financial systems the rest of us now live within the constraints of. For the first time I see it in the man next to me, but it looks uncomfortable, like the white powdered wig doesn't quite fit on his head.

The smell of the Rhode Island salt air wraps around us, as if to pull us apart and out of the security of the car, and each other. Before getting out of the car, he turns to me, his eyes that normally skirt across my face, hopping freckles like lily pads, instead stay frozen on me. It feels like fear, and I've never felt this on him before. I think if I *really* asked him to run away right now, he would do it without a thought. As far as we could go.

He hurries around the car, to meet me at my side. Offering his hand. If we're walking into this, whatever this is, we'll do it together. We climb the steps, our feet always in pace with each other. But we don't make it to the front door before the roar of the engine behind us has him turning on his heel. The red sports car that screams arrogance, only out matched by the man who steps out of it. Leaving it parked at an angle that screams *'someone else's problem.'*

"Cal," Will mouths under his breath to me as we approach the house, not wanting me to be at a disadvantage. He takes the limestone steps two at a time, all golden-boy energy and inherited confidence.

The brothers look alike in that they have the same basic structure, but it takes no time to recognize entirely different substances. And as Cal gets closer, Will's hand slides across my waist, pulling me closer.

"You're here!" Cal's voice calls across the meticulously maintained entrance, bouncing off the pillars that frame the door like exclamation points made of stone. He claps Will on the back with the kind of forceful affection that's meant to establish dominance.

"Mom will be thrilled, no one thought you would actually show, and... with a friend no less."

The word 'friend' drips with the kind of sweetened venom that probably pairs well with the vintage wine they'll serve later. Will doesn't react, instead choosing to let the barb fall into the bushes that line the entrance as his brother strides through the front doors like he owns the place. *Which, given the family dynamics, he probably will someday.*

"Same team, right?" I ask, and feel his grip relax slightly.

"Always," he says, and it sounds like a promise.

"It might not seem like it," Will leans down and whispers, his breath tickling my ear as we head up the staircase, "but I *am* glad you're here." I squeeze his hand twice, and he returns it.

"Why, Will, this couldn't possibly be Newport. I'm fairly certain we've run off to Paris," I say with an affected accent that makes him snort.

We put our things in one of the bedrooms, decorated in shades of blue and white, like someone took the ocean view and decided to bring it inside. I take the moment to freshen up before cocktail hour and then dinner, though Will has already warned me that *'cocktail hour'* here is less about drinks and more about subtle interrogation.

I change into a wrap dress that I specifically packed for tonight. something simple but elegant, the kind of dress that says 'I respect your dress code but I'm not trying too hard.' When I emerge from the bathroom, Will's look makes me wonder if we really need to go downstairs at all.

He's standing in the middle of the room like a beautiful contradiction to everything around him. All black paired with a button down shirt that's *just* formal enough to pass inspection.

"You're beautiful," he says, crossing the room in three long strides. He kisses my cheek but lingers there, his presence warm against my skin. His collar is unbuttoned just enough to show a hint of the tattoo beneath, and my thumb traces the visible ink almost involuntarily.

"We should go down," he says, clearing his throat, but his hands on my hips tell a different story as his finger wraps the sash of fabric tying the dress in place.

"I'd love you to," I say, reaching for his belt, but he catches my hands with a laugh that's half groan.

"I'll fall to my knees right here," he says, his voice deep and challenging between us, "but they're waiting, and as much as I think you like putting on a show for strangers, this isn't the audience you want."

The dining room table can seat twenty but is set for eight. The windows face the ocean, though at this hour it's just a dark presence beyond the glass, marked by the rhythmic sweep of lighthouse beams in the distance as the sound of waves land on the shore.

"Will was telling me about the party tomorrow," I say during a lull in the business talk. "It sounds like it's going to be quite the event."

"And what did Will tell you..." I'm not sure what Alfie feels he's trapped me in, but it comes with a particular brand of aristocratic challenge, crystal stemware clicking against bone china as he sets down his wine glass to focus on me. Will's eyes meet mine across the table, holding me steady as the waves of passive aggression pick up. *Maybe it's just normal aggression.*

"I told her about the year you stole some of the fireworks to impress Luella Carmichael and ended up catching part of the landscaping on fire..." Deliberately rolling up his sleeves just enough to show the edge of his tattoos and cause a different distraction if need be.

"You said that was Franklin's boy!" His father jumps in, fork paused halfway to his mouth.

"*Did I?*" Will's innocence wouldn't fool a kindergartner. "Must have slipped my mind."

"The party tomorrow," his mother cuts in smoothly, clearly trying to steer us back to safer waters, "is a tradition. The Sterling Summer Barbecue."

"Though I should warn you," Will adds, his foot finding mine under the table, "there's nothing remotely barbecue-like about it. Unless you count the way they roast newcomers."

"William," his mother scolds, but there's a demure laugh in her voice. "It's actually quite lovely," she tells me, ignoring her son's commentary. "We've been hosting it for decades. All the families attend, plus some new faces. There's dancing, fireworks over the water..."

"Don't forget the ritual sacrifice," Will dramatically whispers across the table in a way that's not meant to be a whisper but just rile up those around it.

'Same team,' he mouths at me with a wink.

Like I could forget.

Like there's any team I'd rather be on than his.

I hide my smile behind my wine glass, watching them navigate around each other with the precision of ships in a harbor, careful not to crash, but always aware of the possibility. Will might not love it here, but they are his family, and beneath all the sharp edges and sharper wit, he cares more than he admits.

Chapter Thirty

HAPPILY EVER BEFORE

Will

Dinner last night went better than anyone could anticipate. We talked in circles for forty-five minutes about their plans for the merger, my mother ran through the list of societal updates, and I could see Arden's wheels turning the entire time. She works for a big consulting firm, the kind my dad would hire to handle some of his business, and her brain followed with far more interest than mine ever has.

She's a chameleon in the most beautiful way. Adapting to reflect the people around her. I hadn't noticed prior, never seeing a reflection of myself in any conversation, or maybe that's the magic. Maybe no one realizes the honesty she makes them see.

Now, hours later, her hand is in mine as we navigate the crowd of Newport's finest, and more accurately, their worst. Her fingers tap out a silent piano concerto against my knuckles, a habit I've grown to love. She does this when she's thinking, when she's nervous, when she's plotting an escape.

My mother's friends are enchanted, my father's associates intrigued, and my brother Cal... Cal is especially taken. Of course he is. He likes to think of himself as the smartest person in the room, and in many ways he is, because he's able to recognize the second he ceases to be. That's when something far more shrewd switches into place. Charm and manipulation in a smoothness that has coerced more than one contract, and woman. For all he is, I think he sees through people, but not her, and that is driving him crazy.

'The merger would benefit from a third-party oversight,' she had said last night, and I swear Cal almost choked on his roast duck. Not because she was wrong, but because she was right in a way he hadn't considered.

"Let's run away," I whisper, my lips close to her ear. The scent of her perfume, something with notes of vanilla and amber, makes me dizzy in the best way. A silk dress hugs her body down to the floor in a way that makes it easy for me to imagine it's not there at all. There's this sensation between us that pulses like it's beating blood right to my heart.

I lead us away from the crowd, down the hallways until we reach the wine cellar door. It's unlocked, which again feels like the universe conspiring in our favor. *Or caterers needing easy access.*

Rows of bottles catching the low light, the temperature dropping with each step down. The musty cellar air mingles with her scent as ancient wooden shelves creak around us, bottles gleaming like dragon's eyes in the dim light.

'There's an alcove in the back where I used to hide with adventure novels and a flashlight, avoiding whatever was happening upstairs.' I had told her on the drive out.

My hands are on her faster than I can take a breath. Her arms tangle around my neck, the extra height from her heels granting her more access to my mouth than she normally has as her body is pressed against mine. We back into one of the racks and the gentle rattle of glass should distract us from the ferocity with which we consume each other. *It doesn't.* I don't think there's any amount of glass that could shatter around us that would pull us out of each other's arms.

Another bottle quivers in its rack, and Arden breaks our kiss with a breathless laugh.

"If we break anything," she murmurs, eyes crisp even in the dim light, "your mother will have me banned from Newport."

But her hands contradict her words, pulling me closer with a desperation that matches my own.

For all the reasons she is cautious about love, her feelings aren't hidden. She speaks it in a language other's haven't tried to learn. But it's all here. Every so often, I think her lips will part and say the words I swallow down when I watch her drift to sleep. The way her mouth is greedy for more than mine. It's a hunger I can feel that feeds words into silence.

We pick up speed together, in every moment shared, there's no slowing down, and in this moment, she's in my arms with an insatiability that is indescribable. And I would never pretend I had the words to describe it. Because who the fuck am I?

There's noise above us, the rest of the world goes on, but she doesn't care and neither do I.

Our hands race to undress just enough to increase the connection of skin that seems to shock us both into life. Her fingers loop into the knot of my tie, as I grip the silk of her hem so my hands can feel the skin that's meant only for me in this moment. She shimmies in my grip stepping out of the underwear that I pick up from her feet and tuck into my pocket.

Her head lolls back as I press kisses along her jaw and lets out a whisper of desperate desire. Threaded between the letters of my name.

As soon as my name hits the air, my hands grip her thighs and pull her up to me so we're face to face. She's looking right through me full of more than lust. My whole body is throbbing in desperate need to be hers, and the way she's locked around me tells me she agrees.

"Do you think anyone will find us down here?" she asks in a way that indicates she might not be bothered if they did.

"Is that what you want, darling?"

"I want you."

It takes a couple of steps before we're backed into my favorite dark corner. I keep her in my arms as she reaches into my pants where I'm hard in a way only she could command. Her long fingers wrap around me as her thumb circles the head, tensing my entire body.

And as I slide into the grip she has on me in all ways is beyond any reason.

Somewhere between the frenzy of clinging to each other and the orgasm she screams into my mouth, a bottle comes crashing to our feet. Splashing us with red wine as the glass shatters around us. It spreads across the stone floor like spilled secrets, glass shards catching light like scattered stars.

I spin us around and set her down on the wooden table in the middle of the room, where a crystal decanter stands witness to our transgression. Her feet swing off the ledge, and I notice the missing shoe on the ground. It must have fallen off around the same time her leg was wrapped around my back.

When she says my name I don't know how anything could ever sound better than that.

"I love running with you."

"There's nowhere to run for me without you."

There's so much more in that sentence. She's trying it on for size. We don't say the part that lives in the silence. Not yet. I've thought about it. Whispered it once when she inhaled a dream.

I kneel in front of her and take her foot in my hand, slipping the strappy black shoe on and placing it on my shoulder. Pressing kisses up from her ankle to thigh until I am back standing at full height in front of her.

She pulls at my tie, pulls my mouth down onto hers in a way telling me all the things she's not ready to admit beyond the war of our lips.

For now, though, this is enough. She may not wear her heart on her sleeve, but mine is stitched into everything she owns.

"We should go back," she sighs, but makes no move to leave. "Five more minutes," I bargain, pressing my forehead to hers. "Let's just... exist here for five more minutes."

Chapter Thirty-One

HAPPILY EVER BEFORE

Will

As we emerge from the cellar, with each step we get closer and closer to the world I'd love to escape. But maybe, just maybe, there's nothing to run from now. Maybe I was nervous for nothing... Our lungs are filled with each other, but walking back into the main room, slightly more flushed than we left, everyone is already holding a glass. My father and brothers are at the front of the room, and the immediate tightness I have in my chest as I fear whatever is about to come next. This was never just about coming home for summer.

This was a fucking trap.

The waiter hands us each a glass of champagne, some local kid just trying to make a summer-buck. The air in the room is different.

"Here he is, always one for an entrance..." dad says as he uses his whiskey glass to gesture across the room to where we stand. And we're suddenly under the illusion of a spotlight.

"The newest addition to the Sterling Group, my son, William Sterling."

I tighten my grip on her hand, but her fingers loosen from

mine. I squeeze twice. *Same. Team.* Hoping she understands, but her grip goes slack and I can see her confusion.

I know what I'm meant to do, but I just weave my fingers through hers. I'm not moving. I acknowledge the room of sycophants and corporate crows, and rather than falling in line wrap my arm around her back.

How quickly our team lost shape. Maybe because she had no fucking idea what we were getting ourselves into. I did. I tried to warn her. I know she saw all the color drain from my face when we pulled up to the house. My skin rippled with a sense of obligatory stiffness, the stoicism I can use as a shield, one I tried to hide her behind, but it didn't work.

As soon as the announcement was made her hand was pulled from mine as my mother whisked her away to hob-knob with someone who doesn't even realize they've been made to run interference. All so I can be locked in this room, that ironically enough, Arden would love, but right now is the place that my dad and Alfie have decided is the best time and place to do this. I thought they'd save it for breakfast at least.

"You're not going to defend yourself" Alfie asks, or rather accuses.

"I have nothing to defend, you wanted me here, I'm here. But I never agreed to any of this." Between him and our dad, they've been working this angle for a while. The deal being that my time in Boston is up. I had my time to *'figure my life out'* and that the doomsday clock ticked even closer to midnight. But they want more than me just at a family dinner. *Which is not what this is.* They want the press release that the prodigal son has returned. Returned to a role in a company that I have no business doing for any reason other than namesake. And tonight, he thinks he forced my hand.

"You show up here, with a stranger, and don't expect me to say anything after everything you've fucking pulled?!" Alfie snaps like the bulldog dad likes him to be.

"She's not a stranger, dad invited her." I retort with a laugh. I don't sound like myself. I don't feel like myself, but it's the only way to handle them and I know it. It's almost as if the calmer I am the more agitated they become.

"Sarcasm doesn't suit you." Dad jumps in and I know he's eager to get this business sorted. "You should be getting serious about your life, not whatever it is you're doing. There's a standard to be upheld, and you've spit on that idea for long enough."

I turn to face my father, straightening my spine and I think of Arden standing in my office doorway ready to face off against him regardless of who he was.

"I'll sign whatever you want signed, but I'm not leaving my job, I'm not leaving my life."

"You mean you won't leave *her*?" he cracks.

"That's exactly what I mean." I'm not embarrassed about it, but they look at me like I've said something naive.

I watch their faces, the familiar mix of disappointment and frustration, and realize they'll never understand. Not because they can't, but because they don't want to. They think their hand is being forced, to push me, to pressure me, to make this public spectacle. I'd been hoping, foolishly maybe, that this weekend could be different.

I'd pictured this weekend like some sort of waspy psychological warfare. Passive-aggressive jabs traded over vintages, pointed silences between courses, and the occasional swim to wash off the tension. Arden and I would dissect every loaded glance and back-handed compliment on the drive home, turning family drama into something almost entertaining. Leave it to the Sterlings to skip the subtlety and go straight for the jugular, champagne in hand, of course.

I'd hoped we could find common ground, or at least a mutual understanding. But looking at them now, I see the futility in that hope. This board seat, this role they're trying to force me into, it would mean leaving Boston, leaving everything I've built. They present it like an opportunity, but it's a cage constructed of family obligation and corporate ambition. They act like being a docent is something temporary, a rebellion to get out of my system. *That's been said.* Like it's a bad haircut I am growing out of. As if I'm just some tour guide wandering the halls with no purpose beyond killing time until I 'come to my senses.' But I know it wouldn't matter if I were a doctor saving lives or a chef with Michelin stars, anything outside their narrow vision of success might as well not exist.

The only growth they recognize is measured in profit margins and market share. What they've never bothered to see, what they actively choose to ignore, is how much I've already grown, just not in the direction they planned. I sit on three different museum committees now, helping shape the future of art education in Boston. I've developed exhibition programs that bring in schools from underfunded districts, last month, I helped secure a traveling exhibition that will transform our west wing into an interactive space for contemporary artists. But they've never asked about any of it.

Arden gets it. She's sat through countless practice runs of my lectures, offering insights that have helped me refine my approach. Arguing with me as she does. The contrast is stark between her genuine interest and my family's dismissal, between her understanding of what drives me and their refusal to see beyond their own expectations. She sees possibility where they see waste, potential where they see rebellion.

And maybe that's what scares them most, that I've found a different kind of success, one they can't control or quantify. I look back at my father, at the papers scattered across the table that are meant to chart my future without my input. They think they're forcing my hand, but they don't realize I've already chosen my path. They see an ultimatum where I see clarity. Every dismissive comment about my 'silly job,' every condescending reference to 'real work,' has only reinforced that I'm exactly where I need to be.

"Enough of the dramatics, you've had your fun. You've proved your point. You wanted to spend all day focused on the past rather than the future, you've done it. You wanted to flirt and fuck half of Boston? Fine. But your time's up. Now, I've stood by and watched as you've thrown away opportunity after opportunity, but enough's enough. That's over now. I've held a seat for you at this table long enough, delaying deals due to your childish spite. But you're not delaying any longer. Whether you like it or not, you don't just walk away from this family."

It's amazing that just outside there are more than a hundred people in cocktail attire. All here for some version of a formal barbeque. *Laughable.* Meanwhile, Shakespear would have something to say about what's happening in this room. Probably about 30,000 words resulting in regicide.

"I'm happy, I'm not giving *that* up for *this*."

"That's right, the sanctimonious William *fucking* Sterling. How nice it must be to be you." Alfie spits out with resentment so palpable I can taste it from where I stand. And it takes me aback. Maybe it's jealousy. The advantage to being the youngest. But whatever it is doesn't change the intention behind it. Misery will always love company.

"*This* is the reason you're happy. You think you'd like that silly job of yours even a fraction as much if your name wasn't on the wall? You wouldn't."

"I'm leaving. I shouldn't have come. I thought we could be cordial, I thought maybe somewhere you'd understand that this life you have, you *all* have, it's not the one I want."

My father slams his glass on the table, spilling whiskey across the papers meant to finalize the merger and with it, the board seat I would take to solidify it.

"This is it?" he asks "This is the hill you're willing to die on?" The accusation in his voice is laced with betrayal.

"*This* isn't, but *she* is."

I open the double library doors, and there she is. Face fallen with a champagne flute in one hand and my brother Cal to her side. I can't begin to imagine what's going on in her mind. What she's heard. I don't know what I would think if I were on the other side of it. But she was brought here to witness some version of the ugliness that just played out and I'm sick to my stomach.

Maybe this was always their plan, take the pieces of my life that matter most. He would have seen it the second he opened the door and saw Arden. I think the only one who hasn't admitted it yet, is her.

Cal walks off to join them in the library, and leaves us in a moment of pseudo-privacy.

"Let's run away" I say, pleading, as we stand so close our bodies are pressed against each other without any need besides their own self-interest.

"Where can we go?" she asks as she places her hand over my heart.

"New York?" I ask. *I could get us there and checked into a hotel in less than three hours.*

She shakes her head.

"Paris?" I ask, the agreement from earlier. *Hell, we could get to Paris. Get out of here, head straight to the airport, and then straight on till morning.*

"Nah, I don't think Paris was far enough after all... It's gonna have to be Mars."

"Mars it is." I agree. *With no concept of impossibility purely because it's with her.*

"Perfect, I just have to do something first."

She chugs the rest of her champagne and hands me the glass as she stomps forward. She crosses the distance in the hallway and marches right into the library. I can see her momentary pause, and even in just her shape from behind I know she's in awe of the room itself, the books that line every inch. One she'd enjoy under different circumstances. But she doesn't let it slow her, I think she's actually gaining momentum as she marches right up to my father.

"This is all a little cliché don't you think?" she asks.

"I think," he says in a tone that has me striding back into the room, "that my son has potential he's yet to live up to, and I'm tired of waiting around for him to recognize it. If that means I need to force it, so be it."

"That's the thing, Mr. Sterling, you're the only one who hasn't recognized it, because everyone sees it. See's how kind he is, how smart, how generous. How he goes to work everyday and makes peoples lives better, how he celebrates life, how he *lives* it. You don't see any of that because you've never tried."

"You're being..." he begins, with his chest full of hot air, and I'm by her side now.

"I promise, there isn't an end to that you won't regret." It comes out as I mean it to. A near snarl meant to show them I'm deadly serious. I don't think I deserve an ounce of what she's said. But I know there's no amount of casual labeling that can diminish what this is.

"I will not be spoken to this way, not in my own house." I take another step towards him, but Arden places her hand on my arm, to stop me. She just reaches to the table for the glass of whiskey, tipping the small amount back to her lips, emptying it entirely. I don't think anyone else can see the slight twinge, I've never seen her so much as taste a whiskey. But she drinks it down and returns the glass.

"So long as *this* is your opinion, you won't be spoken to by me, ever again." Her chin high as she turns on her heel. Smiling at me before mouthing two words, *same team,* and walking out.

The absence of her hand is replaced by my father's as he reaches for me.

"You're throwing away your future, your family."

"*She* is my future, and one day, she'll be my family."

Chapter Thirty-Two

HAPPILY EVER BEFORE

Arden

I pretended not to hear what he said to his father as we left and we drove back to Massachusetts without stopping. I fell asleep in the car to him singing Abba and awoke to the message of Morse code kisses he left on my forehead.

"Arden," he whispers into my mouth as his lips press against mine and my eyes adjust to him in the moonlight. "We're home." And we are. I've thought it was a convenience, us being neighbors, but I now wonder if it's more than that. The bread crumbs left by the universe so we'd eventually find our way to each other.

I take a deep breath and breathe him in. His eyes are unwavering. I've had men look at me for years, in lust, in affection, and want, in friendship, in jealousy and resentment, in hatred, in anger, in apathy and this is unlike anything.

He exhales a breath and as he does the words live in the air. *"I love you."*

"I–I don't..." his eyes, narrow in concern looking for the answer, for the rest of my sentence. *"You*, dont." His face drops in a way that's filled with fear, and I feel it strangling me. All the things I should say caught in my throat, but I can't get the words

189

out. However bad this is now, however hard it is to love him, it will be so much worse when he realizes he never did.

"You might think that, Will, but it's just the adrenaline, the emotions from today, you should go home tonight, you should take a breath." I grab my bag and start to walk towards my building, knowing his is behind me.

"Arden, stop!" He catches up in a step. "What are you doing?"

"I'm leaving." *I can't stop.* The second I do I'll burst into tears over more than this, over the future end I won't survive this time.

"You're really running this time." It's not a question as he says it, it's a challenge, voice tight with hurt.

"I don't want to fight." I might have held it together earlier, but something about what they said as we left, took root as we drove home.

"*Yes*, you do. I've seen you fight. That's who you are. You're brave and set off by anything you have passion for." He's looking at me in shock. "You have passion for me, I've seen it, I've *felt* it, so why won't you fight for this?"

"Because there's nothing to fight for!" I yell louder than I mean to, maybe that's what he wants, to hear it at a volume that will rattle him back to reality. But he stands there with his eyes narrowed "I heard you earlier, but that's not true. We've kept this casual for a reason." He stands in front of me blocking my path.

"No," he bites out, "we kept this casual because *you* wanted casual, *you* wanted safety. Don't you dare throw it in my face now." His mouth sets in a hard line between words and his nostrils flare. "I *told* you. I would be whatever you wanted, but you have to see," he says, softening ever so slightly. "I'm *so*, incredibly, *in love with you.*"

He takes a step forward towards me, softening still.

"You'd rather date people you can't have or don't really want because you think it means you aren't putting your heart on the line. Well, you can have me and I sure as hell know you want me. *I'll* be here, *I'll* put myself on the line. I just need you to take one small step and meet me here." He takes another step forward, and I don't move.

I swallow tightly, desperate to keep whatever composure I might have left before this all comes crashing down like shattered glass at our feet.

"I know what I'm doing, Will. I know how this plays out... You might think that now, that I'm brave and beautiful, that I'm full of passion. That I'm fucking incredible, the disco ball in the center of the room while the music plays and the crowd dances. I'm a *good* time, the *best* time, your *best* fuck, your best *friend, your best fucking friend.* But the clock will run out, the big light will come on, and you'll see this bright shiny thing didn't have any light but what it could reflect. Eventually, you'll leave, I'll leave, you'll let me leave, you'll take that job, become who you're supposed to be, and no amount of sparkling champagne moments can keep you here. So yeah, I wanted to keep it casual."

"Who told you that?" he demands, stepping closer with fierce protectiveness I saw earlier as well. His eyes scan my face for any indication beyond what I've said, so I help him with the answer and just I shake my head.

"No one," I say, clearly enough for him to accept it. But he doesn't.

"You're lying. That's the kind of intrusive thought that was planted there by someone else."

"Let it go..." I begin to turn but he grabs my hand.

"No, because that means letting you go, and I can't do that. I don't know what happened to make you want to *really* run, to make you think that. But who I'm supposed to be doesn't exist without you anymore. I'm not letting you run away, *not out of fear,* and definitely not without me. Because for all the things I know, there's about a million more I don't. But I do know that the universe, the gods, the whatevers you want to call it, wouldn't knot us together only for me to let you go. I know that and I know *you.*"

"You don't know me." I haven't let him. It hasn't been long

enough. The people who once knew me are all far, or far gone. "I don't even know me." I say in a voice so much softer, so much more scared than the one before. Who I planned to be feels outdated. Who he has seen me be is the collection of in between moments, not someone real.

"Look at me." He takes another step forward and brings his hands to my face. His thumb finding the tears I had hoped to hide from both of us. "I know you... I know the parts you've shown me at three in the morning, while you breath against my chest, I know the parts you dim because you think it's easier, I know that you are terrified, and that fear is your brain working against you in a way I can't fathom. But whatever I don't know I'm begging you to show me. I don't care how complicated you think it is. It doesn't matter, because loving you isn't complicated, darling. It's the easiest thing in the world."

He said love. He said it like I should have known.

He takes a final step forward. His hands are not breaking the connection that keeps our pulses in time.

"Consider that maybe I'm right."

"But...you're never right," I say and he laughs with hope.

"Maybe this time I am. Because I love you and I *know* you love me, too. It's okay if you aren't ready to admit that yet. Because one day we can tell this story to our kids or grandkids about how I had to convince their mother to admit she loved me. But you know what, if it's the only time in the rest of my life that I'm right, that's fine by me. I don't need any more. This is enough for me."

"You really love me?" I want to hear him say it again. I want to know for sure.

"I love you. You can call it casual all you want, but you love me, too."

"Happily ever afters aren't built on casual."

His mouth may have been open waiting to speak but instead the sound that comes out is a short laugh that sounds like relief.

His hand follows the curve from my shoulder slowly and his thumb strokes the column of neck.

"We can build a life on whatever we want. If that means I chase you down the street or out of this city, I will. Because I'm not going to just let you run away from our future. If you can't see it yet, I can see it for the both of us. I'll hold on to it for the both of us. While you figure out the path you want to take to get us there. If you can't see it, I can. Just tell me what you want, and I'll build it. If you want to run away to Paris? To Mars, I'm right behind you."

I take the step forward and his arms wrap around me in something so much more than a kiss, but a promise of what he just said, and I know that our lives will never be the same.

Chapter Thirty-Three

HAPPILY EVER BEFORE

Arden

He said he loved me. He showed me he loves me. He *made* love to me. What a way to say that, even to myself. There's something about the notion of physical intimacy that I've always understood more easily than emotional. Maybe it's the idea that it's more readable. I can see exactly when their view of me changes from friend, classmate, colleague, stranger, into something else. The way it drips down my skin, sometimes in soft ripples and sometimes in unwanted goosebumps. When a man is in my bed, I can see the reaction to my touch, see how it makes them wild, and uncontrolled. Even in the silence of sex there is noise that tells me exactly what they are thinking. The passing breaths, the grunts of desire. But when a man is standing in front of you pouring his soul out, despite all the words he uses, it feels like he's speaking a language I've never heard.

'I love you.' he said.

'Tell me what you want and I'll build it,' he said.

And I stood there as he left all of these promises at my feet, not waiting for me to say it back, but no doubt wanting me to.

But I didn't. I hate that I didn't. Why the fuck didn't I. I kissed him in a way to tell him, and I think he knew. I hope he did. He said I didn't need to say it back, and I believe him.

Each night he comes to bed with me, and in my dreams, the ones that used to evade me, I can hear his breath like the comfort it has become. Each day he pours his soul into mine like filling a glass of water to leave by the bed. The comfort in knowing it's there in the middle of the night when I get thirsty.

My fingers type away, going through the motions of my work day. But there's only him occupying my mind. Every crevice, every corner. The dark ones I stand in when I don't want to be seen, he stands there with me.

I do, I love him. But it's thinking about the last time someone told me they loved me, and the feeling that went along with it that has me spiraling in a way I can't articulate. It's a desperate feeling of grasping at air trying to hold on to anything. Feeling the betrayal of love, and hollowness at the loss of what you perceive as safety in another person.

It all happened so long ago, but still the idea of it has always loomed in some way. The parts I remember, the parts I forced myself to forget. But no matter how much I've tried, it lives in one of those dark corners, and it isn't alone.

I take a breath, and another.

I open my drafts folder and it's just where I've always kept it on ice. The idea that if he had just known, maybe he would change his mind. Despite that he never did.

I open the email and I think I can see the digital dust flutter away as it pulls up on my screen.

Dear Reid,

This isn't the first time I've written a version of this email. One that isn't just cheery updates pretending I'm okay. But I'm not and you don't know that, and worst of all you don't care. I've been so mad at you. And I don't want to be, because it just makes me mad at

myself for ever believing you. I needed you, not as my friend, I have friends, I needed *you*. And you took that from me and so much of me with it. Because I loved you and you just stopped loving me. But even though you broke my heart, I don't have the energy to be mad anymore, because that's the only thing I remember now. So even though I don't understand it, and I may never, if there's ever a chance for us again, for *me* again, I have to forgive you now.
I forgive you for ending it. I forgive you for needing space. I forgive you for making me feel easy to love, and I forgive you for showing me that wasn't true. I even forgive you for not knowing how to love me. But I needed you in ways, and I'm sorry, I can't ever forgive you for not trying.

Arden Bancroft

The person who wrote that was hurt in ways she didn't understand, I'm not sure reading it back now that I do any better. But what I know better now, is myself.

I click into the draft watching the cursor blink and I hold down the delete button without hesitation. It's the breath I've been holding buried under the weight of her sadness and fear for so long.

You don't realize you love someone when you're clinging to an orgasm, or when you're lonely, when you're in bed with someone else, or you're thinking about what they're doing. It's the person you miss when you're busy at two in the afternoon, not bored at two in the morning. And that's what he is, what he became. I miss him in ways of missing the future we haven't experienced yet, not a memory of the past. The person you talk to in the seconds you've found in time that didn't exist before, just because you want to know they are on the other side of the emotional string you choose to tug.

I love him.

I've loved him.

I'm in love with him.

He's become the grains of sand in the glass jar full of marbles. Taking up space in all the smallest moments. Filling all the air pockets surrounding the spheres that make up the bigger moments of my day.

He is sand and I wonder if I could love him more than grains exist. Knowing the limitlessness to determining that number. But suddenly, that's how this feels.

I have been in love before, but it wasn't this, in the way I suddenly believe Plato. That souls are split. Perhaps all this time, we've been in search of each other. Just watching him in the darkness through the glass across the way. In the way our friends have been friends, but not us. As we shared spaces and walked the same streets passing each other in ways to uncover when the time is right.

I didn't want to fall in love with him. I didn't want to fall in love, *period*. I think it's the idea of falling. Being tripped up over a person. But I love him in a way that I haven't before, and more terrifyingly, I don't know that I will again.

Despite all that's happened, maybe because of all that happened, we ended up here.

Inexplicably intertwined.

And he needs to know that I know it, too.

———

"Hey Mack!" I say as I open the door to the museum, the security guard smiles at me the way he has from the first time Will introduced us. *'Arden is a VIP, take good care of her for me.'*

"Hi Ms. Arden... he's just started a tour... I'm sure you can catch up." I thank him and hurry off towards the galleries. I love it here, of course I do, it's because he is here.

The warm tenor of his voice reaches me before I see him, and

I follow it, much like I did that first day, until I reach the small crowd gathered around one of the contemporary exhibits.

Will is crouched down, eye-level with a tiny critic who can't be more than six, earnestly discussing what appears to be a very serious question. His sleeves are just rolled enough to show the edge of his tattoos begin to peer out from their normal hidden view. His hair is slightly mussed like he's been running his hands through it while thinking, something I know the last few days have only increased.

I slip into the crowd just as he rises back to his full height, all six-foot-something of him commanding attention without even trying.

"Are there any other questions?" he asks, and he actually sounds eager for more. I know why it's so easy to hold his own with his family, because of moments like this, where he actually feels rewarded by what he does. Like he could spend forever sharing this passion of his. And I want to share it with him.

My hand shoots up before I can overthink as the smile split across his face

"Ah, yes, the lady in the back with the suspicious timing and the propensity for challenging my expertise," he teases, eyes flaring with excitement and recognition, playing along as he weaves through the crowd toward me.

"Not a question," I say, my voice remaining steadier than my heartbeat. "A correction, actually."

"It seems you think you know something I don't..." He's close enough now that I can see the flecks of gold in his eyes, the way his mouth twitches like he's fighting back a bigger smile, waiting for the moment to let it free.

"That's probably true in most cases," I admit, earning scattered laughter from our impromptu audience. "But I'm actually here to say, that just this once, you're right."

"And what might that be?"

"That I love you." The words come out stronger than I expect, and I feel stronger for saying them.

"Ms. Bancroft," Will says, his voice taking on that professional tour guide tone he uses when he's about to say something decidedly unprofessional, "are you interrupting my carefully planned tour to tell me you love me?"

"Well, you interrupted my carefully planned life to love me, seems only fair. And I'm interrupting your *carefully planned tour* to tell you that Cubism began in 1907, not 1908 like you said." I take a step closer. "But yes, I love you."

"First of all, I said 1907-1908, which is historically accurate," he counters, closing the distance between us. "And second..."

His hands find my waist like they belong there, *which they do*, and he kisses me as the crowd around us breaks into applause. Because apparently we're *that* kind of story now, and I can feel his smile against my lips.

"Say it again" his voice is rough with emotion, not quiet, not hushed or bothered who might hear.

"You're right," I say as his eyes hold mine.

"Not that..."

"I love you," I speak into his kiss, just for him this time.

"There it is," he says softly, resting his forehead against mine, "the only time I'll ever need to be right."

"Don't get used to it," I warn him, but we both know it's too late. I'm already used to this, to him, to us.

Chapter Thirty-Four

HAPPILY EVER BEFORE

Will

The Sterling Financial Group office towers over lower Manhattan, existing on a high floor of another one of the gleaming monuments among the forest of skyscrapers in the Financial District. From street level the building seems to pierce the morning haze, a reminder of everything I've been avoiding for the past month. Not just since the Memorial Day disaster in Newport, if I'm being honest with myself, but that particular spectacle has driven home exactly why I've kept my distance all these years.

The Memorial Day party replays in my mind, crystal champagne flutes catching the evening light, forced laughter from people who'd rather be anywhere else, and my father's booming voice cutting through it all. *'My son William will be joining the board next month.'* Just like that, he'd tried to chain me to his world without an ounce of my agreement.

That night had changed everything, not just with my father, but with Arden too. Sometimes the worst moments spark the best revelations. Standing on the street, still in our formal wear, we'd finally stopped dancing around what we meant to each other.

The three-hour drive from Boston this morning gave me too

much time to think, to second-guess, to rehearse this conversation a hundred different ways. But with the weight of the manila envelope heavy in my hand, I know there's no turning back.

The elevator ride feels longer than usual, each floor bringing me closer to a conversation I've avoided most of my adult life. Up here, the city sprawls beneath us with the morning rush of Wall Street's usual frenetic energy.

My father's secretary, Margaret, looks up as I approach. She's been here since before I was born, her hair grayer now but her smile just as warm. Sometimes I wonder if she knows more about the Sterling men than we know about ourselves, at least three of them.

"William," she says, genuine pleasure warming her voice. "It's been too long."

"Hi Margaret, is he in?"

She nods, already reaching for her phone. "Let me tell him you're here."

"No need," I say, moving past her desk. "I'll surprise him, he likes that, right?" I wink, knowing full well there is nothing my father likes less than a surprise. But in this case, sneak attack is for the best. The element of surprise might be the only advantage I have left.

Learned from the best.

He's standing there, at his floor-to-ceiling windows when I enter, hands clasped behind his back as he surveys his kingdom. The pose is so familiar it almost makes me smile, how many times have I seen him just like this growing up? Before I went 'rogue' as he calls it. Light gleans across his silver hair, and for the briefest of moments, I see him as others must. Powerful, unwavering, a force of nature. But even nature can be destructive.

"Dad."

As he turns, surprise flashes across his face before it settles into a mask of careful neutrality. He's always been good at controlling his expressions, his emotions, everything except his youngest son.

"This is unexpected," he says, and I can hear the unspoken

additions of everything he is holding back until the opportune moment.

"I thought we should talk," I say, closing the door behind me. The soft click echoes in his corner office, high above Manhattan.

"There's nothing to discuss." He moves behind his desk, shuffling papers with practiced dismissal. "When you're ready to stop this—"

"I drove three hours to have this conversation, and you still can't see me as anything but a child having a tantrum."

His eyes narrow, probably noting the wrinkles on my shirt and the one between my brow where frustration is folding itself into my face.

"Some people don't have the luxury of romance, Will. Some of us have responsibilities, obligations—"

"This isn't about romance, this is about the fact that for the first time in your life you're not getting what you want." I interrupt, my voice steady despite the familiar anger rising. "You think any love I have for something that isn't this," I gesture broadly, "isn't valuable. You never wanted to be a husband. You wanted a wife. Not a partner, an asset like everything else. That's why you look at people in my life as a risk, because in yours, it was only you."

There's quiet between us. I can almost hear him thinking through his next move, calculating risks and returns like he does with everything.

He turns back to his view, the one that costs millions to maintain, overlooking the heart of American capitalism.

"She got promoted, I hear," he says, and I'm not surprised he's been keeping tabs on Arden even from here. "She's young for it, especially there."

"She earned it."

"I'm sure she did." His tone suggests otherwise. He strides and takes a seat in his leather chair, large as he is, and perhaps there's something about him trying to come across as fatherly. But it's an ill-fitting role, like a suit bought off the rack, and he's never had one of those.

"Just remember, Will, love is wonderful in theory, but in practice, it needs to be managed like any other asset."

I drop the manila envelope on the desk, the real reason I came here. Inside are the papers that will free us both, my abdication from a throne I never wanted. "Maybe that's where you're right, it is an asset, it's a choice."

"What is this?" he asks, pulling the papers from it, scanning them with a dawning understanding. I watch his face carefully, seeing the moment he realizes what I've done. His fingers tighten on the paper's edge.

"That, is another choice."

My involvement here, in this whole thing, has less to do with me and more the fact that just my existence was allocated a portion of voting power for something I have neither the understanding nor interest to participate in. I began the process months ago, before the great war they waged, before the Memorial Day ambush. They don't need me. This absolves them of that.

"You'll have the vote you need this time, but I've assigned a proxy from here on out."

I think about Simon, my oldest friend, about our conversation when I asked him to take this on. 'Are you sure?' he'd asked, understanding the weight of what I was asking. 'Your father won't take this well.' But he'd agreed. He'd vote with them this time, a compromise to ease the transition, but after that, he'd be free to guide my shares according to his conscience. It's why I asked him, he has one.

The silence stretches between us, heavy with unspoken words. I wonder if my father sees what I see. The merger will still happen, probably. The hostile takeover will wear its sheep's clothing of friendly acquisition, and business will continue as usual. But it will happen without my name attached to it, without my silent complicity.

As I step into the elevator, I catch a glimpse of my father

watching from his office doorway. He raises a hand in what might be a wave, and I nod in return. It's not reconciliation, we're too far past that, but maybe it's pride for something he didn't see coming.

He made his choices long ago, now I'm making mine.

The revolving door spits me out onto the street, and I breathe deeply, feeling lighter than I have in months. Neither the building nor the man in it can cast a shadow over my life any longer. I check my phone, if I leave now, I can make it back to Boston before evening. Back to the life I've chosen and more importantly, the one we are building.

Chapter Thirty-Five

HAPPILY EVER AFTER

Will

Too many of my life's pivotal moments have happened right here. This room has never changed, even when the exhibitions have. I run my finger across the engraved dedication plate and I think of myself as a young man and the couple that inspired it.

We've done this before. Come here when things are tough.

Something I did before her.

Because of her.

With her.

Without *her*.

I remember my face being younger sitting here, less weathered by time and loss. She probably thinks the same thing when she looks at me now, though she'd never say it. The same way I catch glimpses of an easier version of herself, before everything happened. Probably just my mind playing tricks, wanting to see what isn't there anymore.

I knew she had been avoiding me. She looked different today in that old kitchen light.

Her hair is shorter, maybe she's taller. *She's not taller.* She's been avoiding this conversation, too afraid of what it would do to me, but I've known it was coming.

"You turned down Chicago last year," I say quietly. "And San Francisco before that."

"I wasn't ready then," she admits, twisting the ring on her finger, that vertical band of diamonds wrapped around her finger like a stack of books. "But I think... I know, I resent staying in the city just to be nearer to you. And because of that, I began resenting you, too. Even though you never asked me to. Your life was always here and I didn't know how to leave that behind."

I would have rather she'd come home, talk to me about it. It's not a fair expectation, she doesn't owe me any weight in her decisions now. But still, her guilt in that is clear, and why she obviously dragged her feet on the topic.

She came home today for the first time in a year to tell me she's taking a job in Seattle. Finally closing the chapters of her life that took place here. And when she showed up today to tell me, this is the only place I felt we needed to return. I brought her here because she, too, has memories of this place. I don't know if they overwhelm her the same way they do me.

I came to terms with it, she needs to move on, move away, grow away from here, *from me*. Guilt and obligation have held her long enough.

But before she goes, I need her to remember more than just me. I need her to remember...

Arden and I had the greatest of loves, that doesn't just evaporate into the universe. Dissolve into the air. That has to help her through this now. Knowing that love is still in the air we breathe, it's in her blood, no matter how far she needs to run.

We've spent time talking about it all now. Her fears about moving. Her reasons for going. We talked about selling the house. I offered to go with her. But that's not what she needs.

"How did you always make life look so easy?" she asks. She's been struggling recently, I know she has, throwing herself into her work, and being a mother, but taking on *that* role almost makes it all that much harder.

"I think when you love someone, really, it becomes you, and in that way, it can be as easy as breathing."

"What about now?"

"My lungs don't fill the way they used to. I try to take a deep breath, but there just isn't anything left to inhale." I say.

She pushes her glasses up to pull the hair from her face as she presses the base of her hands into her eyes, rubbing the tears free.

"Aren't you disappointed in me?"

And there it is, the thing that's kept her away. How could I ever be disappointed in someone who makes me so proud?

"We're on the same team. *Nothing* changes that."

Chapter Thirty-Six

HAPPILY EVER DURING

Will

The thing about not knowing is that when you do, suddenly recognize this thing that you had no concept of understanding before, there is a ground swell that is uncontrollable. There is no way to return to the moment prior. There is no resetting a course. There is only forward.

I think people have confused death and love. I was always under the impression that when you die your life flashes before your eyes, but if that's the case why did I see hundreds of futures when I looked at her in that moment?

My feet hit the pavement, and I pick up speed.

It wasn't the first time I'd been overcome with this sense of prophecy. That there was some greater entanglement for us as we'd spent time hopping between beds. We were being woven together, we already had been, and just never realized it. But now, it's the music we hear in every silence.

My lungs fill with air that pushes me forward.

I've been sitting on this feeling for longer than makes any sense. I knew I loved her one morning when I had gotten up for this exact purpose, to start my day before the day with my feet against the cement.

And as I kissed her, soft against her temple, light on her cheek, lingering at the corner of her mouth, trailing down to her jaw, catching the spot below her ear that makes her sigh, and finally, inevitably, finding her lips, she stirred in her sleep but still reached for me, muscle memory seeking warmth. As if I was worthy of the attention. In her fog of slumber with eyes barely cracked open she and a whispered sigh escaping her parted lips, she mewled a whimper that had me close to crawling back into bed.

"Why do you do that?" she asked in a way that I could tell was part of a dream, slow and strung together like cursive. In the vulnerability of sleep, she radiates a peace so profound it makes my chest ache, as if I'm witnessing something sacred in these quiet morning hours.

"Do what, darling?" I asked. The first time I used the term of endearment it was in mock necessity, but there is no one and nothing more darling. I twine my fingers in her hair and pick up a morning curl.

"It's always six," she says between a yawn, "whenever you get out of bed, it's always six morning kisses."

I hadn't noticed the pattern, but it makes sense she would. I lean down to her lips and kiss her more deeply than the previous ones. Her mouth awakens and she stretches her arms around my neck. I kick off my running shoes as she pulls the shirt over my head.

Her eyes are open, alert now, pupils wide in the dimness of the morning. The sleepy blur is replaced by something electric, more urgent. And besides the momentary break where she stripped me of my shirt, I can't break our kiss in any way that would separate me from her and it's clear neither can she. I crawl back into bed; I'd crawl on my hands and knees over broken glass to get to her. My hands slide up the curve of her waist, raising her arms as I toss the t-shirt aside and the bareskin of our chests are pressed together with our breathing in tandem. Her eyes are bright and not clouded by any of the sleep she was wrapped in moments ago.

I push up on my elbows, where she's caged underneath me, ironically I'm the one with the inability to leave. I look down to where she lays, and for all the art I've seen, there's nothing more beautiful than this woman.

"Why is it always six?" I repeat back as I kiss the column of her neck. Inching my way up to her ear kiss after kiss. "This is why. One more and I can't bare to leave"

"I noticed." And there's no surprise on my face that she knew the answer before she asked.

Her teeth pull against my lip and the flash narrows her eyes in a smirk. Her leg tightens around me and I'm hers as she has me on my back. Sitting up for me to see as she's straddled across my lap. She is morning-warm and sleep-soft, familiar now but thrilling, like your favorite song coming on unexpectedly. My palms find purchase on her waist as my hands follow her shape to the elastic of the underwear I know are about to find their way to the floor with the rest of our clothes, have me harden beneath her.

We stay in the veil of the moment until we're both sated beyond any sense of reason. And I have no reason. I don't need it. This is enough.

There is this idea that time slows when you realize you love someone. In a way that everyone and everything around you pauses. That's not what it was for me. The world was always slow as I ran through it. But not looking at her. It took six seconds to see all the outcomes of our life, and *know*. I saw them all. All the paths my life could take. And it is undeniable, whatever it may be, there isn't an ounce of sterling in the world worth more than our future.

No choice I would ever make to take me from here, with *her*.

These moments where words are diffused by sleep and kisses stretch like honey being pulled from a jar. The thickness of each shared breath suspended between us, time caught golden and viscous, as morning pours through windows to find us wrapped in amber moments that crystallize rather than break. Preserving every sigh, every touch, every whispered truth, every one of these six-morning-kisses before the world can steal them away.

I don't understand it. I don't need to understand it to know it exists. Like gravity, I can feel it without being able to comprehend why every time my foot hits the pavement it is weighted by a greater force.

That's *her*.

I think people have confused death and love.

They say life flashes before your eyes when you die and that the world comes to a halt when you fall in love.

They are wrong.

It's one and the same.

I'm fairly certain that falling in love is the greatest loss of life one could imagine. It's soul-ripping, world-ending, a beautiful annihilation. And I fall to my knees in painful gratitude at the opportunity, offering myself up to this exquisite destruction. Ceasing to exist as I was before, a willing sacrifice to who I'm becoming. I'll dive headfirst into the River Styx swimming for my life, or rather, to welcome a welcome death.

It turns out love isn't some grand revelation that strikes like lightning. It's more like finally noticing you've been breathing underwater this whole time, your lungs filled with something deeper than air, and somehow that's exactly where you're supposed to be.

Not drowning, but finally, perfectly, alive.

Chapter Thirty-Seven

HAPPILY EVER DURING

Arden

We're surrounded by boxes in our new apartment, which is how it happens. Moving toward the kitchen windowsill, I nearly trip over the small box on the ground and in slow motion, my hands are suddenly empty. The small pot tumbling through air but my hands don't move fast enough to save him. The hollow crack against hardwood can be heard throughout our box-filled apartment, dirt exploding in a tragic halo around my feet. The sharp, fresh scent of crushed basil leaves rises up like a final goodbye.

For a moment, I just stare at my betraying hands, still curved around the ghost of the pot that had become part of my morning routine, coffee brewing, basil check, emails.

"BARRY!" I hear myself yell. I drop to my knees, in part due to the dramatics, but also to begin to address the crime scene of potting soil and shattered dreams.

Will comes running in, his hands full of a box of his own which he sets down on the counter as he rushes to my side.

"I've done so well, he's survived all this time." Almost a year of careful watering, of searching *why are basil leaves turning yellow* at midnight, of feeling stupidly proud every time a new leaf unfurled, of waking up to him bigger than the day before, all ended by one clumsy moment between refrigerator and counter.

While all the other additions to the *'Plant-City-Rollers', the latest plant-band,* eventually moved on, as they say. Barry has survived. He's been my constant through late-night cooking experiments, he survived our first fight, *just like we did*, witnessed countless morning coffees, countless bottles of champagne. Even got a counter-mate with an apothecary jug of collected corks that Will has been collecting since that very first. It feels so much more symbolic than just a little plant because he's been our unofficial timekeeper. Measuring our relationship in new leaves and growth spurts.

And a lot has changed in that time. It's like all the pieces have fallen into place, or they've ended in the spots on the board where we've moved them. I took the promotion, Will finalized his transition to Sterling-in-name-only, giving himself the freedom from family pressure. And since then, we've been talking about expanding our family, a dog, *obviously*. It was one of the things we discussed when moving in together. Getting a friend for Barry.

My hands hover over the wreckage, not quite ready to start cleaning up, as if leaving it might somehow undo it. The soil is still dark and moist from this morning's watering, Barry's last, as it turns out.

"I failed." But his hand is splayed across my back rubbing soothingly the ache that I feel at the loss.

"Darling," Will says in a deeply gentle voice. He's kneeling beside me, as I lay my head on our touching shoulders. "That's not the same basil plant."

The words take a moment to process and suddenly my head is off his shoulder and whipped around to his face.

"What?!"

"That plant died about a month after we brought it home." He drags his fingers across his mouth containing the rest of it until I say something more.

"Well..." as my hands scoop up not-Barry's soggy roots "who is *this* then?"

He starts gathering the larger pieces of pot, his movements careful and methodical.

"*That* would be Barry the..." he looks up to the ceiling as his eyebrows knit together, fingers ticking through invisible numbers. I watch his face cycle through concentration, calculation, and finally, sheepish admission. "Barry the Seventh," he says finally.

"SEVENTH?! The *betrayyyal*... the *basiltrayal*!" I stare at him, this man who shows his love in such unexpected ways, and suddenly everything clicks, the plants mysterious resilience, how it never quite got too leggy despite my haphazard pruning, its ability to bounce back from my *occasional* neglect. Let's not forget how I would constantly say things like *'Barry, you look like a new plant today!'* Turns out. It was.

"You had just been so proud of keeping it alive, so I bought an identical one and replanted it in the same pot. I've been secretly replacing them whenever they start to look rough. The garden center knows me by name now."

"Will..."

"Actually," he continues, a flush creeping up his neck, "once I didn't have time to re-pot it, and you didn't even notice!"

"You've just been running an underground basil replacement operation," I gasp between fits of laughter that bubbles up unexpectedly and unstoppable, shaking my shoulders and rattling my heart as his joins in.

He shrugs, looking adorably embarrassed but equally proud.

I sit back on my heels, wiping tears, formed from laughter and something else, from my eyes.

Once we've cleaned it up together, he stands and dusts off his hands, reaching out for mine.

"Grab your shoes,"

"Where are we going?"

"Time for you to meet my supplier... let's go pick out Barry the Eighth." I take his hand and try not to think about how many times he must have made this trek alone, just to keep my illusion of gardening competence alive.

"And maybe get some rosemary too. Though I expect full disclosure on any future plant casualties."

"Deal," he says, squeezing my hand twice.

Chapter Thirty-Eight

HAPPILY EVER DURING

Will

One day I know I'll be nostalgic for mornings like these. The way life changes overnight. It did for us. The night we met. The night we fought. The night she loved me. The night we moved in. We make decisions at night. We cling to each other at night. We plan our future at night.

All of our boxes are long since unpacked. We've set up the spare room as an office that we share, and there's a perfect nook off the living room that she said looks like it could have been made for an upright piano. So I had one delivered for her a week after we moved in.

I walk back through the space coming back from our run. Mine and Titian's, though despite his collie-esque mix, he's not as much of a runner as the shelter implied he might be. So some days, like today, it's more of a compromise. I slow my pace, he occasionally breaks into an enthusiastic trot, and we both pretend this counts as exercise until we reward ourselves with a treat from the coffee shop. I unclip his leash where he runs laps around until he lands himself on the couch until it's time for lunch.

Through the archway of our kitchen, I spot Arden on her

toes, reaching for something from a high cabinet. A pair of pajama shorts and my old college sweatshirt barely covering her ass can't be keeping her warm in the crisp morning air seeping through the window she always cracks open. I'm behind her and she's wrapped in my arms, the soft roundness of her butt pressed against my torso as I lift her a couple extra feet in the air to reach whatever it is she was struggling for. It flutters down around us and the powder forming a crown on the top of her head, as the bag of flour remains toppled over where it was and it's snowing in the kitchen. I slide her down to her feet and she spins around to face me, and our bodies move in the way they've come to know each other. The remnants of the breakfast she was trying to make, at our feet.

Her hands are in mine and I see the glint in her eye as I stretch my arms away from her, only to pull her into me in a spin. The dusting of flour falling around us as she's in my arms will one day be the snow globe I shake to remember this moment. We're dancing to the same song that is only playing on the shared line between us. Half dressed in the kitchen as the first snow flurry of the season picks up outside and she laughs at the powder on her cheeks.

I take steps and back her into the cabinet, caging her in directly where I found her moments ago. My hands pressed to the counter behind her leaving handprints in the flour, I lean down and kiss her in a way that's full of greed. Not in what I can take from her, but greed for moments like this. There's no limit to how many of them I can consume, how many I want. All of her, always. I've known it for a while. A lot longer than has made any sense, but I know it, despite my lack of understanding it.

When I stood there that night and challenged her to love me back, I knew then what I know now. She loves me wholly in a way I don't think I deserve, but I will crave until the day I die.

Her cheeks are flushed, and our noses brush. The dusting of flour from her face being picked up in the scruff of my facial hair and she laughs into my mouth as she blinks it away. My tongue slips into her mouth as her fingers reach for the waistband of my sweatpants and dips her hand in to grab me. I can't control the sound that reverberates from deep within me. Thinking about how deep in her I could be. As her hand wraps around me tightly my breathing quickens. Being near her everything has always quickened. Her hair sits atop her head in the messy morning bun and as she drops to her knees, taking my pants with her, foregoing any plan for pancakes.

My fingers claw at the counter as she takes me in her mouth, that magical, argumentative, fiery, fucking mouth. The movements are tight and wet and I'm shattering with each hum of her lips as her fingernails dig into my thigh. Leaving the most glorious half moons deep within the ink.

"You're perfect" I grunt out in a voice that only she would know. The tone is so different that it's only ever been used in moments like this where she has me so completely lost to her. She picks up speed and I brush the hair that's fallen in her eyes, the flour leaving fingerprints across her forehead as I frantically try to find her eyes.

She knows this is what does it, everytime fucking time, she can hear it between the breaths and groans in desperate hunger and as she tightens her lips around me and takes me as deeply as she can, using her hands to hold the rest of me. She looks up, her eyes wide but far from doe like. There's nothing simple and confused about them, and when I fall, those are the pools I fall into. And I come as she pulls me deep to the back of her throat.

She sits back against the kitchen cabinets and I join her on the floor. We are sitting side by side, and I feel like my legs have given out. She sucked the blood out of my entire lower half, and now, here we are. Her head on my shoulder as our breathing syncs up, as it always does, and always has. From this vantage point our kitchen is a disaster. The tornado that's gone through it leaving the type of destruction that can only come from two people so wildly in love.

"Come here, come closer..." I whisper into the crown of her head.

We're close, in all the ways that matter and all the ways that don't, but she doesn't mistake my meaning as I pull her onto my bare lap and my hands find themselves pulling off her sweatshirt and I know she can feel me hardening again beneath her, the flimsy fabric of the cotton shorts not any kind of meaningful barrier between us.

The winds of us pick up, whirling in a way things crash around to the ground as she's flipped on her back and she begs, writhing beneath me, this game we play as I tease her. I'd never deny her a fucking thing and like most things, she knows. The idea that I have any control here when I finally slide into her and her back bows from the ground, is ridiculous. My arm catches her beneath me as I keep us pressed together, her entire body responds as mine does. Her teeth sink into my skin to muffle the sound and I lean into her ear, "Scream for me, darling."

Her leg locks around my back and I bury my face in her neck, the taste of sweat on my lips and tongue. Her hands are clawing at my back as her breathing picks up and so does my speed. She lets out a panting cry of pleasure and I release mine before we collapse into the ecstasy of this morning in a pile of sweaty limbs. Her skin is pinked from me and her eyes look weighted in the way of sated contentment that comes only from this type of obsessive intimacy.

There's never going to be enough of this.

Never enough of her.

Chapter Thirty-Nine

HAPPILY EVER DURING

Arden

Is there anything better than a bath? I mean, besides coffee, or finding a parking spot directly in front of your destination in Boston, or the way Will looks when he's concentrating on his crossword puzzle before he tosses it out to me to let me get that hit of crossword dopamine by knowing the answer. But right now, submerged in water hot enough to make my skin bloom pink, I'm voting bath. There's something almost biblical about it, or maybe primordial, this feeling of being wholly embraced by warmth that takes the exact shape of your body's negative space. There's only one other place I feel so safely surrounded.

I sink deeper until only my head remains above the surface, along with my toes, which grip the opposite end of the porcelain tub. It's dangerously easy to lose track of time in here, which isn't ideal given that we're supposed to be meeting our friends for dinner later.

Will's giving some kind of lecture tonight at the museum, it's going to be a big deal, and he's been nervous about it for weeks. It's funny, nerves never really shine through for him, but I think this is the first time I've seen it since he's distanced himself from his parents. And he's got more nerves about it than you would expect. He hasn't practiced in front of me, jokingly saying he'd rather I dismantle his career publicly with a challenge than give him any sort of tip off this time. But I've seen him pacing around the small space silently practicing in his own mind.

Rosealie has already started texting me a series of increasingly dramatic countdown messages making sure we won't be late.

I'm debating whether I can justify another five minutes when Will appears, settling himself on the bathmat beside the tub. He does this sometimes, comes to sit with me while I bathe. It's not sexual, *usually*, most of the time he just sits against the tub and listens to me ramble about my day, about the book I'm reading, about how well Barry the Basil is doing since I started feeding him ice cubes for breakfast. To which he always just smiles. But so often when he comes home from work, if I've already retreated to the bathtub, he just sits next to me to ask about my day, listening to the most mundane details.

But there's something different in his face today. I've learned to read the microscopic shifts in his expressions over time, the way the corner of his mouth twitches when he's trying not to laugh, how his only one eye narrows when he's skeptical. Right now, there's a look in his eyes I'm not sure I've seen before.

I sit up slightly, squeezing water from my hair.

"Aren't you going to ask me about my day?" I ask as he dips his fingers into the water, creating lazy swirls in the bubbles that brush against my skin.

"I will..." he says, that unfamiliar look still dancing across his features. "But you should ask me about mine first." He flicks water at my face playfully.

"How very dare you," I gasp, wiping bubbles from my nose. "I'm in a vulnerable position here."

"You're in a bathtub, not naked at a talent show." There's still something simmering beneath his usual amusement.

"Fine, how was *your* day, Will?" I ask with exaggerated patience.

"Terrible," he says, maintaining an impressively stern face despite the way his eyes are practically sparkling with suppressed something.

I sit up straighter, folding my arms on the edge of the tub. You'd think being naked would make this conversation more charged, but we passed that particular threshold of comfort almost immediately. Now it's just another version of us, me in the bath, him perched beside it.

"Is that so?" I prompt. "Did you get splashed by a car on your way to work?"

"Worse."

"Hmm... did you forget everything you know about art and make a total fool of yourself in front of everyone?"

"So, so much worse..."

"Oh, you must have tripped and fallen face-first on your run this morning, and Titian just sat there in his judgemental-dog way and laughed."

"You're not going to believe me, but it's even worse." His sleeves are rolled up to his elbows, the ink on his forearms contrasting the white porcelain as he covers my folded hands with his own.

"I'm on the edge of my seat."

"It started out like most days, but I just knew it wouldn't be. I knew the minute I woke up, it wouldn't be like any other day. But I tried. I kissed you goodbye, headed off to work, but on my way there I had this gut-wrenching feeling..."

There's a shift in his tone now, something serious beneath the playful setup that makes me pay closer attention.

"It was terrible," he continues. "I made it three blocks from home and I realized, I've completely failed here. I don't think there's any way you could possibly know."

"Know what?"

"How much I love you."

I laugh, because of course I do. Once I finally got to the point of admitting it, it became the clearest view. The shift from the black and white days of Kansas, to the technicolor world of Oz. Even on the most normal of days, the ones that will be like any other, they aren't and they never have been. Most days being up before me, leaving six kisses across my face like a map for him to return home to. And every evening he does. So yes, I know how much he loves me. I know how much I love him. Because I didn't just fall in love with him, I fell in love with myself when I was with him. Not through his eyes, but my own.

His presence wasn't a mirror, but the way light refracts through glass, revealing colors I'd forgotten were there. In those moments together, I discovered corners of myself that had been waiting quietly in shadow. It wasn't that he showed me who I could be, rather, being with him created a space where I finally recognized who I'd been all along. I didn't need his validation to know my worth, instead, his presence somehow gave me permission to acknowledge what had always been true: I was someone worth knowing, worth being, worth loving. Not because he thought so, but because I finally allowed myself to see it.

But mostly, I know it because even in the moments of painful quiet, when we're both lost in our own thoughts, there's something steady in the air between us. A frequency only we can hear. His love isn't just in the grand gestures or the impassioned speeches. It's in the silences. In the spaces between words. Even in our deepest thoughts, our heaviest moments, there is no silence that would ever make me doubt that again. Because loving each other isn't something we just do, it's something we are.

It's such a Will thing to build up to. The idea that I might not know.

"Will, I know you love me." I lean in for a kiss that he deliberately dodges with a slight smile.

"No, Arden. How *much* I love you. You don't. You couldn't possibly. Because it is not possible. And while you of all people could do impossible things..."

For all the places I thought my life would change, I never imagined it would be in our bathroom, but that seems to be our place. Not in the bathroom of a loud bar, and certainly not while I'm naked with my hair dripping onto his rolled-up sleeves. Making the white cotton more translucent to reveal the hidden parts of his tattoos. But the realization that I'm wrong about this, like I've been wrong about so many things when it comes to Will, washes over me along with the lingering bubbles.

"Do you know how much I love you?" he asks, still not looking at me, instead watching his fingers create ripples in the water. His eyes do this sometimes, dancing around the point he's trying to make, like his brain is moving faster than his mouth can keep up with. But they always find their way back to me eventually.

"I think so..." I try again for that kiss, but he shakes his head with a smile that suggests I've walked right into whatever trap he's laying.

"See, that's where I've failed." His fingers continually creating absent patterns in the water. "Because you don't. Then I realized, you couldn't. It's not possible." His eyes find mine, holding something more than my gaze.

"I've thought about it. It's immeasurable. It's math I can't comprehend, poetry I could never write, it's space, time, and all the things I never imagined. The problems of the universe I can't solve. And I don't need to measure it, I don't need to know how it works, I just need you to feel it. Like gravity."

I watch his face as the words fall between us, landing like droplets in the water around me and creating ripples against my skin.

"You need to feel it with every step. Knowing how immensely I love you. In a way that time will only amplify. Our lives and all the moments in them could hang on the walls of any museum. Framed in the most opulent gold for the world to revel at. And it still wouldn't be enough."

I might be completely nude, but as he sits there on our punny 'get naked' bath mat, his eyes are on mine in a way that makes me feel more exposed than my actual nakedness ever could. There's an intimacy in every word that strips away everything else.

Language really is a wild thing. We spend years learning words, how to string them together, how to make them dance. But in moments like this, they become something else entirely, they transform into feelings you can actually touch, like electricity in the air before a storm. The same words I've heard my entire life suddenly arrange themselves into a pattern I know I'll never be able to unhear.

I know what he's saying. It is incomprehensible because I feel it too, in a way I fought against for so long, keeping everything at arm's length. Convinced that slower meant safer, that careful meant protected. Too afraid of what it would mean, too scared we wouldn't get this moment, or worse, what would happen when we did. This happily ever after that's written across his face like the ending of a story I never thought I existed.

"I love you," he continues, his voice soft in the steam-hazed bathroom. "I *will* love you. I have known that I love you longer than makes any sense, and I will continue to love as long as you'll let me, and if the day comes that you decide you don't feel the same, I will love you even beyond that. Let's live our life together, darling. However we want. Please."

Our life. The two words emerge like a prayer to something greater than either one of us. Maybe to just that, a prayer to *our life.* The one we have been building with each shared grocery list. Every time our heads hit adjacent pillows and it's not close enough. The one where we decided unequivocally, whatever life we will have, will be of our choosing.

That last word 'please' lingers in the moisture-laden air like a held breath. It holds everything we've ever been and everything we could become. Every late night conversation, every shared dream, every moment of doubt transformed into certainty. A lifetime of possibilities wrapped in a single syllable, waiting for my answer.

His free hand appears between us, holding out a ring that

catches the bathroom light like it's been waiting for this moment. I laugh, not because it's funny, but because what else do you do when the man you fought so hard against loving proves yet again why fighting was pointless? That he *was* right. And this very well may be the story we tell our kids one day.

This man who never tried to capture my light for himself or dim it for his comfort, who never tried to fix me or put me back together because he never saw me as broken in the first place

"You really want to marry me?"

"Immeasurably," he says. "But I'm *asking* you."

"Immeasurably," I echo, and it's the truest thing I've ever said.

He slips the ring on my finger and finally, finally grants me that kiss I've been chasing. It's not one diamond, but many small rectangular ones lined up like books on a shelf, he explains. Wrapping all the way around the band. *For our story.* Not your typical engagement ring, but there has never been anything typical about Will Sterling, and for the rest of my life, I hope there never is.

He stands, and strips himself of his work clothes before joining me in our much-too-small-for-two-people tub. The water sloshes dangerously close to the edge as he settles behind me, pulling me back against his chest.

"What about your big lecture, dinner?" I ask suddenly, wondering how much time we have to exist before we have to leave this.

"I had a different plan," he says as his body takes shape around me, "but this was the moment."

His arms wrap around me like they were designed for exactly this purpose, one braced under my breasts with his thumb stroking my ribs, the other resting across my collarbones, his palm warm against my shoulder. The way I fit here, have always fit here, makes sense when nothing else has.

"You're going to be my wife," he says it like he's testing out the words.

"You're going to be my husband," I counter, and feel him smile against my shoulder.

"Nothing matters beyond that. Not now, not ever."

"It's that easy, huh?" I whisper, not as much a question as my tone implies, but the revelation he has made so clear.

"Loving you is the easiest thing in the world. Easy as breathing. Even when it's not, and I might forget how, my body remembers."

Chapter Forty

HAPPILY EVER DURING

Arden

"Professor Sterling, your wife is here." The student aide's voice has that particular blend of collegiate enthusiasm and sleep deprivation that feels like looking into a time capsule. 'I know you,' I think.

She can't be much more than nineteen, all bright eyes and university sweatshirt and the kind of confidence that only comes before life has taught you the meaning of consequences. *Poor thing.*

Watching her scurry back to her desk clutching a coffee. I remember being her, clutching my own certainties like talismans. There might have been a time I'd do anything to go back to that blissful ignorance and bravery of collegiate negligence, but there's something about cresting that wave that makes the years that follow that much more rewarding. The way life takes your carefully plotted course and turns it into something entirely different, but somehow better than you could have planned. Perhaps because it wasn't the plan at all.

The aide keeps stealing glances at me from behind her laptop, and I know that look. I've seen variations of it since Will started teaching here, the whispered conversations that stop when he walks by, the suspicious spike in attendance during his office hours, the way his Rate My Professor page has more heart emojis than actual reviews. *Of course I check.* I've even printed some of them out to stick on the fridge.

Will became an adjunct professor three years ago, after trading in that shiny name and all its weighted expectations. It wasn't a straight line from the museum hall to lecture hall, there were pivots and uncertainties, moments of doubt that turned into opportunities. Working with the museum's education program started as a side project, something he loved but didn't think could be a career. Until it was. Until teaching became professing, and suddenly he was exactly where he needed to be.

His classes are always waitlisted, something he attributes to his 'engaging curriculum' refusing to admit any of it has to do with the fact that they most definitely call him the hot-professor. *I would— and sometimes do.*

His office door is propped open with a bronze bust and I can hear him humming behind it. The space beyond is just him exploding into room form. The stack of papers to grade, *because he prefers to print them out,* isn't daunting to him at all. He says there's something meditative about marking papers by hand.

He always looks at me like something he hoped for but wasn't expecting.

"You're here just in time to dismantle one of my lectures if you want to join." he says. Wouldn't be the first time I *'class-crashed'* as he called it. Turned into such a heated discussion on the intersection of commerce and Renaissance art that his students still talk about it, apparently.

"I'm sure there's someone else who can carry that torch," I reply, perching on the edge of his desk.

"None like you...though there is this one sophomore who reminds me of you, he keeps challenging my interpretations of Caravaggio's economic influences."

"Sounds like you need better interpretations."

"Sounds like I need to stop letting you lend my students business books."

I look around his office, at the life he's built here. The collection of student thank-you notes pinned to a cork board. Our wedding photo sits on his desk, right next to one from a karaoke night many chapters ago, both of us younger, slightly drunk, infinitely happy. So in love before we ever admitted it.

"I have news," I say, and watch his expression shift to attentive.

"Good news or champagne news?"

"Good. I think. *Scary-good.*" I take a deep breath, feeling the weight of the decision I've already made. It wont come as a huge surprise to him, given that we spent months talking and planning for it. But, now that it's done, I came running to tell him.

"I quit my job today. Officially starting my own firm." And he's on his feet and I'm in his arms.

"You're going to be amazing. Terrifying, incredible, but amazing." His hands cradle my face, "I'm so proud of you. Tell me everything."

"You've heard it!" And he has, of course he has, because there isn't a step in this life that we don't take together.

"I want to hear it again." So I tell him everything, *again*. I can focus less on corporate ladder-climbing, and more on actual impact. I climbed the ladder I had been so desperate to, but eventually found that the accounts and people I liked working with most weren't the corporate behemoths, but the smaller ones actually pushing boundaries, not just profit margins.

My younger self would never believe this is where we'd end up. Walking away from the office and the titles I'd fought so hard to reach. But that version of me, the one who thought success only looked one way, didn't know what I know now. That *up* isn't the only option for movement. Even the version of me from a few years ago, the one winning pitched battles in boardrooms and chasing promotions like they were oxygen, would be proud.

What's that song? Yo-ho, yo-ho, start-up life for me? Maybe

that's just about pirates. Either way, there's something about walking away from the safe path, about choosing the uncertain adventure over the guaranteed success. Will has done it time and time again, each pivot bringing him closer to who he really is. *Now it's my turn.*

"I have a class in ten minutes. Want to stay and help me scandalize the students with tales of corporate influence on contemporary creative expression?"

"Tempting, but not this time."

He kisses me quickly, aware of the open door and potentially lurking students, but as usual unbothered and unapologetic about how loudly he loves me.

"Go forth and conquer, darling."

It's funny to be back on campus, funnier still that this is the second time in our lives we've been here simultaneously. The first time, of course we were strangers. Now it's his career, and my re-established access to the libraries because of him.

I pass groups of students lounging on the lawn, their entire futures spread out before them. I remember being them, so certain of my path, never imagining I'd end up here, happier than any of my carefully planned futures could have made me.

Chapter Forty-One

HAPPILY EVER DURING

Arden

Somewhere along our skipping down the yellow brick road, and singing *goodbye* to it, our lives evolved without us knowing. Time began spiraling around us like a Kansas tornado, the narrow base widening up to the heavens like the vastness of our lives was only expanding.

The emerald city gleamed different shades of green as the years passed, sometimes brilliant and full of promise, other times muted by storm clouds of reality. Some people staying to walk beside us, others taking different paths through their own poppy fields.

The wicked witches weren't always cackling, sometimes they wore white coats and other times old arguments and expectations roaring their same heads. But my ruby slippers have carried me farther than I ever thought possible, with Will being my home that was there all along.

Chapter Forty-Two

HAPPILY EVER DURING

Will

My phone vibrates against the kitchen counter for the third time tonight, the screen lighting up with 'Dad' in harsh letters. I watch it move across the granite like some kind of technological poltergeist before hitting decline, again. Arden's eyes follow the motion from where she's stirring risotto at the stove, but she doesn't say anything.

We've perfected this over the last few years, the careful navigation of family events, the polite nods across crowded museum galas where my parents' names still grace the donor wall in ironic gold letters. The way my mother cornered me last spring behind a Degas sculpture to show me pictures of Alfie's new baby, her voice careful and measured as she mentioned how we should come back to the Newport house for a visit. Arden and I sent a carefully selected baby gift, a peace offering wrapped in tissue paper and possibility.

The thing about making the choices I did, when I did, was that it was never just about my career. To them, it was about control. It was about disappointing an entire legacy of men I never knew for a birthright that was only mine to the benefit of the boardroom. My father likes to remind me that there's still an empty office waiting for me, as if the years peppered with silence can be erased by the promise of a corner view.

The idea of returning to their home court advantage always fills me with a great deal of unease. But even during the happiest of times, the most blissful undisruptable moments, my father has managed to color them with disappointment.

'You have a wife to think about now,' he'd said, swirling his glass in the dim light.

'The museum has been a nice hobby, but it's time to think about real success.'

Arden's voice breaks me out of the memory and calls me back to the present for dinner.

"The risotto is almost ready," she says now, her voice gentle in that way that tells me she's giving me an out from whatever conversation I'm having in my head. The declined invitations, the terse exchanges at charity events, the holiday cards sent with carefully worded notes that never quite bridge the gap, and don't intend to.

"Can you grab a bottle of wine?" she asks, taking two wine glasses from the cabinet and handing them to me.

"Anything particular?"

"Hmm, what do you think goes well with mushroom risotto *and* avoiding difficult conversations?"

And there it is, her uncanny ability to call your bullshit with devastating accuracy.

"Definitely a red." I say. "But I thought we weren't talking about it." My hands pull the cork from the bottle with perhaps more force than necessary.

"*We're* not. But you were clearly talking about it in your own head, so I figured, might as well let me in on the conversation. We've been not *not* talking about it for a while now. We're existing in this weird quantum state of talking-not-talking where I pretend, *poorly*, that I don't notice you declining calls from your family at a higher frequency than ever before, and you pretend not to notice me noticing."

"Schrödinger's family drama?"

"Exactly." She accepts the glass of wine I hand her, her fingers brushing mine in that intentional way she has, like every point of contact between us is worth savoring. "Though I think the cat's definitely alive in this scenario, and it's getting pretty loud in that box."

"He made his choice," I say, the words familiar and bitter on my tongue.

"Actually, you both made choices. He chose to give you an ultimatum, and you chose not to take it. And now, they are making a choice to change things, and you are the one choosing to keep this distance."

"You sound like you're on his side." It comes out sharper than I intend, and I immediately want to take it back.

"I'm on the side of not watching my husband flinch every time his phone rings. I'm on the side of maybe not spending another holiday pretending that your family doesn't exist. I'm on the side of you being happy, Will. Always. Of course I'm on your side, but here in our home? I can also tell you that I think you are being stubborn about something that life gives you a finite amount of time to resolve."

His heart attack had been mild, all things considered. The doctors called it a warning shot, the kind that leaves you alive but just more aware of mortality. Dad recovered quickly, was back to pacing the office within weeks, but we all knew this was the real reason behind everything else. Men like him spend their whole lives fortifying their hearts against anyone's ability to penetrate them. Feeling a false sense of security behind an organ of stoicism and duty.

It's funny how nature has its ways of making metaphors manifest, these proud, strong men, taken down not by any external force, but by their own hearts demanding to finally be heard.

Cal called me from the hospital that night, his voice carrying that strange mix of efficiency and fear that comes with medical emergencies. I sat in our kitchen, phone pressed to my ear, while Arden's hand found mine under the table. The same table where we now sit, having variations of the same conversation we've been having since that night. Not about forgiveness exactly, that's too simple a word for what lies between us, but about time, and its finite nature, and what we choose to do with it.

"They don't understand our life, I've made a conscious effort to not let them infect it." I say finally.

"They don't need to understand something to respect it," she says, tearing off a piece of the french bread and popping it into her mouth, always powered by carbohydrates.

"When did you get so wise?".

"Therapy." She steals a bite from my plate, despite having her own perfectly full serving.

Thanksgiving will take place at the Newport house. Sprawling with views of the ocean, where summer memories are stored in every corner. A place I fell in love with so much, with history, had my first kiss, a place where so many pivotal moments occurred for me. My brothers and I used to race through the halls, my mother hosted parties that made the society pages of a different era, and where the library still holds the art books I used to read while Alfie and Cal played water polo in the pool. Now, Alfie's kids have their own rooms, holidays happen there without us, and while we still get the annual invitations in the mail, we haven't attended in years.

I think one day our children will also have rooms there, but as I learned, when you let yourself dream beneath someone else's roof, it's easy to surrender them to their architecture. Your infinite possibilities are reshaped to fit into rooms already built. Your wings clipped to not escape through someone else's windows.

And yet... she's right. *Of course she is.*

"It's not forgiveness I'm struggling with," I admit. "It's that I know the second we walk through the doors it will be an ambush. No matter how much we want to pretend it isn't."

Arden's hand finds mine. "Then we run away. Anywhere you want to go. But we'll never know if anything's changed if we don't give them a chance to show us. Even if that means a potentially awkward family Thanksgiving where your father will definitely comment on my career choices and your mother will absolutely make at least one passive-aggressive remark about the museum's endowment fund and how her name is no longer the gala headliner."

Arden's career has become one of the safer harbors in conversation with my father. He tracks her successes like a harbormaster tracking ships, noting each promotion, each victory as she navigated the corporate seas. Until she surprised everyone, except me, by jumping from the big ship and starting to steer her own. Maybe because in her, he sees the kind of ambition he always wanted for me, though hers burns differently. When she officially opened her own firm, he sent a bottle of champagne to her office. The same vintage he opened when I graduated from college, though I doubt he remembers that detail.

Sometimes I catch him watching her at charity functions, as she navigates rooms full of potential investors with charm, and in some ways the fact that she took his name is a sense of pride he would never admit, but counts as a silver coin in his bank all the same.

"God, why do you want to subject yourself to this?"

She's quiet for a moment, thoughtful in that way that usually precedes something profound.

"Because I chose to become a Sterling, which means I'm involved. And if anything, it's been years since we've been in that wine cellar."

I recall what it was like meeting her parents. It hit me like that Miami heat when we stepped off the plane, all-encompassing, impossible to hide from. They didn't treat love like a limited resource, didn't measure it out in careful spoonfuls or check the levels like it might run dry. That weekend, watching them move around their home, finishing each other's stories with shared narration, and sliding past each other in practiced dance steps, I realized I'd been reading love in a foreign language my whole life. The way they folded me into their life, no questions asked, no permissions needed.

She's like them in so many ways, and in so many others she's this incredible distinct blend of existence. Sharing that when she was younger, she struggled with some of the same ideas of familial expectations, only to discover their only expectations of her were those that she had set for herself.

I watch her pull her bottom lip between her teeth, the plumpness of her lips due to the depth of the red wine. I look at my wife, this woman who believes in second chances and the importance of choosing happiness over expectations. Who would walk into the Sterling family lion's den with me, armed with nothing but each other knowing that would be enough.

"If we do this," I say slowly, "we do it on our terms."

"The only terms I like," she affirms with that fierce protectiveness I've come to rely on, nodding vigorously enough that her curls bounce.

"We leave if it gets uncomfortable." My voice comes out firmer now, finding its footing.

"We'll run anywhere you want to go," she promises softly, reaching across to still my fidgeting hands with hers.

"We don't stay at their house." I list each condition like I'm building a wall, brick by careful brick.

"There's that great boutique hotel in town we've always talked about!"

"And you have to promise to run interference if my father starts talking about profit margins."

"One of my favorite topics!"

"Okay." I say through a sigh, letting my shoulders drop. It's not defeat. I know I could hold the line, and she would be right there with me, standing guard against the past.

"You don't have to decide right now," her voice is gentle but sure, like she's leading me through a dark room. "But maybe... maybe it's time to stop declining the call and see what happens when you answer."

I finally take a bite of the risotto in front of me. It's gone cold. But like most things, it can be reheated.

Chapter Forty-Three

HAPPILY EVER DURING

Arden

We're standing on different sides of a room so carefully designed that even our places in it feel predetermined. Everything here screams careful curation from the hand painted wallpaper to the antique Persian rug. The numerous throw pillows on the king sized bed between us seem to mock the distance they create, each one a small fortress in what has always been a place we can connect easily.

Now it's bearing witness to the single worst fight of our married lives. In the same house we ran from years ago. Some of the original cast of characters returning for this encore performance.

"The last thing I need is for these people to know that this..." I gesture between us, the space feeling wider with each word, "is something they can actually impact."

I inject the words with more venom than I mean to, but we so rarely find ourselves across this gaping crater of views that I don't know how else to bridge it except with anger. The tears threatening to spill feel like betrayal.

"These people? These people are family. I never see them but you pushed me to come, and now you're mad..." His hands run through his hair trying to keep his composure. "I don't even know what you're mad about!" he bursts out, frustration breaking through. *And I hate that neither do I.*

It became one of those arguments that manifested out of nothing more than a tense situation and suddenly you're looking at the only person who can absorb every sharp edge you possess, every jagged piece of yourself you wish you could file smooth. The fight started over something real, his family's subtle digs, my pushing too hard for this visit, but somewhere along the way it morphed into this ugly thing.

The worst part? I see it happening. I watch myself say things I know will hurt him, watch him flinch and return fire. The argument loses its original shape, becomes formless and mean, until we're just two people who love each other more than anything standing on opposite sides of a room, trying to hurt each other because we've hurt ourselves. Loving someone like this makes you both stronger and more vulnerable all at once. How the person who knows exactly how to hold you together also knows exactly where your seams are weakest.

The knock at the door adjusts our postures automatically, where we'd both bent over the bed between us. The love we normally found for each other in bed is lost now, replaced by the ugliness this house breeds.

We straighten at the intrusion as the door opens and his brother Cal, pops his head in. The tears running down my face are clearly visible, and I watch his judgment land there first, emotion being such a gauche thing, after all.

"Everything alright? We can hear you in the library," he asks with no care in his voice. And somehow it's all so much worse, not just that they can hear us, though I had hoped to prevent that at all costs. But that of all places, the room with the greatest stories of all, is hearing the ripples of this fight, like it will infect the printed pages with ugliness.

"It's fine," Will clips out, tension evident in every syllable, clearly trying to urge Cal along. Not wanting to allow anyone else access to this raw moment, not wanting himself exposed to people he quite literally has kept himself covered around.

"Things don't *seem* fine." Cal swings his head to me, not outright assigning blame but acknowledging that I must again be the presence that disrupts this household.

"It's been a stressful week," Will says, sobering in the presence of his family in a way only years of experience could perfect.

"Don't let a lovers quarrel ruin a perfectly good evening, dad is waiting for you." Cal turns to leave but it's the bite in Will's delivery that halts him in the doorway.

"For fucks sake." Something raw breaking through his careful facade. "She's not my lover, Cal, she's my *wife*. And he can keep waiting."

As Cal exits, so do I, pausing before I've fully retreated into the bathroom to hide.

"I'm not going to dinner. I'll see you when you're back. Apologize for me."

"There's no part of you I need to apologize for."

I shut the bathroom door behind me, turning the knob of the bathtub faucet and tossing in some of the spa products that never get any used in this guest room. Wasted like so much else in this house.

The water begins to fill, turning it to scolding. The aroma overwhelms the room as I step out of my clothes, leaving them puddled by the claw foot of the tub. I sink down into a bath as I have countless times before when I need an escape. *No one can tell if you're crying underwater.*

I can feel the footsteps in the bedroom adjacent where I've just left my husband standing mid-argument. No. Not mid. His brother's intrusion ended it. And I hear the echo of the door shut as it reverberates through the water. Finally breaking the surface and taking a breath.

I don't know how long I soak. Four full drains and refills. Full prune. And one more total sob. Each time I empty and refill the tub, I think about the first time we came here as a couple, how terribly that went. But I was naive in thinking things had changed.

It's the soft knock on the door, as it slowly opens, that pulls me from my memories. The man standing there is very different from the one I left standing on the other side of it. His eyes remain bloodshot, but it's not alcohol causing it now, the tears are as evident as mine. He hangs a white fluffy robe on the back of the door, bringing it in as a gesture. An offering. But clearly the least important one he has.

"How was dinner?" I ask flatly, devoid of any real interest.

"Arden." He breathes my name like a confession containing whole paragraphs of an apology that follow it, as he drops down to his knees by the side of the bath.

"Never again."

His forearms rest on the rim of the tub, his head hanging towards his chest. Looking more hungover from the emotional turmoil than the alcohol he was drunk on not that long ago.

"Same team," he says, scanning my face. "We won't do this. I'm never going to put you in a position like this again. Ever again. I'm sorry. I let the situation get the better of me... Being with these people... The stress of it....I'm sorry."

"I don't want that at the expense of your family. I feel awful. And you looked at me like I was awful. Like I am who they think I am. The one who took you from them." The words catch in my throat, old fears rising to the surface like the bubbles in the bath.

"You could never take me from my family," he declares with quiet certainty. "*You* are my family." His hand finds mine under the water, our fingers interlacing automatically.

"How was dinner?" I ask again, needing to know what story they're telling about us now.

"I didn't go. I went for a run. I cleared my head. And have been sitting outside the bathroom door for the last hour." The admission makes my heart clench. I picture him there, leaning against the door, listening to the water drain and refill, waiting for the right moment.

He pulls the plug from the drain and I watch as his eyes follow the spiral water spout emptying the tub. I lean forward towards the wall of the tub, not to be wholly exposed as the bath empties. While the water might be transparent, it feels safer somehow.

He pulls the robe from the door and I stand in the bath as he wraps it around me. He tightens the tie around my waist and leans down slightly, heaving me into his arms. I'm bundled and warm. I'm where I belong nestled against him. Though an hour ago I couldn't fathom this.

He kisses me, with apology. The one he just verbalized. And holds me tight against him wrapped in the thickness of the terrycloth robe.

"Never again" he whispers to himself as much as to me, as he carries me the ten paces to the bedroom. Setting me down atop it and curling his body around mine.

"I love you. Nothing matters beyond that. Not now, not ever. I'm sorry I let myself forget that. It's you and me on this team, no one else."

Chapter Forty-Four

HAPPILY EVER DURING

Arden

There's something electric about wanting someone you already have. It should be impossibly mundane, the way his fingers curl around a wine glass, how his collar sits slightly askew, the familiar curve of his smile when he catches me looking. I've seen it all thousands of times before. But tonight, in the glow of the restaurant, surrounded by conversation and clinking glasses, the laughter of our friends, I'm struck by the same lightning that hit me years ago.

Our friends are deep in conversation about their latest home renovation disaster, but all I can focus on is the way he's looking at me across the table. His attention is a compass, always pointing to me, to the way his eyes hold me with a darkness that isn't about color, but about depth. About wanting and desire, the kind that makes my skin prickle with anticipation. He takes a deliberately slow sip of his wine, and I watch his throat work. The scruff that once defined his twenties has softened, grown more intentional, and I remember how it feels against the contours of my body.

We've gotten good at this. The subtle signals, the practiced timing. I excuse myself from the table with a casual mention of touching up my lipstick. Our friends barely pause their story about catastrophic wallpaper choices. As I walk away, I can feel his eyes following me, knowing without looking that he's already planning his exit strategy, probably an important call he *'has to take.'* We've always known how to run away to our own world.

The bathroom door barely closes before we collide. His lips pepper kisses up my skin in a frenetic way. The *I-couldn't-survive-another-second* kind of way. *I get it.* His lips are a fevered language against my skin, speaking desperate translations that require no words and my body responds in its own dialect, urgent, knowing that only he understands.

I frantically reach for his belt as his hands sink into my thighs. Pulling down my underwear and tucking them into his pocket. There was a time that might have been to satisfy a kink, now, after years together, I think it's more the courtesy of not leaving clean panties on the public bathroom floor.

He walks us backwards, and with his hands never leaving my waist, spins me toward the mirror.

"Is this what you wanted?" he whispers, and the words are both a question and a statement. His lips brush my ear, and I can hear the smile.

The *mmm-hmm* that slips from my lips as much a plea as it is involuntary. But this is who we are. We can be sitting at a table of a half dozen people, with numerous conversations, and yet no one hears the unspoken thing between us. No one sees the pulsing desperation between us. And we just sneak off to find ourselves a pocket of passion amidst the banality of the rest of life. Though I often wonder if our friends know the truth. That sometimes, we are exactly who we were that first night. And we chose not to deny ourselves anything. At least not from each other in moments of outright pleasure

We move together with the practiced ease of two people who have spent years learning each other's rhythms. The mirror reflects us, not just our bodies, but the way we see each other when no one else is watching.

And that's exactly how we got here. Where he has me braced forward over the sink as my hands leave their grip on the porcelain sides.

My head hangs down, unable to bear the weight of itself on my neck, instead rolling from side to side with the sensation of him. His body bent over mine. His body *in* mine. He drags his teeth across my shoulder, up to my ear as he pulls out and thrusts deep within me again.

Our friends are outside. There is an entire restaurant outside. But when he looked at me tonight, there was no world where I could have waited to have him. And the look on his face told me he agreed, as he always does. His hand wraps around my neck, not as a domination, but as stability.

"Let's make a baby," he says, and suddenly the entire world narrows to this moment.

My response is half laugh, half gasp.

"Now?" We're perpetually on the edge of propriety, on the edge of orgasm, chasing life changing decisions in a bathroom.

But that's always been us.

He drapes his body over me, and wraps his arms around me tightly. Not disconnecting us where it matters, us both teetering on the edge as he holds me, and whispers, "Whenever you're ready."

"We can't make a baby in this bathroom, so tonight you'll have to settle for just making me come."

I say as his hand slips between my legs, increasing the pleasure only I can feel as his body drives home the rest of it.

"Darling," he says, his other hand gripping on my jaw, straightening it forward to capture our shared gaze in the reflection, "there is nothing about you that could ever be settling," his breath is labored, meaning he is ready to dive head first into orgasm with me. He picks up his pace, and I tighten in his arms. His moans heighten, and I slap my hand behind me to capture the sounds ready to escape him.

I keep him tightly inside of me as we both finish. Knowing we have limited time before we have to return to the casual conversation of dinner and everyone can pretend that we aren't both glistening in a new layer of sweat.

But before we sneak back into the version of our life for public consumption, I am curious how serious he is. The probability I conceived a child on this day, in this bathroom, isn't likely. Considering I've been on the pill since I was eighteen. But the thrill of knowing what primal intention he had in that moment, was surprising. Some psychological wiring circuited in my brain when he said it. Not because I am or have ever been baby crazed, never one of those people who had baby fever, but somehow, I have always seen a family with *him*.

I'm fixing my hair in the mirror when he wraps his arms around my waist from behind, resting his chin on my shoulder.

"You really want to start our family in a public bathroom?" I tease, watching his reflection smile back at me.

"We started our family in a public bathroom years ago," he says softly, tucking a strand of hair behind my ear. "I want to grow it."

Maybe I've seen a family with him, because for longer than I ever realized, he has been my family.

"You know," I muse, reaching back to straighten his collar, our bodies swaying slightly together, "most people have these conversations somewhere a little more sensible."

He laughs, the sound rumbling through both our bodies as he presses a kiss to my temple. "When have *we* ever been sensible?"

"Fair point." I smooth my dress, checking my reflection one final time. "Think they know?"

"That we just had a life changing conversation in a bathroom?" he whispers conspiratorially. "Probably not." He opens the door, gesturing for me to go first. "That we snuck away for a quickie?" He opens the door with a flourish, gesturing for me to go first. "Almost definitely."

We make our way back to the table, where our friends are now debating the merits of various countertop materials. They barely acknowledge our return, though I catch Amanda hiding a knowing smile behind her wine glass.

I settle back into my seat, the weight of our conversation sitting warm in my chest. His hand finds mine under the table, thumb running across my knuckles. It's strange how a single moment can shift everything and nothing at all. The world keeps spinning, our friends keep talking, the wine keeps flowing. But somewhere along the way, we made a decision far bigger than what we would order for dessert.

Chapter Forty-Five

HAPPILY EVER DURING

Arden

I wake to cold sheets and the familiar absence beside me. I have no doubt he scattered kisses across my face before he left, but I've been sleeping just a little bit deeper in a way I don't always stir when he leaves.

Those kisses each morning took root in the early years of our lives, not delicate seeds requiring tender care, but ancient acorns buried deep in fertile soil, destined to rise as oaks whose branches would shelter all generations in their steadiness. Within them all the power of patient, inevitable becoming.

Through our bedroom window, dawn is just starting to crack open the sky like a fresh egg, spreading its golden yolk across the horizon. Will's running shoes are missing from their usual spot by the door. Some things you can set your watch by: taxes, death, and Will Sterling's morning run. *Though now he drags Titian with him. Though I am unconvinced the dog goes for any reason more than a pup-cup at the end of it.*

I roll over, watching the early morning shadows painted across our ceiling, thinking about the small white stick hiding in my purse. *Actually, several boxes.* I bought them yesterday three neighborhoods away, because this may be a city, but it's also the kind of place where you always run into someone you know at the worst possible moment and I didn't want the usual cashier to give me that kind of face next month when I showed up to buy tampons instead of prenatal vitamins.

Instead, the unknown cashier just gave me that knowing look, that made me feel like I was a teen-mom not a grown-adult-woman pretending to be fascinated by the gum display. There's something strange about the fact that even though sex might be the most natural thing on the planet to do, having someone see me buy a pregnancy test, *or the shelf of them*, feels more vulnerable than them seeing me by Plan B. *For which I never went to a different neighborhood.*

What started out as a *'whatever happens, happens,'* situation when we decided to stop trying *not to*, eventually became a bit more methodical. We had wanted to avoid it as long as possible with the fear that introducing more regimen to our sex life would be pressure. Instead ending up with the kind of casual approach that actually requires tremendous effort to maintain. Like when he catches me reading parenting books or when I catch him lingering a little too long in front of the window display at that baby boutique in Beacon Hill. The benefit to not-really-trying meant that we also weren't really failing. It wasn't until one night a few months ago we were laying in tangled sheets as his fingers twirled around my belly button. Us both staring up at the same ceiling fan with the painful dichotomy of being wholly completely content but also wanting more.

For all important moments of my life, I prepared. So, for this, I would also prepare. It was then, I pulled out my phone and marked the date to begin tracking. Will simply rolled over in silent understanding, pressed his lips to mine, and whispered, *'same team.'*

Now, the thing about being married to a runner is that you

learn their rhythms, their routes, the way they mark time in foot-falls and miles. Six miles along the Charles, regardless of weather or season or how late we stayed up the night before watching *'just one more episode'* of whatever show we're binging, or what book ending he has to comfort me through.

I swing my legs over the side of the bed, my bare feet meeting the cool hardwood. The pregnancy test feels like it's screaming at me, a Chekhov's gun waiting to go off in the first act of whatever play we're about to start. Or maybe worse, a red herring of hope.

In the bathroom, I go through the motions of my morning routine on autopilot, everything but peeing of course, because I'd read it's more effective when it's the first pee of the morning. Which is why it stayed hidden until now. It's not that it's contraband, but more the idea that just knowing it was there, Will would want to be here, as he has been for so many negatives.

Three minutes that feel like three years.

I set the test on the counter and decide I'm just going to go ahead and add another layer of skin serum to keep my hands busy rather than pace in what suddenly feels like a space that's too small, too warm, too everything. I think about Will, probably hitting his stride right about now, his feet carrying him past the universities, past the boathouses. I wonder if he can feel it, this moment happening miles away, the way I swear I can sometimes feel when he's about to call before my phone even rings.

Two minutes.

I think about how we met. More than once. But eventually at the right time.

One minute.

I think about our apartment, how the extra bedroom is currently part home office, part book hoarders dream, but could be... something else. We'd talked about it. How this would work for a time longer. How the morning fills the space and how it has its own bathroom that would be perfect for...

The timer on my phone chimes and I wish he was here.

I check his location, right on track, making the loop home, meaning he's only about a mile away.

Suddenly I'm moving, pulling on the first clothes I can find. Will's old college sweatshirt, a pair of leggings, running shoes I bought with good intentions but mainly use for errands. As I start frantically doing SAT level math in my head.

Let's see… if he's just a mile from home, and on average runs a seven minute mile, I am one mile from him, and can run… my mouth.

Ugh not helpful Arden.

Okay okay.

I can probably run a thirteen minute mile if I'm lucky. But then again, he's already running, so… *back to SAT math.*

I'm shoving my foot in a shoe and tripping out the door with nothing but my phone and a stick, *though capped,* suspiciously covered in pee.

Let's see, if Person A is running at a speed of 7 minutes per mile. And Person B is running at a speed of 13 minutes per mile. They are one mile apart. How soon will they meet in the middle. Lowest common denominator… seven and thirteen… is… ninety-one…

I'm stumbling down the street, not so much a run, not in any coordinated effort, though I'm surprised no one has stopped me to make sure I'm okay. *Which obviously I am not.*

So, our combined speed is… 20 over 91 miles-per-minute. Whatever the fuck that actually means. Time is the distance of combined speed… so… one mile over 20/91 miles-per-minute. Which would be one times 91/20… what is that… four minutes and… who the fuck cares.

I know his route by heart, could probably run it backwards in my sleep, *or at least, walk it.* Out the door, down our street where the cherry trees are just starting to bloom, past the coffee shop where I sneak out to sometimes meet him and wait for him on the course. The air hits my face, cool and sharp, filling my lungs as I start to run.

I'm not really a runner. *Not literally.* Only in the ways Will and I run away together, and that is rarely on foot. Despite the occasions when I need to expel energy and we just take off down the path as fast as possible. But this isn't that.

Somewhere ahead of me, Will is running, probably lost in whatever podcast he's listening to.

I scan the path ahead, looking for the back of him. Will runs, like he does everything else, with a kind of effortless grace that makes me both envious and hopelessly fond. I'd know his stride anywhere, the way I'd know his laugh in a crowded room or his footsteps coming to bed.

My lungs are burning now. *God, how does he do this every morning?* I've only been running for a couple minutes and I'm already questioning every life choice that led me here. But then I see him, his form silhouetted against the morning sky.

"Will!" My voice comes out embarrassingly breathless. A couple of other runners turn to look, but not him, his earbuds probably drowning out everything else.

I push harder, ignoring the protest in my muscles. "William Sterling!"

Nothing.

"TITIAN!" The name bounces across the path as our black-and-white collie freezes mid-stride, nearly taking Will down with him. The leash goes taut and he whips around at my voice, dragging Will with him as he bounds back toward me. Will's face morphs from confusion to surprise, finally giving way to concern as he sees me running toward him. He pulls out his airpods, already moving in my direction faster than imaginable.

I crash into him, Titian jumping at my side. My momentum carries us all a few stumbling steps but he doesn't let us fall. His hands come up to steady me automatically, and he's warm and solid against me.

"Arden, what's wrong?" His hands are on me frantically. Holding my face in fear as I catch my breath.

He's glistening in sweat, so am I, as he brushes the hair from my eyes and tilts my face up to his for a better assessment.

"Are you okay? What's going on?" He tries again. But as we take breaths long enough to fill out lungs something on my face relaxes him.

"I'm fine," I manage between gasps. "Everything's fine. I mean... my math skills aren't what they used to be..." He looks at me more perplexed. "I just—" I look up at him, at his worried face, at the way the rising sun is turning his hair to gold at the edges, maybe even catching a single strand of silver, and suddenly I'm laughing as I seem to in all the most important moments of our life.

"Arden?" His hands cup my face, thumbs wiping at tears I didn't even realize were falling. "You're scaring me, darling."

"I just couldn't wait until you got home. I needed to find you."

"You never need to find me. Call me, and I will come home, to wherever you are." He says as a promise.

"I'm pregnant—"

His kiss cuts me off, tasting of salt and joy and morning air. When he pulls back, he's crying too, or maybe still laughing, his smile so bright it rivals the sunrise. Right there on the running path, with people streaming past and the whole city waking up around us. I saw the sun rise in his eyes and I realized the longer I stared, it was me. And for him, nothing would ever eclipse that.

The words spread into my chest like warm honey, sweet and golden and perfect. I hadn't given myself a moment to feel them before needing to share them.

"Oh god." I look down at my hand, still clutching the test. "I just ran through Boston carrying my own pee stick... Chapter One of the baby book... *'How Your Mother Lost All Dignity Before You Were Even the Size of a Poppy Seed'.*"

He laughs and stares confirming the same thing I did. "I can hold on to that for us." Slipping it into his pocket for safe keeping. I half expect him to label it and drop it in the canister with all the champagne corks we've collected.

We start the float home, not quite walking, but moving all the same. Carried by something much more than our feet.

"Hey Will?" I say, turning to face him. "Same team?"

"Same team. All three of us."

Chapter Forty-Six

HAPPILY EVER DURING

Arden

"What's a better word for cock? And please don't say 'member' again." Heads turn from all corners of the coffee shop and converge right on our table, not clearly as tucked away and remote as we thought.

"First of all, I have absolutely never said 'member,' and second, you do realize we're still in public, right?"

"And when has that ever stopped you?"

Both are rhetorical questions. Mine, because we have been at this same table nearly every Sunday for months as Amanda writes her seventh contemporary romance novel. Hers, because our friends have all us sneak off to find moments of sanctuary together regardless of crowds.

"Fine, Arden, you've never said member, but I'm not going to whisper the word cock when half the people in here have them." She shakes her head with a light laugh and looks back to her computer as she continues her original thought. "It's just that, I don't think she'd say cock when this scene is melancholy. Cock is just so aggressive, it's like COCKK." She says the word again, this time with additional emphasis on the harshness of the hard K.

The sound that bookends the word to prove her point, in turn earning a few extra glares in our direction.

"Is this the breakup scene?" I empty the rest of my mug, sipping down that end-of-cup-was-once- hot-coffee and sugar mixture.

"Yep! Breakup sex scene to be specific. It's more them accepting closure this time, but something isn't quite right yet. I need more perspective, preferably from a male point of view. And considering I can't go back to the source on this one and ask my ex..." She'd said she was most excited about this book, because it was inspired by her actual love story.

"I always welcome more inspiration if you want to share whatever's got your mind churning." Amanda tips her chin up and replies with a wink. She's not wrong; my mind is churning with the memory of Reid that I haven't thought about in years.

I was nineteen. We hadn't been together that long, but it was an important relationship for me, until he ended it one night after a few too many drinks and external influences pushed us to be the worst versions of ourselves. And at that point, he decided I was never going to be enough. Too young, too immature. And even though he granted me the one-last-time I asked for when I showed up at his door hoping he would take me back, we eventually moved on.

Reid had never been one to mince words, or hold back what he means. So after he dumped me, I never rehashed the breakup, or reminisced over our time together. No matter how long I spent thinking we would end up together. I never told him, terrified of what would have happened having him reject me a second time. Eventually, that thought became as distant as the person I was when I met him.

He had so much more impact on how I viewed love than I ever really admitted. Both in the good and bad. Making me feel both easy to love, and then not at all, was something it took time for me to unravel. And while for a time I skirted from relationship to relationship keeping them casual enough for him to come back,

I lived in a constant state of anticipation. Every relationship felt like holding a door open with trembling arms, waiting for him to walk through. I'd catch myself imagining the weight of his footsteps approaching that door I held open with such desperate hope. It terrified me how much power I gave him, how I'd built my romantic life around the possibility of his return, I measured every new connection against the ghost of what we had, keeping everyone at arm's length so they couldn't take up the space I was saving for him.

Eventually, I met someone who showed me all the ways loving someone is not a choice and all the ways it is. And Will has continued to choose me, and I him without question, ever since.

"I was just thinking about when I was dumped." I wince as I say it, because in your thirties, who would want to think about their college breakup? My early twenties were enough of that. "Aside from being the only time I've been broken up with, it's also my only reference for breakup sex. The rest of the time I was doing the dumping, and at that point the last thing I really wanted from any of them was sex. Reid is the only reference." I shrug.

"Don't hold back…"

"For starters, I spoke to him recently."

"Okay, now I'm even more curious!"

"It's far from what you think. He had something at work and was curious about an alternative approach. It's just something we've done on and off for years, reaching out for perspective on different projects. It's not a big deal."

"Not even to Will?" she asks clearly in disbelief. "You guys just chat without any of the old feelings burning through?"

"Nope, not even to Will. Those old feelings burnt out when we were children. He's engaged, there's nothing left in the space between us except friendship." I know so. They've even met once. I'm not sure who it was more clarifying for. Will had no doubt at the time, but I think walking away from it he could see that there was nothing left besides some old camaraderie and shared work-experiences.

"Okay, Amanda. I'll prove it. You want a male perspective on the breakup sex scene? I'll text him and ask Reid."

me: A friend of mine is writing a book, and it has a big plot point around breakup sex as closure. I offered you up as a male perspective on the topic about when you ended things between us! Hope you don't mind sharing your thoughts!

I don't have time to worry about a potential miscommunication over one too many exclamation points, and he doesn't read that much into anything. I set my phone back down on the table, ready to pick up a different conversation while we waited for his eventual reply. I used to obsess over just every comma and word. *Is my tone too much. Am I coming on too strong.* But not anymore, not considering our very full lives. I saw his engagement post six months ago, someone he works with, and he liked the recent photo of me sitting at the piano with a new puppy seated next to me on the bench, the one I captioned 'Barktoven.'"

Reid Jennings: Arden, what are you talking about when I ended things?

I drag my teeth across my bottom lip. Is he kidding? Trying to be avoidant? It's been years and while we have never actually talked about our breakup, surely he remembers it.

me: I know we're getting old, but try and remember 2008 ;)
I told her about how you dumped me when we were in college because I thought it would be helpful for her book
Reid Jennings: got that part, AB
Reid Jennings: but I didn't dump you

It's Amanda who finally breaks the silence, slowly closing her laptop. Forgoing her own writing in this moment exchanging it for the real life dramedy playing out in front of her.

"What are you texting back?"

"I-I'm not... I mean, I don't..."

Seriously, though. What did I just step into? Was it too bold to outright text him about our relationship, about our breakup, about our breakup sex? This was outside the bounds of our normal conversations, but I trusted him and the friendship we have built over the last 14 years. It was a friendship based on mutual respect and time. More than anything else, I respect myself, my marriage.

He drew clear lines around who we were post breakup, and I never crossed them. Never crying to him that I missed him, except almost once, and I never made that mistake again. Erasing all drafts of him I had saved so long ago I don't even remember what they once said.

Besides today's text which I shot off without too much fore-thought, he had texted me a few months ago looking for some advice about a potential acquisition of a small company.

Our careers sometimes overlapped. Had similar starts too, but eventually after feeling like I was in a rat race of men only to get a pat on the head, I left to focus on somewhere that I could define. Rather than climbing a ladder where everyone behind me was just trying to look up my skirt while beating me to the top.

I look between the phone and back to Amanda. My best friend was staring at me like she just struck romance novelist gold, her big brown eyes absolutely on fire with the possibility of what was about to play out in front of her.

"I don't really know what to text back to that. I don't even know what to think about that."

His initial response shocked me; his follow up paralyzed me. And now I am flooded with the doubt that bringing up our romantic relationship wasn't wise. We had never directly discussed it. We had never *indirectly* discussed it. Not until enough time had passed and we started more seriously dating other people, at which point we would casually throw out an inquiry, a litmus test to ensure our boundaries were still firmly in place. They always were.

We give it a few minutes, but his response never comes. *Yep, that's Reid.* So we move on to the next plot point until it's time to go.

"Same time next week?" Amanda asks as we both gather up our things to leave the coffee shop. The same people who were offended by the colorful language and explicit conversation are now leaping for our perfectly positioned table. *I always could pick a good seat.*

"You got it!" I kiss her cheek goodbye and grab a couple croissants to bring home with me, though they usually don't make it out of the car.

———

"Will?" I call out as I push open the door and drop my bag on our entryway bench—a flea market find that Will swears was 'liberated' from the university sometime in the 1960s.

"In here!" He responds from the kitchen, and I follow his voice through our gentle maze. And there he is, standing over our kitchen sink, hands slightly soapy, wearing a university sweatshirt we both would have sported when we were actual students, but now, he's been upgraded to professor.

Now a fully tenured professor teaching some of the same courses we both took, *how full circle.*

"How was coffee?" he asks as I join him at the sink, throwing my hair into a messy bun atop my head.

"Well, you actually wouldn't believe it..." I start, grabbing a dish towel and falling into our choreography of wash and dry while I begin to tell him how today's session of drawing out sex scenes for the practicality of them, shifted into mind fuckery I didn't see coming.

"Okay, walk me through this again," Will says, handing me another plate. His mouth is doing that thing where he's trying not to smile too much at my predicament, but the corners keep twitching upward anyway. The late afternoon sun streaming through our kitchen window catches on my wedding ring as I gesture trying with all my might to explain, sending little prisms dancing across our cabinets.

"You just casually texted Reid... about your breakup... for Amanda's book?"

I groan and bump his hip with mine, nearly knocking over the tiny potted succulent that's somehow survived three months on our windowsill despite my best efforts to kill it with neglect. Though given Will's history, it very well could be an imposter.

"When you say it like that, it sounds ridiculous."

"That's because it *is* ridiculous. Gloriously ridiculous, and very you." He reaches over and tucks a loose strand of hair behind my ear, his hands still slightly soapy. A drop of water rolls down my neck, and he kisses it away.

"What does *that* mean?"

"Arden, objectively speaking, people don't stay friends with their exes like you do. And they definitely don't *'casually text'* them about what is arguably the greatest romantic fumble in history asking for details about a sexual encounter that happened more than a decade ago... And now he's saying he didn't break up with you?"

"Right?" I set down the dish towel and hop up onto the counter, legs dangling. From this perch, I can see into our spare room-turned-office, turned-nursery, turned-back-into-an-office, turned-cautious-place-we-are-storing-everything-until-it-becomes-a-nursery.

"I mean, I was there. I lived it." I say returning to the conversation between us, recapping the one from earlier.

Will abandons the dishes entirely now, coming to stand between my knees.

"And you're absolutely sure about this memory?"

"I mean..." I start picking at a loose thread on his sweatshirt, the logo is so faded it's barely legible anymore. "I was nineteen. And there was a party, beer pong, and that questionable kind of punch that was served out of a giant plastic tub. I vaguely remember gummy worms. *But still!*"

"The plot thickens!" Will throws his head back laughing, and I'm momentarily distracted by the way the fading light catches on his jawline. Even in marriage, he still sometimes catches me off guard with how stupidly handsome he is.

"So you're telling me that the great breakup of freshman year might have been a tequila-induced hallucination?"

"You're enjoying this way too much," I pout, but I'm fighting a smile too. He fills our apartment with laughter the same way he fills it with art, deliberately and with absolute devotion.

"I'm just trying to picture nineteen-year-old you showing up at his door for breakup sex, possibly tequila-fueled, after he maybe-didn't-actually break up with you." He's grinning now, full and unrestrained.

"Stop," I groan, hiding my face in his shoulder, breathing in the familiar scent of his laundry detergent mixed with the warm amber musk he wears. "This is insane enough without you narrating it like it's the plot of a bad romance novel."

"Sounds like a pretty good romance novel to me... I bet Amanda agrees." His hands find their way to my waist, thumbs brushing the strip of skin where my shirt has ridden up. "Girl mistakenly thinks boy breaks up with her, has dramatic breakup sex, goes on to become happy, successful, marries the love of her life... " his thumb rubbing my stomach means so much more now. "The way I see it, we're here because of all of that, not in spite of it. Do I actually want to talk about my wife's sex life before me? No. But that was a lifetime ago. We were different people then."

He pulls back just enough to look at me, his expression softening, but I lean in, and his kiss tastes like mint tea he has sitting on the counter.

I'm about to respond when my phone pings again. We both

freeze, staring at it like it might explode. But it's just Amanda, asking if there are any updates.

Will sets the phone down and takes both my hands in his.

"Well, first of all, you're going to tell Amanda she owes you big time for this plot twist. And second..." He pauses, and I can see him choosing his words carefully, the same way he does when he's trying to explain why a particular brushstroke in a Monet matters. "Maybe it's time to finally clear up whatever happened that night. You're not nineteen anymore, Arden."

He gestures around our kitchen, with its mismatched mugs and the vases full of champagne corks from celebrations we've shared, the takeout menus magneted to the fridge next to paint swatches for the accent wall we keep talking about doing but haven't gotten around to yet.

"Whatever he says doesn't change who you are now, maybe just how you got here."

It's going to be a long Monday; I can feel it already. Especially after the last 24 hours and yesterday's great revelation.

I've been obsessing over what I can control about this pregnancy, nausea and heartburn *not* in the I can control this column, so instead, I've been fixated on preparing for my departure from work. There was a time when I was afraid that if I wasn't the hardest working person in the room, that no one would see my value. But as with most things, that view changed with age and the awareness that men often reach for bronze and treat it like gold because it gives them the chance to win without setting expectations too high. Whereas for me, I spent years being an overachiever thinking it would be noticed, but instead it became the floor of what was expected of me.

This morning when I settled in at my desk, looking around my office at the collection of items, photos, moments of my life I have around me. I'd be lying to myself to say I didn't also think about Reid and his message. I hadn't come up with anything to say in response to his 'but-I-didn't-dump-you' text, and he didn't seem to have anything else to say either. So we left it where we leave all of our history. In the past. And in all the places my mind is wandering, there's no path that isn't landing me at my very own front door.

Nineteen year old me might be incredibly impressed with the career I've made for myself, so would twenty-three year old me, but none of that will matter if I let this all turn into a dumpster fire right before I take parental leave. I draft an email to get some clarity around this latest mess, *at work, not my personal life*, in the hopes some of it can be resolved without too much pressure or worse, more delay. Because someday soon, this still modest protrusion from my middle may have my arms out of reach of a keyboard.

I reach them out in front of me to imagine just how big that would be.

Team,
Let's discuss incentives or resources needed to rectify the latest hurdles. We cannot afford another three-month delay.
- ABS

Arden Bancroft Sterling
President & Founder

I always sign my name with my initials. It feels like a subtle feminist power move before you drop to the next line and see the autogenerated signature. Despite our shared origins, I *don't* pull the tech-bro Mark Zuckerberg inspired *'I'm CEO bitch.'* Opting for the much more widely acceptable President. *Still humbling to see.*

But my initials are ungendered and detached; they let me email with the power of a man. A habit I started a long time ago–

the anonymity behind initials, protecting a bit of yourself, and also, as Will once told me, it 'just sounds cool.'

Like most things, they have a history of their own. I sink a bit more into my chair, thinking about the day Reid scribbled them onto a scrap of paper and used it to knight me with a nickname that stuck around longer than he did. And just like that, Reid's email pops into my inbox like the memory I'm not ready to decode.

Subject: Different sides.

Laughable subject line, but really, what else could he have put? The 'I'm sorry I miss you' that I spent years waiting for would be unwelcomed now, and he must know that. After Will and I moved in together I heard from him. He was coming back to Boston and we met up for the coffee that became less and less frequent as time went on.

And while we had stayed up to date about relationship statuses thanks to social media, I think he knew as well as I did, that this time was different. His only response at the time, *that feels fast.'*

But now, after yesterday, I've spent time trapped in my own mind, thinking through absolutely everything that I remember, and worse, the parts I don't. I don't often deep dive on social media anymore looking for ghosts of *best fucking friends* past, but for my own sanity it felt like it was the right time. Looking through every character that might have been cast in our original play, where we were the main characters of our downfall. And everyone, including Reid, is exactly where they should be.

Chapter Forty-Seven

HAPPILY EVER DURING

Arden

"Come on, Pearl Sterling?! She sounds like she went down on the Titanic." Will and I are both laying in bed with notebooks full of names, and in some cases, just random words. "Veto." I say, as I lean across his chest to the yellow striped spiral pages in his hand, and cross it off the list.

His glasses sitting on the bridge of his nose make him look more like a professor than I think he intended. But it wasn't a fashion choice as much as an ophthalmological need. One I'm desperately avoiding myself, even though when he leaves them at home I often borrow them to sharpen my own sight, though I tell myself it's so I don't burn my retinas from staring at a screen for twelve hours a day. And when they are never in the same spot he leaves them, I just shrug and plead ignorance. Not willing to admit to any more aging that I've already had to.

Only women would have the existence where your age is a complete contradiction of *'you're too old'* and *'you're too young'* at the exact same point in time. I gently rub my hand over the curve of my stomach. *Geriatric.* There's no definition of that word that makes it less offensive. Trust me, we looked it up. But of course, up until now, I wouldn't have even been able to run for President of the country, and now, I'm considered a geriatric pregnancy.

"Fine. Pearl is off the list... Your turn, *hit me*." Will adjusts his position, the mattress dipping as he flips to a new page in his notebook.

"What about Alexandra? Defender of mankind, that's pretty powerful." I offer.

"Alexandra Sterling sounds like she exclusively wears tennis whites and summers in the Hamptons," he counters.

"As opposed to Newport?"

"See, I'm qualified to make that assessment. Plus, every other girl in boarding school was either Alexandra or Victoria. Hard pass."

He taps his pen against the page thoughtfully.

"Okay, what about something mythology-based? Athena?"

"You want to name our daughter after the goddess who sprung fully formed from her father's forehead? I'll tell you what, if you have her spring from your forehead, Athena it is."

"Alright then, *no to Athena*." He says as he vigorously scratches it from the list.

"Besides, Athena Sterling sounds like she teaches advanced Latin and has strong opinions about the Oxford comma." I say doubling down on my veto.

Will laughs, his chest vibrating against my shoulder. "As opposed to her mother, who has no strong opinions whatsoever?"

"I have exactly the right amount of opinions, thank you very much. All of them correct." I poke him in the ribs. "What about Matilda, we could call her Tilly."

"Sure, I'll prepare her dowry of petticoats... *veto*."

"Kennedy."

"Too presidential." I cross it off the list.

"What about... Aurora?"

"Do you want our daughter to spend her entire life hearing 'Oh, like Sleeping Beauty?' Absolutely not." I shake my head.

Will is quiet for a moment, his fingers run against the flesh on my arm, occasionally drifting to my stomach where our daughter, *still nameless*, kicks as if joining the debate. His fingers read my skin like scripture, following paths only he knows. The way my fingertips trace his illustrated skin, some pieces he carried before me, their meaning woven into who he was, and others he added in the chapters of us, two words not an illustration at all added near his heart. Fragments of our story etched permanent as stars. While his canvas tells tales to any observer, he finds the invisible art written on mine. Maps of freckles, the silver whispers of some scars, the invisibility of others. Places life has left its marks in ways only he can read, the constellation of beauty marks that led him home.

"You know," he says slowly, "there's one name we haven't considered."

"If you say Pearl again, I swear—"

"Think about it," Will continues, warming to his own idea. "It's strong without being pretentious. It sounds like someone who could either run Wall Street or dismantle it, depending on her mood... we could call her Banks for short."

"Your father would have an aneurysm over the implications," I say, but I'm smiling. *'A Sterling heir named after his financial legacy?'* I tease the idea, but it fits.

"It's you. Your name, *your* legacy." He shifts to face me, his expression earnest behind his glasses.

"The weight of a name, I wonder if we're giving her armor or a burden."

I think about my own name, how it shaped me and challenged me and gave me something to live up to. How Will's name opened every door for him, even the ones he never wanted.

"You don't think it's arrogant?"

"How many men name their sons after themselves, juniors or thirds, or hell, we've all heard of Henry VIII."

"Is that really the example you want to go with?" I lean back against him and write on my notepad the future permutations of her pen.

Bancroft Sterling. Banks Sterling. Banks. BS. B. Croft. Sterling. Banny. Banksy.

"Banks Sterling. God help the world." The name takes shape like a prophecy in the dim light.

"God help *us*," Will corrects with a laugh that rumbles through his chest and into mine, pulling me closer as if preparing for the beautiful chaos we've just named into being.

Chapter Forty-Eight

HAPPILY EVER DURING

Arden

This is the kind of house that makes you believe in past lives, the sort that has you thinking maybe, just maybe, you were meant to live here in another timeline. That's how it feels standing in front of it the first time.

And when I told Will, he said *then it should be ours in this timeline.*

We'd seen maybe a dozen houses all in different parts of the city, before this one. All in different outskirts and on train lines that take us farther and farther from our youth. It's classic New England brick, that deep, weathered red that somehow gets more beautiful with each passing winter, like the house is aging into itself the way people do.

The wrought iron gate creaks when it opens to a brick pathway that someone laid by hand decades ago, now charmingly uneven with spots where stubborn moss peeks through. The garden is deliberately wild, and when the ground isn't covered in snow, there are massive daylilies lining the front stairs.

The house itself sits back from the street like it's being modest about its own grandeur. Which, it is. Not in that over-the-top kind of way. But definitely in the *'what did Kevin's parent's do for work to afford that house and take everyone on a trip to Europe'* kind of way. The rom-com *'this is a totally realistic multi-million dollar home but made to feel attainable'* kind of way.

It's three stories of architectural showing-off. Each with windows marching in neat rows across the facade with their own set of black shutters.

Once it was officially ours, the first thing we did was go pick out paint for the front door. The yellow is almost offensive in its cheerfulness. But against the brick and beneath the trim of the doorframe, it works like a laugh at a funeral. Inappropriate, necessary, and somehow perfect.

My hands are gloved and still wrapped tightly around the thermos taking a sip to warm my insides. But this is the first snow of the season, and our new front yard is coated in the blanket of winter that screams for hot cocoa. Exactly what I promised Banks and Ollie if they'd ever be willing to come inside. *They have yet to oblige.*

But like usual, these two peas in a pod, are on some kind of mission communicating in a language they formed together in infancy.

The other benefit of this house? The Victorian one around the corner that Ethan moved into just last month. Our kids are both bundled up like little michelin men crunching in the snow with their faces barely exposed.

Oliver was born only a few days before Banks, and they have never spent more than a flu diagnosis apart. At least, that was until Banks caught it and we let them ride it out together. At the time it felt like a great idea, but immediately we realized toddlers are not really looking for conversational company when feverish.

There's something special about this generational friendship of our children. And when Ethan told us the news, we were confused because we were about to tell him of our own soon-to-be arrival.

Sometimes I watch them together and my life flashes forward

fifty years wondering what kind of life we will have given them. The burdens of our parents' expectations, the burden of ourselves? It's hard to say. I blow out my breath and the warm air takes the shape of the thought I expel.

"STERLING IS HOME!" A little voice yells as her boots crunch towards the front gate. Banks meets him there, standing on the inside of the iron gate that opens into the path of our front lawn as he leans over the top of it, dusting snow off the top of her hood as Ollie rushes to her side.

Her little mittened hands gripping the gate as she looks up to him, snowflakes catching in her eyelashes just like Will's do.

"Password pleaseee" she says.

Every inch of our house, *our life,* has been transformed by Banks's imagination, fueled by Will's nightly readings. First it was Narnia. His voice bringing Aslan to life while she spent weeks searching every closet and cupboard for her own pathway to another world. When she finally declared our coat closet 'definitely magical, but just sleeping,' we didn't have the heart to correct her. Then came The Secret Garden, and suddenly our front gate became her own mysterious entrance to wonder. She spent hours examining the ivy growing along the brick wall, convinced it held secrets only she could unlock. The garden isn't hidden, but she treats it like it's full of magic anyway.

The scene unfolds like a snow globe coming to life. One of those precious winter moments that feels both frozen in time and impossibly fleeting. Banks is more and more precocious with each passing day, but her mind swirls around things of beauty like Will's does. Even as she stands guard at our gate in her powder blue puffer coat.

"Sterling is home!" she announces again, bouncing on her toes as Will approaches, his messenger bag slung across his chest.

"Pass-word puh-leaseee," Banks repeats, more insistent this time, while Ollie nods solemnly beside her, their matching winter hats making them look like coordinated conspirators.

Will pretends to think deeply, stroking his chin in an exaggerated gesture that makes both kids giggle. "Is it... 'Banks'?"

"Noooo," Banks draws out the word. "That's way too easy, Sterling."

I can't help but smile into my thermos.

She started calling him Sterling a few weeks ago, after a day at school that came home written on her face in tear tracks and confusion. During the inevitable school project about name origins, some kid had declared that 'Bancroft wasn't a real first name' with the kind of cruelty children specialize in, learning from their parents. And while we tried to talk to her about it, the truth really poured out later that night when Ethan texted us a photo of the note from her and Ollie's teacher about a 'playground disagreement' where Ollie apparently declared that 'Banks is the best name ever' with a little more mudslinging, the real kind, than any of us should laugh about. That night, over mac and cheese that she barely touched, we stumbled through explanations of names, mine from my mother's side, Will's from somewhere long-ago, many branches up a tree.

We talked about how names can be bridges to our past or doorways to our future, how sometimes they're heavy with meaning and sometimes they're just sounds that feel right in your heart. How one day she might get to choose a name for someone else, the way we chose hers, if she wants. We talked about Titian's name and Sally's nickname (after Salvador Dali) but the naming methodology behind our family pets wasn't what she cared about. Watching her push pasta around her plate, I knew she wasn't ready for the poetry of names, she just wanted to make sense of her own. That's when she lifted her chin with a determination I recognized from my own mirror and declared that if her name was going to be a last name, then so was her dad's.

'I'm Bancroft. You're Sterling,' she announced, her voice still wobbly but sure. We never thought it would stick around, yet here we are, four weeks into 'Mommy and Sterling.' Even in her small form, she has my bones and Will's soul, but her way of

reshaping the world into something more beautiful is entirely her own, turning other people's walls into her own secret gardens.

Will scoops her up over the gate and pushes it open into the walkway towards home. She is every late-night conversation we've ever had about our future without ever knowing it.

"Hot chocolate time?" Ollie pipes up hopefully, reminding us all of the promised reward for coming inside.

"Hot chocolate time," I confirm, watching as Banks squirms down from Will's arms to grab Ollie's hand, both of them racing toward the door that glows like a lighthouse in the growing dusk.

Will catches me around the waist before I can follow, pulling me close.

"Hello darling," he murmurs, pressing a cold kiss to my temple.

"Forgot the password again, I see." reply, breathing in the familiar scent of wool and winter and home.

"She keeps changing it!"

We make our way up the steps, following the sound of children's laughter and the promise of warm chocolate. The yellow door swings open to welcome us in.

"Do you ever feel like you stumbled into the end of a novel? Just tripped into someone else's perfect life."

"Not someone else's," he corrects gently. "Ours. Every bit of it."

Chapter Forty-Nine

HAPPILY EVER DURING

Arden

Well, I've made it through the day. I think to myself as my hands ring the leather of the steering wheel. I've pulled into the driveway and put the car in park and am now just sitting here. Waiting. Not for anything in particular, not even hiding. Just that sometimes you need that extra minute, or fifteen, to finish the song that's being played, give yourself a few extra minutes of reading time. Or just, experience the silence.

It's acknowledged by all of our friends and family, even those that pre-date the 'our' portion of that sentence, that I am and always have been the most insufferable person on my birthday. And yet, I married the man who has always found a reason to celebrate, and of the things he would let pass without celebration, it would never be me. I understand why, we *do* have too much to celebrate now. Having reached that shockingly picture-perfect epilogue of our novel, even though the story has kept going.

At work I thought I escaped the usual lets-all-pile-into-the-conference-room-for-cake ordeal, but they caught me on the way out the door. I don't actually blame them. As Will reminded me as we both left this morning, *'birthdays give people a reason to do lots of things, but at a minimum, it gives everyone else a break from their day and a slice of cake. And you wouldn't deny anyone cake, would you?'*

The November air is in cahoots with that autumn golden hour light, and it catches on our bright marigold front door like it's winking at me.

Will claimed the garage door was broken, which is suspicious enough but more than that, our typically quiet street has a few additional and familiar cars. I smile despite myself, remembering how just this morning he'd kissed me goodbye with a reminder not to work too late. And now, even from where my car sits unmoving in our driveway, I can see that despite the curtains being drawn, there's the slightest movement inside. Walking up the path, past Banks's scattered chalk drawings, and a magnifying glass and dry brush from her current obsession with archeology, *'I swear, Will,'* I mutter under my breath at the sneaking suspicion I know what I'm walking into... Though, what promise I am making and to whom, I have no idea.

I push open the front door and step into our entryway with the patterned wallpaper that we spent three weeks debating before finally agreeing on. Even going so far as putting up a panel on each side of the wall to negate the other's point. The house is hushed, but not silent. And the absence of the dogs rushing to my feet tells me everything I already knew.

"SURPRISE!"

The shout comes from everywhere all at once, and suddenly our home is alive with faces I love. They emerge from behind furniture, from doorways, from corners I didn't even know could hide people. And there at the center of it all is Will, holding Banks on his hip, both of them beaming like they've just pulled off the greatest heist in history. And maybe we all have.

"Happy birthday, love," Will says, and I can hear the satisfaction in his voice.

"I guess you forgot about the no birthdays rule?" I manage, still taking in the scene.

"More like *reinterpreted* the no birthdays rule." He passes Banks to Amanda, who's appeared beside him wearing what appears to be...

"Is that a beret?"

Because now I'm noticing the details, everyone is dressed in art museum-worthy attire. Ethan, emerging from behind our sofa, sports a Vincent van Gogh-style bandage over one ear *'Too soon?'*. Rosalie and Simon are done up as American Gothic, complete with pitchfork. Amanda, besides the beret, has what appears to be a fake mustache and a sign reading *'This is not a pipe.'*

"Welcome," Will announces grandly, "to the Museum of Arden: A Retrospective Exhibition... definitely *not* a birthday."

Our living room has been transformed into a gallery space. The walls are lined with photos from throughout my life, each with its own little museum didactic plate offering Will's distinctive commentary. I move closer to read one.

'MOTHERHOOD: A SELF-PORTRAIT'
MIXED MEDIA: COFFEE, CHAOS, AND INFINITE LOVE
ON LOAN FROM WILL STERLING'S PRIVATE COLLECTION.

A photo of me and Banks, she can't be more than a few weeks old here. We're both asleep, likely passed out from our same hungry cry because she wouldn't latch. But you would never have known it from this photo. It looks incredibly serene. So much so, that Will must have taken the picture to preserve the peace and quiet which we definitely rarely felt early on. We stayed in that apartment as just the family of five (including the dogs of course) for as long as we could. But eventually we outgrew the space, as we had with the others before. Somehow, our lives and all that was in them needed more room. But leaving that apartment was the hardest because it meant leaving her first moments behind as well.

The crowd of guests are all mingling as I tour my personal exhibition. Walking up to another...

'BULLSEYE (2009)'
MIXED MEDIA: PIZZA GREASE AND LAUGHTER
ON LOAN FROM ETHAN HAYES' ARCHIVAL COLLECTION.

Ethan and I at the bar. A dart tucked behind my ear and another one between my fingers as I pretend to smoke it like a cigarette. My red lips pursed as I put on a show for the camera as I so often did. Never being good at darts, just good enough at distracting my partners. Which worked for most except Ethan.

'THE LITERARY ESCAPE'
MIXED MEDIA: DOG-EARED PAGES, MARGIN NOTES, AND STOLEN MOMENTS
ON LOAN FROM WILL STERLING'S PRIVATE COLLECTION.

This wasn't taken that long ago. The image of me curled up in the big reading chair in our bedroom with both dogs at my feet. My hand covering my mouth as I got to the plot twist I never saw coming that had me all too eager to throw the book across the room.

Finally reaching my favorite one yet. I wouldn't exactly call it modern-impressionism, but those guys had similar paint strokes. This one, unlike the others, is not a photo.

'MOMMY - A PORTRAIT'
BANCROFT STERLING
WATERCOLOR ON PAPER.
ON LOAN FROM THE ARTIST.

I walk past photos of me, different places and times. Concerts, coffee shops, holidays, and just Mondays. Photos of Will and I in Paris, and Rome. Sitting on the steps of the Met after we got a stern talking to from *their* tour guide about what they consider 'inappropriate heckling.' *Which we standby was not heckling but a very appropriate, and well needed correction.* Pictures from my parents, of us becoming parents, dog first, then human. So much of it is here. Some strung up, others propped up on easels. Even the occasional installation.

'WOMAN DANCING TO ABBA WHILE THINKING NO ONE CAN SEE HER'
MIXED MEDIA: JOY, TERRIBLE CHOREOGRAPHY, AND COMPLETE ABANDON
ON LOAN FROM WILL STERLING'S PRIVATE COLLECTION.

"You didn't," I breathe, but I'm already laughing.

"Oh, but I did." Will appears beside me, warm and solid and impossibly pleased with himself. "Wait until you see the installation in the dining room. It's called *Coffee Cups I Have Known: A Love Story in Caffeine.'* That, however, is a temporary piece and *will* be dismantled once the show is over. The rest, I'm still considering leaving."

I turn to face him properly, taking in his outfit. Crisp black shirt, the cuff of his sleeves rolled up to expose some of his forearms, now adorning matching friendship bracelets we made with Banks last week. He's dressed as a museum docent, complete with the name tag he used to wear, though it's long since retired since he moved into academia full time. I know he still strolls the halls on occasion. We've even made a habit to go back and sit on that bench when we need to run away, to have a serious conversation, or just to remember our youth. The man pictured is younger than the one in front of me, with the shyest whisper of grey tucked by his temples.

"How long have you been planning this?" I'm unable to keep the amazement from my voice.

"Planning? Please," he scoffs with theatrical indignation. "You know I don't plan. This was completely spontaneous. I just happened to have several dozen professionally printed museum plates lying around."

"And the catering?" I gesture to the spread of food I can see in the kitchen, all my favorites arranged like still life paintings.

"Pure coincidence. You know how sometimes you accidentally order exactly the right amount of food for thirty-seven people?"

"And Banks kept this secret?" Our daughter, now sitting with Ethan and his son Oliver, both kids wearing tiny matching Museum-Geek shirts and berets, waves at us.

"That," Will admits, "was the real masterpiece."

I shake my head, taking in more details. The way the furniture has been rearranged to create perfect viewing galleries, the soft museum-style lighting, the gentle classical music playing in the background. "I can't believe you did all this."

"Really? Because this is kind of my thing." He pulls me closer, speaking softly so only I can hear. "Besides, I had help. Turns out our friends are good at keeping secrets especially when they think they might get some embarrassing photos out of it. *Of course I delivered.*"

"I hate you." My smile betrays me completely.

"You love me," he corrects with absolute certainty. "It's been extensively documented. There's a whole exhibit about it in the study. *'The Evolution of Love: From Bathroom Hookups to Bathroom Remodels.'*" The soft wink tells me he's joking and my shock of horror dissipates as his hand wraps my face. His thumb stroking my cheek which is round with joy as he brings his mouth to mine granting me a kiss of all the moments not pictured on the walls.

Simon appears beside us, still in his American Gothic costume. "Please tell me you got to the guest book yet. Will made us all leave reviews. He *really* wanted to make sure we shouted out the tour guide. You'd think he had a complex about it or something."

I let Will lead me to a leatherbound book on a pedestal in the corner. Opening it, I find messages from our friends written in their best art critic voices:

"The piece titled 'Arden Attempts to Cook Dinner' was particularly moving. The smoke alarm really tied the whole experience together. Five stars." - Ethan

"The early works showing the subject pining were a bit derivative, but the later pieces displaying domestic bliss really demonstrate artistic growth." - Amanda

"The collaborative piece *'Banks's First Steps'* brings tears to the eyes, though the artists' commentary of *'holy shit she's moving'* perhaps lacks sophistication." - Rosalie

"Hey," Will protests, reading over my shoulder. "That was very sophisticated."

I'm about to respond when Banks breaks away from her game with Ollie and runs to us, her beret askew. I'm already being pulled along by Banks toward the dining room, where indeed, every coffee cup I've ever owned seems to be arranged in chronological order, including the *'ceci n'est pas une mug'* mug from Will's old apartment.

I'm standing in our kitchen as Will taps his champagne glass ringing the rooms to attention. I don't mind being the center of attention, I used to revel in it. But the illumination of it now is less of a spotlight and more of a soft glow.

"To my wife," he starts, "Who, as everyone knows, absolutely despises her birthday with the burning passion of, well... her." Our friends laugh, because of course they do. Will has always known how to work a room.

"You see, everyone has a glass of champagne. And as you know, darling, we can't waste champagne, even on the worst of days, we pop a bottle of champagne and find reasons to celebrate. But I'm sorry, I can't commiserate with you this time, because there is nothing in my life I would rather celebrate, than you." He raises his glass higher, and I notice how the golden liquid catches the light. The same way it reflects in his eyes right back to me. "To the woman who somehow makes everyone's life better just by existing. Who probably has a much cleverer, and definitely *dirtier* toast prepared, because let's be honest, she always does."

"To Arden," he continues, his voice getting that soft quality it gets when he's being completely sincere. "Who hates being celebrated but deserves it more than anyone I know. So here's to you, darling. You can sulk about your birthday with your champagne, and we'll all just keep right on adoring you anyway."

He winks at me across our large kitchen island, past the ridiculous number of small basil plants mingled with flower arrangements, and there is no part of my smile, or myself I could ever hide from him.

———

The house settles into that particular kind of quiet that follows a really good party, the kind where the walls seem to still sing with laughter and the air holds onto fragments of joy like fireflies. Streamers droop lazily from our ceiling beams with their shadows across the walls in the dim light.

Banks and Oliver fell asleep in her room hours ago, somewhere in the middle of Mamma Mia. Their latest obsession. *I blame Will.* Even with the guests and music, we could hear their little feet bouncing and singing along. It wasn't until they fell silent Ethan went to check on them and confirmed they were both completely knocked out. The sugar rush from the birthday cake and nonstop Super Trooper marathon exhausted them.

Ethan helps straighten up some, asks if Oliver can stay the night, wishes me a happy birthday and heads home. We've talked before about how lucky they are to have each other, and while we hope they stay friends as we have, *maybe without some of the detours,* it's nice for them to have each other now.

The crowd dissipates as it does. And I find Will by the kitchen sink with his sleeve rolled up washing up a bit. The music has changed back to the playlists of our home as I hear him harmonizing with the running water. *And I would walk five-hundred miles... and I would walk five-hundred more.*

I duck under his arm to join him as he kisses the top of my head. Taking my spot next to him at the sink and grabbing a dish towel to dry.

"So," Will says, his hands deep in soapy water, "should we address the fact that our daughter is currently having a sleepover with a boy?"

I snort, taking in the aftermath of what Will has dubbed *'The Greatest Exhibition of Our Time'* and it feels like it. Empty champagne bottles standing like tiny glass soldiers on every surface, glitter scattered across the hardwood floors like daisies.

"This isn't the first time, we literally used to put them in a crib together to stop them from crying. Plus, they fell asleep watching Meryl Streep and Colin Firth wearing spandex and singing about the Greek islands."

"Still," he says, absently handing me another dish, "I wasn't expecting them to be curled up like puppies in her reading nook."

"You mean the reading nook we built specifically so she could, and I quote, *'have a place to run away?'*"

"I just didn't think it would be with a boy. I don't know when we need to be concerned about it." In some ways I know what he means. They are best friends now. They are young and don't understand the societal divisions structured around gender in a way that will pressure them out of this ignorant bliss.

"I think we have a little more time before this becomes a Joey and Dawson situation" I say as I take another dish.

I reach for a champagne cork that was left on the counter and a sharpie from the 'everything drawer' scrawling '40th' on the side of it to add to the collection. The glass apothecary style jars where we've kept all the champagne moments over the years. We've filled up more than a few, always slightly different shapes and sizes. When we can adding the reason to the cork. Some are better than others. *Taylor Swift Eras Tour* was a great cork. *IKEA trip*, not so much. Though Will stills swears that successfully assembling the three bookshelves without divorce, *or murder*, was worth celebrating.

"Should we clean up?" I ask, making absolutely no move to do so more than the handful of dishes I wiped down.

"Definitely," Will agrees, pulling me closer. "Right after I finish cataloging this moment for the next exhibition."

"Oh? And what would you call this piece?"

He pretends to think, adopting his former museum docent voice with practiced precision, and I hear him as clearly as I did that first day, where his voice called to something sleeping inside me, waking up parts I didn't know were dreaming.

"Happily Ever After."

The song changes like it was part of the plan. It plays in a way our feet always find familiarity as we danced to it in black tie for the first time as husband and wife. His soapy hands grab mine and slowly spins me as does regardless of music, location, or audience. We dance through the gallery of our life, celebrating mine, buzzed on the bubbles of commiseration that taste so much like happiness.

I look at this man who turns ordinary moments into exhibitions and bad days into celebrations. I lean into him, breathing in the familiar scent of warm amber and fresh laundry, the smells of home. In the window, I can see our reflection, the two of us, surrounded by love and art and memories, dancing in our own private museum. And I think about the college girl who lost herself in the rejection of love, the young woman who was desperate to prove herself in her choices, the sleepless new mother who googled *is it normal if baby breathes this way* while clutching cold coffee, the associate who decided that victory is not in climbing the highest ladder but the right one, the wife who knows that love isn't just about grand gestures but about someone who just knows when to pick up a box of tampons.

Now here I am at forty, somehow all of these women at once.

Their collective wisdom, battle scars and triumphs, wrapped up in this moment, swaying to music in our kitchen as they watch from some part deep within me, knowing that they all have their happily ever after.

Right here.

In the middle of our life.

Chapter Fifty

—————————

HAPPILY EVER AFTER

Bancroft

He looks older here, or maybe just more tired. The house must feel so empty now. I want to ask but don't know how without it sounding like pity.

"What's scaring you?" he asks, trying not to pull too hard. But the words settle between us like fallen leaves after a storm. *What's scaring me? Too many things to name.*

I pull my legs up onto the bench, wrapping my arms around my knees like I used to do when we'd spend hours here as I waited for him to be done. Because even when he became a professor, and committed to teaching full time, he always came back here like he could never abandon the roots he planted.

Guess that makes one of us.

He used to say that every person who's ever stood in front of these paintings has brought their own story to it and left with it changed, somehow. Even in tiny ways. I look at him, and know, no one has left as much of a story here as he has. This bench being the support in all of it.

"I'm absolutely terrified what will happen to you if I go. The idea of leaving you alone, in that house..."

That's what's made this all so hard.

It's not the decision, I know it's time.

But I can picture him there still, standing at the kitchen sink in the fading light, staring out into the garden beyond. In the farthest corner of the yard, past where the grass gives way to wild things, there's a perfect view of the stone bench nestled amidst what's become an unexpected forest of basil. The same bench where he used to watch me with my books and steaming mugs on Sunday mornings. Each plant a story of rescue. Valentine's Days, anniversaries, birthdays, celebrations where roses were never enough to capture the depth of love that existed. No matter how many times they withered under, he'd just smile and carry them out to the backyard, one by one, transplanting them into soil that seemed to understand exactly what they needed. Now years of nearly-dead plants surround that bench like faithful guardians, their leaves reaching toward the sky as if stretching for second chances. He always did that. Believed in saving things that seemed too far gone, saw life in places others had given up on. Even the most wilted stem could find its way back to blooming, and that's how I know I need to go. But he treats himself as the keeper of these things. These memories are his obligation, the cornerstone he's built his life around, the ship he would sink with. Like gravity will keep him here.

He's grown roots here, anchored himself to this place where every leaf and stone holds life that was built. But some things need to be transplanted to grow, need to stretch toward different skies. I learned that from him, though I don't think either of us were prepared for the moment I was the one stretching away from him.

"*That house* has some of the greatest moments of my life."

It had been just the two of us for so long, that now, I think about when that all began to change. It's almost as if he has the same thought I do. He spins the wedding band on his finger, and I look down at the one on mine, stacked with another that holds the weight of a love story much greater than just mine.

"Do you ever think about the wedding?"

"Some of the greatest moments of my life..." he repeats softly.

Chapter Fifty-One

HAPPILY EVER AFTER (ISH)

Bancroft

My childhood bedroom hasn't changed. I like that it's never changed, even if I have. I'm sitting on the window seat, tufted and upholstered in some pattern I picked when I thought rainbows on a window seat would be a good-long term choice. And my parents didn't try to talk me out of it. Even as the rest of the room developed, when pictures and posters were rotated through frames and the walls changed colors, eventually in high school settling on this forest green, the room is the same. It grew up like I did, but unlike me, was preserved. The way some things stay frozen when they hold all of your secrets.

The walls have witnessed everything from first crushes to the last, college acceptance letters, late-night study sessions to early morning doubts. I don't have doubts sitting here now, now about this.

I don't fit here as well as I remember, but it might be the outfit. I scoop some of the dress onto the seat so it isn't just hanging on the floor. My toes scrunch into the cushion and I rest my head against the glass, the sun beaming into my room cutting across my lap and lighting a direct path to the door. *That feels like a good sign. It's literally lighting the way.*

Guests have begun to arrive and I can see him there talking to his dad. He's beaming much like this setting sun telling me to get my butt down there. The hour is golden and so is he. In some ways, this already feels like a memory. One that can be hung on the wall next to my parents wedding photo.

This was what I wanted, to get married at home, nothing too elaborate, just people who love us, in a place I have always felt love. The backyard is set up with a collection of round tables, clusters of greenery and baby's breath in the center. Simple. Understated. Part of the garden is overgrown, and it's always my favorite. I love that this room has a view of it. Even before it became my secret garden, before it became as wild and completely overgrown as it is now, I could look out this window and see this patch of garden so loved by my parents. Now, it has nearly completely overtaken the stone bench that sits nestled amongst it.

I have music playing on a small speaker that is about a decade old and it clashes with the string quartet outside. It kind of makes sense. I look down at people beginning to take their seats. And his glare cuts through the crowd, through the glass, through me. I know people might say we're too young, maybe we are. But I can see him, and I see my future. I'm smiling as my dad knocks on the door. He opens it slowly and pops his head through the crack.

"You ready sweetheart?"

"Just about... shoes and bouquet"

"Bouquet is getting final touches downstairs, we can pick it up on the way to the altar."

I slip on my shoes, a pair of silver glitter keds, felt like a fun nod to the *Sterling* of it all. Plus, I have no interest in trying to wear high heels in grass, and these will allow me to not trip over my own feet when dancing.

My father is tall, standing in the doorway full of pride and memory as I give myself one more glance in the mirror. The a-line dress hangs across my body in a way I didn't know something could actually fit someone. It's not adorned anywhere but the hem, where it has lace trim, the *something old*. Goes perfectly with the small sapphire earrings. Made using a pair from my mom, we had them surrounded in small diamonds to wear today. Taking care of the *new, borrowed, and blue.*

My hair is barely pulled back and pinned with some baby's breath. The few freckles across the bridge of my nose are not shy and buried under foundation, my eyes have some sparkle, and my cheeks are pink, but I look like me. Which is exactly what I wanted. I brush my hands to smooth out my dress, and I know the butterflies in my stomach are fluttering to meet their mates, like I am, at the end of the green path.

"Ready."

"You absolutely are," he says with a smile.

This house elicits all the senses, triggered by my favorite parts of my childhood. I'm wrapped in all the warmth of my mother as I descend the stairs. I hear my father's laugh as we reach the kitchen island. As we approach the french doors in the family room, we're standing there, just the two of us.

The wedding coordinators are waiting, poised to open the doors. I see him there, and he sees me. Like our eyes would never have been able to keep apart. And while the world outside is still watching him, his eyes are here. He taps his nose twice, discreetly, and points right at me. I do the same back.

And with that, I'm handed my bouquet and the doors are opened. I realize the *'final touches'* are the touches of basil. It's everywhere. The boutonnieres, the center pieces, it's in my memories, my future. He did this for me, knowing what it would mean. The sweet smell of basil is subtle in the air, but it's the distinct memories that flood my senses with each breath. For some, red roses hold the romance, but for me? It will always be a small hardware-store potted basil plant. I always imagine it, just sitting there on the ledge above the sink, right by the kitchen window. I think about how many times it died and he secretly replaced it. That's a type of love not everyone is lucky to know. But I am. It made me.

I hold on to my father step by step and we're all in tears by the time we reach the altar. For reasons known and unknown, said and unsaid.

With a kiss on my cheek, he whispers he loves me, and he steps to the side.

It feels different than I thought. My stomach is anxious for more reasons than I can count, but none have to do with the man standing with me.

The way we know each other isn't fair. No one could ever compete. I'm looking at him as he takes my hands, and I know with my whole heart he's the one who owns it forever.

In some ways I feel like I am watching this all through someone else's eyes, I'd think that except the way he mouths *'I love you'* amidst the officiants speech where he wrinkles his nose at me in jest, I couldn't be anyone but myself. I can hear the background noise of the ceremony, but it's only him I hear, as he begins his vows.

"I can't think of a more perfect place to marry you, my best friend, *than right here*, mere feet away from our first kiss... Actually... I think we should..." his hands are placed on my upper arms, running his fingers across my skin and he steps forward toward me and pushes me slightly backwards, mere feet, just like he said.

"There. That's better," he says with our feet now rooted in our past while our hands hold each other's future. The place in my childhood backyard where we had our kiss.

"I know that no matter how much today should be pure joy, there is something missing. *Someone* missing." I glance over at my dad, who is wiping away tears for more than just me. He's missing *her* like I am. But missing her is always his way of making sure she is here, even though she hasn't been for years now.

"I know that you wanted for your mom to see you get married... and I could say that she is here with us, and I do believe that..." He subtly signals to someone behind me. "You may not know this, you might not remember, but she saw you get married. She saw *us* get married. The first time."

I'm confused, and look to my dad for confirmation. But his lips are held together with a nod and smile that tells me he knows something I don't, at least not yet. His hands turn me towards the back of the house, and wraps his arms around me. Everyone in their seats turning with me. And just like that, the speakers crackle and come to life with the sound of her voice on an old recording.

"What are you two doing?" she laughs and then the projection flickers on. There she is. Larger than life, like always. Glowing. And then I come into frame can't be more than four with one of her white slip dresses drowning my small body as I trip over my feet squealing and laughing. And then he comes running into frame behind me, clutching a small handful of basil he had pulled from the garden.

"We're getting married!" I scream and jump into her arms.

"Can you believe it, darling!? Our only daughter is already getting married?!" My father's younger voice from behind the camera. This home video of us as children is one I've never seen, I don't even know exactly when it's from. But it's in this house.

It plays for a few minutes, the whole ceremony, and when my mom pronounces us 'husband and wife' he throws his arms around me and tackles me to the ground and we laugh like children do. And so does she.

The camera shifts, and it's back on my mom, even with her hair wild, wearing just one of my dads t-shirts and a pair of leggings, she was perfect.

"Can you please introduce yourself, and share a message for the lovely bride and groom?" My dad teases her. She holds up a banana as a fake microphone, and looks right at him.

"Hiii, I'm Arden Sterling, I'm the mother of the bride... and on this glorious day of your wedding, I have a toast just for you..."

Her voice sounds like music from a jewelry box, one I can't easily open anymore. But it's lyrical and light as she taps the banana microphone again asking *is this thing on.*

"What *kind* of toast, darling?" My father chides knowing as well as I do the flare she always had for something that caused a little stir. But she ignores him, clearing her throat to continue.

"There are tall ships, there are small ships, there are a lot of ships at sea. But the best ships are friendships, so here's to Banks and Ollie... I wish you a lifetime of happiness on your wedding day, today, the 18th of September... I love you both!"

My hands fly to my mouth as the video ends, the freeze-frame remains projected on the house as she's frozen there in time, in a memory I didn't know I had.

I turn to him, my soon to be husband, my first-husband, my lifetime best friend and he turns back to me.

"Banks, most people don't get to marry their best friend, and they definitely don't get to marry them *twice... on the same day.* I love you, then...today...tomorrow and I know I'll love growing old with you, because I loved growing up with you. And I vow, no matter how many steps we are away from this sacred spot, no matter how many days we are away from our wedding day, my love for you is rooted deeper than anything else to ever exist."

It's my turn for my vows, I don't know how to vow anything more to this man than my entire self, which he already has so completely.

"Ollie," my own tears are flowing, and I see myself reflected in the glistening of his own eyes. "My dad always told me that his life began when he fell in love with my mom." I take a breath hoping it's enough to power me through. "But that's not true for us, because my life has never existed without you. People search for lifetimes to feel the way I do about you, and when they do find that person they have to open their heart and fit the pieces together. But not me. I didn't have to search, I've known you as long as I've known myself. Our hearts never needed to fit together, because mine has always had you in it." The pads of his thumbs are wiping tears from my cheeks as his own meet the holy ground we stand on.

"Most people find their best friends in their soulmates, but not for me, I found my soulmate in my best friend."

I've never been filled with as much emotion as I have right now. I didn't know this much emotion could exist within a person.

My hands grab his face and pull him to me. His lips and mine smiling against each other slick by tears.

It's the kiss of husband and wife at their second wedding, years later.

Chapter Fifty-Two

HAPPILY EVER AFTER

Arden

"We need champagne." My voice catches, and I see him register it. I watch him register it, the way his shoulders tense slightly, the careful way his expression doesn't change tells me everything about how well he knows me after all these years together. I drop my keys in the ceramic bowl by the door, the one Banks made in art class that looks more like an anatomically correct heart than the bowl it was meant to be.

"Champagne?" he asks softly, already moving toward the cabinet where we keep the special bottles.

"Yep. Because today we need to find something to celebrate." My voice breaks on 'celebrate' and I watch Will's face do that thing, that terrible, beautiful thing, where he's trying to prepare himself for whatever's coming while pretending he's not terrified. "Will you grab it? The good bottle we've been saving?"

We've been saving that bottle since an anniversary, tucked away behind the everyday wines. We'd agreed to open it for 'something special.' Now I'm going to make my husband open it to toast to the fact that... *well*, I haven't exactly decided what to toast yet.

Will works the cork free with steady hands as it makes a soft pop instead of the celebratory bang we usually aim for. Another metaphor I don't need right now. He takes down two mugs, slides one across the counter to me, and I take a sip, letting the bubbles burn my tongue, hoping they'll somehow burn away the words stuck in my throat.

"So," he says, settling into the seat beside me, his knee brushing mine in that way that our limbs have always tangled without our consent. "Tell me, what are we celebrating?"

I take another sip of champagne from my *'Freak in the Excel Sheets'* mug.

"Well, for starters, Banks didn't burn down the kitchen making toast this morning."

Will's lips twitch. He knows this game intimately, and has played it with me a thousand times before. In those first weeks of us testing our waters, even though we dove straight in, we played this game. I went running to him after every bad day, and he listed every small celebration sipping right from the bottle until we were more drunk off every bit of each other than the alcohol. When we lost jobs, when we lost pregnancies, when we lost parents, when we lost friends, even in moments we lost ourselves, we always did this. Silly in some ways, but in others, it became the way to preserve the joy in the gratitude of grief and pain. No matter how big or small that pain might be.

He takes a long sip from his own mug with the words *'Decent Docent'* and his old museum id printed on it. I got him for his birthday a few years ago.

"I finally fixed that squeaky floorboard in the hallway," he offers, his eyes never leaving my face.

"You mean you threw a rug over it." A laugh joins the bubbles in the carbonation despite everything.

"I solved the problem," he counters, and for a moment, we're just us again, not a couple facing whatever's coming next.

"We're celebrating that the garden didn't die when I forgot to water it for two weeks." I say, my fingers tracing the rim of my mug, focusing on the smooth ceramic.

"We're celebrating that after all this time, you still don't realize I've been the one watering it." His voice is as stabilizing as the hand rubbing slow circles around my back.

"Of course you are" I try to keep my voice light, but something must slip through because his thumb starts twisting his wedding ring.

I take another sip of champagne, wondering how many more small moments we'll have like this. How many more chances to catalogue our ordinary celebrations.

"We're celebrating that I finally learned to make my Rosalie's gluten-free banana bread recipe."

"After only seventeen attempts," he adds.

"And only three minor fires." I admit. This rhythm between us that has been there since the beginning.

"We really shouldn't be so hard on Banks about the whole *'can barely make toast'* thing." He lifts our joined hands, presses a kiss to my knuckles. His lips linger there, warm against my skin, and I know he can feel my pulse.

"We're celebrating," he says carefully, "that you went to the doctor's appointment today..."

And there it is. The thing we've been dancing around, the reason we're drinking champagne from mugs in the afternoon. I look at our joined hands, at the way his thumb is still tracing those steady circles, and try to find the right words. The same way I practiced them in the car, in every moment since leaving the doctor's office.

"Will..." Something in my voice must give me away again because his grip tightens.

His hand stills in mine but doesn't let go.

"We're celebrating that we know what we're fighting." *The words feel like glass in my mouth, sharp and dangerous and impossibly fragile.*

Will's breath catches, just for a moment, but I hear it. All these years of loving someone teaches you all their sounds, all their silences.

"Okay," he says finally. "Okay. Then we're celebrating that you're the strongest person I know."

"Will— "

"No, let me finish." His voice is steady but his eyes are shining. "We're celebrating that we have the best doctors in the state. We're celebrating that we can go anywhere. Get any opinion. We're celebrating that you're stubborn as hell and..."

"Will."

"Arden," Somehow, of all the voices I hear in him, he sounds exactly like he did the day he proposed. Full of promise surging from somewhere. We were young then, not so much now. "We're celebrating that we have options, that you're here drinking champagne, that you're actually fucking extraordinary. And I will go get another bottle right now for us to keep going... but we will be okay, *you* will be okay."

I have to close my eyes against that, against the fierce love in his voice. "We need a plan."

"We'll figure it out," he says with that unwavering certainty he has always had.

"We have to tell Banks." Just saying her name makes my chest ache.

"We will. But first, tell me everything. Every detail."

I squeeze his hand so hard it must hurt, but he just holds on tighter. I start talking, laying out every detail shared. Options, statistics, things I've googled myself. Will listens like he's studying for the most important test of his life, which I suppose he is. Though regardless of his landing in academia, preparedness and studying were not his usual way.

Will pulls me into his arms, and he presses his lips to my hair. "I love you. Beyond any sense of science."

When Banks walks in, she's humming like he does. She looks so much like Will when she's lost in thought, that same little furrow between her eyebrows, that same slight tilt to her head.

"You're both home early," she says, dropping her bag to survey the scene, and her face changes. "What's wrong?"

She's always been too perceptive for her own good. Will's hand finds mine again, his wedding ring cool against my fingers. Our daughter's eyes dart between us, taking in the champagne mugs, the way we're seated, and how her father's shoulders are tense and set in a stance she's seen so rarely.

"Sweetheart," he says, we need to talk."

And just like that, our story shifts into a new chapter, one I never thought we'd write.

Chapter Fifty-Three

HAPPILY EVER AFTER

Bancroft

Somehow, everything here is slightly dream-like, slightly magical, the way memories tend to be when you're trying desperately to hold onto them. Though, it's a weird way to describe a diner. Mom always said this place had the best fries in all of Boston, but I think what she really meant was that there was a saltiness to them that is a reminder of her and dad's youth.

I slide into our corner booth, the one with the wobbly table that rocks whenever anyone puts their elbows on it. It's the outcast table for the three black sheep. This is the booth nobody else wants, which makes it perfect for us. We've come back to this place more often because of the proximity to mom's appointments. Doesn't matter the year, the season, or the time of day, a diner's menu can satisfy anyone and this one remains unchanged.

Dad's already ordering before any of us can even think about opening our menus. *Fries for the table,'* he says to our regular waitress who's known me through a few seasons of my own.

"French fries are a love language," mom says, her voice carrying that particular lilt that always makes her sound like she's about to share some profound secret. Even now, after everything, she still has that way about her, like she's carrying around this endless source of light inside her chest and we're all just lucky enough to bask in it. Even though the fact that we're back here *again* tells us it isn't endless at all. "Our first date was in a diner like this..."

"Sharing my french fries pretty much sealed the deal," dad adds, and I watch their hands find each other under the table, the way they always do, like magnets that can't help but pull together.

"The deal was already sealed..." she starts, and I can't help but roll my eyes, channeling my best Cher Horowitz. They both gasped when I called Clueless vintage last week, one of her favorites, but technically speaking, it is.

"Can you *not*?" I groan, but there's no real annoyance behind it. How could there be? These are the moments I collect like seashells, storing them away for when the tide goes out. The cyclic nature of this whole thing, of the tests, the results, the options, the treatments, the *real* celebrations, the tests, the results, the options, the treatments... Well, that's why we spend so much time in this diner.

Mom looks tired today. The kind of bone deep exhaustion that seems to follow us home from every appointment like an unwanted shadow. But when she looks at him, her eyes still light up with the same spark I've seen in every photo album, every video, and every stolen glance across this very table.

"Your father's right, it sealed the deal," she continues, her voice warm with memory. "Then he ordered a piece of pie..."

"And he pretended he didn't want any but ended up eating half," I finish, because I know all their stories by heart now. The way some kids memorize fairy tales, I've memorized my parents as the blueprint, even now.

"I never pretended," dad protests, his mock offense making Mom laugh.

The fries arrive, golden and perfectly crisp, steam rising from them like little prayers. Dad automatically pushes them closer to her side of the table, and I pretend not to notice how she takes smaller bites these days, how she sometimes has to pause between them, and how she still shows up here anyway.

She casually talks about the next phases of treatment, as if she's talking about the weather or tomorrow's homework. *'The doctors are optimistic.'* She says this last part with a slight frown.

She is busy picking around her omelet and I'm two bites into a burger when she decides to fully pivot the conversation.

"How's Ollie?" she asks as my dad mouths the words *'apple pie'* to the waitress as if we can't see it.

"Ollie is... Ollie. He's good. He's busy. You know him." And they do know him. They've known him since before I was born. Though she says that based on the time I was her 'womb-mate' — *gross* — that technically she's known me longer than she's known him. Oliver has been my on-again-off-again everything since we were infants. Currently, we're back into the same space which seems to be our default setting post puberty.

They've had front row seats to the Bancroft-and-Oliver show for our entire lives after all. Both the ones we made them watch when we got super into Meryl Streep, and the ones where I spent a week crying after he pop-kissed Lindsey Lovewell, *yes that was her real name,* in truth or dare.

I watch them, these two people who've built their entire world around each other and then somehow made room for me in it too.

"Same time next month?" I ask as we're getting ready to leave, and I see something flicker across mom's face, quick as a shooting star, gone before you can make a wish on it.

"Same time," she agrees, her voice steady even though her hand trembles slightly as she reaches for her purse. Dad pretends not to notice, just like he pretends not to notice how she leans on him a little more heavily as we walk to the car. And you can see in the way he looks at her, he would carry any part of her for as far as she needed.

The evening air wraps around us like a blanket as we make our way across the parking lot, our shadows stretching long beneath the street lights. I trail slightly behind them, watching how they still walk in perfect step with each other, how his hand finds hers without either of them having to look.

He whispers something softly to her, and even from behind, I can see how her whole body softens at his words, like a flower turning toward the sun. For a moment, watching them, I can almost believe that nothing's changed, that nothing will change, that we'll keep coming back to this wobbly table until we're all old and gray and still arguing about who gets the last french fry.

But then I catch her reflection in the car window as she gets in, see the careful way she holds herself now, like she's made of something a little more delicate. I see the way his hands linger on her shoulder just a second longer than they used to and the way his eyes follow her every movement more than I recall him doing ever before.

Chapter Fifty-Four

HAPPILY EVER AFTER

Will

I find her asleep in our bed. Arden never naps, or she didn't, before. She used to joke that she'd sleep when she was dead, *which isn't funny anymore*, not even in that dark way she sometimes needs it to be. The sight of her curled on her side of the bed stops me in the doorway, my messenger bag still slung across my chest, full of student essays about Baroque architecture that feels impossibly trivial.

The house is quiet in a way that it feels like holding its breath. Even the maple tree outside our window, the one that usually tap-tap-taps against the glass like an impatient visitor, seems to have stilled its branches to respect the moment she needs. I remember the day we bought this house, how Arden had spun in circles in every empty room, her laughter seeping into the bare walls. Walls we didn't keep bare for long.

We had good years after the first diagnosis. Years of clear scans and cautious optimism, of planning trips we'd take and arguing about what color to paint the guest room. Years of almost believing we'd dodged the bullet, that we were the lucky ones, that statistics were just numbers on a page that had nothing to do with us. Now those years feel like a cruel joke, like one of those trompe l'oeil paintings where something that looks real until you reach out to touch it and your hand meets flat canvas instead of depth.

'*It's not fair,*' I said to her recently. A childish remark as I braced myself against the kitchen island gripping it for my own stability. My head hanging low as I stared at my own feet begging them to carry us all away from this.

'*It's actually incredibly fair,*' she replied with an infuriating amount of honesty. '*It patently sucks. It's completely frustrating. It's all around the shittiest of things to ever happen to us... but, it's not unfair. I've spent so much time thinking why me, why us? But we've had everything. Why anyone else and not us?*'

I set my bag down quietly, trying not to wake her, but the old floorboard by the door creaks, the one we talk about fixing but somehow never do. And she stirs ever so slightly at my tattletale step, her face scrunching in that way that always reminds me of Banks when she was little, fighting sleep with every fiber of her being.

"Hey, stranger," she mumbles, not fully opening her eyes. "Come be horizontal with me."

She must have been reading when she dozed off as the book lays next to her patiently waiting for her to return to their shared adventure.

I toe off my shoes and climb onto the bed beside her, still in my work clothes, my shirt getting hopelessly wrinkled with folds of this moment. She immediately curls into me like a quotation mark seeking its pair as her head finds the spot on my chest that she has been permanently indented by her profile over time.

'*Well, at least I'll finally get some sleep.*' She'd said when we got the news. She'd been right about that, in the cruel ironic way the universe sometimes has of granting wishes. Though we never wished for sleep. We spent nights watching the moon from our bedroom window, from Banks's nursery window, from our front steps, from anywhere we could. Never afraid of sleepless nights or what the sunrise would bring.

"How was your day, Professor?" she asks, her voice and dry still thick with sleep. "Did you dazzle young minds with tales of dead artists and their influences?"

"Today was a riveting lecture on the architectural significance of flying buttresses." I press a handful of kisses plus one to the top of her head. "Only two students fell asleep this time, so I'm counting it as a win."

She snorts against my chest. "Defending Gothic Architecture to students who probably were just hoping you'd make some kind of butt joke," she teases, her voice muffled by my shirt. I run my fingers through her hair, threads of gold with hints of silver.

"How about you?" I ask softly, matching her quiet tone. "Productive day of horizontal contemplation?"

"Oh, very productive. I've been lying here thinking about running away."

"Where are we running to this time?" I play along, the way I always do.

"No where this time," she breathes, each word careful and measured. "Not us, just me."

"Arden..." Her name clings to my lips as a desperate two-syllable plea.

"Will..." She uses mine in protest.

"Do you ever feel like we've lived this life before?" she asks quietly, her voice soft in the stillness of our bedroom. Her fingers follow the familiar lines of my palm, each known crease and paper-grading callus with the precision of a cartographer. With her ear pressed against my chest I know she can feel my heartbeat steady beneath her.

"I sometimes think that we could have had another hundred years together, and it wouldn't have been enough. I would never have been able to fit all my love for you into just this one lifetime," she confesses into the quiet space between heartbeats. She pauses, watching sunspots dance in the beams streaming through the window. "So we leave pieces of it behind, don't we? We pass it on to Banks, this love that's too big for one life to hold. We leave it tucked between the pages of books she'll read someday, hung on walls in photographs she'll show her children. And when I have to leave this world before you," her voice breaks, "because I will," she continues, "I'll build our new house, wherever I end up. I'll fill it with all the love that couldn't fit here, because this one world, this one lifetime was never going to be enough to contain it all."

My hand finds her cheek, thumb brushing across the roundness of it. Her eyes are clear now, more awake than she's been all afternoon.

"I don't know what's going to happen, Will. I don't know if any book got it right, if any dream holds the truth. I don't know if I'll be able to take any of it with me. All these memories we've made, this life we've built together. Do I just pack them up like precious treasures in a suitcase? Choose the minutes and moments I love most and carry them with me when I go?" She shifts to look at me fully, her eyes bright with unshed tears. "I'll board whatever transport the universe has waiting, heading to whatever destination has been planned. It's not fear I feel when I think about it, but it is envy for all the things I'll have to leave behind."

Her voice grows stronger, more certain. "But I need you to know something. When it's time, I'll go with more gratitude than sadness, because this life... this beautiful life with you and Banks, with the families we chose, and even the ones we haven't, it's been well lived, and so well loved. Because this time, it will be my turn to build the future *you* can't see yet. And I'll be there waiting, patient and sure, until it's time for you to find me again."

Her voice drops to a whisper and a plea, not the kind I make in every moment of silence I can find, but one for my ears only.

"But please, my love, for everything we've built and everything we are, don't rush. Let time unfold the way it's meant to for once. And when you meet me, whenever, wherever that may be, you'll sink into the warm bath behind me and tell me all the small things I missed from the day."

I want to argue, to rage against this quiet acceptance, this gentle planning for an after I refuse to contemplate. But she's right, as she's always been right about the important things. *Except one.* The thing that mattered most. The love she has for me, that turned into the love of so much more. My brilliant wife, who can take even this darkest moment and transform it into a promise for a future.

"Now, Will, can you please tell me about your day and the flying buttresses... and there better be at least one ass-joke."

I can feel my own tears trailing the lines of my face that we earned together as she moves from one topic to another with the implication they are equal in density of discussion. But there's no request I wouldn't grant her.

"Well, for starters... they support what seems impossible," I whisper into her hair.

"Oh yeah, tell me more..."

"What's really beautiful is that they turned a structural necessity into art. These buttresses could have been purely functional, but they look like they are holding up heaven. It's like they refused to accept the limitations of gravity."

So I lie here, being her buttress, and I pray to every god I've ever lectured about to grant us more time. So I can pretend, *just for a little while,* that we can exist here together, that we have all the time in the world.

I pull the blanket over us, as she settles back into me to rest more deeply with the vibration of my voice. She's already drifting off, her breathing evening out into the rhythm I know better than my own heartbeat. And as she does, I am lost to her, as I always have been, in all the ways I will remain long past this moment and any to come.

Chapter Fifty-Five

Will

I resent every second my eyes close because each second is one I carelessly toss away. I can't afford to do that. She needs them. I need them for her. The hospital room has become our universe recently, its dimensions shrinking and expanding with each beep of the machines that were supposed to keep me alert but have instead become white noise. The steady rhythm of medical equipment has replaced the soft rustle of pages turning late at night when she couldn't sleep.

Her skin is so cold despite my hands being wrapped around her fingers. I've spent hours trying to warm them, as if I could transfer my own heat into her body through sheer force of will. Her knuckles have left an imprint on my cheek from where my head had fallen, and my eyes have stolen the rest that I'm furious at taking.

My body is curved over the side of the bed, and it aches as I straighten. The hospital chair creaks beneath me, its institutional green cushioning flattened from constant vigil. The pain in my bones is nothing compared to the metaphysical shattering and ache that my body is adjusting to like growing pains. It's the opposite of growth. I'm shrinking. The skin is tightening around me. I straighten, and roll my neck from side to side, hearing the soft pops of protest. Closing my eyes for just one more second before I land again on her.

She's sleeping. I know because I've become hyper-aware of the smallest rises and falls of her chest. Better than any of the machines tracking her pulse. It reminds me of when we watched Banks together after she was first born. We were terrified she would stop breathing, hovering over her crib like anxious satellites constantly googling for reassurance. We just sat there waiting for each rise of her tiny chest so we knew she was okay. I get no reassurance now. I'm terrified now.

Then, we were new parents worried about the unknown. Now, I'm her husband watching the known approach with terrible certainty.

"Don't." The voice is so light, barely a whisper, and I know the energy it must have taken for her to scold me for wallowing. The things I want to say crowd my throat but I don't want her to force out any more words. Not when I know how much it costs her to speak.

The words used to tumble from her mouth like water over stones, bright and musical and endless. Not anymore. I wonder if she feels the unformed brilliance trapped in her mind trying to escape, like stars caught behind cloud cover. Arden always had the right words, even when she was wrong, throwing them at some unsuspecting, over-eager, docent. Now each word is precious, rationed like wartime supplies.

She forces a swallow and I reach for a lollipop, the wrapper crinkling too loudly in the quiet room. Sliding into the hospital bed next to her, I'm careful of the tubes and wires that have become extensions. The shape of her is different now, hollowed out like sea glass, but no matter what shape she takes she doesn't lose any of the shape of her. One I could recognize in any form.

I slip the lollipop between her lips, which are dry like pressed flowers. The manifestation of her body sucking every ounce of her to fight itself. And she has fought, as she's done for everything in her life. For me. For our daughter. The cherry scent of the candy mingles with the antiseptic hospital smell, creating a strange sweetness.

She shifts herself so slightly into me, and I wrap myself around her like a shroud. If only I could shield her from all of this, become armor against the enemy that lives in her own cells.

When we first found out, when we sat down with our fourth 'second opinion' my only response was *I won't let this happen.* It was such a stupid thing to say, as if I could command any part of her to behave differently. All she said was *I know you won't. But we should be prepared anyways.*

And as usual, my wife, in all her brilliance, was right.

I hate her for that.

Of all the times for her to be right. She started preparing immediately. Organizing files, writing letters, making lists. I couldn't even look at the papers without feeling sick.

I hate every second we ever spent not just ferociously loving each other. Every second I blinked was a waste. She would say we didn't waste any of it. That we lived it all, and again, she'd be right. But right now looking at her shallow breathing, I just know we are nearing an end I'm in no way prepared for. One I prayed for any god to delay. A god I didn't know I even believed in. I offered any deal to the devil, but my soul isn't worth hers. So my bargains and begging fell on deaf ears.

I spoke to the doctors a few hours ago in the hallway, their faces grave under the fluorescent lights. There's no more hope in their tones. Just resolution, like that's what they expect from me. As if I could ever be resolved to this. As if I could ever accept that the universe would take her and leave so many lesser people behind.

I notice the movement of her lips, and slowly remove the lollipop that's meant to help some of the thirst, or the sores in her mouth from treatment, meant to do who-knows-what. Maybe just because she always liked them when she was sick. Even when we were dating, I'd bring her bags of Dum Dums whenever she had a cold. She'd line them up by color on her coffee table, saving the cherry ones for last.

I see her beginning to form words, and I'm terrified every time she opens her mouth that they will be her goodbyes. The ones she said long before this moment. Leaving letters in the safe for Banks for all the big days in her future. Having enough conversations with me leading up to these moments so 'when it happens it can just happen' as if it's that simple.

As if anything about this could be simple.

"Can we run away?" She asks, the whisper of her voice is one I've been trying to thread into my mind. Stitching together every thought so I never lose the sound of it.

"Anywhere you want to go... Paris?" I offer, thinking of how she used to talk about walking along the Seine, eating baguettes still warm from the oven, getting lost in narrow streets with names we couldn't pronounce.

She blinks tightly, and despite the I.V. in her arm, I think the tear that forms in the slight of her eye might be the last bit of water her body has to spare. I run the pad of my thumb to wipe it away. To save it. Hoping to absorb any part of her into my skin.

Every cell, every tear, every breath, I hold on to them all.

"How about Narnia..." I offer up instead. Her eyes are up on mine, bright despite everything, and I just wish I could fall into them and drown with her. But we made a deal. I don't get to drown when we have a child who can't swim in this alone. Banks needs at least one parent who's still breathing.

"Mars," she eeks out in the softest rasp, and my heart clenches. Mars was always the most desperate destination in our game. The place to take us as far as we could go, the moon always feeling too attainable. We'd double-moon watch. We'd lounge on the red sand beaches. We'd joke about growing rose bushes on Mars, and she'd say *'if I can't keep a basil plant alive on earth, how am I going to grow roses on Mars.'* My response was always the same. *'Because you can do anything.'*

"Let's run away to Mars..." I'm trying so hard to be strong for this woman who has been so strong her whole life, remains strong even in weakness. But I'm failing miserably as I can feel the tears slip from the corners of my eyes. I don't make an effort to wipe them away. Knowing what she's saying. That my fear has been right all along. Knowing that when she speaks she's doing it with intention and warning. This is her way of telling me it's time.

My physical hold on her tightens in a way that she settles into. Settling into all of this. Her eyes cut to the perfect figure draped under one of our many failed knitting experiments, a blanket that's more holes than yarn, with dropped stitches creating accidental patterns we pretended were intentional. It was Arden's idea, of course. *We shouldn't waste our time while we sit around in hospitals,' she'd* announced one day, pulling yarn and needles from her bag like she'd been planning an ambush for weeks. As if waiting rooms and IV drips were just another excuse for one of her projects, as if we could knit ourselves a shield against what was coming. So we all took up knitting, our clicking needles filling the sterile silence of hospital corridors.

As with most things, she was brilliant and I was a mess. Her hat ended up perfect, even stitches, beautiful pattern. Unfortunately for Banks, in this case, she took after me. But Arden wore them all, rotating between them with equal pride. She used to say they were the warmest things she'd ever put on, and then we moved on to blankets.

Banks sleeps the way she always has, one arm flung over her head, curls a mess against the pillow. The fierce flame who is made in every spark of her mother's image, right down to her laugh.

Before she looks back to me wordlessly, her lips are not able to form the words this time. So I try to.

"You just have a bit of a head start this time, okay? I'll have to meet you there, up in the stars, okay, my darling?" I feel her chest move again, the shallowest sinking feeling as I press a kiss to the top of her head as she leans into me.

She moves her hand grasping for the button to release medication, to subside the pain she pretends she's not in, but her grip is gone, so I do it for her. Her fingers, once so strong she would sit at the piano and run scales until she broke into whatever song was in her mind, now can't even manage this small task. And she sinks into me further. I think knowing like I do, this form of her isn't much longer for this world.

"I will never have enough words or enough time to thank you for this life you've given me." I drop the words like kisses into the crown of her head, the words falling like benedictions. Knowing the tears that draw tracks down my cheeks, through the scruff of my facial hair, are landing somewhere I can't see. "Thank you for always being on my team. You were the only teammate I ever needed. I promise... I swear, I'll take care of our rookie, now. You don't have to worry, okay?" I'm raw and ragged like I've been screaming though I've barely spoken above a whisper. "You can run if you need to, I have a teammate. And she's perfect because of you."

I don't know if she's awake. She doesn't respond, though the shallow breaths I can feel against where my forearm wraps around her selfishly comfort me. I press six kisses against her. Six kisses, like always.

We slip into a commingled sleep, my body gently curled around hers. She's been burning for so long, and I fanned the flames any chance I could get. Willing to be burned alive to just be in her presence. She burned so bright but her fire became the shelter for all of us. The burning moat to protect the ones she loves. Even now, that fire can never burn out completely. Not really. It lives in Banks, in me, in every life she touched.

It's an unfamiliar stillness that has me opening my eyes. Her body ever so slightly more slouched into mine, and a different noise coming from the machines that we've all accepted as the background noise to our lives. The steady beeping has changed to something more urgent, more final. Some people enter the room. Logic would tell me it's doctors. But it doesn't matter now. I can see their mouths moving, telling me something my body detected long before any machine of theirs could.

She prepared us for this moment, though nothing could prepare me for this moment, not even her.

I lean down to offer her one more I love you, though of all the things I don't know in my life, I know this. And so did she. The words feel different now. Like they're trying to bridge the growing distance between the world with her in it and the one without.

I press six kisses to her temple, each one burning with all the moments we'll never have and all the ones we did. "Goodbye, my love." My voice shatters on the words.

These six mourning kisses, each one a desperate attempt. My body doesn't quite believe it yet, my muscle memory already aching for tomorrow's morning that will never come.

In a few minutes, I'll have to start making calls to let people know.

In a few days, I'll have to put on a suit and bury my wife.

But for now, l have to figure out how to keep breathing in a world without her, for *her*.

She ran ahead without me, that was the deal, but she left a map in Banks' smile in the memories we built together. Someday, I'll follow that map back to her.

Chapter Fifty-Six

HAPPILY EVER AFTER

Bancroft

He walks to the front, his shoulders look heavy, but he straightens them, he knows the weight of what he's about to do. I've never been a front row kind of girl, but I wasn't given a choice this time. I turn back in my seat and look at all the people here, and I'm reminded why I hate the front row. Everyone can see me, and I am the one they are staring at.

It starts with an inhale, like he is about to dive into the deep-end and needs a single breath to carry him all the way. Maybe he does.

"There haven't been many times in my life that I've been right when the person on the other side was my wife and I've been okay with that, reveled in it even. You see, I made a deal a long time ago that I wouldn't need to be, because there was only one thing I needed to be right about, and it would be worth everything, nothing else would matter. And it was."

The thought looks like it makes him want to smile, but his heart won't allow it. *My* heart won't allow it.

"When this happened, when it *began*, she sat me down and said, 'we have to talk' I thought she was going to tell me it was over. It was far-fetched, but it was all I could imagine that would merit that level of severity in her voice. Because *losing* her felt more possible than *losing her.* She looked at my face, one that undoubtedly was washed with fear and was gearing up for a fight, and she said *'You can calm down, Will, no one is dead... at least not yet.'"*

There are a few huffs in the crowd, what might under different circumstances form laughter, but not here, not now.

"And then, when I told her I wouldn't let it happen. She said she believed me like she had for so many things, for so many years, *'but we should probably have a backup plan just in case'* and this time, I hate that she was right. *This...* was her backup plan. Her *backup* backup plan. Because her original plan was some version of an iron-man suit, but Robert Downey Jr. didn't have a working one." He rubs his hands over his face and fills his lungs with air as he dives deeper into the sea that is my mother.

"She was funny. Funnier in private in a way that wasn't curated for anyone but her own brain, and it made her laugh. And that made me laugh... I was right years ago, when I said she loved me. What I didn't know at the time... is what that would mean for our lives." The way he talks about her it's like he's sharing the deepest secret to exist.

"She loved me, more fiercely than I had any right to be loved by her." He forces a swallow that looks painful. "Arden and I, we were neighbors, sort of, it's one of the ways we met. And when people would ask *'how did you meet?'* we could change the answer, because there had been so many times our lives had crossed paths slowly knotting us together. But for a time she was right there, and the universe mocked us for how much time we wasted being so near. One of the first times I saw her, really saw her, she didn't even notice me. It was one morning getting a cup of tea from a shop on the corner, and there she was, before the world woke up. It looked like something she did regularly. I was out for a run, before the sun had fully risen, trying to clear my mind. And she did. As soon as I saw her. My mind went completely blank. I went to say something, to introduce myself, maybe it was the fact she was hurrying out the door or what I later found out was *'the worst day ever'...* "he recalls it so easily.

"Huh," he laughs to himself and shakes his head softly. You can tell his eyes have unfocused and he's looking at a memory, not this crowd of people. "I think this one has yours beat, darling." He presses his lips together with a sad smile meant for her. He takes a breath, and another. "Love at first sight can mean a lot of things. But the undeniable way she was someone I wanted to know, changed my life. And falling in love with her was something I never deserved to do. That we existed in the same time, however the universe had destined, is enough. Being in her orbit in any way, is...*was,* enough."

There's a reverence and discomfort in the adjustment he made, one that makes me sick to my stomach, but he continues painting this picture that so few here would have been lucky enough to have seen.

"Then one day she walked through the doors of my life, one that I had been subconsciously holding open just for her. That despite the fact we had classes, coffees, friends, we spent years sharing without knowing. When the time came, I never knew she was on the other side of the street. Like the universe was mocking us..."

I spent my life hearing their love story, but growing up as their daughter meant I also lived it. Watching him share it now, like some great unveiling to the world, has everyone in silence. They are all just sitting in awe in all shades of black. But I have to look away from him, my dad who is trying so desperately to not fall apart, and I look around me to so many people I've never seen, doing exactly that.

"What happened next, I don't know how to explain it. I've never tried to anyone but myself... But I think people confuse love and death. Standing here now, I know it. I died then. The most welcome death. There was no version of a life to exist without her."

I watch the audience lean forward, caught in the gravity of their love story, but all I can see is my father trying to piece together a universe that no longer has its center.

"We became knotted together like wild vines seeking sunlight, our paths intertwined long before we were willing to acknowledge them. We had been weaving our threads into an intricate tapestry of a life we would one day have without ever knowing. Golden strings of fate pulling taut across time and space, creating a pattern so complex and beautiful that even destiny must have held her breath in anticipation. And when we finally gave in to that, it was a sense of déjà vu. The feeling of coming home to a place you've never been, but somehow always knew.

"And now, even without her here, all that's left is love. Even in the physical absence of her, that love is left. If you don't believe me as blindly as she would, it's all," he lets the tears fall without any reservation, "that love is all right here."

He nods in my direction.

"I'm not going to stand here and talk about her accomplishments, she would just laugh it off. The big things she did, in school, at work, she was impressive, but more than that, she was captivating. She could make anyone feel seen. She adapted to what people needed, and it was marvelous to watch. How she could wrap anyone in kindness. She raised the bar for everyone in her life, never making them feel bad if they couldn't reach it, she just gave them a boost."

"So let me tell you about my wife..." His hands are wrapped around the podium in a way you'd think his years of teaching would have prepared him for, but it's clearly for stability above all else now.

"She *loved* a birthday. As long as it wasn't hers.

"She kept a list of words that she adored, because she learned them, because the definitions surprised her, because she just liked the way they sounded.

"There are few things she couldn't do, except keep a basil plant alive.

"Books were her best friends, but she was mine.

"She filled my life, she gave life, she made life worth living.

"She had a face that could launch a thousand ships and a mind that could sink them.

"Even on the days it took a little longer to climb high in the sky, on the nights it slept earlier, the sun would rise and set with her.

"When we got married, we were young, we didn't know what we were doing, but we knew we needed to do it together. We were on the same team."

My father isn't known for meticulous preparation of things, and so far it's clear to anyone listening he is pouring himself out at our feet. And I know she'd like that. Which is why his unfolding and straightening of papers against the podium feels out of character.

"I told you, she had a plan b. I've been given explicit instructions to read this exactly as she wrote it and not open it until I was standing here... so, here we go..."

I scoot to the edge of my seat, as if that will get me closer to her, but I feel fingers interlock with mine. Holding me steady. Ollie, of course. I can see my grief in those around me, and Ollie is one of those people. Though to him, she was so much more than my mother, she's been in his life just as long.

My dad clears his voice from the front, preparing himself to continue.

"Dearly beloved, we are gathered here today to celebrate the marriage of... oh wait, this is the wrong speech... go ahead and file this one away for Banks' wedding one day and skip to the next page..." he starts about as confused as the rest of us, but realizes, even in death, my mother loves a joke. He chuckles through tears and flips to the next sheet.

"Now that I have your attention. We *are* gathered here to celebrate. Maybe it doesn't seem like that right now, but in preparation for this day, it started to feel more and more like a wedding, preparing a guest list, planning a reception, *hell*, I even got to pick out an outfit. I just don't get to be there for any of it. At least not in a way that wouldn't make this really weird. Because if you were at my wedding, or anywhere I have a glass, you know I love a reason to make a toast."

He flips another page, and continues reading, and it's as if their voices have blended together. It may be him, but no one could deny her presence in the words.

"I've made a few in my day. And as much as I want to stand here and raise a glass of champagne with a toast that would have made my parents, *or now-a-days my daughter,* blush, this one is a little different. But as you taught me, Will, no matter how much it doesn't feel like celebrating, there's still something to celebrate and it still deserves champagne..."

I see my uncle Ethan move from his seat next to Ollie to approach my dad handing him a small bottle. He looks back at the paper as his hand covers his mouth in disbelief. His eyes are bright like she was, but reflective with tears he can't control and would never try to.

In all my life, there was nothing he tried to limit for her.

"If everyone could look under their seats, and join me in one final toast."

The space shifts around me, the sounds of people adjusting to reach beneath them to find small bottles. I look around the room, more people than fit in this space. Despite the size, like everything she did, she overflowed it. They are all here for her, in varying stages of life and shades of black.

I reach beneath my seat and find a small bottle of my own, like everyone holding on to it waiting for her direction, even now.

He takes a breath as deep as she was, and continues.

"My life wouldn't have been worth celebrating if it weren't for all of you. So thank you. No ending, no matter how unexpected or premature, changes that. No ending, no matter how sad, makes my life any less full of joy and happiness.

"Will, my love, you once told me that a day might come and things might change, but you would love me beyond that. You once told me that you didn't need to understand it, but you needed me to feel the gravity of your love. You once told me that if I couldn't see the future, you would see it enough for the both of us.

"Well, if you're reading this, I'm sorry, things have changed. But I love you and Banks, beyond any sense of gravity. And you were right, you saw the future, you built it and because of you the love of my life became the love of my life."

I've stopped hearing his voice, and instead the only voice I hear is hers.

"Cheers... to all of you."

The pops of corks go off around me. And it makes sense. Only my mother would have her funeral go off with a resounding bang. I look around the room at these people who loved her, taking sips from the bottles. As the bubbles hit my tongue the tears hit my cheeks.

"That's Arden for you. Once again saying it better than I could... Cheers, to you, my darling." He takes a swig from his bottle and presses his eyes closed as tears run down his cheeks in what feels like a silent prayer, to the only god he ever believed in, her.

Chapter Fifty-Seven

HAPPILY EVER AFTER

Bancroft

I hate how many people are here, people I've never even heard of. It was one thing for them to be at the actual funeral service, but this is our house. This is where she lived. This is *my* space. And the more people traipse through these rooms they will soak up all the smell of her. I can hear them downstairs, I can see them through the window in the backyard, a few of them gathered by the patch of basil that has nearly overtaken everything. The story she always told about my dad, where in that moment she knew she'd love him forever, the story that has undoubtably fucked me up when it comes to believing in love, because lets face it, they were fucking perfect and even that didn't guarantee them an ending.

I sit on the floor with my back braced against the foot of my bed and take a deep breath inhaling the warmth of the cardigan I'm wearing that I took from her closet this morning. I stretch the sleeves to cover more of my hands and squeeze them tightly like I can conjure the feeling of her hand holding mine. It's unfair that she spent her whole life comforting me, and now in the moment I need that comfort most, she isn't here. That the person

I need most now, is my mother. And she's the only person I can't have.

There is a gentle knock at the door and it creaks open as I peer around the bedpost to see who it is.

He looks exhausted in a way I've never seen, and it scares me a little bit. He knows as well as I do, it's just us now, and neither one of us could replace the massive void for the other. It's not a void. It's a full blown black hole and everything that should bring me joy gets sucked in never to be seen again. I wipe the tears from my eyes, that are more boiling hot with fury than just sadness. Maybe it would be better if I could just be sad, but he's sad enough for the both of us.

He takes a seat next to me on the floor.

"You should eat something, Bancroft," he says as he hands me a small plate of mixed appetizers from the reception happening downstairs.

"Thanks, Sterling," I say to him, as I always do. Even in this moment, there is something comforting about pretending things are the same. And even though I have his eyes, his height, and his aversion to pickles, for as long as I can remember, I've called him by his name.

We both hear the voices outside the door, no doubt it's my grandparents. I know the boom of his voice anywhere, and so does my dad.

The door swings open, and we both duck our heads as Grandpa Sterling does a quick sweep of the room looking for one or both of us. But misses what's right in front of him as he shuts the door and we hear him say *'can't find him'* and stomp off.

They may not be at odds the way I've heard stories of before, but that doesn't mean on a day like today, he's the person either of us will find comfort in. There's something about it, maybe the act of hiding, that makes us both laugh in a way that feels unnatural. I can see it on his face, that it hurts him. Because it's the first time I've heard him laugh in weeks. And maybe worse, because I know I laugh like *she did.*

"Shouldn't you be with everyone downstairs?" I ask as I wrap a piece of prosciutto around a slice of brie.

"Should? Maybe," he says as he reaches for my plate making the same combination bite. "But there's only one thing that matters now, and we can stay here all day. Just the two of us."

My eyes fill with tears faster that I can even try to control.

The two of us.

It wasn't supposed to be the two of us.

They were the pair. It was always so clear how much they loved each other beyond any sense of reality. And they loved me, too. I know that. But we-two, are the wrong two. She was my best friend, and she was his. So now we both just have each other? Second string? It's not fair.

"I can't do this." Without my mother I feel alone. A type of alone I didn't know existed. He pulls me into a hug and I cry on his shoulder. I miss her, it hasn't been a week, and I miss her. I miss her from my future, the one every girl is promised. I can tell by his breathing he is also in tears, he's never hidden them from me.

"It's alright, sweetheart. It will be alright," he whispers. He shushes softly into my hair as he rubs my cashmere covered back. But the tears are coming in a way he is absorbing completely.

"No matter what else is going on, who else is around, we are an impenetrable force. If you can't handle something, I can, I will. Okay? We can do this." His voice cracks ever so slightly before hardening in a way to prove that he means it, swallowing down the pain for me.

"You and me," he says, so softly, "we're on the same team."

Chapter Fifty-Eight

HAPPILY EVER AFTER

Will

I've always considered grief to be a man, that's kind of just how we talk about it, the Grim Reaper is some cloaked male figure in every story, but once you know her, you know better. She could only ever be female. The way she wraps around you, with mortality's measured touch, she can rip you to shreds. There's nothing masculine about it. Somehow, she has become the worst friend I've ever had.

Her visits are always unannounced, when it was newer, it felt like she had moved in completely.

And now, sometimes I'll just be sitting on the couch, reading a book, and I can feel her sidle up next to me, as her hand soothingly rubs my back. Her long nail draws down my spine in a way to remind me it would be one stroke to split me in half for good. But she doesn't, that would be too generous.

Then there are days that she's the most wicked, cursing me with chronic pain that makes every movement feel like shattered glass trapped beneath the thinnest layer of skin, but never able to break free and spare me the discomfort.

She's possessive, she's jealous of my every happiness. She doesn't want to share, but she's patient. She is multitasking. She's ironic. She's consistent yet unpredictable. She's the gilded frame around images of devastation. The rotten milk in the perfect cup of coffee. It doesn't make sense and doesn't have to.

It's the worst club you can ever be a part of, no matter how good the company is. It's the most human and universal experience. Something not unique but in no way would those experiencing it ever believe they aren't the only ones to be in that much pain. How could pain like this exist in droves? How can I not be experiencing all that could possibly exist?

Loving someone is learning a language, word by word over time immersed in it. Being in love is a language only you both speak, the shared whispers and secrets of lovers unheard by anyone else. And when that person is gone you feel like the only person left on this planet fluent in something no one else can understand. Wandering the earth looking for someone to translate, but they never can.

As I lay in our bed, the wrinkles of the sheets we once shared are long gone, but the shape of you in them will exist with me forever.

I don't like to be lost in my own mind, but sometimes that's the only place you're left whole. There are parts of you everywhere. In people and places we loved. But the only place you exist now completely is in my memories. And the mind is a cruel thing, men have gone mad over less than this. Like a hedge maze I'm constantly wandering following the trail of you with just my senses.

This place was ours, you built it with your love, and we filled it with every happily ever after anyone could wish for. But a happily ever after doesn't mean it's over. And now, in this after without you, I hold onto that. Because as long as I exist, so do you. Known in every room I enter, simply because I am there.

. . .

People think sadness is the most all consuming emotion of all. It's not, it's gratitude. It's just funny how often we confuse them.

Chapter Fifty-Nine

HAPPILY EVER AFTER

Will

Bancroft turns to me, and for a moment, she's five years old again, all wild curls, untied shoelaces and unfinished stories. Time folds in on itself here in this museum, I can see her at every age, spinning through these halls like a living exhibit of joy. She was so fearless when she was little, so unafraid of taking a leap off anything, diving from her bed into the pillow fort, or from my shoulders into the deep end of a pool. But the woman before me now came home with fear, weighted by guilt she has no responsibility to bear, her shoulders carrying a burden I never meant for her to hold.

She carries herself with Arden's grace, that same quiet determination in her eyes. I see her mother in every careful movement, every thoughtful pause.

"Sterling, I," she starts to speak, then stops, dropping her knees from where they had been pulled up to her chest, and lands them back on the floor.

I can see the worry. For me.

"You've been afraid to tell me," I finish for her, my voice soft with understanding, "Because you think I can't handle being alone." She turns, and I see Arden in every line of her face, in the way she holds herself brave even when she's breaking inside. My brilliant, beautiful daughter, who has spent too many years trying to fill the space her mother left behind.

"I'll be alright, you know." I don't think I'm convincing, and it breaks a part of my heart I didn't know I had left.

"But you'll be all alone."

I laugh softly, wrapping an arm around her shoulders.

"I have colleagues who won't leave me alone even when I want them to, I have my students, I have my family, I have this museum, I have your uncle Ethan, your aunt Rosalie, *and I have your mother.* Yes, she's not *here*, but there's not a breath I take that I don't have your mother. She exists in everything I do."

Looking at my daughter on the precipice of the rest of her life is something I didn't think I would be doing alone. But even worse is the idea that I could be the thing that prevents her from living it.

"But it's different," she insists. "I know I haven't come home a lot, and I'm sorry I've avoided it, but it was easier for me not to deal with it if I stayed away. But now, this move, this job, it feels more permanent. As long as I was in the same city, it felt like I wasn't abandoning you, or *her...*"

Her eyes are welled with tears that drip with guilt, as she bites down on her lip, and it's like a flashback to all the reasons she carries this burden.

"The only thing worse than living in the present without her, is being trapped in the past. I wouldn't wish that for anyone, least of all you. You have a life, and so much more of it ahead of you. I would be on the first plane out if I thought it's what you needed. But sweetheart, it's time for you to live the life you want. Not the one you think you owe her, and definitely not the one you think you owe me."

I run my finger across the small gold plate that we had affixed to the bench not long after Arden passed.

TAKE SEATS TOGETHER AS STRANGERS AND STAY
LONG ENOUGH TO FALL IN LOVE LIKE WE DID.
IN LOVING MEMORY OF ARDEN BANCROFT STERLING

The engraving of it was inspired by an elderly couple we used to see here. They'd come once a week, and take their respective seats and talk about their lives as if they hadn't lived them together for the last sixty years.

They once told me that sometimes, they would sit together feeling like strangers and fall in love all over again.

That's what Arden and I did. We took seats as strangers, and in each seat we took, every bed we claimed, every moment we stole, and every place we ran, we fell deeper and deeper in love. And even still, I come sit here with her.

She is in every minute that exists, and all the ones that don't.

Bancroft and I have shared this space long enough now that I think she understands, that I think she's accepting the love for herself. That she sees for all the reasons to do something in her life, and all the reasons not to, it should never be me.

"Ms. Bancroft," Mack's voice is also slower now, as is his pace around the museum, but she looks up all the same. "Some folks are here for you."

And with that, little feet come running into the hall.

"Mama!" he screams as he runs towards her and jumps right into her arms.

Ollie strolls in just a few paces behind his son, able to cut across the room to his little family, and plants himself right next to his wife.

"What are you doing here?" she asks him.

"Your dad called me." *I did. The second she told me.*

The way he looks at our daughter settles something in my chest I didn't know was still unsettled. In his eyes, I see all the proof I need that she'll be okay, that she'll be loved the way she deserves to be loved, completely, steadily, without reservation.

And just like that their whole life can begin again because

they've made the choice. Right where ours began, right where we did. I leave the two of them. Not strangers needing to fall in love with each other, but two people choosing their next happily ever after.

As I walk back through the hall, a place filled with parts of our lives, I hear my grandson's giggles follow me down the corridor. It mingles with memories of Bancroft's own childhood laughter, of Arden's. The sounds layer over each other like strokes painting a picture of time that doesn't move in straight lines but circles back on itself, creating patterns we can only see when we step far enough away.

"Dad!" Bancroft's voice catches me before I reach the end of the hall. Not just her voice, but the fact that in her life, I've so rarely been 'dad' when she called for me. I turn to find her standing there, appearing lighter than I've seen her in as long as I can remember. While grief may never fully dissipate, she carries it differently now. A warm scarf rather than a noose. She leaps into me for a hug, and I catch her, as I always will, though she hasn't needed me to for some time. "Thank you."

———

The drive home is quiet, but it's a different kind of quiet than it's been lately. It's not the hollow silence of absence, but acceptance.

I reach our house, and it is still ours, it will always be ours. No matter how far Banks runs, and she should, it will be hers, too. The front gate cries as I push it open, watching the shadows of a lifetime lengthen across our front steps.

In our bedroom, I sit on the edge of the bed and let out a long breath. On the nightstand, there's a photo of us from a different chapter of our youth. Both of us laughing at something long forgotten, our faces turned toward each because there would be nowhere else worth looking.

"You would be so proud of her," I say to the empty room, knowing that it's not really empty at all. "She's so much like you, darling. So brave and beautiful and finally, about to live her life on her own terms."

Sadness and gratitude are sisters, I've learned. They walk hand in hand through our lives, each making the other more profound, more meaningful. The ache of missing Arden will never fully fade, but it lives alongside the joy of having loved her, of loving her still.

That's the real happily ever after, isn't it? Not the absence of pain or the promise of forever, but the courage to love completely, knowing it will change you irrevocably.

Here in this house filled with memories, I'll continue adding chapters to ours. And somewhere, in every moment of joy and grace and love, Arden's story goes on.

We keep waiting for endings, for neat conclusions, for some grand moment when everything falls into place and stays there. But life doesn't work that way, it's not about finding closure or reaching a final chapter. Our happily ever after isn't waiting at the end of the story, it's in all the scattered moments we collect. It's in the memories we keep making, even without those we thought would possess them all. Because in all the versions of love that exist, it isn't about endings at all. It's about beginnings, the endless beginnings that we choose.

The End

Authors Note

If you've made it this far, I know your heart might be heavy. Perhaps you're moving through your own stages of grief, and for that, I'm sorry.

This book was drafted (in some form) immediately following When We Were. At a time when people were clamoring for a happily ever after, and I began thinking more and more about how we define that. For the most part, I know how the romance community defines it. And for that reason, I'm not always sure I fit amongst the authors and novels I love. Because for me the expectations about what constitutes a happily ever after, put too much weight on the *after* portion of that.

I've always struggled with the notion that happiness is this singular, perfect moment that can only be followed by even more perfection. The wedding, the babies, the dream house, the successful career, the self actualization. We close these books at these 'perfect' moments, as if life simply stops there, frozen in eternal bliss. The idea that whether or not someone has a happily ever after depends simply on when we stop paying attention to their story.

But life doesn't work that way.

Real happiness isn't just a destination. It's countless moments scattered throughout our lives. It's in the beginning, the middle, and yes, even in the end. Some of these moments might be tinged with sadness, others with joy, but they're all part of a life well-lived. And *that* is a happily ever after no matter where, when, or how often, it occurs in the story.

I deliberately chose not to name Arden's illness, I kept her age vague. In fact, a lot of details and timelines were intentionally left undefined so that the reader could find themselves in portions of this story they needed to.

While much of this story was influenced by watching my grandmother – the original Diane – pass away in 2017, and how her death shifted our family's universe, this story is about something larger than any specific diagnosis. Because like Arden, my grandmother's happily ever after wasn't confined to a single chapter of her life, nor was it erased by its ending. It lived on without her.

While so much of this book feels like Arden should just be blasting 'The Man' by Taylor Swift, the fact is, even in 2025, women in the workplace are underpaid, and met with internalized and intentional gender bias on a daily basis, with minority groups impacted at even greater rates.

With that said, it's also important to acknowledge the privilege in this book, of which there is *a lot*. Both Arden and Will have a great deal of privilege in how they navigate their lives, careers, trauma, and even illness.

Even as the story explores themes of healing and resilience, it's crucial to acknowledge how privilege shapes these characters' journeys. Their ability to take time off work, access quality healthcare, and pursue therapy, speaks to advantages many in the United States, and around the world, don't share. Their family connections, their education, and their implied financial safety nets in the form of their parents, allow them the space and security to navigate their lives in ways many people never get.

This isn't to diminish their struggles. Pain is pain, and trauma leaves its marks regardless of circumstance. But their paths to healing are undeniably different due to social capital that remain out of reach for many.

As an author, it's important to recognize this reality while still telling their love story.

Love stories don't end when tragedy enters. Sometimes, they become even more beautiful for having existed at all. Arden and Will's love story isn't tragic because it ended. Their happily ever after isn't undone. It could never be. Because it changed them both, because it created Banks, because the ripple effects of one love story, of one person, are so much bigger than just the last chapter of a book.

Acknowledgments

To you, the reader. First and foremost thank you for putting up with my absolutely insufferable gamification of releasing this book. What can I say besides that, I like Taylor Swift a little too much and love puzzles.

To those of you who got snippets of it while it was disjointed, to you who received it stitched up, to you reading it right now. Thank you.

My Framily. No, not a typo. *(Though I'm sure you'll find those in here also)* The framily I chose and the one that chose me, my life has been full of so much more because of you. You make the happy ever afters of my life that much happier.

To Diane. My grandmother. My pen-namesake. Thank you for reading smut unapologetically at a time when there were no discrete covers. And thank you for showing me a happily ever after that spanned a life of so much love. Thank *you* for this beautiful life and for continuing to inspire me and my writing every single day.

To my mother. I'm sorry, I couldn't write a funny book. Not this time. (Though I did make myself laugh at the *plantslaughter puns*.) But thank you for being proud of me regardless, even though this one will absolutely have us upping our Lexapro dosages.

To my husband, thank you for letting me use parts of you in this story. (To the readers, no, I won't tell you which parts.) There has never been a future you weren't willing to build. To quote you: When we got married, we were young and didn't know what we were doing... Well, now, we're not young, and we still don't know what we're doing. But we're having an amazing time doing it. Thank you for endlessly choosing a happily ever after for us.